DISCUSSIONS AND ARGUMENTS

ON VARIOUS SUBJECTS.

EIGHTH EDITION.

PRINTED BY
KELLY AND CO., GATE STREET, LINCOLN'S INN FIELDS, W.C.
AND KINGSTON-ON-THAMES.

DISCUSSIONS

AND

ARGUMENTS

ON VARIOUS SUBJECTS

BY

JOHN HENRY CARDINAL NEWMAN

NEW EDITION.

LONDON

LONGMANS, GREEN, AND CO.

AND NEW YORK: 15 EAST 16th STREET

1891

TO

THE REV. HENRY ARTHUR WOODGATE, B.D.,

RECTOR OF BELBROUGHTON, HONORARY CANON OF
WORCESTER.

My dear Woodgate,

Half a century and more has passed since you first allowed me to know you familiarly, and to possess your friendship.

Now, in the last decade of our lives, it is pleasant to me to look back upon those old Oxford days, in which we were together, and, in memory of them, to dedicate to you a Volume, written, for the most part, before the currents of opinion and the course of events carried friends away in various directions, and brought about great changes and bitter separations.

Those issues of religious inquiry I cannot certainly affect to lament, as far as they concern myself: as they relate to others, at least it is left to me, by such acts as you now allow me, to testify to them that affection which time and absence cannot quench, and which is the more fresh and buoyant because it is so old.

I am, my dear Woodgate,

Your attached and constant friend,

JOHN HENRY NEWMAN.

January 5, 1872.

ADVERTISEMENT.

This Volume is a fresh contribution, on the part of the Author, towards a uniform Edition of his publications.

Of the six portions, of which it consists, the first appeared in the *British Magazine* in the spring of 1836, under the title of " Home Thoughts Abroad." As that title was intended for a series of papers which were never written, and is unsuitable to a single instalment of them, another heading has been selected for it, answering more exactly to the particular subject of which it treats.

The second and third are the 83rd and 85th numbers of the "Tracts for the Times," and were published in the 5th volume, in the year 1838.

The fourth, " The Tamworth Reading Room," was written for the *Times* newspaper, and appeared in its columns in February 1841, being afterwards published as a pamphlet. The letters, of which it consists, were written off as they were successively called for by the parties who paid the author the compliment of employing him, and are necessarily immethodical as compositions.

The same may with still more reason be said of the Letters which follow, entitled, "Who's to blame?" written in the spring of 1855, for an intimate friend, at that time the editor of the newspaper in which they appeared.

The Review, which closes the Volume, was published in the *Month* Magazine of June 1866.

January, 1872.

CONTENTS.

I.

HOW TO ACCOMPLISH IT.[*]

I.

WHEN I was at Rome, I fell in with an English acquaintance, whom I had met occasionally in his own county, and when he was on a visit at my own University. I had always felt him a pleasant, as rather engaging companion, and his talent no one could question; but his opinions on a variety of political and ecclesiastical subjects were either very unsettled or at least very uncommon. His remarks had often the effect of random talking; and though he was always ingenious, and often (as far as I was his antagonist) unanswerable, yet he did not advance me, or others, one step towards the conviction that he was right and we were wrong in the matter which happened to be in dispute. Such a personage is no unusual phenomenon in this day, in which every one thinks it a duty to exercise the "sacred right of private judgment;" and when, consequently, there are, as the grammar has it, "quot homines, tot

---

* [The discussion in this Paper is carried on by two speculative Anglicans, who aim at giving vitality to their Church, the one by uniting it to the Roman See, the other by developing a nineteenth-century Anglo-Catholicism. The narrator sides on the whole with the latter of these.]

sententiæ;" nor should I have distinguished my good
friend from a score of theorists and debaters, producible
at a minute's notice in any part of the United Kingdom,
except for two reasons—first, that his theories lay in
the different direction from those now in fashion, and
were all based upon the principle of "bigotry," (as he,
whether seriously or paradoxically, avowed)—next, that
he maintained they were not novelties, but as old as the
Gospel itself, and possessing as continuous a tradition.
Yet, in spite of whatever recommendations he cast about
them, they did not take hold of me. They seemed unreal; this will best explain what I mean:—*unreal*, as if
he had raised his structure in the air, an independent,
self-sustained pile of buildings, *sui simile*, without historical basis or recognized position among things existing,
without discoverable relations to the wants, wishes, and
opinions of those who were the subjects of his speculations.

We were thrown together at Rome, as we had never
been before; and, getting familiar with him, I began to
have some insight into his meaning. I soon found him
to be quite serious in his opinions; but I did not think
him a wit the less chimerical and *meteoros* than before. However, as he was always entertaining, and could
bear a set-down or a laugh easily, from the sweetness
and amiableness of his nature, I always liked to hear him
talk. Indeed, if the truth must be spoken, I believe, in
some degree, he began to poison my mind with his extravagances.

One day I had called at the Prussian Minister's, and
found my friend there. We left together. The landing
from which the staircase descended looked out over
Rome; affording a most striking view of a city which
the Christian can never survey without the bitterest, the

most loving, and the most melancholy thoughts. I will not describe the details of the prospect; they may be found in every book; nothing is so common now as panoramic or dioramic descriptions. Suffice it to say, that we were looking out from the Capitol all over the modern city; and that ancient Rome, being for the most part out of sight, was not suggested to us except as the basis of the history which followed its day. The morning was very clear and still: all the many domes, which gave feature to the view before us, rose gracefully and proudly. We lingered at the window without saying a word. News of public affairs had lately come from England, which had saddened us both, as leading us to forebode the overthrow of all that gives dignity and interest to our country, not to touch upon the more serious reflections connected with it.

My friend began by alluding to a former conversation, in which I had expressed my anticipation, that Rome, as a city, was still destined to bear the manifestation of divine judgments. He said, " Have you really the heart to say that all this is to be visited and overthrown ?" His eye glanced at St. Peter's. I was taken by surprise, and for a moment overcome, as well as he; but the parallel of the Apostles' question in the Gospel soon came to my aid, and I said, by way of answer, " Master, see what manner of stones and what buildings are here!" He smiled ; and we relapsed into our meditative mood.

At length I said, "Why, surely, as far as one's imagination is concerned, nothing is so hard to conceive as that evil is coming on our own country : fairly as the surface of things still promises, yet you as well as I expect evil. Not long before I came abroad, I was in a retired parish in Berkshire, on a Sunday, and the inestimable blessings of our present condition, the guilt of those who are destroying them, and moreover, the difficulty of believing they could be lost, came forcibly upon me. When everything looked so calm, regular, and smiling, the church bell going for service, high and low, young and old flocking in, others resting in the porch, and others delaying in the churchyard, as if there were enjoyment in the very cessation of that bodily action which for six days had worried them, (but I need not go on describing what both of us have seen a hundred times,) I said to myself, 'What a heaven on earth is this! how removed, like an oasis, from the dust and dreariness of the political world! And is it possible that it depends for its existence on what is without, so as to be dissipated and to vanish at once upon the occurrence of certain changes in public affairs?' I could not bring myself to believe that the foundations beneath were crumbling away, and that a sudden fall might be expected."

He replied by one of his occasional flights—"If Rome itself, as you say, is not to last, why should the daughter who has severed herself from Rome? The amputated limb dies sooner than the wounded and enfeebled trunk which loses it."

"Say this anywhere in Rome than on this staircase," I answered. "Come, let us find a more appropriate place for such extravagances;" and I took him by the arm, and we began to descend. We made for the villa on the Palatine, and in our way thither, and while strolling in its walks, the following discussion took place, which of course I have put together into a more compact shape than it assumed in our actual conversation.

2.

"What I mean," said he in continuation, "is this: that we, in England, are severed from the centre of unity, and therefore no wonder our Church does not flourish. You may say to me, if you please, that the Church of Rome is corrupt. I know it; but what then? If (to use the common saying) there are remedies even worse than the disease they practise on, much more are remedies conceivable which are only not as bad, or but a little better. To cut off a limb is anyhow a strange mode of saving it from the influence of some constitutional ailment. Indigestion may cause cramp in the extremities, yet we spare our hands or feet, notwithstanding. I do not wish to press analogies; yet, surely, there is such a religious *fact* as the existence of a great Catholic body, union with which is a Christian privilege and duty. Now, we English are separate from it."

I answered, "I will grant you thus much,—that the present is an unsatisfactory, miserable state of things; that there is a defect, an evil in existing circumstances, which we should pray and labour to remove; yet I can grant no more. The Church is founded on a doctrine— the gospel of *Truth;* it is a means to an end. Perish the Church Catholic itself, (though, blessed be the promise, this cannot be,) yet let it perish *rather* than the Truth should fail. Purity of faith is more precious to the Christian than unity itself. If Rome has erred grievously in doctrine (and in so thinking we are both of one mind), then is it a duty to separate even from Rome."

"You allow much more," he replied, "than most of us; yet even you, as it seems to me, have not a deep sense enough of the seriousness of our position. Recollect, at the Reformation we did that which is a sin, *unless* we prove it to be a duty. It was, and is, a very solemn protest. Would the seraph Abdiel have made his resistance a triumph and a boast,—spoken of the glorious stand he had made,—or made it a pleasant era in his history? Would he have gone on to praise himself, and say, 'Certainly, I am one among a thousand ; all of them went wrong but I, and they are now in hell, but I am pure and uncorrupt, in consequence of my noble separation from those rebels'? Now, certainly, I have heard you glory in an event which at best was but an escape as by fire,—an escape at a great risk and loss, and at the price of a melancholy separation."

I felt he had, as far as the practical question went, the advantage of me. Indeed it must be confessed that we Protestants are so satisfied with intellectual victories in our controversy with Rome as to think little of that charity which "vaunteth not herself, is not puffed up, doth not behave herself unseemly."

He continued:—"Do you recollect the notion entertained by the primitive Christians concerning Catholicity? The Church was, in their view, one vast body, founded by the Apostles, and spreading its branches out into all lands,—the channel through which the streams of grace flowed, the mystical vine through which that sap of life circulated, which was the possession of those and those only who were grafted on it. In this Church there can be no division. Pass the axe through it, and one part or the other is cut off from the Apostles. There cannot be two distinct bodies, each claiming descent from the original stem. Indeed, the very word *catholic* witnesses to this. Two Apostolic bodies there may be without actual contradiction of terms ; but there is necessarily but one body Catholic." And then, in illustration of this view, he went on to cite from memory the substance of passages from Cyril and Augustine, which I suspect he had picked up from some Romanist friend at the English College. I have since turned them out in in their respective authors, and here give them in translation.

The first extract occurs in a letter written by Augustine to a Donatist bishop :—

" I will briefly suggest a question for your consideration. Seeing that at this day we have before our eyes the Church of God, called Catholic, diffused throughout the world, we think we ought not to doubt that herein is a most plain accomplishment of holy prophecy, confirmed as it was by our Lord in the Gospel, and by the Apostles, who, agreeably to the prediction, so extended it. Thus St. Paul preached the Gospel, and founded churches, etc. John also writes to seven Churches, etc. With all these churches we, at this day, communicate, as is plain ; and it is equally plain that you Donatists do not communicate with them. Now, then, I ask you to assign some reason why Christ should . . . all at once be pent up in Africa, where you are, or even in the whole of it. For your community, which bears the name of Donatus, evidently is not in all places —that is, catholic. If you say ours is not the Catholic, but nickname it the Macarian, the rest of Christendom differs from you ; whereas you yourselves must own, what every one who knows you will also testify, that yours is known as the Donatist denomination. Please to tell me, then, how the Church of Christ has vanished from the world, and is found only among you ; whereas our side of the controversy is upheld, without our saying a word, by the plain fact, that we see in it a fulfilment of Scripture prophecy." *

The next is from one of the same Father's treatises, addressed to a friend :—

" We must hold fast the Christian religion, and the communion of that Church which is, and is called, Catholic, not only by its members, but even by all its enemies. For, whether they will or no, even heretics themselves, and the children of schism, when they speak, not with their own people, but with strangers, call that Church nothing else but Catholic ? Indeed they would not be understood, unless they characterized it by that name which it bears throughout the world." †

* Ep. 49, Ed. Benedict.   † De vera Rel., c. 7, n. 12.

The last was from Cyril's explanation of the doctrine
of the One Holy Catholic Church :—

"Whereas the name (*church*) is used variously . . . . as (for
instance) it may be applied to the heresy or persuasion of the
Manichees, etc., therefore the creed has carefully committed to thee
the confession of the One Holy Catholic Church, in order that thou
mayest avoid their odious meetings, and remain always in the Holy
Catholic Church, in which thou wast regenerated.   And if perchance thou art a traveller in a strange city, do not simply ask,
'Where is the house of God?' for the multitude of persuasions
attempt to call their hiding-places by that name ; nor simply,
'Where is the Church?' but, 'Where is the *Catholic* Church?'
for such is the peculiar name of this the holy Mother of us all, who
is the spouse of the Only-Begotten Son."*

3.

After giving some account of these passages, he continued : "Now, I am only contending for the *fact* that
the communion of Rome constitutes the main body of
the Church Catholic, and that we are split off from it,
and in the condition of the Donatists ; so that every
word of Augustine's argument to them, could be applied
to us.   This, I say, is a *fact ;* and if it be a grave fact,
to account for it by saying that they are corrupt is only
bringing in a second grave fact.   Two such serious facts
—that we are separate from the great body of the
Church, and that it is corrupt—should, one would think,
make us serious ; whereas we behave as if they were
plus and minus, and destroyed each other.   Or rather,
we *triumph* in the Romanists being corrupt, and we *deny*
they are the great body of Christians, unfairly merging
their myriad of churches under the poor title of '*the*
Church of Rome ;' as if unanimity destroyed the argument from numbers."

* Cyril Hieros. Catech., xviii. 12.

"Stay! not so fast!" I made answer; "after all, they are but a part, though a large part, of the Christian world. Is the Greek communion to go for nothing, extending from St. Petersburg to Corinth and Antioch? or the Armenian churches? and the English communion which has branched off to India, Australia, the West Indies, the United States, Canada, and Nova Scotia? The true state of the case is this: the condition of the early Church, as Augustine and Cyril describe it, exists no more; it is to be found nowhere. You may apply, indeed, the terms which they used of it to the present time, and call the Romanists Catholics, as they claim to be; but this is a fiction and a theory, not the expression of a visible fact. Is it not a mere theory by which the Latin Church can affect to spread itself into Russia? I suspect, in spite of St. Cyril, you might ask in vain for their churches under the name of Catholic throughout the autocrat's dominions, or in Greece, as well as in England or Scotland. Where is the Catholic Bishop of Winchester or Lincoln? where the Catholic Church in England as a visible institution? No more is it such in Scotland; not to go on to speak of parts of Germany or the new world. All that can be said by way of reply is, that it is a very considerable communion, and venerable from its consistency and antiquity."

"That is the point," interrupted my companion; "they maintain that, such as they are, such they ever have been. They have been from the first 'the Catholics.' The schismatical Greeks, the Nestorians, the Monophysites, and the Protestants have grown up at different times, and on a novel doctrine or foundation."

"Have a care," I answered, "of diverging to the question of Apostolicity. We are engaged upon the Catholicity of the Latin Church. If we are to speak of

Antiquity, you yourself will be obliged to abandon its cause, for you are as decided as myself upon its corruptions from primitive simplicity. Foundation we have as apostolical as theirs, (unless you listen to the Nag's-head calumny,) and doctrine much more apostolical. Please to keep to the plain tangible *fact*, as you expressed it when you began, of the universal or catholic character of the Roman communion."

He was silent for a while, so I proceeded.

"Let me say a word or two more on the subject I had in hand when you interposed. I was observing that the state of things is certainly altered since Augustine's time—that is, in matter of fact, divisions, cross divisions, and complicated disarrangements have taken place in these latter centuries which were unknown in the fifth. We cannot, at once, apply his words as the representatives of things now existing; they are, in great measure, but the expression of principles to be adopted. May I say something further without shocking you? I think dissent and separatism present features unknown to primitive Christianity—so unknown that in its view of the world a place is not provided for them. A state of things has grown up, of which hereditary dissent is an element. All the better feelings of stability, quietness, loyalty, and the like, are in some places enlisted in its favour. In some places, as in Scotland, dissent is the religion of the state and country. I am not supposing that such outlying communities have blessings equal to the Church Catholic; only, while I condemn them as outlying, I would still contend that they retain so much of privilege, so much of the life and warmth of that spiritual body, from the roots of which they spring, as irregular shoots, as to secure their individual members from the calamity of being altogether cut off from it. In the latter ages of Judaism, the ten tribes, and afterwards the Samaritans, and then the proselytes of the gate, present a parallel, as having a position beyond the literal scope of the Mosaic law. I shall scruple, therefore, to apply the strong language which Cyprian uses against schismatics to the Scottish presbyterians or to the Lutherans. At least, they have the Scriptures. You understand why I mention this—to show, by an additional illustration, that not every word that the Fathers utter concerning the Church Catholic applies at once to the Church of this day. The early Christians had not the complete canon, nor were books then common, nor could most of them read. Other differences between their Church and our Church might be mentioned ;—for instance, the tradition of the early Church was of an historical character, of the nature of testimony ; and possessed an authority superadded to the Church's proper authority as a divine institution. It was a witness, far more perfect in its way, but the same in kind, as the body of ancient writers may be for the genuineness of Cæsar's works. It was virtually infallible. Now, however, this accidental authority has long ceased, or, at least, is indefinitely weakened ; and to resist it is not so obviously a sin against light. Here, then, is another reason for caution in applying the language of the Fathers concerning schism to our own times, since they did not in their writings curiously separate the Church's intrinsic and permanent authority as divine, from her temporary office of bearing witness to the Apostolic doctrine as to an historical fact."

"I must take time to think of this," he replied; "meanwhile, you at least grant me that the Latin communion is the main portion of Christendom—that participation with it is especially our natural position—and that our present separation from it is a grievous calamity as such, and, under the circumstances, nothing short of a solemn protest against corruptions in it, of which we dare not partake."

"I grant it," said I.

"And, in consequence, you discard, henceforth and for ever, the following phrases, and the like—'our glorious emancipation from Rome,' 'the noble stand we made against a corrupt church,' 'our enlightened times,' 'the blind and formal papists,' etc. etc."

"We shall see," I answered—"we shall see."

4.

We walked some little way in silence; at length, he said, "I wonder what use you intend to make of the view you just now so eagerly propounded, of the difference of circumstances between the present and the ancient Church. It leads, I suppose, to the justification of some of those ill-starred theories of concession which are at present so numerous?"

To tell the truth, I did not see my way clearly how far my own view ought to carry me. I saw that, without care, it would practically tend to the discarding the precedent of Antiquity altogether, and was not unwilling to have some light thrown by my friend upon the subject; so I affected, for the moment, a latitudinarianism which I did not feel.* "Certainly," I replied, "it would appear to be our duty to take things as we find them; not to dream about the past, but to imitate, under changed circumstances, what we cannot fulfil literally. Christianity is intended to meet all forms of society; it is not cast in the rigid mould of Judaism. Forms are transitory — principles are eternal: the Church of the

* [*Vid.* Note on "Essays Crit. and Histor.," vol. i., p. 288; also p. 308.]

day is but an accidental development and type of the invisible and unchangeable. It will always have the properties of truth; it will be ever (for instance) essentially conservative and aristocratic; but its policy and measures will ever vary according to the age. Our Church in the seventeenth century was inclined to Romanism; in the nineteenth, it was against Catholic emancipation. The orange ribbon, the emblem of a whig revolution, is now the badge of high tory confederations. Thus, the spirit of the Church is uniform, ever one and the same; but its relative position and ordinances change. At least, all this might be said; and I should like to see how you would answer it."

" That is," he interposed, " you grant that a Jew *would* have been wrong in philosophizing after the pattern you are setting, and talking of the nature of things, and transitory forms, and eternal truths, though you are privileged to do so ? "

" May we not suppose that the rules of the early Church were expedient then—nay, expedient now—as far as they could conveniently be observed, without considering them absolutely binding ? "

"Will you allow," he asked, in reply, "that St. Cyprian would have been in sin had he dispensed with episcopal Ordination, or St. Austin had he recognized the Donatists, or St. Chrysostom had he allowed the deacons to consecrate the elements ? "

" They would have committed sin," I answered.

" And in what would that sin have consisted ? "

" I suppose in doing that which they thought to be contrary to the continued usage of the Church."

" That is," he said, "in doing what they thought contrary to *apostolic* usage ? "

I granted it.

"And, of course," he said, "what they thought to be of apostolic usage, in such matters, was really such?"

I allowed this also.

"So it seems," he continued, "that they might not, and we may, do things contrary to apostolic usage."

"That," I said, "is the very assertion I am making; outward circumstances being changed, we may alter our rule of conduct."

He made answer: "I will give you my mind in a parable. Not many days since, I had scrambled into the rubbish yonder, which marks the site of the Apollo library, when I found what would be a treasure in the eyes of all the antiquarians in Europe, but which, to me, has a value of another kind—a MS. vindication of himself by a Jewish courtier of Herod the Great, for not observing the rites and customs of Judaism. It is well argued throughout. He sets out with owning the divinity of the Mosaic law, its beauty and expediency; the associations of reverence and interest cast around it; the affection it stirs within the mind; and the abstract desirableness of obeying it. 'But, after all, I confess,' he continues, 'I do not think its precepts binding at this day, because we are at such a distance from the age of Moses, and all the nations around us, not to say ourselves are changed, though the Law is not.' He proceeds to argue that he is not bound to go up to Jerusalem at the Passover, because there are synagogues about the country, which did not exist in the time of Moses; and, though it is true that purifications may be performed at the Temple, which the synagogues do not allow of, yet, 'after all,' he asks, 'how can we possibly know that the line of priests and Levites has been kept pure? Who can tell what irregularities may not have been introduced into their families during the captivity? Then, again, what a set of men these said priests are! Tainted with pharisaical pride, or rather polluted with pharisaical hypocrisy: especially the high priests: the very office has become altogether secular—very much changed, too, in form and detail from the original institution. What enormities have occurred in the history of the Asmoneans! Who can suppose that they have any longer extraordinary gifts, prophecy, or the like, as of old time? Besides, there is a temple at Alexandria now, not to say another at Gerizim. Again, Herod, a man of Edom, is king, and has remodelled the state of things; for centuries we have had secular alliances, and religion is now to be supported by ordinary, not extraordinary, means. From the time that these political changes took place, the rites have been superfluous. Events have proved this. A number of Jews once attempted to keep the Sabbath strictly, when an enemy came who surprised them in consequence, and killed them. They were pious but plainly narrow-minded and extravagant men. In short, since the Captivity, the former system has been superseded.'"

"Enough, enough," I interrupted; "perhaps I have spoken more strongly than I meant as to our liberty of acquiescing in innovations. However, I still must hold that we have no right to judge of others at this day, as we should have judged of them, had all of us lived a thousand years earlier. I do really think, for instance, that in the presbyterianism of Scotland we see a providential phenomenon, the growth of a secondary system unknown to St. Austin—begun, indeed, not without sin, but continued, as regards the many, ignorantly, and compatibly with some portion of true faith: I cannot at once apply to its upholders his language concerning schismatics,"

"Well, perhaps I may grant you this, under explanations," he replied, "if you, indeed, will grant that we, on our part, should deviate in practice from primitive rules *as. little* as we can help—only so much as the sheer necessity of our circumstances obliges us. For instance, no plain necessity can ever oblige us to bury an unbaptized person ; though a necessity (viz., of climate), may be urged for baptizing by sprinkling, not by immersion. This will serve as an illustration."

I assented to him, and was glad to have gained a clearer view on this point than I had ever obtained before. I have since seen the principle expressed, in a Tract that has fallen in my way, as follows, the immediate point argued in it being the Apostolical Succession :—

"Consider the analogy of an absent parent, or dear friend, in another hemisphere. Would not such an one naturally reckon it one sign of sincere attachment, if, when he returned home, he found that in all family questions respect had been shown especially to those in whom he was known to have had most confidence ? . . . If his children and dependents had searched diligently where, and with whom, he had left commissions, and, having fair cause to think they had found such, had scrupulously conformed themselves, as far as they could, to the proceedings of those so trusted by him, would he not think this a better sign than if they had been dexterous in devising exceptions, in explaining away the words of trust, and limiting the prerogatives he had conferred ?"*

The principle herein set forth is one which the law manifestly acts upon, as does every prudent statesman or man of business—viz., to go as near as he can to the rules, etc., which come into his hands, when he cannot observe them literally in all respects. But, to continue our conversation.

* [By Mr. Keble.]

5.

My companion went on in his ardent way: "After all, there is no reason why the ancient unity of Christendom should not be revived among us, and Rome be again ecclesiastical head of the whole Church."

"You will," said I, "be much better employed, surely, in speculating upon the means of building up our existing English Church, the Church of Andrewes and Laud, Ken and Butler, than attempting what, even in your own judgment, is an inconsistency. Tell me, can you tolerate the practical idolatry, the virtual worship, of the Virgin and Saints, which is the offence of the Latin Church, and the degradation of moral truth and duty which follows from these?"

"These are corruptions of the Greek Church also," he answered.

"Which only shows," said I, "that we are in the position of Abdiel—one against a many, to take your own comparison. However, this is nothing to the purpose. It is plain, to speak soberly and practically, we never can unite with Rome; for, even were we disposed to tolerate in its adherents what we could not allow in ourselves, they would not listen to our overtures for a moment, unless we began by agreeing to accept all the doctrinal decrees of Trent, and that about images in the number. No; surely, the one and only policy remaining for us to pursue is, not to look towards Rome, but to build up upon Laud's principles."

"Here you are theorizing, not I," returned he. "What is the ground of Andrewes and Laud, Stillingfleet and the rest, but a theory which has never been realized? I grant that the position they take in argument is most admirable, nearer much than the Romanist's to that of the primitive Church, and that they defend and develop their peculiar view most originally and satisfactorily; still, after all, it is a *theory*,—a fine-drawn theory, which has never been owned by any body of churchmen, never witnessed in operation in any system. The question is not, how to draw it out, but how to do it. Laud's attempt was so unsuccessful as to prove he was working upon a mere theory. The actual English Church has never adopted it: in spite of the learning of her divines, she has ranked herself among the Protestants, and the doctrine of the Via Media has slept in libraries. Nay, not only is Anglicanism a theory; it represents, after all, but an imperfect system; it implies a return to that inchoate state, in which the Church existed before the era of Constantine. It is a substitution of infancy for manhood. Of course it took some time, after its first starting, to get the Ark of Religion into her due course, which was at first somewhat vacillating and indeterminate. The language of theology was confessedly unformed, and we at this day actually adopt the creeds and the canons of the fourth century; why not, then, the rites and customs also?"

"I suppose," said I, "no follower of Laud *would* object to the rites and customs then received."

"Why, then," he asked, "do not we pay to the See of Rome the deference shown by the Fathers and Councils of that age?"

"Rome is corrupt," I answered. "When she reforms, it will be time enough to think about the share of honour and power belonging to her in the Universal Church. At present, her prerogative is, at least, suspended, and that most justly."

"However, what I was showing," continued he, "was that the Anglican principle is scarcely fair, as fastening the Christian upon the very first age of the Gospel for evidence of all those necessary developments of the elements of Gospel truth, which could not be introduced throughout the Church except gradually. On the other hand, the Anglican system itself is not found complete in those early centuries; so that the principle is self-destructive. Before there were Christian rulers, there was no doctrine of 'Church and King,' no union of 'Church and State,' which we rightly consider to be a development of the Gospel rule. The principle in question, then, is both in itself unfair and unfairly applied, as it is found in our divines. It is also the result of a very shallow philosophy: as if you could possibly prevent the completion of given tendencies, as if Romanism would not be the inevitable result of a realized Anglicanism, were it ever realized.* However, my main objection to it is, that it is not, and never has been, realized. Protestantism is embodied in a system; so is Popery: but when a man takes up this Via Media, he is a mere doctrinarian —he is wasting his efforts in delineating an invisible phantom; and he will be judged, and fairly, to be trifling, and bookish, and unfit for the world. He will be set down in the number of those who, in some matter of business, start up to suggest their own little crotchet, and are for ever measuring mountains with a pocket ruler, or improving the planetary courses. The world moves forward in bold and intelligible parties; it has its roads to the east and north—nay, to points of the compass

---

* ["As to the resemblance of the author's opinions to Romanism,—if Popery be a perversion or corruption of the Truth, as we believe, it must, by the very force of the terms, be like that Truth which it counterfeits; and therefore the fact of a resemblance, as far as it exists, is no proof of any essential approximation in his opinions to Popery. Rather, it would be a serious argument against their primitive character, if to superficial observers they bore no likeness to it. Ultra-Protestantism could never have been silently corrupted into Popery."—*Advert. 3rd vol. Par. Serm., Ed. 1.*]

between them, to the full number of the thirty-two;
but not to more than these. You *must* travel along
a ready-made road ; you cannot go right ahead across-
country, or, in spite of your abstract correctness, you
will be swamped or benighted. When a person calling
himself a ' Reformed Catholic,' or an ' Apostolical Christian,' begins to speak, people say to him, ' What are
you ? If you are a Catholic, why do you not join the
Romanists ? If you are ours, why do you not maintain
the great Protestant doctrines ?' Or, in the words of
Hall of Norwich, addressed, it is said, to Laud :

> ' I would I knew where to find you ; then I could tell how to
> take direct aims ; whereas now I must pore and conjecture. To-
> day you are in the tents of the Romanists—to-morrow in ours ; the
> next day between both—against both. Our adversaries think you
> ours—we, theirs ; your conscience finds you with both and neither.
> I flatter you not : this of yours is the worst of all tempers. Heat
> and cold have their uses—lukewarmness is good for nothing, but to
> trouble the stomach. . . . How long will you halt in this indiffer-
> ence ? Resolve one way, and know, at last, what you do hold—
> what you should. Cast off either your wings or your teeth, and,
> loathing this bat-like nature, be either a bird or a beast.'

" This was the character of his school down to the
Non-jurors, in whom the failure of the experiment was
finally ascertained. The theory sunk then, once and for
all."

" My dear fellow," I made answer, " I see you are of
those who think success and the applause of men everything, not bearing to consider, *first*, whether a view be
true, and then to incur boldly the ' reproach ' of uphold-
ing it. Surely, the Truth has in no age been popular,
and those who preached it have been thought idiots, and
died without visible fruit of their labours."

He smiled, and was silent, as if in thought.

I continued : " Now listen to me, for I have it in purpose to turn your own words against yourself, to show that you are the theorist, and I the man of practical sense ; and at the same time to cheer you with the hope, that the Anglican principle, though the true one, yet may perchance be destined, even yet, in the designs of Providence, to be expanded and realized in us, the unworthy sons of the great Archbishop.

6.

As I said these words, I caught a sight of one of the companions of my excursion making towards us, who was well known to the friend with whom I was conversing. Instead, then, of beginning my harangue upon the prospects of the English Church, I said, " Here comes a friend in need, just in time. I was but going to repeat what I have picked up from him. He is the great theorist, after all, and he will best do justice to his own views himself."

We went forward to meet him ; and, after some indifferent topics had passed between us, I told him the position in which he had found us, and asked him to take upon himself the exposition of his own speculations. I will pass over all explanations on his part, hesitations, disclaimers of the character I gave of him, and the like, and will take up the conversation when he was fairly implicated in the task which we had imposed upon him. For the future, I will call him Basil, and my first friend Ambrose, to avoid circumlocution.

" Nothing seems so chimerical, I confess," said he, " as the notion that the Church temper of the seventeenth century will ever return in England ; nor do I ever expect it will, on a large scale. But the great and small in extent are not conditions of moral or religious strength

and dignity. The Holy Land was not larger than Wales.
We can afford to give up the greater part of England to
the spirit of the age, and yet develop, in a diocese, or a
single city, those principles and tendencies of the Caroline era which have never yet arrived at their just
dimensions."

"You presuppose, of course, a King like the Martyr,
in these anticipations?" said Ambrose.

"In speaking of a *single* diocese, or city," returned
the other, " I have obviously implied a system of which
political arrangements are not the mainspring. Alas! we
can no longer have such a king. The Monarchy is not
constitutionally now what it was then ; nay, the Church,
perchance, may not even be allowed the privilege of
being loyal in time to come, though obedient and
patient it always must be. The principle of national
religion is fast getting out of fashion, and we are relaps-
ing into the primitive state of Christianity, when men
prayed for their rulers, and suffered from them, neither
giving nor receiving temporal benefits. The element of
high-churchmanship (as that word has commonly been
understood) seems about to retreat again into the
depths of the Christian temper, and Apostolicity is to
be elicited instead, in greater measure.

  ' 'Tis true, 'tis pity ; pity 'tis, 'tis true.'

It would be well, indeed, were we allowed to acknowledge
the magistrate's divine right to preside over the Church;
but if the State declares it has itself no divine right over
us, what help is there for it ? We must learn, like Hagar,
to subsist by ourselves in the wilderness. Certainly, I
never expect the *system* of Laud to return, but I do
expect the due continuation and development of his
principles. High-churchmanship—looking at the m tr

historically—will be regarded as a temporary stage of a course. The (so-called) union of Church and State, as it then existed, has been a wonderful and most gracious phenomenon in Christian history. It is a realization of the Gospel in its highest perfection, when both Cæsar and St. Peter know and fulfil their office. I do not expect anything so blessed again. Charles is the King, Laud the prelate, Oxford the sacred city, of this principle; just as Rome is the city of Catholicism, and modern Paris of infidelity. I give up high-churchmanship. But, to return——"

"First, however," interrupted Ambrose, "I have it in purpose to imprison you in a dilemma, which you must resolve before you can discuss your subject with any ease or convenience. Either you expect this substitution of apostolicity for high-churchmanship at an early or at a distant date. If you say at an early, such keen anticipation of so deplorable a calamity as the unchristianizing of the State savours of disloyalty; if at a distant, of fanaticism, as if the spirit of the seventeenth century could, on ever so contracted a field, revive centuries hence."

"I intend," he answered, "neither to be disaffected nor fanatical, and yet shall retain my anticipations. As to the charge of disloyalty, I repel it at once by stating, that I *am* looking forward to events as yet removed from us by centuries. It is no disloyal or craven spirit to suppose that, in the course of generations, changes may occur, when change is the rule of the world, and when, in our own country especially, not one hundred and fifty years perhaps has ever passed without some great constitutional change, or violent revolution. It is no faintness of heart to suppose that the eras of 1536, 1649, and 1688 are tokens of other such in store.

We all know that dynasties and governments are, like individuals, mortal; and to provide against the un-churching of the monarchy, is not more disrespectful to it than to introduce a regency bill beforehand, in the prospect of a minority. The Church alone is eternal; and, being such, it must, by the very law of its nature, survive its friends, and is bound calmly to anticipate the vicissitudes of its condition. We are consulting for no affair of the day; we are contemplating our fortunes five centuries to come. We are labouring for the year 2500. By that time we may have buried our temporal guardians: their memory we shall always revere and bless; but the Successors of the Apostles will still have their work—if the world last so long—a work (may be) of greater peril and hardship, but of more honour, than now.

"Nor, on the other hand, is it idle to suppose that former principles, long dormant, may, like seed in the earth, spring up at some distant day. History is full of precedents in favour of such an anticipation. At this very time the nation is beginning to reap the full fruits of the perverse anti-ecclesiastical spirit to which the Re-formation on the Continent gave birth. Three centuries and more have not developed it. Again, three centuries and more were necessary for the infant Church to attain her mature and perfect form, and due stature. Atha-nasius, Basil, and Austin are the fully instructed doctors of her doctrine, discipline, and morals."

7.

I could not but look at Ambrose, and smile at hearing the argument he had used, before the other came up incidentally made available against himself. Basil continued:

"Again, Hildebrand was the first to bring into use the donations made by Pepin and Charlemagne to the Church; yet these were made between A.D. 750—800, and Hildebrand's papacy did not commence till 1086. The interval was a time of weakness, humiliation, guilt, and disgrace to the Church, far exceeding any ecclesiastical scandals in our own country, whether in the century before or after the Caroline era. Gibbon tells us that the Popes of the ninth and tenth centuries were 'insulted, imprisoned, and murdered by their tyrants;' that the illegitimate son, grandson, and great grandson of Marozia, a woman of profligate character, were seated in St. Peter's chair; and the second of these was but nineteen when elevated to that spiritual dignity. He renounced the ecclesiastical dress, and abandoned himself to hunting, gaming, drinking, and kindred excesses. This, too, was the season of anti-popes, one of whom actually opposed Hildebrand himself, and eventually obliged him to retreat to Salerno, where he died. Yet now that celebrated man stands in history as if the very contemporary and first inheritor of Charlemagne's gifts, and reigns in the Church without the vestige of a rival. So little has time to do with the creations of moral energy, that Guiberto ceases in our associations to have lived with him, or the first Carlovingians to have been before him. He obliterated an interval of three hundred years."

"You were somewhat too conceding, methinks, when you began," said Ambrose, "if you are not exorbitant now. It is not much more to ask that a king like Charles should ascend the throne, than that a mind like Hildebrand's should be given to the Church."

"And yet Father Paul, a sagacious man," Basil answered, "did look with much anxiety towards the English hierarchy of his day (1617), as likely to develop an apostolical spirit which even kings could not control. So far, indeed, he was mistaken in his immediate anticipation, because the English Church was far too loyal to be dangerous to the State; yet it may chance that, in the course of centuries there is no king to whom to be loyal. His words are these:—

'Anglis nimium timeo; episcoporum magna illa potestas, licet sub rege, prorsus mihi suspecta est. Ubi vel regem desidem nacti fuerint, vel magni spiritûs archiepiscopum habuerint, regia authoritas pessundabitur, et episcopi ad absolutam dominationem aspirabunt. Ego equum ephippiatum in Angliâ videre videor, et ascensurum propediem equitem antiquum divino.' *

"Now, is it not singular that this Church should so close upon these words have developed Laud, a prelate (if any other) aspiring and undaunted? And again, that within fifty years of him the king actually was in the power of the primate, as the umpire between him and the nation, though Sancroft (as he himself afterwards understood) was not alive to his position, nor equal to the emergency? These are omens of what may be still to come, inasmuch as they show the political and moral temper, the presiding genius of the Anglican Church, which had produced, at distant intervals, before Laud, prelates as high-minded, though doubtless less enlightened and more ambitious. It is not one stroke of fortune, one political revolution, which can chase the *genius loci* from his favourite haunt. Canterbury and Oxford are a match for many Williams of Nassau."

I here interrupted him to corroborate his last remarks, without pledging myself to approve his mode of conveying them. I said that "Leslie, one of the last of

* [I think this is to be found in Sarpi's Letters, a book lent to me by Dr. Routh.]

the line of apostolical divines, had expressed the same opinion concerning the Church at large, in his Case of the Regale and Pontificate. His words are as follows:

'I say, if the Church would trust to Him more than to the arm of flesh, she need not fear the power of kings. No; Christ would give her kings, not as heads and spiritual fathers over her, but as nursing fathers, to protect, love, and cherish her, to reverence and to save her, as the Spouse of Christ. Instead of such fathers as she has made kings to be over herself, and of whom she stands in awe, and dare not exert the power Christ has given her, without their good liking, she should then have " children whom she might make princes in all the earth." Kings would become her sons and her servants, instead of being her fathers.

' My brethren, let me freely speak to you. These promises must be fulfilled, and in this world, for they are spoke of it, and belong not to the state of heaven, but to the condition of the Church in all the earth. All the prophets that have been, since the world began, have spoken of these days ; therefore, they will surely come ; and " though ye have lien among the pots, yet she shall be as the wings of a dove, that is covered with silver, and her feathers like gold." '

"Having been led to quote from an author who wrote a century since, let me here add the witness of an acute observer of our own century, whose Letters and Remains have been published since the date of the conversation I am relating—Mr. Alexander Knox. The following was written just two centuries after Sarpi's letter :

' No Church on earth has more intrinsic excellence, [than the English Church,] yet no Church, probably, has less practical influence. Her excellence, then, I conceive, gives ground for confiding that Providence will never abandon her ; but her want of influence would seem no less clearly to indicate, that Divine Wisdom will not always suffer her to go on without measures for her improvement. . . . Shall then the present negligence and insensibility always prevail? This cannot be ; the rich provision made by the grace and providence of God, for habits of a noble kind, is evidence that those habits shall at length be formed, that men shall arise, fitted, both by inclination and ability, to discover for themselves, and to display to others, whatever yet remains undisclosed, whether in the words or works of God. But if it be asked, how shall fit instruments be prepared for this high purpose, it can only be answered, that in the most signal instances times of severe trial have been chosen for divine communications.—Moses, an exile, when God spoke to him from the bush; Daniel, a captive in Babylon, where he was cheered with those clearest rays of Old Testament prophecy; St. John, a prisoner in Patmos, where he was caught up into heaven, and beheld the apocalyptic vision. . . . . My persuasion of the radical excellence of the Church of England does not suffer me to doubt, that she is to be an illustrious agent in bringing the mystical kingdom of Christ to its ultimate perfection.'"

8.

When the conversation had arrived at this point, my friend Ambrose put in a remark. "It must be confessed," he said, "that your triumphant Church will, after all, be very much like what the papal was in its pride of place. The only difference would seem to be, that the Popes deposed kings; but you, in effect, wait till there are no kings to depose, leaving it to the (so-called) 'radical reformers' to bring upon themselves the odium of the acts which are to introduce you. Why not, then, avail ourselves of what is ready to our hands in the Church of Rome? Why attempt, instead, to form a second-best and spurious Romanism?"

"Pardon me," I said, in answer, "Basil thinks the Roman Church corrupt in doctrine. We cannot join a Church, did we wish it ever so much, which does not acknowledge our Orders, refuses us the Cup, demands our acquiescence in image worship, and excommunicates us, if we do not receive it and all other decisions of the Tridentine Council. While she insists on this, there must be an impassable line between her and us; and while she claims infallibility, she must insist on what she has once decreed; and when she abandons that claim she breaks the principle of her own vitality. Thus, we can never unite with Rome."

"This is true and certain," said Basil; "but even though Rome were as sound in faith as she is notoriously unsound, our present line would remain the same. What, indeed, might come to pass at a distant era, when monarchies had ceased to be, it would be impertinent to ask; but, though I have been anticipating the future, we have nothing really to do with the future. Our business is with things as they are. We want to *begin* at once, and must not, dare not start upon a basis which is not to be realized for some hundred years to come. Of course;—and to do anything effectually, we must build upon principles and feelings already recognized among us. I grant all this: let us leave the future to itself: we are concerned, not with illusions, (as the French politicians say,) but with things that are. But this holds of other illusions besides those against which you have warned such as me. For what we know, by the time we are without kings Rome may be without a Pope; and it would be a strange policy to go over to them now, by way of anticipating a distant era, which, for what we know, may, in the event, be preceded by their coming over to us. You have heard of the two brothers in the seventeenth century, papist and puritan, who disputed together and convinced each other. Let us take warning from them.

"I repeat, to do anything effectually, certainly we must start upon *recognized* principles and customs. Any other procedure stamps a person as wrong-headed, ill-judging, or eccentric, and brings upon him the contempt and ridicule of those sensible men by whose opinions society is necessarily governed. Putting aside the question of truth and falsehood—which of course is the main consideration—even as aiming at success, we must be aware of the great error of making changes on no more definite basis than their abstract fitness, their alleged scripturalness, their adoption by the ancients. Such changes are rightly called *innovations;* those which spring from existing institutions, opinions, or feelings, are called *developments,* and may be recommended without invidiousness as being *improvements.* I adopt, then, and claim as my own, that position of yours, 'that we must take and use what is ready to our hands.' To do otherwise, is to act the *doctrinaire,* and to provide for simple failure : for instance, if we would enforce observance of the Lord's Day, we must not, at the outset, rest it on any theory (however just) of Church authority, but on the authority of Scripture. If we would oppose the State's interference with the distribution of Church property, we shall succeed, not by urging any doctrine of Church independence, or by citing decrees of General Councils, but by showing the contrariety of that measure to existing constitutional and ecclesiastical precedents among ourselves. Hildebrand found the Church provided with certain existing means of power; he vindicated them, and was rewarded with the success which attends, not on truth as such, but on this prudence and tact in conduct. St. Paul observed the same rule,— whether preaching at Athens or persuading his countrymen. It was the gracious condescension of our Lord Himself, not to substitute Christianity for Judaism by any violent revolution, but to develop Judaism into Christianity, as the Jews might bear it. Now, Popery is *not* here ready to our hands ; on the contrary, we find among us, at this day, an intense fear and hatred of Popery ; and that, ill-instructed as it confessedly is, still based upon truth. It is mere headstrong folly, then, to advocate the Church of Rome. It is to lose our *position* as a Church, which never answers to any, whether body or individual. If, indeed, salvation were not in our Church, the case would be altered ; as it is, were Rome as pure in faith as the Church of the Apostles, which she is not, I would not join her, unless those about me did so too, lest I should commit schism. Our business is to take what we have received, and build upon it : to accept, as a legacy from our forefathers, this ' Protestant' spirit which they have bequeathed us, and merely to disengage it from its errors, purify it, and make it something more than a negative principle ; thus only have we a chance of success. All your arguments, then, my dear Ambrose, in favour of Romanism, or rather your regrets on the sub-ject—for you are not able to go so far as to design, or even to hope on the subject—seem to me irrelevant, and recoil upon your own professed principle ; and, instead of persuading others, only lead them to ask the pertinent question, ' Why do you stay among us, if you like a foreign religion better ? ' "

The other smiled with an expression which showed that he was at once entertained and as unconvinced as before. For myself, I was not quite pleased with the tone of political expedience which my friend had assumed, though I agreed in his general sentiment ; except, indeed, in his patience towards the word " Protestant," which is a term as political as were his arguments.

" You have surely been somewhat carried beyond your own excellent judgment," I said, " by your earnestness in advocating a view. A person who did not know you as well as I do would take such avowals as the offspring of a Florentine, not an English school. It is certainly *safer* in so serious a matter to go upon more obvious, more religious grounds than those you have selected ; for I agree with you most entirely in the conclusion you arrive at. I will give you a reason, which has had particular weight with me. Of course, one must not say, 'Whatever is, is right,' in such a sense as to excuse what is wrong, whether committed or permitted, violence or cowardice ; yet, at the same time, it certainly is true, that the external circumstances under which we find ourselves, have a legitimate influence, nay, a sort of claim of deference, upon our conduct. St. Paul says that every one should remain in the place where he finds himself. This, so far, at least, applies to our ecclesiastical position, that, unless where conscience comes in, it is our duty to submit to what we are born under. I do not insist here on the engagements of the clergy to administer the discipline of Christ as the Church and Realm have received the same ; here, I only assert that we find the Church and State united, and must therefore maintain that Union."

"The said Union," interrupted Ambrose, "being much like the union of the Israelites with the Egyptians, in the house of bondage."

"So it may be," I replied,—"but recollect that the chosen people were not allowed to disenthral themselves without an intimation of God's permission. When Moses attempted, of himself, to avenge them, he only got into trial and distress. It was in vain he killed the Egyptian, there was neither voice, nor any to answer, nor any that regarded. Providence always says, ' *Stand still,* and see the salvation of God.' We must not dare to move, except He bids us. How different was the success of Moses afterwards, when God sent him ! In like manner, the deliverers of Israel, in the period of the Judges, were, for the most part, expressly commissioned to their office. At another time, 'the Lord delivered Sisera into the hand of a woman.' It is not for us 'to know the times and the seasons which the Father hath put in His own power.'

"And so, once more, Daniel, though he prayed towards the Temple during his captivity, made no attempt to leave Babylon for his own country, to escape from the mass of idolaters and infidels, scorners and profligates, among whom his lot was cast in this world. We, too, who are in captivity, must *bide our time.*"

9.

Here there was a pause in the conversation, as if our minds required rest after sharing in it, or leisure to digest it. We were in the terrace walk overlooking the Trastevere: we stood still, and made such disconnected remarks as the separate buildings and places in the view suggested. At length, the Montorio, where St. Peter was martyred, and some discourse it suggested, recalled us to our former subject, and we began again with fresh life.

"Hildebrand," said Ambrose, "had a basis to go upon; and we, in matter of fact, have none. However true your policy may be of our availing ourselves of things existing, I repeat we have no *church* basis,—we have nothing but certain merely political rights. Hildebrand had definite powers, though dormant or obsolete. The Exarchate of Ravenna had been formally ceded to the popedom by Pepin, though virtually wrested from it in the interval. The supposed donation of Constantine and the Decretals were recognized charters, which churchmen might fall back upon. We have nothing of this kind now."

* *

3

"Let us make the most of what we have," returned the other; "and surely we have enough for our purpose. Let us consider what that purpose is, and what it is we want: our one tangible object is to restore the connexion, at present broken, between bishops and people;—for in this everything is involved, directly or indirectly, which it is a duty to contend for;—and to effect this, we want no temporal rights of any sort, as the Popes needed, but merely the recognition of our Church's existing spiritual powers. We are not aiming at any kingdom of this world; we need no Magna-Chartas or Coronation oaths for the object which we have at heart: we wish to maintain the faith, and bind men together in love. We are aiming, with this view, at that commanding moral influence which attended the early Church, which made it attractive and persuasive, which manifested itself in a fascination sufficient to elicit out of paganism and draw into itself all that was noblest and best from the mass of mankind, and which created an internal system of such grace, beauty, and majesty, that believers were moulded thereby into martyrs and evangelists. Now let us see what materials we have for a similar spiritual structure, if we keep what, through God's good providence, has descended to us.

"First, we have the Ordination Service, acknowledging three, and three only, divinely appointed Orders of ministers, implying a Succession, and the bishop's divine commission for continuing it, and assigning to the presbytery the power of retaining and remitting sins: these are invaluable, as being essential, possessions.

"Next, we have the plain statements of the general necessity of the sacraments for salvation, and the strong language of the services appointed for the administration of them. We have Confirmation and Matrimony recognized as spiritual ordinances. We have forms of absolution and blessing.

"Further, we have the injunction of daily service, and the solemnization of fast and festival days.

"Lastly, we have a yearly confession of the desirableness of a restoration of the primitive discipline.

"On these foundations, properly understood, we may do anything."

"Still you have not touched upon the real difficulty," interrupted Ambrose. "Hildebrand governed an existing body, and was only employed in vindicating for it certain powers and privileges; you, on the other hand, have to make the body, before you proceed to strengthen it. The Church in England is not a body now, it has little or no substantiveness; it has dwindled down to its ministers, who are as much secular functionaries as they are rulers of a Christian people. What reason have you to suppose that the principles you have enumerated will interest an uninstructed, as well as edify an already disciplined, multitude? Still the problem is, How to do it?"

10.

When he stopped, Basil looked at me. "Cyril," said he, mentioning my name, "has much to say on this argument, and I leave it to him to tell you how to do it." Thus challenged, I began in my turn.

"I will tell you," I said, "Hildebrand really had to create as well as we. If the Church was not in his time laid prostrate before the world, at least it was incorporated into it—so I am told, at least, by those who have studied the history of his times: the clergy were dissolved in secular vocations and professions; a bishop was a powerful baron, the feudal vassal of a temporal prince, of whom he held estates and castles, his Ordination being virtually an incidental form, necessary at the commencement of his occupancy; the inferior clergy were inextricably entangled in the fetters of secular alliances, often criminal and scandalous. In planting his lever, which was to break all these irreligious ties, he made the *received* forms and rules of the Church his fulcrum. If masterminds are ever granted to us, to build us up in faith and unity, they must do the same; they must take their stand upon that existing basis which Basil has just now described, and must be determined never to extravagate from it. They must make that basis their creed and their motive; they must persevere for many years, in preaching and teaching, before they proceed to act upon their principles, introducing terms and names, and impressing members of the Church with the real meaning of the truths which are her animating element, and which her members verbally admit. In spite of opposition, they must persevere in insisting on the episcopal system, the apostolical succession, the ministerial commission, the power of the keys, the duty and desirableness of Church discipline, the sacredness of Church rites and ordinances.

"So far well; but you will say, how is all this to be made interesting to the people? I answer, that the topics themselves which they are to preach are of that striking and attractive nature which carries with it its own influence. The very notion, that representatives of the Apostles are now on earth, from whose communion we may obtain grace, as the first Christians did from the Apostles, is surely, when admitted, of a most transporting and persuasive character; it will supply the desideratum which exists in the actual teaching of this day. Clergymen at present are subject to the painful experience of losing the more religious portion of their flock, whom they have tutored and moulded as children, but who, as they come into life, fall away to the dissenters. Why is this? Because they desire to be stricter than the mass of Churchmen, and the Church gives them no means; they desire to be governed by sanctions more constraining than those of mere argument, and the Church keeps back those doctrines, which, to the eye of faith, give a reality and substance to religion. He who is told that the Church is the treasure-house of spiritual gifts, comes for a definite privilege; he who has been taught that it is merely a duty to keep united to the Church, gains nothing, and is tempted to leave it for the meeting-house, which promises him present excitement, if it does nothing more. He who sees Churchmen identified with the world, naturally looks at dissent as a separation from it. The first business, then, of our Hildebrand will be to stop this continual secession to the dissenters, by supplying those doctrines which nature itself, I may say, desiderates in our existing institutions, and which the dissenters attempt to supply. This should be well observed, for it is a remarkable circumstance, that most of the more striking innovations of the present day are awkward and unconscious imitations of the provisions of the old Catholic system. 'Texts for every day in the year' are the substitute for the orderly calendar of Scripture Lessons; prayer-meetings stand for the daily service; farewell speeches to missionaries take the place of public Ordinations; public meetings for religious oratory, the place of the ceremonies and processions of the middle ages; charitable societies are instead of the strict and enthusiastic Religious Institutions. Men know not of the legitimate Priesthood, and therefore are condemned to hang upon the judgment of individual and self-authorized preachers; they defraud their children of the initiatory sacrament, and therefore are forced to invent a rite of dedication instead of it ; they put up with legends of private Christians, distinguished for an ambiguous or imperfect piety, narrow-minded in faith, and tawdry and discoloured in their holiness, in the place of the men of God, the meek martyrs, the saintly pastors, the wise and winning teachers of the Catholic Church. One of the most striking illustrations of this general remark, is the existing practice and feeling about psalmody :—formerly great part of the public service was sung ; part of this, as the Te Deum, being an exhibition of the peculiar gospel doctrines. We let this practice go out ; then, feeling the want of singing, we introduce it between the separate portions of the services. There is no objection to this, so far ; it has primitive sanction. But observe,—we have only time for one or two verses, which cannot show the drift and spirit of the Psalm, and are often altogether unintelligible, or grammatically defective. Next, a complaint arises, that no *Christian* hymns constitute part of the singing ; so, having relinquished the Te Deum, we have recourse to the rhymes of Watts, Newton, and Wesley. Moreover, we sing as slow as if singing were a penitential exercise. Consider how the Easter hymn affects a congregation, and you will see their natural congeniality to musical services of a more animated, quicker, and more continued measure. The dissenters seem to feel this in their adoption of objectionable secular tunes, or of religious tunes of a *cantabile* character ; our slow airs seem to answer no purpose, except that of painfully exhausting the breath—they will never allure a congregation to sing. So, again, as to the Services generally ; they are scarcely at all adapted to the successive seasons and days of the Christian year : the Bible is rich in materials for illustrating and solemnizing these as they come; but we make little use of it. Consider how impressive the Easter anthem is, as a substitute for the *Venite:* why should not such as this be appointed at other Seasons, in the same and other parts of the service? How few prayers we possess for particular occasions! Reflect, for instance, upon Jeremy Taylor's prayers and litanies, and I think you will grant that, carefully preserving the Prayer Book's majestic simplicity of style, we might nevertheless profitably make additions to our liturgical services. We have but matins and evensong appointed: what if a clergyman wishes to have prayers in his church seven times a day?

"I touched just now on the subject of the Religious Institutions of the middle ages. These are imperatively called for to stop the progress of dissent; indeed, I conceive you necessarily must have dissent or monachism in a Christian country;—so make your choice. The more religious minds demand some stricter religion than that of the generality of men; if you do not gratify this desire religiously and soberly, they will gratify it themselves at the expense of unity. I wish this were better understood than it is. You may build new churches, without stint, in every part of the land, but you will not approximate towards the extinction of Methodism and dissent till you consult for this feeling; till then, the sectaries will deprive you of numbers, and those the best of your flock, whom you can least afford to lose, and who might be the greatest strength and ornament to it. This is an occurrence which happens daily. Say that one out of a number of sisters in a family takes a religious turn; is not her natural impulse to join either the Wesleyans or the irregulars within our pale? And why? all because the Church does not provide innocent outlets for the sober relief of feeling and excitement: she would fain devote herself immediately to God's service—to prayer, almsgiving, attendance on the sick. You not only decline her services yourself,—you drive her to the dissenters: and why? all because the Religious Life, though sanctioned by Apostles and illustrated by the early Saints, has before now given scope to moroseness, tyranny, and presumption."

II.

"I will tell you," interrupted Basil, "an advantage which has often struck me as likely to result from the institution (under sober regulations) of religious Sisterhoods—viz., the education of the female portion of the community in Church principles. It is plain we need schools for females: so great is the inconvenience, that persons in the higher ranks contrive to educate their daughters at home, from want of confidence in those schools in which alone they can place them. It is speaking temperately of these to say, that (with honourable exceptions, of course, such as will be found to every rule) they teach little beyond mere accomplishments, present no antidotes to the frivolity of young minds, and instruct in no definite views of religious truth at all. On the other hand, what an incalculable gain would it be to the Church were the daughters, and future mothers, of England educated in a zealous and affectionate adherence to its cause, taught to reverence its authority, and to delight in its ordinances and services! What, again, if they had instructors, who were invested with even more than the respectability which collegiate foundations give to education in the case of the other sex, instructors placed above the hopes and fears of the world, and impressing the thought of the Church on their pupils' minds, in association with their own refinement and heavenly serenity! But, alas! so ingrained are our unfortunate prejudices on this head, that I fear nothing but serious national afflictions will give an opening to the accomplishment of so blessed a design."

"For myself," said I, "I confess my hopes do not extend beyond the vision of the rise of this Religious Life among us ; not that even this will have any success, as you well observe, till loss of property turns the thoughts of the clergy and others from this world to the next. As to the rise of a high episcopal system, that is, again to use your notion, a dream of A.D. 2500. We can but desire in our day to keep alive the lamp of truth in the sepulchre of this world till a brighter era : and surely the ancient system I speak of is the providentially designed instrument of this work. When Arianism triumphed in the sees of the eastern Church, the Associated Brethren of Egypt and Syria were the witnesses prophesying in sackcloth against it. So it may be again. When the day of trial comes, we shall be driven from the established system of the Church, from livings and professorships, fellowships and stalls ; we shall (so be it) muster amid dishonour, poverty, and destitution, for higher purposes ; we shall bear to be severed from possessions and connexions of this world ; we shall turn our thoughts to the education of those middle classes, the children of farmers and tradesmen, whom the Church has hitherto neglected ; we shall educate a certain number, for the purpose of transmitting to posterity our principles and our manner of life ; we shall turn ourselves to the wants of the great towns, and attempt to be evangelists in a population almost heathen.

"Till then, I scarcely expect that anything will be devised of a nature to meet the peculiar evils existing in a densely peopled city. Benevolent persons hope, by increasing our instruments of usefulness, to relieve them. Doubtless they may so relieve them ; and no charitable effort can fail of a blessing. New churches and lay co-operation will do something ; but, I confess, I think that some instrument different in kind is required for the present emergency: great towns will never be evangelized merely by the parochial system. They are beyond the sphere of the parish priest, burdened as he is with the endearments and anxieties of a family, and the secular restraints and engagements of the Establishment. The unstable multitude cannot be influenced and ruled except by uncommon means, by the evident sight of disinte-rested and self-denying love, and elevated firmness. The show of domestic comfort, the decencies of furniture and apparel, the bright hearth and the comfortable table, (good and innocent as they are in their place,) are as ill-suited to the missionary of a town population as to an Apostle. Heathens, and quasi-heathens, (such as the miserable rabble of a large town,) were not converted in the beginning of the Gospel, nor now, as it would appear, by the sight of domestic virtues or domestic comforts in their missionary. Surely Providence has His various means adapted to different ends. I think that Religious Institutions, over and above their intrinsic recommendations, are the legitimate instruments of working upon a populace, just as argument may be accounted the medium of conversion in the case of the educated, or parental authority in the case of the young.

12.

"I have been watching with some interest," said Ambrose, who had been silent all this while, "how near, with all your protestations against Popery, you would advance towards it in the course of your speculations. I am now happy to see you will go the full length of what you yourselves seem to admit is considered one of its most remarkable characteristics—monachism."

"I know," answered I, "that is at present the popular notion; but our generation has not yet learned the distinction between Popery and Catholicism. But, be of good heart; it will learn many things in time."

The other laughed; and, the day being now someway advanced into the afternoon, we left the garden, and separated.

March, 1836.

THE PATRISTICAL IDEA OF ANTICHRIST.

IN FOUR LECTURES.

I.

The Times of Antichrist.

THE Thessalonian Christians had supposed that the
coming of Christ was near at hand. St. Paul
writes to warn them against such an expectation. Not
that he discountenances their looking out for our Lord's
coming,—the contrary ; but he tells them that a certain
event must come before it, and till that had arrived the
end would not be. "Let no man deceive you by any
means," he says ; "for that Day shall not come, except
there come a falling away first,"—and he proceeds
"and" except first "that man of sin be revealed, the
son of perdition."

As long as the world lasts, this passage of Scripture
will be full of reverent interest to Christians. It is their
duty ever to be watching for the advent of their Lord,
to search for the signs of it in all that happens around
them ; and above all to keep in mind this great and
awful sign of which St. Paul speaks to the Thessalonians.
As our Lord's first coming had its forerunner, so will the

second have its own. The first was "One more than a prophet," the Holy Baptist: the second will be more than an enemy of Christ; it will be the very image of Satan, the fearful and hateful Antichrist. Of him, as described in prophecy, I propose to speak; and, in doing so, I shall follow the exclusive guidance of the ancient Fathers of the Church.

I follow the ancient Fathers, not as thinking that on such a subject they have the weight they possess in the instance of doctrines or ordinances. When they speak of doctrines, they speak of them as being universally held. They are witnesses to the fact of those doctrines having been received, not here or there, but everywhere. We receive those doctrines which they thus teach, not merely because they teach them, but because they bear witness that all Christians everywhere then held them. We take them as honest informants, but not as a sufficient authority in themselves, though they are an authority too. If they were to state these very same doctrines, but say, "These are our opinions: we deduced them from Scripture, and they are true," we might well doubt about receiving them at their hands. We might fairly say, that we had as much right to deduce from Scripture as they had; that deductions of Scripture were mere opinions; that if our deductions agreed with theirs, that would be a happy coincidence, and increase our confidence in them; but if they did not, it could not be helped—we must follow our own light. Doubtless, no man has any right to impose his own deductions upon another, in matters of faith. There is an obvious obligation, indeed, upon the ignorant to submit to those who are better informed; and there is a fitness in the young submitting implicitly for a time to the teaching of their elders; but, beyond this, one man's opinion is not better than another's. But this is not the state of the case as regards the primitive Fathers. They do not speak of their *own private* opinion; they do not say, "This is true, *because* we see it in Scripture"—about which there might be differences of judgment—but, "this is true, because in matter of fact it is held, and has ever been held, by all the Churches, down to our times, without interruption, ever since the Apostles:" where the question is merely one of testimony, viz., whether they had the means of knowing that it had been and was so held; for if it was the belief of so many and independent Churches at once, and that, on the ground of its being from the Apostles, doubtless it cannot but be true and Apostolic.

This, I say, is the mode in which the Fathers speak as regards *doctrine*; but it is otherwise when they interpret prophecy. In this matter there seems to have been no catholic, no formal and distinct, or at least no authoritative traditions; so that when they interpret Scripture they are for the most part giving, and profess to be giving, either their own private opinions, or vague, floating, and merely general anticipations. This is what might have been expected; for it is not ordinarily the course of Divine Providence to interpret prophecy before the event. What the Apostles disclosed concerning the future, was for the most part disclosed by them in private, to individuals—not committed to writing, not intended for the edifying of the body of Christ,—and was soon lost. Thus, in a few verses after the passage I have quoted, St. Paul says, "Remember ye not, that when I was yet with you, I told you these things?" and he writes by hints and allusions, not speaking out. And it shows how little care was taken to discriminate and authenticate his prophetical intimations, that the Thessalonians had adopted an opinion, that he had said—what in fact he had not said—that the Day of Christ was immediately at hand.

Yet, though the Fathers do not convey to us the interpretation of prophecy with the same certainty as they convey doctrine, yet, in proportion to their agreement, their personal weight, and the prevalence, or again the authoritative character of the opinions they are stating, they are to be read with deference; for, to say the least, they are as likely to be right as commentators now; in some respects more so, because the interpretation of prophecy has become in these times a matter of controversy and party. And passion and prejudice have so interfered with soundness of judgment, that it is difficult to say who is to be trusted to interpret it, or whether a private Christian may not be as good an expositor as those by whom the office has been assumed.

I.

Now to turn to the passage in question, which I shall examine by arguments drawn from Scripture, without being solicitous to agree, or to say why I am at issue, with modern commentators: "That Day shall not come, except there come a falling away first." Here the sign of the second Advent is said to be a certain frightful apostasy, and the manifestation of the man of sin, the son of perdition—that is, as he is commonly called, Antichrist. Our Saviour seems to add, that that sign will immediately precede Him, or that His coming will follow close upon it; for after speaking of "false prophets" and "false Christs," "showing signs and wonders," "iniquity abounding," and "love waxing cold," and the like, He adds, "When ye shall see all these things, know that it is near, even at the doors." Again

He says, "When ye shall see the Abomination of
Desolation . . . stand in the holy place . . . then let
them that be in Judea flee into the mountains."* Indeed,
St. Paul also implies this, when he says that Antichrist shall be destroyed by the brightness of Christ's
coming.

First, then, I say, if Antichrist is to come *immediately*
before Christ, and to be the sign of His coming, it is
manifest that Antichrist is not come yet, but is still to
be expected; for, else Christ would have come before now.

Further, it appears that the time of Antichrist's tyranny
will be three years and a half, or, as Scripture expresses
it, "a time, and times, and a dividing of time," or "forty-
two months,"—which is an additional reason for believing he is not come; for, if so, he must have come quite
lately, his time being altogether so short; that is, within
the last three years, and this we cannot say he has.

Besides, there are two other circumstances of his
appearance, which have not been fulfilled. First, a time
of unexampled trouble. "Then shall be great tribulation, such as was not from the beginning of the world
to this time, no, nor ever shall be; and except those days
should be shortened, there should no flesh be saved."†
This has not yet been. Next, the preaching of the
Gospel throughout the world—"And this Gospel of the
kingdom shall be preached in all the world for a witness
unto all nations, and then shall the end come."‡

2.

Now it may be objected to this conclusion, that St.
Paul says, in the passage before us, that "the mystery
of iniquity doth already work," that is, even in *his* day, as
if Antichrist had in fact come even then. But he would

* Matt. xxiv. 16, 33.   † Ib. 21, 22.   ‡ Ib. 14.

seem to mean merely this, that in his day there were shadows and forebodings, earnests, and operative elements, of that which was one day to come in its fulness. Just as the types of Christ went before Christ, so the shadows of Antichrist precede him. In truth, every event of this world is a type of those that follow, history proceeding forward as a circle ever enlarging. The days of the Apostles typified the last days : there were false Christs, and risings, and troubles, and persecutions, and the judicial destruction of the Jewish Church. In like manner, every age presents its own picture of those still future events, which, and which alone, are the real fulfilment of the prophecy which stands at the head of all of them. Hence St. John says, " Little children, it is the last time ; and as ye have heard that the Antichrist shall come, *even now* are there many Antichrists ; whereby we know that it is the last time."* Antichrist was come, and was not come ; it was, and it was not the last time. In the sense in which the Apostles' day might be called the "last time," and the end of the world, it was also the time of Antichrist.

A second objection may be made as follows : St. Paul says, "Now ye know what withholdeth, that he (Antichrist) might be revealed in his time." Here a something is mentioned as keeping back the manifestation of the enemy of truth. He proceeds : " He that now withholdeth, will withhold, until he be taken out of the way." Now this restraining power was in early times considered to be the Roman Empire, but the Roman Empire (it is argued) has long been taken out of the way ; it follows that Antichrist has long since come. In answer to this objection, I would grant that he "that withholdeth," or "hindereth," means the power of Rome, for all the ancient

* 1 John ii. 18.

4

writers so speak of it. And I grant that as Rome
according to the prophet Daniel's vision, succeeded
Greece, so Antichrist succeeds Rome, and the Second
Coming succeeds Antichrist.* But it does not hence follow that Antichrist is come : for it is not clear that the
Roman Empire is gone. Far from it : the Roman Empire in the view of prophecy, remains even to this day.
Rome had a very different fate from the other three mon-
sters mentioned by the Prophet, as will be seen by his
description of it. "Behold a fourth beast, dreadful and
terrible, and strong exceedingly ; and it had great iron
teeth : it devoured and brake in pieces, and stamped the
residue with the feet of it : and it *was diverse from all
the beasts that* were before it, and it *had ten horns.*"† These
ten horns, an Angel informed him, "are ten kings that
shall rise out of this kingdom" of Rome. As, then, the ten
horns belonged to the fourth beast, and were not separate
from it, so the kingdoms, into which the Roman Empire
was to be divided, are but the continuation and termination of that Empire itself,—which lasts on, and in some
sense lives in the view of prophecy, however we decide the
historical question. Consequently, we have not *yet* seen
the end of the Roman Empire. "That which withholdeth" still exists, up to the manifestation of its ten
horns ; and till it is removed, Antichrist will not come.
And from the midst of those horns he will arise, as the
same Prophet informs us : "I considered the horns, and
behold, there came up among them another little horn ;
. . . and behold, in this horn were eyes like the eyes of
a man, and a mouth speaking great things."

Up to the time, then, when Antichrist shall actually
appear, there has been and will be a continual effort to
manifest him to the world on the part of the powers

* Chrysostom in loco.   † Dan. vii. 7.

of evil. The history of the Church is the history of that long birth. "The mystery of iniquity doth *already* work," says St. Paul. "*Even now* there are many Antichrists,"* says St. John,—"every spirit that confesseth not that Jesus Christ is come in the flesh, is not of God ; and *this* is that spirit of the Antichrist, whereof ye have heard that it should come, *and even now already is it in the world.*"† It has been at work ever since, from the time of the Apostles, though kept under by him that "withholdeth." At this very time there is a fierce struggle, the spirit of Antichrist attempting to rise, and the political power in those countries which are prophetically Roman, firm and vigorous in repressing it. And in fact, we actually have before our eyes, as our fathers also in the generation before us, a fierce and lawless principle everywhere at work—a spirit of rebellion against God and man, which the powers of government in each country can barely keep under with their greatest efforts. Whether this which we witness *be* that spirit of Antichrist,‡ which is one day at length to be let loose, this ambitious spirit, the parent of all heresy, schism, sedition, revolution, and war—whether this be so or not, at least we know from prophecy that the present framework of society and government, as far as it is the representative of Roman powers, is that which withholdeth, and Antichrist is that which will rise when this restraint fails.

3.

It has been more or less implied in the foregoing remarks, that Antichrist is one man, an individual, not a power or a kingdom. Such surely is the impression left on the mind by the Scripture notices concerning him, after taking fully into account the figurative character

* 1 John ii. 18. † 1b. iv. 3. ‡ [ὁ ἄνομος.]

of prophetical language. Consider these passages together, which describe him, and see whether we must not so conclude. First, the passage in St. Paul's Epistle : " That day shall not come, except there come a falling away first, and that man of sin be revealed, the son of perdition, who is the adversary and rival of all that is called God or worshipped ; so that he sitteth as God in the temple of God, proclaiming himself to be God. . . . Then shall that Wicked One be revealed, whom the Lord shall consume with the spirit of His mouth, and shall destroy with the brightness of His coming . . . . whose coming is after the working of Satan, with all power and signs and lying wonders."

Next, in the prophet Daniel : "Another shall rise after them, and he shall be diverse from the first, and he shall subdue three kings. And he shall speak great words against the Most High, and shall wear out the saints of the Most High, and think to change times and laws : and they shall be given into his hand until a time and times, and the dividing of time. But the judgment shall sit, and they shall take away his dominion, to consume and to destroy it unto the end." Again : "And the king shall do according to his will ; and he shall exalt and magnify himself above every god, and shall speak marvellous things against the God of gods, and shall prosper till the indignation be accomplished. . . . Neither shall he regard the God of his fathers, nor the Desire of women, nor regard any god ; for he shall magnify himself above all. But in his estate shall he honour the God of forces, and a god whom his fathers knew not shall he honour with gold and silver, and with precious stones, and pleasant things."* Let it be observed, that Daniel elsewhere describes other kings, and that the event has shown them

* Dan. vii.; xi.

certainly to be individuals,—for instance, Xerxes, Darius, and Alexander.

And in like manner St. John : "There was given unto him a mouth speaking great things, and blasphemies ; and power was given unto him to continue forty and two months. And he opened his mouth in blasphemy against God, to blaspheme His Name, and His taber-nacle, and them that dwell in heaven. And it was given unto him to make war with the saints, and to overcome them ; and power was given him over all kindreds and tongues and nations. And all that dwell upon the earth shall worship him, whose names are not written in the book of life of the Lamb slain from the foundation of the world."†

Further, that by Antichrist is meant some one person, is made probable by the anticipations which, as I have said, have already occurred in history, of the fulfilment of the prophecy. Individual men have arisen actually answering in a great measure to the above descriptions ; and this circumstance creates a probability, that the absolute and entire fulfilment which is to come will be in an individual also. The most remarkable of these shadows of the destined scourge appeared before the time of the Apostles, between them and the age of Daniel, viz., the heathen king Antiochus, of whom we read in the books of Maccabees. This instance is the more to the purpose, because he is actually described, (as we suppose) by Daniel, in another part of his pro-phecy, in terms which seem also to belong to Antichrist, and, as belonging, imply that Antiochus actually was what he seems to be, a type of that more fearful future enemy of the Church. This Antiochus was the savage persecutor of the Jews, in their latter times, as Anti-

† Rev. xiii.

christ will be of the Christians.   A few passages from
the Maccabees will show you what he was.   St. Paul in
the text speaks of an Apostasy, and then of Antichrist as
following upon it ; and thus is the future of the Christian
Church typified in the past Jewish history.   " In those
days went there out of Israel wicked men, who persuaded
many, saying, Let us go and make a covenant with the
heathen that are round about us : for since we departed
from them, we have had much sorrow.   So this device
pleased them well.   Then certain of the people were so
forward herein, that they went to the king, who gave
them licence to do after the ordinances of the heathen ;
whereupon they built a place of exercise at Jerusalem,
according to the custom of the heathen ; and made
themselves uncircumcised, and forsook the holy covenant,
and joined themselves to the heathen, and were sold to
do mischief."   Here was the Falling away.   After this
introduction the Enemy of truth appears.   " After that
Antiochus had smitten Egypt, he returned again, ...
and went up against Israel and Jerusalem with a great
multitude, and entered proudly into the sanctuary, and
took away the golden altar, and the candlestick of light
and all the vessels thereof, and the table of the shew-
bread, and the pouring vessels, and the vials, and the
censers of gold, and the veil, and the crowns, and
the golden ornaments that were before the temple ;
all which he pulled off.   And when he had taken all
away, he went into his own land, having made a great
massacre, and spoken very proudly."   After this he set
fire to Jerusalem, "and pulled down the houses and
walls thereof on every side. . . . Then built they the
city of David with a great and strong wall, . . . and
they put therein a sinful nation, wicked men, and forti-
fied themselves therein."   Next, " King Antiochus wrote

to his whole kingdom, that all should be one people, and every one should leave his laws: so all the heathen agreed according to the commandment of the king. Yea, many also of the Israelites consented to his religion, and sacrificed unto idols, and profaned the sabbath." After this he forced these impieties upon the chosen people. All were to be put to death who would not "profane the sabbath and festival days, and pollute the sanctuary and holy people, and set up altars, and groves, and chapels of idols, and sacrifice swine's flesh and unclean beasts," and "leave their children uncircumcised." At length he set up an idol, or, in the words of the history, "the Abomination of Desolation upon the altar, and builded idol altars throughout the cities of Juda on every side. . . . And when they had rent in pieces the books of the law which they found, they burnt them with fire." It is added, "Howbeit many in Israel were fully resolved and confirmed in themselves not to eat any unclean thing, wherefore they chose rather to die . . . and there was very great wrath upon Israel."* Here we have presented to us some of the lineaments of Antichrist, who will be such, and worse than such, as Antiochus.

The history of the apostate emperor Julian, who lived between 300 and 400 years after Christ, furnishes us with another approximation to the predicted Antichrist, and an additional reason for thinking he will be one person, not a kingdom, power, or the like.

And so again does the false prophet Mahomet, who propagated his imposture about 600 years after Christ came.

Lastly, that Antichrist is one individual man, not a power,—not a mere ethical spirit, or a political system, not a dynasty, or succession of rulers,—was the universal

---

* 1 Mac. i.

tradition of the early Church. "We must say," writes St.
Jerome upon Daniel, "what has been handed down to us
by all ecclesiastical writers, that, in the end of the world,
when the Roman Empire is to be destroyed, there will
be ten kings, to divide the Roman territory between
them, and that an eleventh will rise up, a small king,
who will subdue three of the ten, and thereupon receive
the submission of the other seven. It is said that 'the
Horn had eyes, as the eyes of a man,' lest we should, as
some have thought, suppose him to be the evil spirit, or
a demon, whereas he is one man, in whom Satan shall
dwell bodily. 'And a mouth speaking great things;'
for he is the man of sin, the son of perdition, so that he
dares to 'sit in the Temple of God, making himself as if
God.' 'The beast has been slain, and his carcase has
perished;' since Antichrist blasphemes in that united
Roman Empire, all its kingdoms are at one and the
same time to be abolished, and there shall be no earthly
kingdom, but the society of the saints, and the coming
of the triumphant Son of God." "And Theodoret:
"Having spoken of Antiochus Epiphanes, the prophet
passes from the figure to the Antitype; for the Antitype
of Antiochus is Antichrist, and the figure of Antichrist
is Antiochus. As Antiochus compelled the Jews to act
impiously, so the Man of Sin, the son of perdition, will
make every effort for the seduction of the pious, by false
miracles, and by force, and by persecution. As the Lord
says, 'Then will be great tribulation, such as never was
from the beginning of the world till this time, nor ever
shall be.'" *

What I have said upon this subject may be summed
up as follows:—that the coming of Christ will be
immediately preceded by a very awful and unparalleled

* Jerom. in Dan. vii ; Theodor. in Dan. xi.

outbreak of evil, called by St. Paul an Apostasy, a falling away, in the midst of which a certain terrible Man of sin and Child of perdition, the special and singular enemy of Christ, or Antichrist, will appear; that this will be when revolutions prevail, and the present framework of society breaks to pieces; and that at present the spirit which he will embody and represent is kept under by "the powers that be," but that on their dissolution, he will rise out of their bosom and knit them together again in his own evil way, under his own rule, to the exclusion of the Church.

4.

It would be out of place to say more than this at present. I will but insist on one particular circumstance contained in St. Paul's announcement which I have already in part commented on.

It is said there will "come a falling away, and the man of sin will be revealed." In other words, the Man of Sin is born of an Apostasy, or at least comes into power through an apostasy, or is preceded by an apostasy, or would not be except for an apostasy. So says the inspired text: now observe, how remarkably the course of Providence, as seen in history, has commented on this prediction.

First, we have a comment in the instance of Antiochus previous to the actual events contemplated in the prophecy. The Israelites, or at least great numbers of them, put off their own sacred religion, *and then* the enemy was allowed to come in.

Next the apostate emperor Julian, who attempted to overthrow the Church by craft, and introduce paganism back again: it is observable that he was preceded, nay, he was nurtured, by heresy; by that first great heresy which disturbed the peace and purity of the Church.

About forty years before he became emperor, arose the
pestilent Arian heresy which denied that Christ was
God. It ate its way among the rulers of the Church
like a canker, and what with the treachery of some, and
the mistakes of others, at one time it was all but dominant throughout Christendom. The few holy and faithful men, who witnessed for the Truth, cried out, with
awe and terror at the apostasy, that Antichrist was coming. They called it the "forerunner of Antichrist."*
And true, his Shadow came. Julian was educated in
the bosom of Arianism by some of its principal upholders. His tutor was that Eusebius from whom its
partizans took their name; and in due time he fell
away to paganism, became a hater and persecutor of the
Church, and was cut off before he had reigned out the
brief period which will be the real Antichrist's duration.

And thirdly, another heresy arose, a heresy in its consequences far more lasting and far-spreading; it was of
a twofold character; with two heads, as I may call them,
Nestorianism and Eutychianism, apparently opposed to
each other, yet acting towards a common end: both in
one way or other denied the truth of Christ's gracious incarnation, and tended to destroy the faith of Christians
not less certainly, though more insidiously, than the
heresy of Arius. It spread through the East and through
Egypt, corrupting and poisoning those Churches which
had once, alas! been the most flourishing, the earliest
abodes and strongholds of revealed truth. Out of this
heresy, or at least by means of it, the impostor Mahomet sprang, and formed his creed. Here is another
especial Shadow of Antichrist.

---

* πρόδρομος ᾿Αντιχρίστου.—"Now is the Apostasy; for men have fallen
away from the right faith. This then is the Apostasy, and the enemy must
be looked out for."—*Cyril. Catech.*, 15, n. 9.

These instances give us warning :— Is the enemy of Christ, and His Church, to arise out of a certain special falling away from GOD ? And is there no reason to fear that some such Apostasy is gradually preparing, gathering, hastening on in this very day ? For is there not at this very time a special effort made almost all over the world, that is, every here and there, more or less in sight or out of sight, in this or that place, but most visibly or formidably in its most civilized and powerful parts, an effort to do without Religion ? Is there not an opinion avowed and growing, that a nation has nothing to do with Religion ; that it is merely a matter for each man's own conscience ?—which is all one with saying that we may let the Truth fail from the earth without trying to continue it in and on after our time. Is there not a vigorous and united movement in all countries to cast down the Church of Christ from power and place ? Is there not a feverish and ever-busy endeavour to get rid of the necessity of Religion in public transactions ? for example, an attempt to get rid of oaths, under a pretence that they are too sacred for affairs of common life, instead of providing that they be taken more reverently and more suitably ? an attempt to educate without Religion ?—that is, by putting all forms of Religion together, which comes to the same thing ;—an attempt to enforce temperance, and the virtues which flow from it, without Religion, by means of Societies which are built on mere principles of utility? an attempt to make *expedience*, and not *truth*, the end and the rule of measures of State and the enactments of Law? an attempt to make numbers, and not the Truth, the ground of maintaining, or not maintaining, this or that creed, as if we had any reason whatever in Scripture for thinking that the many will be in the right, and the

few in the wrong ? An attempt to deprive the Bible of
its one meaning to the exclusion of all other, to make
people think that it may have an hundred meanings all
equally good, or, in other words, that it has no meaning
at all, is a dead letter, and may be put aside ? an attempt to supersede Religion altogether, as far as it is
external or objective, as far as it is displayed in ordinances, or can be expressed by written words,—to confine it to our inward feelings, and thus, considering how
variable, how evanescent our feelings are, an attempt, in
fact, to destroy Religion ?

Surely, there is at this day a confederacy of evil,
marshalling its hosts from all parts of the world, organizing itself, taking its measures, enclosing the Church of
Christ as in a net, and preparing the way for a general
Apostasy from it. Whether this very Apostasy is to
give birth to Antichrist, or whether he is still to be
delayed, as he has already been delayed so long, we
cannot know ; but at any rate this Apostasy, and all its
tokens and instruments, are of the Evil One, and savour
of death. Far be it from any of us to be of those simple
ones who are taken in that snare which is circling around
us ! Far be it from us to be seduced with the fair
promises in which Satan is sure to hide his poison ! Do
you think he is so unskilful in his craft, as to ask you
openly and plainly to join him in his warfare against the
Truth ? No ; he offers you baits to tempt you. He
promises you civil liberty ; he promises you equality ;
he promises you trade and wealth ; he promises you a
remission of taxes ; he promises you reform. This is
the way in which he conceals from you the kind of work
to which he is putting you ; he tempts you to rail against
your rulers and superiors ; he does so himself, and in-
duces you to imitate him ; or he promises you illumina-

tion,—he offers you knowledge, science, philosophy, enlargement of mind. He scoffs at times gone by ; he scoffs at every institution which reveres them. He prompts you what to say, and then listens to you, and praises you, and encourages you. He bids you mount aloft. He shows you how to become as gods. Then he laughs and jokes with you, and gets intimate with you ; he takes your hand, and gets his fingers between yours, and grasps them, and then you are his.

Shall we Christians allow ourselves to have lot or part in this matter ? Shall we, even with our little finger, help on the Mystery of Iniquity which is travailing for birth, and convulsing the earth with its pangs ? " O my soul, come not thou into their secret ; unto their assembly, mine honour, be not thou united." * " What fellowship hath righteousness with unrighteousness ? and what communion hath light with darkness ? Wherefore, come out from among them, and be ye separate," . . . lest you be workers together with God's enemies, and be opening the way for the Man of Sin, the son of perdition.

2

The Religion of Antichrist.

ST. JOHN tells us that "every spirit that confesseth not that Jesus Christ is come in the flesh, is that spirit of Antichrist, which even now already is in the world." It was the characteristic of Antichrist, that he should openly deny our Lord Jesus Christ to be the Son of God come in the flesh from heaven. So exactly and fully was this description to answer to him, that to deny Christ might be suitably called the spirit of Antichrist; and the deniers of Him might be said to have the spirit of Antichrist, to be like Antichrist, to be Antichrists. The same thing is stated in a former chapter. "Who is the Liar, but he that denieth that Jesus is the Christ? he is the Antichrist, that denieth the Father and the Son. Whosoever denieth the Son, the same hath not the Father;"* from which words, moreover, it would appear that Antichrist will be led on from rejecting the Son of God to the rejecting of God altogether, either by implication or practically.

I shall now make some further observations on the characteristic marks of the predicted enemy of the Church; and, as before, I shall confine myself to the interpretations of Scripture given by the early Fathers.

My reason for doing so is simply this,—that on so difficult a subject as unfulfilled prophecy, I really can

---

* 1 John ii. 22, 23.

have no opinion of my own, nor indeed is it desirable I should have, or at least that I should put it forward in any formal way. The opinion of any one person, even if he were the most fit to form one, could hardly be of any authority, or be worth putting forward by itself; whereas the judgment and views of the early Church claim and attract our special regard, because for what we know they may be in part derived from traditions of the Apostles, and because they are put forward far more consistently and unanimously than those of any other set of teachers. Thus they have at least greater claims on our attention than those of other writers, be their claims little or great; if they are little, those of others are still less. The only really strong claim which can be made on our belief, is the clear fulfilment of the prophecy. Did we see all the marks of the prophecy satisfactorily answered in the past history of the Church, then we might dispense with authority in the parties setting the proof before us. This condition, however, can hardly be satisfied, because the date of Antichrist comes close upon the coming of Christ in judgment, and therefore the event will not have happened under such circumstances as to allow of being appealed to. Nor indeed is any history producible in which are fulfilled all the marks of Antichrist clearly, though some are fulfilled here and there. Nothing then is left us, (if we are to take up any opinion at all,—if we are to profit, as Scripture surely intends, by its warnings concerning the evil which is to come,) but to go by the judgment of the Fathers, whether that be of special authority in this matter or not. To them therefore I have had recourse already, and now shall have recourse again. To continue, then, the subject with the early Fathers as my guides.

I.

It seems clear that St. Paul and St. John speak of the same enemy of the Church, from the similarity of their descriptions. They both say, that the spirit itself was already at work in their day. "That spirit of the Antichrist," says St. John, "is *now already* in the world." "The mystery of iniquity doth *already* work," says St. Paul. And they both describe the enemy as characterized by the same especial sin, open infidelity. St. John says, that "he is the Antichrist that *denieth the Father and the Son;*" while St. Paul speaks of him in like manner as "*the adversary and rival of all that is called God, or worshipped;*" that "he sitteth as God in the Temple of God, setting forth himself that he is God." In both these passages, the same blasphemous denial of God and religion is described ; but St. Paul adds, in addition, that he will oppose all existing religion, true or false, "*all* that is called God, or worshipped."

Two other passages of Scripture may be adduced, predicting the same reckless impiety ; one from the eleventh chapter of Daniel : "The king shall do according to his will ; and he shall exalt himself and magnify himself *above every god,* and shall speak marvellous things *against the God of gods,* and shall prosper till the indignation be accomplished. . . . Neither shall he regard the *God of his fathers,* nor the Desire of women, nor *regard any god*—for he shall magnify himself *above all.*"

The other passage is faintly marked with any prophetic allusion in itself, except that all our Saviour's sayings have a deep meaning, and the Fathers take this in particular to have such. "I am come in My Father's Name, and ye receive Me not ; if *another shall come in his own name,* him ye will receive." * This they consider

* John v. 43.

to be a prophetic allusion to Antichrist, whom the Jews were to mistake for the Christ. He is to come "in *His own* name." Not from God, as even the Son of God came, who if any might have come in the power of His essential divinity, not in God's Name, not with any pretence of a mission from Him, but in his own name, by a blasphemous assumption of divine power, thus will Antichrist come.

To the above passages may be added those which speak generally of the impieties of the last age of the world, impieties which we may believe will usher in and be completed in Antichrist :—

"Many shall run to and fro, and knowledge shall be increased. . . . Many shall be purified, and made white, and tried : but the wicked shall do wickedly ; and none of the wicked shall understand, but the wise shall understand."* "In the last days perilous times shall come, for men shall be lovers of their own selves, covetous, boasters, proud, blasphemers, disobedient to parents, unthankful, unholy, without natural affection, trucebreakers, false accusers, incontinent, fierce, despisers of those that are good, traitors, heady, high-minded, lovers of pleasures more than lovers of God, having a form of godliness but denying the power thereof : "† "scoffers walking after their own lusts, and saying, Where is the promise of His coming ?"‡ "despising government, presumptuous . . . self-willed, not afraid to speak evil of dignities . . . promising men liberty, while themselves the servants of corruption : "§ and the like.

2.

I just now made mention of the Jews : it may be well

---

* Dan. xii. 4, 10. ‡ 2 Pet. iii. 3, 4.
† 2 Tim. iii. 2—5. § 2 Pet. ii. 10, 19.

then to state what was held in the early Church concerning Antichrist's connexion with them.

Our Lord foretold that many should come in His name, saying, "I am Christ." It was the judicial punishment of the Jews, as of all unbelievers in one way or another, that, having rejected the true Christ, they should take up with a false one ; and Antichrist will be the complete and perfect seducer, towards whom all who were previous are approximations, according to the words just now quoted, "If another shall come in his own name, him ye will receive." To the same purport are St. Paul's words after describing Antichrist ; "whose coming," he says, "is . . . with all deceivableness of unrighteousness in them that perish, because they received not the love of the Truth, that they might be saved. And *for this cause* God shall send them strong delusion that they should believe a lie, that they all might be damned who believed not the Truth, but had pleasure in unrighteousness."

Hence, considering that Antichrist would pretend to be the Messiah, it was of old the received notion that he was to be of Jewish race and to observe the Jewish rites.

Further, St. Paul says that Antichrist should "sit in the Temple of God ;" that is, according to the earlier Fathers, in the Jewish Temple. Our Saviour's own words may be taken to support this notion, because He speaks of "the Abomination of Desolation" (which, whatever other meanings it might have, in its fulness denotes Antichrist) "standing in the *holy place.*" Further, the persecution of Christ's witnesses which Antichrist will cause, is described by St. John as taking place in Jerusalem. "Their dead bodies shall lie in the street of the great city, (which spiritually is called Sodom and Egypt,) where also our Lord was crucified."

Now here a remark may be made. At first sight, I suppose, we should not consider that there was much evidence from the Sacred Text for Antichrist taking part with the Jews, or having to do with their Temple. It is, then, a very remarkable fact, that the apostate emperor Julian, who was a type and earnest of the great enemy, should, as he did, have taken part with the Jews, and set about building their Temple. Here the history is a sort of comment on the prophecy, and sustains and vindicates those early interpretations of it which I am reviewing. Of course I must be understood to mean, and a memorable circumstance it is, that this belief of the Church that Antichrist should be connected with the Jews, was expressed long before Julian's time, and that we still possess the works in which it is contained. In fact we have the writings of two Fathers, both Bishops and martyrs of the Church, who lived at least one hundred and fifty years before Julian, and less than one hundred years after St. John. They both distinctly declare Antichrist's connexion with the Jews.

The first of them, Irenæus, speaks as follows: "In the Temple which is at Jerusalem the adversary will sit, endeavouring to show himself to be the Christ."

And the second, Hippolytus: "Antichrist will be he who shall resuscitate the kingdom of the Jews." *

3.

Next let us ask, Will Antichrist profess any sort of religion at all? Neither true God nor false god will he worship: so far is clear, and yet something more, and

---

* Iren Hær. v. 25. Hippol. de Antichristo, § 25. St. Cyril of Jerusalem also speaks of Antichrist building the Jewish Temple; and he too wrote before Julian's attempt, and (what is remarkable) prophesied it would fail, because of the prophecies.—*Vide* Ruff. Hist. i. 37.

that obscure, is told us.   Indeed, as far as the prophetic
accounts go, they seem at first sight incompatible with
each other.   Antichrist is to "exalt himself over all
that is called God or worshipped." He will set himself
forcibly against idols and idolatry, as the early writers
agree in declaring.   Yet in the book of Daniel we read,
" In his estate *shall he honour the god of forces ; and a
god whom his fathers knew not shall he honour* with
gold and silver, and with precious stones and pleasant
things.   Thus shall he do in the most strongholds with
a *strange god, whom he shall acknowledge* and increase
with glory." *   What is meant by the words translated
"god of forces," and afterwards called "a strange god,"
is quite hidden from us, and probably will be so till the
event ; but anyhow some sort of false worship is certainly predicted as the mark of Antichrist, with this
prediction the contrary way, that he shall set himself
against *all idols*, as well as against the true God.   Now
it is not at all extraordinary that there should be this
contrariety in the prediction, for we know generally that
infidelity leads to superstition, and that the men most
reckless in their blasphemy are cowards also as regards
the invisible world.   They cannot be consistent if they
would.   But let me notice here a remarkable coincidence,
which is contained in the history of that type or shadow
of the final apostasy which scared the world some forty
or fifty years ago,—a coincidence between actual events
and prophecy sufficient to show us that the apparent
contradiction in the latter may easily be reconciled,
though beforehand we may not see how ; sufficient to
remind us that the all-watchful eye, and the all-ordain-
ing hand of God is still over the world, and that the
seeds, sown in prophecy above two thousand years since,

* Dan. xi. 38, 39.

are not dead, but from time to time, by blade and tender shoot, give earnest of the future harvest. Surely the world is impregnated with the elements of preternatural evil, which ever and anon, in unhealthy seasons, give lowering and muttering tokens of the wrath to come!

In that great and famous nation over against us, once great for its love of Christ's Church, since memorable for the deeds of blasphemy, which leads me here to mention it, and now, when it should be pitied and prayed for, made unhappily, in too many respects, our own model—followed when it should be condemned, and admired when it should be excused,—in the Capital of that powerful and celebrated nation, there took place, as we all well know, within the last fifty years, an open apostasy from Christianity; nor from Christianity only, but from every kind of worship which might retain any semblance or pretence of the great truths of religion. Atheism was absolutely professed;—and yet in spite of this, it seems a contradiction in terms to say it, a certain sort of worship, and that, as the prophet expresses it, "a strange worship," was introduced. Observe what this was.

I say, they avowed on the one hand Atheism. They prevailed upon a wretched man, whom they had forced upon the Church as an Archbishop, to come before them in public and declare that there was no God, and that what he had hitherto taught was a fable. They wrote up over the burial-places that death was an eternal sleep. They closed the churches, they seized and desecrated the gold and silver plate belonging to them, turning, like Belshazzar, those sacred vessels to the use of their impious revellings; they formed mock processions, clad in priestly garments, and singing profane hymns. They annulled the divine ordinance of marriage, resolving it into a mere civil contract to be made and dissolved at pleasure. These things are but a part of their enormities.

On the other-hand, after having broken away from all restraint as regards God and man, they gave a name to that reprobate state itself into which they had thrown themselves, and exalted it, that very negation of religion, or rather that real and living blasphemy, into a kind of god. They called it LIBERTY, and they literally worshipped it as a divinity. It would almost be incredible, that men who had flung off all religion should be at the pains to assume a new and senseless worship of their own devising, whether in superstition or in mockery, were not events so recent and so notorious. After abjuring our Lord and Saviour, and blasphemously declaring Him to be an impostor, they proceeded to decree, in the public assembly of the nation, the adoration of Liberty and Equality as divinities: and they appointed festivals besides in honour of Reason, the Country, the Constitution, and the Virtues. Further, they determined that tutelary gods, even dead men, may be canonized, consecrated, and worshipped; and they enrolled in the number of these some of the most notorious infidels and profligates of the last century. The remains of the two principal of these were brought in solemn procession into one of their churches, and placed upon the holy altar itself; incense was offered to them, and the assembled multitude bowed down in worship before one of them—before what remained on earth of an inveterate enemy of Christ.

Now, I do not mention all this as considering it the fulfilment of the prophecy, nor, again, as if the fulfilment when it comes will be in this precise way, but merely to point out, what the course of events has shown to us in these latter times, that there *are* ways of fulfilling sacred announcements that seem at first sight contradictory,— that men may oppose every existing worship, true and false, and yet take up a worship of their own from pride, wantonness, policy, superstition, fanaticism, or other reasons.

And further, let it be remarked, that there was a tendency in the infatuated people I have spoken of, to introduce the old Roman democratic worship, as if further to show us that Rome, the fourth monster of the prophet's vision, is not dead. They even went so far as to restore the worship of one of the Roman divinities (Ceres) by name, raised a statue to her, and appointed a festival in her honour. This indeed was inconsistent with exalting themselves "above *all* that is called god;" but I mention the particular fact, as I have said, not as throwing light upon the prophecy, but to show that the spirit of old Rome has not passed from the world, though its name is almost extinct.

Still further, it is startling to observe, that the former Apostate, in the early times, the Emperor Julian, he too was engaged in bringing back Roman Paganism.

Further still, let it be observed that Antiochus too, the Antichrist before Christ, the persecutor of the Jews, he too signalized himself in forcing the Pagan worship upon them, introducing it even into the Temple.

We know not what is to come; but this we may safely say, that, improbable as it is that Paganism should ever be publicly restored and enforced by authority for any period, however short, even three years and a half, yet it is far less improbable now than it was fifty years ago, before the event occurred which I have referred to. Who would not have been thought a madman or idiot, before that period, who had conjectured such a porten-

tous approximation towards Paganism as actually then
took place?

4.

Now let us recur to the ancient Fathers, and see
whether their further anticipations do not run parallel
to the events which have since happened.

Antichrist, as they considered, will come out of the
Roman Empire just upon its destruction;—that is, the
Roman Empire will in its last days divide itself into ten
parts, and the Enemy will come up suddenly out of it
upon these ten, and subdue three of them, or all of them
perhaps, and (as the prophet continues) "shall speak
great words against the Most High, and shall wear out
the saints of the Most High, and think to change times
and laws, and they shall be given into His hand until a
time, and times, and the dividing of time."* Now it is very
observable, that one of the two early Fathers whom I
have already cited, Hippolytus, expressly says that the
ten states which will at length appear, though kingdoms,
shall also be *democracies*. I say this is observable, considering the present state of the world, the tendency of
things in this day towards democracy, and the instance
which has been presented to us of democracy within the
last fifty years, in those occurrences in France to which
I have already referred.

Another expectation of the early Church was, that the
Roman monster, after remaining torpid for centuries,
would wake up at the end of the world, and be restored
in all its laws and forms; and this, too, considering those
same recent events to which I have referred, is certainly
worth noticing also. The same Father, who anticipates
the coming of democracies, expressly deduces from a
passage in the xiiith chapter of the Apocalypse, that

* Dan. vii. 25.

"the system of Augustus, who was founder of the Roman Empire, shall be adopted and established by him (Antichrist), in order to his own aggrandizement and glory. This is the fourth monster whose head was wounded and healed; in that the empire was destroyed and came to nought, and was divided into ten diadems. But at this time Antichrist, as being an unscrupulous villain, will heal and restore it; so that it will be active and vigorous once more through the system which he establishes." *

I will but notice one other expectation falling in with the foregoing notion of the re-establishment of Roman power, entertained by the two Fathers whom I have been quoting; viz., one concerning the name of Antichrist, as spoken of in the xiiith chapter of the Revelation: "Here is wisdom," says the inspired text; "let him that hath understanding count his number, for it is the number of a man, and his number is six hundred threescore and six." Both Irenæus and Hippolytus give a name, the letters of which together in Greek make up this number, characteristic of the position of Antichrist as the head of the Roman Empire in its restored state, viz., the word Latinus, or the Latin king.

Irenæus speaks as follows: "Expect that the empire will first be divided into ten kings; then while they are reigning and beginning to settle and aggrandize themselves, suddenly one will come and claim the kingdom, and frighten them, having a name which contains the predicted number (666); him recognize as the Abomination of Desolation." Then he goes on to mention, together with two other words, the name of Lateinos as answering to the number, and says of it, "This is very probable, since it is the name of the last empire;—for the Latins" (that is, the Romans) "are now in power." †

* Ibid., **27, 49.**   † He adds, that he himself prefers one of the other words.

And Hippolytus: "Since . . the wound of the first monster was healed . . . . and it is plain that the Latins are still in power, therefore he is called the Latin King (Latinus), the name passing from an empire to an individual." *

Whether this anticipation will be fulfilled or not, we cannot say. I only mention it as showing the belief of the Fathers in the restoration and re-establishment of the Roman Empire, which has certainly since their day been more than once attempted.

It seems then, on the whole, that, as far as the testimony of the early Church goes, Antichrist will be an open blasphemer, opposing himself to every existing worship, true and false,—a persecutor, a patron of the Jews, and a restorer of their worship, and, further, the author of a novel kind of worship. Moreover, he will appear suddenly, at the very end of the Roman Empire, which once was, and now is dormant ; that he will knit it into one, and engraft his Judaism and his new worship (a sort of Paganism, it may be) upon the old discipline of Cæsar Augustus ; that in consequence he will earn the title of the Latin or Roman King, as best expressive of his place and character ; lastly, that he will pass away as suddenly as he came.

5.

Now concerning this, I repeat, I do not wish to pronounce how far the early Church was right or wrong in these anticipations, though events since have seriously tended to strengthen its general interpretations of Scripture prophecy.

It may be asked, however, What practical use is there in speaking of these things, if they be doubtful ?

---

* Hippol. de Antichristo, § 50.   The Greek text seems corrupt.

I answer, first, that it is not unprofitable to bear in mind that we are still under what may be called a miraculous system. I do not mean to maintain that literal miracles are taking place now every day, but that our present state is a portion of a providential course, which began in miracle, and, at least at the end of the world, if not before, will end in miracle. The particular expectations above detailed may be right or wrong; yet an Antichrist, whoever and whatever he be, is to come; marvels are to come; the old Roman Empire is not extinct; Satan, if bound, is bound but for a season; the contest of good and evil is not ended. I repeat it, in the present state of things, when the great object of education is supposed to be the getting rid of things supernatural, when we are bid to laugh and jeer at believing everything we do not see, are told to account for everything by things known and ascertained, and to assay every statement by the touchstone of experience, I must think that this vision of Antichrist, as a supernatural power to come, is a great providential gain, as being a counterpoise to the evil tendencies of the age.

And next, it must surely be profitable for our thoughts to be sent backward and forward to the beginning and the end of the Gospel times, to the first and the second coming of Christ. What we want, is to understand that we are in the place in which the early Christians were, with the same covenant, ministry, sacraments, and duties;— to realize a state of things long past away;—to feel that we are in a sinful world, a world lying in wickedness; to discern our position in it, that we are witnesses in it, that reproach and suffering are our portion,—so that we must not "think it strange" if they come upon us, but a kind of gracious exception if they do not; to have our hearts awake, as if we had seen Christ and

His Apostles, and seen their miracles,—awake to the
hope and waiting of His second coming, looking out for
it, nay, desiring to see the tokens of it ; thinking often
and much of the judgment to come, dwelling on and
adequately entering into the thought, that we individually
shall be judged.   All these surely are acts of true and
saving faith ; and this is one substantial use of the Book
of Revelation, and other prophetical parts of Scripture,
quite distinct from our knowing their real interpretation,
viz., to take the veil from our eyes, to lift up the cover-
ing which lies over the face of the world, and make us
see day by day, as we go in and out, as we get up and
lie down, as we labour, and walk, and rest, and recreate
ourselves, the Throne of God set up in the midst of us,
His majesty and His judgments, His Son's continual
intercession for the elect, their trials, and their victory.

3.

The City of Antichrist.

THE Angel thus interprets to St. John the vision of the Great Harlot, the enchantress, who seduced the inhabitants of the earth. He says, " The woman which thou sawest is that great city, which reigneth over the kings of the earth." The city spoken of in these words is evidently Rome, which was then the seat of empire all over the earth,—which was supreme even in Judæa. We hear of the Romans all through the Gospels and Acts. Our Saviour was born when His mother the Blessed Virgin, and Joseph, were brought up to Bethlehem to be taxed by the Roman governor. He was crucified under Pontius Pilate, the Roman governor. St. Paul was at various times protected by the circumstance of his being a Roman citizen ; on the other hand, when he was seized and imprisoned, it was by the Roman governors, and at last he was sent to Rome itself, to the emperor, and eventually martyred there, together with St. Peter. Thus the sovereignty of Rome, at the time when Christ and His Apostles preached and wrote, which is a matter of historical notoriety, is forced on our notice in the New Testament itself. It is undeniably meant by the Angel when he speaks of "the great city which reigneth over the earth."

The connexion of Rome with the reign and exploits of Antichrist, is so often brought before us in the controversies of this day, that it may be well, after what I have already had occasion to say on the subject of the last enemy of the Church, to consider now what Scripture prophecy says concerning Rome; which I shall attempt to do, as before, with the guidance of the early Fathers.

I.

Now let us observe what is said concerning Rome, in the passage which the Angel concludes in the words which I have quoted, and what we may deduce from it.

That great city is described under the image of a woman, cruel, profligate, and impious. She is described as arrayed in all worldly splendour and costliness, in purple and scarlet, in gold and precious stones, and pearls, as shedding and drinking the blood of the saints, till she was drunken with it. Moreover she is called by the name of "Babylon the Great," to signify her power, wealth, profaneness, pride, sensuality, and persecuting spirit, after the pattern of that former enemy of the Church. I need not here relate how all this really answered to the character and history of Rome at the time St. John spoke of it. There never was a more ambitious, haughty, hard-hearted, and worldly people than the Romans; never any, for none else had ever the opportunity, which so persecuted the Church. Christians suffered ten persecutions at their hands, as they are commonly reckoned, and very horrible ones, extending over two hundred and fifty years. The day would fail to go through an account of the tortures they suffered from Rome; so that the Apostle's description was as signally fulfilled afterwards as a prophecy, as it was accurate at the time as an historical notice.

This guilty city, represented by St. John as an abandoned woman, is said to be seated on "a scarlet-coloured monster, full of names of blasphemy, having seven heads and ten horns." Here we are sent back by the prophetic description to the seventh chapter of Daniel, in which the four great empires of the world are shadowed out under the figure of four beasts, a lion, a bear, a leopard, and a nameless monster, "diverse" from the rest, "dreadful and terrible, and strong exceedingly;" "and it had ten horns." This surely is the very same beast which St. John saw: the ten horns mark it. Now this fourth beast in Daniel's vision is the Roman Empire; therefore "the beast," on which the woman sat, is the Roman Empire. And this agrees very accurately with the actual position of things in history; for Rome, the mistress of the world, might well be said to sit upon, and be carried about triumphantly on that world which she had subdued and tamed, and made her creature. Further, the prophet Daniel explains the ten horns of the monster to be "ten kings that shall arise" out of this Empire; in which St. John agrees, saying, "The ten horns which thou sawest are ten kings, which have received no kingdom as yet, but receive power as kings one hour with the beast." Moreover in a former vision Daniel speaks of the Empire as destined to be "divided," as "partly strong and partly broken."* Further still, this Empire, the beast of burden of the woman, was at length to rise against her and devour her, as some savage animal might turn upon its keeper; and it was to do this in the time of its divided or multiplied existence. "The ten horns which thou sawest upon him, these shall hate" her, "and shall make her desolate and naked, and shall eat her flesh and burn her with fire." Such was to be the end of the great city. Lastly, three of the kings, perhaps all, are said to be subdued by Antichrist, who

* Dan. ii. 41, 42.

is to come up suddenly while they are in power; for such is the course of Daniel's prophecy: "Another shall rise after them, and he shall be diverse from the first, and he shall subdue three kings, and he shall speak great words against the Most High, and shall wear out the saints of the Most High, and think to change times and laws; and they shall be given into his hands until a time, times, and the dividing of time." This power, who was to rise upon the kings, is Antichrist; and I would have you observe how Rome and Antichrist stand towards each other in the prophecy. Rome is to fall before Antichrist rises; for the ten kings are to destroy Rome, and Antichrist is then to appear and supersede the ten kings. As far as we dare judge from the words, this seems clear. First, St. John says, "The ten horns shall hate and devour" the woman; secondly, Daniel says, "I considered the horns, and behold, there came up among them another little horn," viz., Antichrist, "before whom" or by whom "there were three of the first horns plucked up by the roots."

2.

Now then, let us consider how far these prophecies have been fulfilled, and what seems to remain unfulfilled.

In the first place, the Roman Empire did break up, as foretold. It divided into a number of separate kingdoms, such as our own, France, and the like; yet it is difficult to number ten accurately and exactly. Next, though Rome certainly has been desolated in the most fearful and miserable way, yet it has not exactly suffered from ten parts of its former empire, but from barbarians who came down upon it from regions external to it; and, in the third place, it still exists as a city, whereas it was to be "desolated, devoured, and burned with fire." And, fourthly, there is one point in the description of the ungodly city, which has hardly been fulfilled at all in the case of Rome. She had "a golden cup in her hand full of abominations," and made "the inhabitants of the earth drunk with the wine of her fornication;" expressions which imply surely some seduction or delusion which she was enabled to practise upon the world, and which, I say, has not been fulfilled in the case of that great imperial city upon seven hills of which St. John spake. Here then are points which require some consideration.

I say, the Roman Empire has scarcely yet been divided into ten. The Prophet Daniel is conspicuous among the inspired writers for the clearness and exactness of his predictions; so much so, that some unbelievers, overcome by the truth of them, could only take refuge in the unworthy, and, at the same time, unreasonable and untenable supposition, that they were written after the events which they profess to foretell. But we have had no such exact fulfilment in history of the ten kings; therefore we must suppose that it is yet to come. With this accords the ancient notion, that they were to come at the end of the world, and last for but a short time, Antichrist coming upon them. There have, indeed, been approximations to that number, yet, I conceive, nothing more. Now observe how the actual state of things corresponds to the prophecy, and to the primitive interpretation of it. It is difficult to say whether the Roman Empire is gone or not; in one sense, it is gone, for it is divided into kingdoms; in another sense, it is not, for the date cannot be assigned at which it came to an end, and much might be said in various ways to show that it may be considered still existing, though in a mutilated and decayed state. But if this be so, and if it is to end in ten vigorous kings, as Daniel says, then it must one day *revive*. Now observe, I say, how the prophetic description answers to this account of it. " The wild Beast," that is, the Roman Empire, " the Monster that thou sawest, *was and is not*, and *shall* ascend out of the abyss, and go into perdition." Again mention is made of " the Monster that was, and *is not, and yet is*." Again we are expressly told that the ten kings and the Empire shall rise together; the kings appearing at the time of the monster's resurrection, not during its languid and torpid state. " The ten kings . . . have received no kingdom as yet, but receive power as kings one hour with the beast." If, then, the Roman Empire is still prostrate, the ten kings have not come ; and if the ten kings have not come, the destined destroyers of the woman, the full judgments upon Rome, have not yet come.

3.

Thus the full measure of judgment has not fallen upon Rome ; yet her sufferings, and the sufferings of her Empire, have been very severe. St. Peter seems to predict them, in his First Epistle, as then impending. He seems to imply that our Lord's visitation, which was then just occurring, was no local or momentary vengeance upon one people or city, but a solemn and extended judgment of the whole earth, though beginning at Jerusalem. " The time is come," he says, " when judgment must begin at *the house* of God " (at the sacred city) ; "and, if it first begin at us, what shall the end be of them that obey not the Gospel of God ? And if the righteous scarcely be saved,"— (*i. e.*, the remnant who should go forth of Zion, according to the prophecy, that chosen seed in the Jewish Church which received Christ

when He came, and took the new name of Christians,
and shot forth and grew far and wide into a fresh Church,
or, in other words, the elect whom our Saviour speaks
of as being involved in all the troubles and judgments
of the devoted people, yet safely carried through); "if
the righteous scarcely be saved, where shall the ungodly
and the sinner appear,"—the inhabitants of the world at
large? *

Here is intimation of the presence of a fearful scourge
which was then going over all the ungodly world, beginning at apostate Jerusalem, and punishing it. Such
was the case : vengeance first fell upon the once holy
city, which was destroyed by the Romans : it proceeded
next against the executioners themselves.† The empire
was disorganized, and broken to pieces by dissensions
and insurrections, by plagues, famines, and earthquakes,
while countless hosts of barbarians attacked it from the
north and east, and portioned it out, and burned and
pillaged Rome itself. The judgment, I say, which began
at Jerusalem, steadily tracked its way for centuries round
and round the world, till at length, with unerring aim,
it smote the haughty mistress of the nations herself, the
guilty woman seated upon the fourth monster which
Daniel saw. I will mention one or two of these fearful
inflictions.

Hosts of barbarians came down upon the civilized
world, the Roman empire. One multitude—though
multitude is a feeble word to describe them,—invaded
France, ‡ which was living in peace and prosperity under
the shadow of Rome. They desolated and burned town
and country. Seventeen provinces were made a desert.

---

* Pet. iv. 17, 18. *Vide* also Jer. xxv. 28, 29. Ezek. ix. 6:
† *Vide* Is. xlvii. 5, 6.
‡ A.D. 407. *Vide* Gibbon, Hist. vol v chap. 30.

Eight metropolitan cities were set on fire and destroyed. Multitudes of Christians perished even in the churches.

The fertile coast of Africa was the scene of another of these invasions.* The barbarians gave no quarter to any who opposed them. They tortured their captives, of whatever age, rank, and sex, to force them to discover their wealth. They drove away the inhabitants of the cities to the mountains. They ransacked the churches. They destroyed even the fruit-trees, so complete was the desolation.

Of judgments in the course of nature, I will mention three out of a great number. One, an inundation from the sea in all parts of the Eastern empire. The water overflowed the coast for two miles inland, sweeping away houses and inhabitants along a line of some thousand miles. One great city (Alexandria) lost fifty thousand persons.†

The second, a series of earthquakes; some of which were felt all over the empire. Constantinople was thus shaken above forty days together. At Antioch 250,000 persons perished in another.

And in the third place a plague, which lasted (languishing and reviving) through the long period of fifty-two years. In Constantinople, during three months, there died daily 5,000, and at length 10,000 persons. I give these facts from a modern writer, who is neither favourable to Christianity, nor credulous in matters of historical testimony. In some countries the population was wasted away altogether, and has not recovered to this day.‡

Such were the scourges by which the fourth monster

* A.D. 430.　*Vide* Gibbon, Hist. vol. vi. chap. 33.
† A.D. 365.　Ibid. vol. iv. chap. 26.
‡ A.D. 540.　Ibid. vol. vii. chap. 43.

of Daniel's vision was brought low, "the Lord God's sore judgments, the sword, the famine, and the pestilence." *   Such was the process by which "that which withholdeth," (in St. Paul's language) began to be "taken away ;" though not altogether removed even now.

And, while the world itself was thus plagued, not less was the offending city which had ruled it. Rome was taken and plundered three several times. The inhabitants were murdered, made captives, or obliged to fly all over Italy. The gold and jewels of the queen of the nations, her precious silk and purple, and her works of art, were carried off or destroyed.

4.

These are great and notable events, and certainly form part of the predicted judgment upon Rome ; at the same time they do not adequately fulfil the prophecy, which says expressly, on the one hand, that the ten portions of the Empire itself which had almost been slain, shall rise up against the city, and "make her desolate and burn her with fire," which they have not yet done ; and, on the other hand, that the city shall experience a *total* destruction, which has not yet befallen her, for she still exists. St. John's words on the latter point are clear and determinate. "Babylon the great is fallen, is fallen ; and is become the habitation of devils, and the hole of every foul spirit, and a cage of every unclean and hateful bird ;"† words which would seem to refer us to the curse upon the literal Babylon ; and we know how that curse was fulfilled. The prophet Isaiah had said, that in Babylon "wild beasts of the desert should lie there, and their houses be full of doleful creatures, and owls should dwell there, and satyrs," or wild beasts "dance there."‡

* Ezek. xiv. 21.   † Rev. xviii. 2.   ‡ Isa. xiii. 21.

And we know that all this has in fact happened to Babylon; it is a heap of ruins; no man dwells there; nay, it is difficult to say even where exactly it was placed, so great is the desolation. Such a desolation St. John seems to predict, concerning the guilty persecuting city we are considering; and in spite of what she has suffered, such a desolation has not come upon her yet. Again, "she shall be utterly burnt with fire, for strong is the Lord God, who judgeth her." Surely this implies utter destruction, annihilation. Again, "a mighty Angel took up a stone, like a great millstone, and cast it into the sea, saying, Thus with violence, shall that great city Babylon be thrown down, and *shall be found no more at all.*"

To these passages I would add this reflection. Surely Rome is spoken of in Scripture as a more inveterate enemy of God and His saints even than Babylon, as the great pollution and bane of the earth : if then Babylon has been destroyed wholly, much more, according to all reasonable conjecture, will Rome be destroyed one day.

It may be farther observed that holy men in the early Church certainly thought that the barbarian invasions were not all that Rome was to receive in the way of vengeance, but that God would one day destroy it by the fury of the elements. "Rome," says Pope Gregory, at a time when a barbarian conqueror had possession of the city, and all things seemed to threaten its destruction, " Rome shall not be destroyed by the nations, but shall consume away internally, worn out by storms of lightning, whirlwinds, and earthquakes." * In accordance with this is the prophecy ascribed to St. Malachi of Armagh, a mediæval Archbishop (A.D. 1130), which declares, "In the last persecution of the Holy Church,

* Greg. Dial. ii. 15.

Peter of Rome shall be on the throne, who shall feed his flock in many tribulations. When these are past, *the city upon seven hills shall be* destroyed, and the awful Judge shall judge the people."*

5.

This is what may be said on the one side, but after all something may be said on the other; not indeed to show that the prophecy is already fully accomplished, for it certainly is not, but to show that, granting this, such accomplishment as has to come has reference, not to Rome, but to some other object or objects of divine vengeance. I shall explain my meaning under two heads.

First, why has Rome not been destroyed hitherto? how was it that the barbarians left it? Babylon sank under the avenger brought against it—Rome has not: why is this? for if there has been a something to procrastinate the vengeance due to Rome hitherto, peradventure that obstacle may act again and again, and stay the uplifted hand of divine wrath till the end come. The cause of this unexpected respite seems to be simply this, that when the barbarians came down, God had a people in that city. Babylon was a mere prison of the Church; Rome had received her as a guest. The Church dwelt in Rome, and while her children suffered in the heathen city from the barbarians, so again they were the life and the salt of that city where they suffered.

Christians understood this at the time, and availed themselves of their position. They remembered Abraham's intercession for Sodom, and the gracious announcement made him, that, had there been ten righteous men therein, it would have been saved.

* *Vide* Dr. Burton, Antiq. of Rome, p. 475.

When the city was worsted, threatened, and at length overthrown, the Pagans had cried out that Christianity was the cause of this. They said they had always flourished under their idols, and that these idols or devils (gods as they called them) were displeased with them for the numbers among them who had been converted to the faith of the Gospel, and had in consequence deserted them, given them over to their enemies, and brought vengeance upon them. On the other hand, they scoffed at the Christians, saying in effect, "Where is now your God? Why does He not save you? You are not better off than we;" they said, with the impenitent thief, "If thou be the Christ, save Thyself and us;" or with the multitude, "If He be the Son of God, let Him come down from the Cross." This was during the time of one of the most celebrated bishops and doctors of the Church, St. Augustine, and he replied to their challenge. He replied to them, and to his brethren also, some of whom were offended and shocked that such calamities should have happened to a city which had become Christian.* He pointed to the cities which had already sinned and been visited, and showed that they had altogether perished, whereas Rome was still preserved. Here, then, he said, was the very fulfilment of the promise of God, announced to Abraham;—for the sake of the Christians in it, Rome was chastised, not overthrown utterly.

Historical facts support St. Augustine's view of things. God provided visibly, not only in His secret counsels, that the Church should be the salvation of the city. The fierce conqueror Alaric, who first came against it, exhorted his troops "to respect the Churches of the Apostles St. Peter and St. Paul, as holy and inviolable sanctuaries;" and he gave orders that a quantity of plate, consecrated

* August. de Urbis Excidio, vol. vi. p. 622. ed. Ben. et de Civ. Dei, i. 1–7.

to St. Peter, should be removed into his Church from the place where it had been discovered.*

Again, fifty years afterwards, when Attila was advancing against the city, the Bishop of Rome of the day, St. Leo, formed one of a deputation of three, who went out to meet him, and was successful in arresting his purpose.

A few years afterwards, Genseric, the most savage of the barbarian conquerors, appeared before the defenceless city. The same fearless pontiff went out to meet him at the head of his clergy, and though he did not succeed in saving the city from pillage, yet he gained a promise that the unresisting multitude should be spared, the buildings protected from fire, and the captives from torture.†

Thus from the Goth, Hun, and Vandal did the Christian Church shield the guilty city in which she dwelt. What a wonderful rule of God's providence is herein displayed which occurs daily!—the Church sanctifies, yet suffers with, the world,—sharing its sufferings, yet lightening them. In the case before us, she has (if we may humbly say it) suspended, to this day, the vengeance destined to fall upon that city which was drunk with the blood of the martyrs of Jesus. That vengeance has never fallen; it is still suspended ; nor can reason be given *why* Rome has not fallen under the rule of God's general dealings with His rebellious creatures, and suffered (according to the prophecy) the fulness of God's wrath begun in it, except that a Christian Church is still in that city, sanctifying it, interceding for it, saving it. We in England consider that the Christian Church there has in process of time become infected with the sins of Rome itself, and has learned to be ambitious and cruel after the fashion of those who possessed the place aforetimes. Yet, if it were what many would make it, if it were as reprobate as

* *Vide* Gibbon, Hist. vol. v. chap. 31.   Ibid. vol. vi. chap. 35, 36.

heathen Rome itself, what stays the judgment long ago begun? why does not the Avenging Arm, which made its first stroke ages since, deal its second and its third, till the city has fallen? Why is not Rome as Sodom and Gomorrah, if there be no righteous men in it?

This then is the first remark I would make as to that fulfilment of the prophecy which is not yet come; perhaps through divine mercy, it may be procrastinated even to the end, and never be fulfilled. Of this we can know nothing one way or the other.

Secondly, let it be considered, that as Babylon is a type of Rome, and of the world of sin and vanity, so Rome in turn may be a type also, whether of some other city, or of a proud and deceiving world. The woman is said to be Babylon as well as Rome, and as she is something more than Babylon, namely, Rome, so again she may be something more than Rome, which is yet to come. Various great cities in Scripture are made, in their ungodliness and ruin, types of the world itself. Their end is described in figures, which in their fulness apply only to the end of the world; the sun and moon are said to fall, the earth to quake, and the stars to fall from heaven.* The destruction of Jerusalem in our Lord's prophecy is associated with the end of all things. As then their ruin prefigures a greater and wider judgment, so the chapters, on which I have been dwelling, may have a further accomplishment, not in Rome, but in the world itself, or some other great city to which we cannot at present apply them, or to all the great cities of the world together, and to the spirit that rules in them, their avaricious, luxurious, self-dependent, irreligious spirit. And in this sense is already fulfilled a portion of the chapter before us, which does not apply to heathen Rome;—I

* *Vide* Isaiah xiii. 10, etc.

mean the description of the woman as making men drunk with her sorceries and delusions ; for such, surely, and nothing else than an intoxication, is that arrogant, ungodly, falsely liberal, and worldly spirit, which great cities make dominant in a country.

6.

To sum up what I have said. The question asked was, Is it not true (as is commonly said and believed among us) that Rome is mentioned in the Apocalypse, as having especial share in the events which will come at the end of the world by means, or after the time, of Antichrist? I answer this, that Rome's judgments have come on her in great measure, when her Empire was taken from her; that her persecutions of the Church have been in great measure avenged, and the Scripture predictions concerning her fulfilled ; that whether or not she shall be further judged depends on two circum-stances, first, whether "the righteous men" in the city who saved her when her judgment first came, will not, through God's great mercy, be allowed to save her still ; next, whether the prophecy relates in its fulness to Rome or to some other object or objects of which Rome is a type. And further, I say, that if it is in the divine counsels that Rome should still be judged, this must be before Antichrist comes, because Antichrist comes upon and destroys the ten kings, and lasts but a short space, but it is the ten kings who are to destroy Rome. On the other hand, so far would seem to be clear, that the prophecy itself has not been fully accomplished, what-ever we decide about Rome's concern in it. The Roman Empire has not yet been divided into ten heads, nor has it yet risen against the woman, whomsoever she stands for, nor has the woman yet received her ultimate judgment.

We are warned against sharing in her sins and in her punishment;—against being found, when the end comes, mere children of this world and of its great cities; with tastes, opinions, habits, such as are found in its cities; with a heart dependent on human society, and a reason moulded by it;—against finding ourselves at the last day, before our Judge, with all the low feelings, principles, and aims which the world encourages; with our thoughts wandering (if that be possible then), wandering after vanities; with thoughts which rise no higher than the consideration of our own comforts, or our gains; with a haughty contempt for the Church, her ministers, her lowly people; a love of rank and station, an admiration of the splendour and the fashions of the world, an affectation of refinement, a dependence upon our powers of reason, an habitual self-esteem, and an utter ignorance of the number and the heinousness of the sins which lie against us. If we are found thus, when the end comes, where, when the judgment is over, and the saints have gone up to heaven, and there is silence and darkness where all was so full of life and expectation, where shall we find ourselves then? And what good could the great Babylon do us then, though it were as immortal as we are immortal ourselves?

4.

The Persecution of Antichrist.

WE have been so accustomed to hear of the persecutions of the Church, both from the New
Testament and from the history of Christianity, that it
is much if we have not at length come to regard the
account of them as words of course, to speak of them
without understanding what we say, and to receive no
practical benefit from having been told of them; much
less are we likely to take them for what they really are,
a characteristic mark of Christ's Church. They are
not indeed the necessary lot of the Church, but at least
one of her appropriate badges; so that, on the whole,
looking at the course of history, you might set down
persecution as one of the peculiarities by which you
recognize her. And our Lord seems to intimate how
becoming, how natural persecution is to the Church, by
placing it among His Beatitudes. "Blessed are they
who are persecuted for righteousness' sake, for theirs is
the kingdom of heaven;" giving it the same high and
honourable rank in the assemblage of evangelical graces,
which the Sabbath holds among the Ten Commandments,—I mean, as a sort of sign and token of His
followers, and, as such, placed in the moral code, though
in itself external to it.

He seems to show us this in another way, viz., by in-
timating to us the fact, that in persecution the Church
begins and in persecution she ends. He left her in perse-

cution, and He will find her in persecution. He recognizes her as His own,—He framed, and He will claim
her,—as a persecuted Church, bearing His Cross. And
that awful relic of Him which He gave her, and which
she is found possessed of at the end, she cannot have
lost by the way.

The prophet Daniel, who shadows out for us so many
things about the last time, speaks of the great persecution yet to come. He says, " There shall be a time of
trouble, such as never was, since there was a nation,
even to that same time: and at that time thy people
shall be delivered, every one that shall be found written
in the Book." To these words our Lord seems to refer,
in His solemn prophecy before His passion, in which He
comprises both series of events, both those which attended His first, and those which will attend at His
second coming—both persecutions of His Church, the
early and the late. He speaks as follows : " Then shall
be great tribulation, such as was not since the beginning
of the world to this time, no, nor ever shall be ; and except those days should be shortened, there should no
flesh be saved ; but for the elect's sake, those days shall
be shortened." *

Now I shall conclude what I have to say about the
coming of Antichrist by speaking of the persecution
which will attend it. In saying that a persecution will
attend it, I do but speak the opinion of the early Church,
as I have tried to do all along, and as I shall do in
what follows.

I.

First, I will cite some of the principal texts which
seem to refer to this last persecution.

* Matt. xxiv. 21, 22.

"Another shall rise after them, and . . . he shall speak great words against the Most High, and shall wear out the saints of the Most High, and think to change times and laws; and they shall be given into his hand until a time, times, and the dividing of time :" * that is, three years and a half.

"They shall pollute the Sanctuary of strength, and shall take away the Daily Sacrifice, and they shall place the Abomination that maketh desolate, and such as do wickedly against the Covenant shall he corrupt by flatteries; but the people that do know their God shall be strong and do exploits. And they that understand among the people, shall instruct many; yet they shall fall by the sword, and by flame, by captivity, and by spoil, many days." †

"Many shall be purified, and made white, and tried; but the wicked shall do wickedly ; . . . . and from the time that the Daily Sacrifice shall be taken away, and the Abomination that maketh desolate set up, there shall be a thousand two hundred and ninety days." ‡

"Then shall be great tribulation, such as was not since the beginning of the world," § and so on, as I just now read it.

"And there was given unto him a mouth speaking great things and blasphemies; and power was given unto him to continue forty and two months. And he opened his mouth in blasphemy against God, to blaspheme His name, and His tabernacle, and them that dwell in heaven: and it was given unto him to make war with the saints, and to overcome them . . . . and all that dwell upon the earth shall worship him, whose

---

* Dan. vii. 24, 25. ‡ Dan. xii. 10, 11.
† Dan. xi. 31—33. § Matt. xxiv. 21

names are not written in the book of life of the Lamb
slain from the foundation of the world ." *

"I saw an Angel come down from heaven, having the
key of the bottomless pit, and a great chain in his hand ;
and he laid hold on the dragon, that old serpent, which
is the devil and Satan, and bound him a thousand years
. . . . and after that he must be loosed a little season
. . . . and shall go out to deceive the nations which are
in the four quarters of the earth, Gog and Magog, to
gather them together to battle : the number of whom is
as the sand of the sea. And they went up on the
breadth of the earth, and compassed the camp of the
saints about and the beloved city." †

These passages were understood by the early Christians to relate to the Persecution which was to come in
the last times ; and they seem evidently to bear upon
them that meaning. Our Lord's words, indeed, about
the fierce trial which was coming, might seem at first
sight to refer to the early persecutions, those to which
the first Christians were exposed ; and doubtless so they
do also : yet, violent as these persecutions were, they were
not considered by those very men who underwent them
to be the proper fulfilment of the prophecy; and this surely
is itself a strong reason for thinking they were not so.
And we are confirmed by parallel passages, such as the
words of Daniel quoted just now, which certainly speak
of a persecution still future ; if then our Lord used
those very words of Daniel, and was speaking of what
Daniel spoke of, therefore, whatever partial accomplishment His prediction had in the history of the early
Church, He surely speaks of nothing short of the last
persecution, when His words are viewed in their full
scope. He says, " There shall be great tribulation, such

* Rev. xiii. 5—8.   † Rev. xx. 1—9.

as was not since the beginning of the world to this time, no, nor ever shall be : and except those days should be shortened, there shall no flesh be saved ; but for the elect's sake those days shall be shortened." And immediately after, " There shall arise false Christs and false prophets, and shall show great signs and wonders ; insomuch that, if it were possible, they shall deceive the very elect." In accordance with this language, Daniel says, " There shall be a time of trouble, such as never was since there was a nation, even to that same time : and at that time thy people shall be delivered, every one that shall be found written in the book." One of the passages I quoted from the Revelation says the same, and as strongly : " It was given him to make war with the Saints, and to overcome them . . . . and all that dwell on the earth shall worship him, whose names are not written in the book of life ." *

2.

Let us then apprehend and realize the idea, thus clearly brought before us, that, sheltered as the Church has been from persecution for 1500 years, yet a persecution awaits it, before the end, fiercer and more perilous than any which occurred at its first rise.

Further, this persecution is to be attended with the cessation of all religious worship. "They shall take away the Daily Sacrifice,"—words which the early Fathers interpret to mean, that Antichrist will suppress for three years and a half all religious worship. St. Augustine questions whether baptism even will be administered to infants during that season.

And further we are told : " They shall place the Abomination that maketh desolate " in the Holy Place

* Rev. xiii 7, 8.

—they shall " set it up : " our Saviour declares the same.
What this means we cannot pronounce. In the former
fulfilment of this prophecy, it has been the introduction
of heathen idols into God's house.

Moreover the reign of Antichrist will be supported, it
would appear, with a display of miracles, such as the
magicians of Egypt effected against Moses. On this
subject, of course, we wait for a fuller explanation of the
prophetical language, such as the event alone can give
us. So far, however, is clear, that whether false miracles
or not, whether pretended, or the result, as some have
conjectured, of discoveries in physical science, they will
produce the same effect as if they were real,—viz., the
overpowering the imaginations of such as have not the
love of God deeply lodged in their hearts,—of all but
the elect." Scripture is remarkably precise and consistent in this prediction. " Signs and wonders," says
our Lord, " insomuch that, if it were possible, they shall
deceive the very elect." St. Paul speaks of Antichrist
as one " whose coming is after the work of Satan, with
all powers and signs, and lying wonders, and with all
deceivableness of unrighteousness in them that perish ;
because they received not the love of the Truth, that they
might be saved. And for this cause God shall send them
strong delusion, that they should believe a lie."*   And St.
John : " He doeth great wonders, so that He maketh fire
come down from heaven on the earth in the sight of men,
and deceiveth them that dwell on the earth by the means
of those miracles which He had power to do in the sight
of the beast."†

In these four respects, then, not to look for others,
will the last persecution be more awful than any of the
earlier ones : in its being in itself fiercer and more hor-

* 2 Thess. ii. 9—11.   † Rev. xiii. 13, 14.

rible; in its being attended by a cessation of the Ordinances of grace, "the Daily Sacrifice;" and by an open and blasphemous establishment of infidelty, or some such enormity, in the holiest recesses of the Church; lastly, in being supported by a profession of working miracles. Well is it for Christians that the days are shortened!—shortened for the elect's sake, lest they should be overwhelmed,—shortened, as it would seem, to three years and a half.

3.

Much might be said, of course, on each of these four particulars; but I will confine myself to making one remark on the first of them, the sharpness of the persecution.—It is to be worse than any persecution before it. Now, to understand the force of this announcement, we should understand in some degree what those former persecutions were.

This it is very difficult to do in a few words; yet a very slight survey of the history of the Church would convince us that cruelties more shocking than those which the early Christians suffered from their persecutors, it is very difficult to conceive. St. Paul's words, speaking of the persecutions prior to his time, describes but faintly the trial which came upon the Church in h's own day and afterwards. He says of the Jewish saints, "They were tortured, not accepting deliverance" . . . they "had trials of cruel mockings and scourgings, yea moreover, of bonds and imprisonment: they were stoned, they were sawn asunder, were tempted, were slain with the sword: they wandered about in sheepskins and goatskins; being destitute, afflicted, tormented." Such were the trials of the Prophets under the Law, who in a measure anticipated the Gospel, as in creed, so in suffering;

yet the Gospel suffering was as much sharper as the Gospel creed was fuller than their foretaste of either.

Let me take, as a single specimen, a portion of a letter, giving an account of some details of one of the persecutions in the south of France. It is written by eye-witnesses.

" . . . The rage of the populace, governor, and soldiers especially lighted on Sanctus, a deacon ; on Maturus, a late convert ; on Attalus, and on Blandina, a slave, through whom Christ showed that the things which are lowly esteemed among men have high account with God. For when we were all in fear, and her own mistress was in agony for her, lest she should be unable to make even one bold confession, from the weakness of her body, Blandina was filled with such strength, that even those who tortured her by turns, in every possible way, from morning till evening, were wearied and gave it up, confessing she had conquered them. And they wondered at her remaining still alive, her whole body being mangled and pierced in every part. But that blessed woman, like a brave combatant, renewed her strength in confessing ; and it was to her a recovery, a rest, and a respite, to say, ' I am a Christian.' . . Sanctus also endured exceedingly all the cruelties of men with a noble patience . . and to all questions would say nothing but ' I am a Christian.' When they had nothing left to do to him, they fastened red-hot plates of brass on the tenderest parts of his body. But though his limbs were burning, he remained upright and unshrinking, steadfast in his confession, bathed and strengthened from Heaven with that fountain of living water that springs from the well of Christ. But his body bore witness of what had been done to it, being one entire wound, and deprived of the external form of man."

After some days they were taken to the shows where the wild beasts were, and went through every torture again, as though they had suffered nothing before. Again they were scourged, forced into the iron chair (which was red-hot), dragged about by the beasts, and so came to their end. " But Blandina was hung up upon a cross, and placed to be devoured by the beasts that were turned in." Afterwards she was scourged ; at last placed in a basket and thrown to a bull, and died under the tossings of the furious animal. But the account is far too long and minute, and too dreadful, to allow of my going through it. I give this merely as a specimen of the sufferings of the early Christians from the malice of the devil.

As another instance, take again the sufferings which the Arian Vandals inflicted at a later time. Out of four hundred and sixty Bishops in Africa, they sent forty-six out of the country to an unhealthy place, and confined them to hard labour, and three hundred and two to different parts of Africa. After an interval of ten years they banished two hundred and twenty more. At another time they tore above four thousand Christians, clergy and laity, from their homes, and marched them across the sands till they died either of fatigue or ill-usage. They lacerated others with scourges, burned them with hot iron, and cut off their limbs.*

Hear how one of the early Fathers, just when the early persecutions were ceasing, meditates on the prospect lying before the Church, looking earnestly at the events of his own day, in order to discover from them, if he could, whether the predicted evil was coming :

"There will be a time of affliction, such as never happened since there was a nation upon the earth till that time. The fearful monster, the great serpent, the unconquerable enemy of mankind, ready to devour. . . The Lord knowing the greatness of the enemy, in mercy to the religious, says, ' Let those that are in Judea flee to the mountains.' However, if any feel within him a strong heart to wrestle with Satan, let him remain, (for I do not despair of the Church's strength of nerve,) let him remain, and let him say, ' Who shall separate us from the love of Christ ?' . . . Thanks to God, who limits the greatness of the affliction to a few days ; ' for the elect's sake those days shall be cut short.' Antichrist shall reign

* Gibbon, Hist., chap. 37.

only three years and a half, a time, times, and the dividing of
times. . . . "Blessed surely he who then shall be a martyr for
Christ ! I consider that the martyrs at that season will be greater
than all martyrs ; for the fo.mer ones wrestled with man only, but
these, in the time of Antichrist, will battle with Satan himself personally. Persecuting emperors slaughtered the former ; but they
did not pretend to raise the dead, nor make show of signs and
wonders : but here there will be the persuasion both of force and of
fraud, so as to deceive, if possible, even the elect. Let no one at
that day say in his heart, ' What could Christ do more than this or
that ? by what virtue worketh he these things ? Unless God willed
it, He would not have permitted it.' No : the Apostle forewarns
you, saying beforehand, ' God shall send them a strong delusion,'—
not that they may be excused, but condemned—viz., those who
believe not in the Truth, that is, the true Chris', but take pleasure
in unrighteousness, that is, in Antichrist. . . . Prepare thyself,
therefore, O man ! thou hearest the signs of Antichrist ; nor remind
only thyself of them, but communicate them liberally to all around
thee. If thou hast a child according to the flesh, delay not to instruct him. If thou art a teacher, prepare also thy spiritual children,
lest they take the false for the True. ' For the mystery of iniquity
doth already work.' I fear the wars of the nations, I fear the
divisions among Christians, I fear the hatred among brethren.
Enough ; but God forbid that it should be fulfilled in our day.
However, let us be prepared."—*Cyr. Catech.* xv. 16, 17.

4.

I have two remarks to add : first, that it is quite certain, that if such a persecution has been foretold, it has
not yet come, and therefore is to come. We may be
wrong in thinking that Scripture foretells it, though it
has been the common belief, I may say, of all ages ; but
if there be a persecution, it is still future. So that every
generation of Christians should be on the watch-tower,
looking out,—nay, more and more, as time goes on.

Next, I observe that signs do occur from time to time,
not to enable us to fix the day, for that is hidden, but to
show us it is coming. The world grows old—the earth

is crumbling away—the night is far spent—the day is at hand. The shadows begin to move—the old forms of empire, which have lasted ever since our Lord was with us, heave and tremble before our eyes, and nod to their fall. These it is that keep Him from us—He is behind them. When they go, Antichrist will be released from "that which withholdeth," and after his short but fearful season, Christ will come.

For instance: one sign is the present state of the Roman Empire, if it may be said to exist, though it does exist; but it is like a man on his death-bed, who after many throes and pangs at last goes off when you least expect, or perhaps you know not when. You watch the sick man, and you say every day will be the last; yet day after day goes on—you know not when the end will come—he lingers on—gets better—relapses,—yet you are sure after all he must die—it is a mere matter of time, you call it a matter of time: so is it with the Old Roman Empire, which now lies so still and helpless. It is not dead, but it is on its death-bed. We suppose indeed that it will not die without some violence even yet, without convulsions. Antichrist is to head it; yet in another sense it dies to make way for Antichrist, and this latter form of death is surely hastening on, whether it comes sooner or later. It may outlast our time, and the time of our children; for we are creatures of a day, and a generation is like the striking of a clock; but it tends to dissolution, and its hours are numbered.

Again, another anxious sign at the present time is what appears in the approaching destruction of the Mahometan power. This too may outlive our day; still it tends visibly to annihilation, and as it crumbles, perchance the sands of the world's life are running out.

And lastly, not to mention many other tokens which might be observed upon, here is this remarkable one. In one of the passages I just now read from the book of Revelation, it is said that in the last times, and in order to the last persecution, Satan, being loosed from his prison, shall deceive the nations in the extremities of the earth, Gog and Magog, and bring them to battle against the Church. These appellations had been already used by the prophet Ezekiel, who borrows the latter of them from the tenth chapter of Genesis. We read in that chapter, that after the flood the sons of Japheth were "Gomer, and Magog, and Madai, and Javan, and Tubal, and Meshech, and Tiras." Magog is supposed to be the ancestor of the nations in the north, the Tartars or Scythians. Whatever then Gog means, which is not known, here is a prophecy that the northern nations should be stirred up against the Church, and be one of the instruments of its suffering. And it is to be observed, that twice since that prophecy was delivered the northern nations have invaded the Church, and both times they have brought with them, or rather (as the text in the Revelation expresses it) they have been deceived into, an Antichristian delusion,—been deceived into it, not invented it. The first irruption was that of the Goths and Vandals in the early times of the Church, and they were deceived into and fought for the Arian heresy. The next was that of the Turks, and they in like manner were deceived into and fought for Mahometanism. Here then the after history, as in other instances, is in part a comment upon the prophecy Now, I do not mean that as to the present time, we see how this is to be accomplished in its fulness, after the pattern of the Shadows which have gone before. But thus much we see—we see that in matter of fact the nations of the North * are gathering strength, and beginning to frown over the seat of the Roman Empire as they never have done since the time when the Turks came down.   Here then we have a sign of Antichrist's appearance—I do not say of his instant coming, or his certain coming, for it may after all be but a type or shadow of things far future ; still, so far as it goes, it is a preparation, a warning, a call to sober thought—just as a cloud in the sky (to use our Lord's instance) warns us about the weather.   It is no sure proof that it precedes a storm, but we think it prudent to keep our eye upon it.

5.

This is what I have to say about the last persecution and its signs.   And surely it is profitable to think about it, though we be quite mistaken in the detail.   For instance, after all perhaps it may not be a persecution of blood and death, but of craft and subtlety only—not of miracles, but of natural wonders and powers of human skill, human acquirements in the hands of the devil. Satan may adopt the more alarming weapons of deceit —he may hide himself—he may attempt to seduce us in little things, and so to move Christians, not all at once, but by little and little from their true position. We know he has done much in this way in the course of the last centuries.   It is his policy to split us up and divide us, to dis'odge us gradually from off our rock of strength. And if there is to be a persecution, perhaps it will be then ; then, perhaps, when we are all of us in all parts of Christendom so divided, and so reduced, so full of schism, so close upon heresy.   When we have cast ourselves upon the world, and depend for protection upon

* [*E. g.,* The Chinese ?]

it, and have given up our independence and our strength, then he may burst upon us in fury, as far as God allows him. Then suddenly the Roman Empire may break up, and Antichrist appear as a persecutor, and the barbarous nations around break in. But all these things are in God's hand and God's knowledge, and there let us leave them.

This alone I will say, in conclusion, as I have already said several times, that such meditations as these may be turned to good account. It will act as a curb upon our self-willed, selfish hearts, to believe that a persecution is in store for the Church, whether or not it comes in our days. Surely, with this prospect before us, we cannot bear to give ourselves up to thoughts of ease and comfort, of making money, settling well, or rising in the world. Surely, with this prospect before us, we cannot but feel that we are, what all Christians really are in the best estate (nay, rather would wish to be, had they their will, if they be Christians in heart), pilgrims, watchers waiting for the morning, waiting for the light, eagerly straining our eyes for the first dawn of day—looking out for our Lord's coming, His glorious advent, when He will end the reign of sin and wickedness, accomplish the number of His elect, and perfect those who at present struggle with infirmity, yet in their hearts love and obey Him.

POSTSCRIPT.

THE above expositions of the teaching of the Fathers on the subject treated, were preached by the Author in the form of Sermons in Advent, 1835, and are illustrated by the following remarkable passage in a letter of Bishop Horsley's, written before the beginning of this century ; vide *British Magazine*, May, 1834.

"The Church of God on earth will be greatly reduced, as we may well imagine, in its apparent numbers, in the times of Antichrist, by the open desertion of the powers of the world. This desertion will begin in a professed indifference to any particular form of Christianity, under the pretence of universal toleration ; which toleration will proceed from no true spirit of charity and forbearance, but from a design to undermine Christianity, by multiplying and encouraging sectaries. The pretended toleration will go far beyond a just toleration, even as it regards the different sects of Christians. For governments will pretend an indifference to all, and will give a protection in preference to none. All establishments will be laid aside. From the toleration of the most pestilent heresies, they will proceed to the toleration of Mahometanism, Atheism, and at last to a positive persecution of the truth of Christianity. In these times the Temple of God will be reduced almost to the Holy Place, that is, to the small number of real Christians who worship the Father in spirit and in truth, and regulate their doctrine and their worship, and their whole conduct, strictly by the word of God. The merely nominal

Christians will all desert the profession of the truth, when the powers of the world desert it. And this tragical event I take to be typified by the order to St. John to measure the Temple and the Altar, and leave the outer court (national Churches) to be trodden under foot by the Gentiles. The property of the clergy will be pillaged, the public worship insulted and vilified by these deserters of the faith they once professed, who are not called apostates because they never were in earnest in their profession. Their profession was nothing more than a compliance with fashion and public authority. In principle they were always, what they now appear to be, Gentiles. When this general desertion of the faith takes place, then will commence the sackcloth ministry of the witnesses. . . . There will be nothing of splendour in the external appearance of their churches ; they will have no support from governments, no honours, no emoluments, no immunities, no authority, but that which no earthly power can take away, which they derived from Him, who commissioned them to be His witnesses."— *B. M.*, vol. v., p. 520.

June, 1838.

III.

HOLY SCRIPTURE IN ITS RELATION TO THE CATHOLIC CREED.

IN EIGHT LECTURES.

I.

Difficulties in the Scripture Proof of the Catholic Creed.

I PROPOSE in the following Lectures to suggest some thoughts by way of answering an objection, which often presses on the mind of those who are inquiring into the claims of the Church, and the truth of that system of doctrine which she especially represents, and which is at once her trust and her charter. They hear much stress laid upon that Church system of doctrine; they see much that is beautiful in it, much that is plausible in the proof advanced for it, much which is agreeable to the analogy of nature—which bespeaks the hand of the Creator, and is suitable to the needs and expectations of the creature,—much that is deep, much that is large and free, fearless in its course, sure in its stepping, and singularly true, consistent, entire, harmonious, in its adjustments; but they seem to ask for more rigid proof in behalf of the simple elementary propositions on which it rests; or, in other words, by way of speaking more clearly, and as a chief illustration of what is meant (though it is not quite the same thing), let me say, they desire more adequate and explicit *Scripture proof* of its truth. They find that the proof is *rested* by us on Scripture, and therefore they require more explicit *Scripture proof*. They say, " All this that you say about the Church is very specious, and very attractive ; but where is it to be found in the inspired Volume ? " And that it is *not* found there (that is, I mean not found as fully as it might be), seems to them proved at once by the simple fact, that all persons (I may say all, for the exceptions are very few),—all those who try to form their Creed by Scripture only, fall away from the Church and her doctrines, and join one or other sect or party, as if showing that, whatever is or is not scriptural, at least the Church, by consent of all men, is not so.

I am stating no rare or novel objection : it is one which, I suppose, all of us have felt, or perhaps still feel : it is one which, before now (I do not scruple to say), I have much felt myself, and that without being able satisfactorily to answer : and which I believe to be one of the main difficulties, and (as I think) one of the intended difficulties, which God's providence puts at this day in the path of those who seek Him, for purposes known or unknown, ascertainable or not. Nor am I at all sanguine that I shall be able, in what I have to say, to present anything like a full view of the difficulty itself, even as a phenomenon ; which different minds feel differently, and do not quite recognize as their own when stated by another, and which it is difficult to bring out even according to one's own idea of it. Much less shall I be able to assign it its due place in that great Catholic system which nevertheless I hold to be true, and in which it is *but* a difficulty. I do not profess to be able to account for it, to reconcile the mind to it, and to dismiss it as a thing which was in a man's way, but is henceforth behind him ;—yet, subdued as my hopes may be, I have too great confidence in that glorious Creed, which I believe to have been once delivered to the Saints, to wish in any degree to deny the difficulty, or to be unfair to it, to smooth it over, misrepresent it, or defraud it of its due weight and extent. Though I were to grant that the champions of Israel have not yet rescued this portion of the sacred territory from the Philistine, its usurping occupant, yet was not Jerusalem in the hands of the Jebusites till David's time ?—and shall I, seeing with my eyes and enjoying the land of promise, be over-troubled with one objection, which stands unvanquished (supposing it) ; and, like haughty Haman, count the King's favour as nothing till I have all my own way, and nothing to try me ? In plain terms, I conceive I have otherwise most abundant evidence given me of the divine origin of the Church system of doctrine: how then is that evidence which *is* given, *not* given because, *though* given in Scripture, it might be there given more explicitly and fully, and (if I may so say) more consistently ?

One consideration alone must create an anxiety in entering on the subject I propose. It is this :—Those who commonly urge the objection which is now to be considered, viz., the want of adequate Scripture evidence for the Church creed, have, I feel sure, no right to make it ; that is, *they* are *inconsistent* in making it ; inasmuch as they cannot consistently find fault with a person who believes more than they do, unless they cease to believe just so much as they do believe. They ought, on their own principles, to doubt or disown much which happily they do not doubt or disown. This then is the direct, appropriate, polemical answer to them, or (as it is called) *an argumentum ad hominem.* "Look at home, and say, if you can, *why* you believe this or that, which you do believe : whatever reasons you give for your own belief in one point, this or that article, of your Creed, those parallel reasons we can give for our belief in the articles of our Creed. If you are reasonable in believing the one, we are reasonable in believing the other. Either we are reasonable, or you are not so. You ought not to stand where you are ; you ought to go further one way or the other." Now it is plain that if this be a sound argument against our assailants, it is a most convincing one ; and it is obviously very hard and very unfair if we are to be deprived of the use of it. And yet a cautious mind will ever use it with anxiety ; not that it is not most effective, but because it may be (as it were) too effective : it may drive the parties in question the wrong way, and make things worse instead of better. It only undertakes to show that they are inconsistent in their present opinions ; and from this inconsistency it is plain they can escape, by going further either one way or the other—by adding to their creed, or by giving it up altogether. It is then what is familiarly called a kill-or-cure remedy. Certainly it is better to be inconsistent, than to be consistently wrong—to hold some truth amid error, than to hold nothing but error—to believe than to doubt. Yet when I show a man that he is inconsistent, I make him decide whether of the two he loves better, the portion of truth or the portion of error, which he already holds. If he loves the truth better, he will abandon the error ; if the error, he will abandon the truth. And this is a fearful and anxious trial to put him under, and one cannot but feel loth to have recourse to it. One feels that perhaps it may be better to keep silence, and to let him, in shallowness and presumption, assail one's own position with impunity, than to retort, however justly, his weapons on himself;—better for oneself to seem a bigot, than to make him a scoffer.

Thus, for instance, a person who denies the Apostolical Succession of the Ministry, because it is not clearly taught in Scripture, ought, I conceive, if consistent, to deny the divinity of the Holy Ghost, which is nowhere literally stated in Scripture. Yet there is something so dreadful in his denying the latter, that one may often feel afraid to show him his inconsistency; lest, rather than admit the Apostolical Succession, he should consent to deny that the Holy Ghost is God. This is one of the great delicacies of disputing on the subject before us: yet, all things considered, I think, it only avails for the cautious use, not the abandonment, of the argument in question. For it is our plain duty to preach and defend the truth in a straightforward way. Those who are to stumble must stumble, rather than the heirs of grace should not hear. While we offend and alienate one man, we secure another; if we drive one man further the wrong way, we drive another further the right way. The cause of truth, the heavenly company of saints, gains on the whole more in one way than in the other. A wavering or shallow mind does perhaps as much harm to others as a mind that is consistent in error, nay, is in no very much better state itself; for if it has not developed into systematic scepticism, merely because it has not had the temptation, its present conscientiousness is not worth much. Whereas he who is at present obeying God under imperfect knowledge has a claim on His Ministers for their doing all in their power towards his obtaining further knowledge. He who admits the doctrine of the Holy Trinity, in spite of feeling its difficulties, whether in itself or in its proof,—who submits to the indirectness of the Scripture evidence as regards that particular doctrine,—has a right to be told those other doctrines, such as the Apostolical Succession, which are as certainly declared in Scripture, yet not more directly and prominently, and which will be as welcome to him, when known, because they are in Scripture, as those which he already knows. It is therefore our duty to do our part, and leave the event to God, begging Him to bless, yet aware that, whenever He visits, He divides.

In saying this, I by no means would imply that the only argument in behalf of our believing more than the generality of men believe at present, is, that else we ought in consistency to believe less—far from it indeed ; but this argument is the one that comes first, and is the most obvious and the most striking. Nor do I mean to say—far from it also—that all on whom it is urged, *will* in fact go one way or the other ; the many will remain pretty much where education and habit have placed them, and at least they will not confess that they are affected by any new argument at all. But of course when one speaks of anxiety about the effect of a certain argument, one speaks of cases in which it will have effect, not of those in which it will not. Where it *has* effect, I say, that effect may be for good *or* for evil, and that is an anxious thing.

I.

Now then, first, let me state the objection itself, which is to be considered. It may be thrown into one or other of the following forms : that "if Scripture laid such stress, as we do, upon the ordinances of Baptism, Holy Eucharist, Church Union, Ministerial Power, Apostolical Succession, Absolution, and other rites and ceremonies, —upon external, or what is sometimes called formal religion,—it would not in its general tenor make such

merely indirect mention of them ;—that it would speak
of them as plainly and frequently as we always speak of
them now ; whereas every one must allow that there is
next to nothing on the surface of Scripture about them,
and very little even under the surface of a satisfactory
character." Descending into particulars, we shall have
it granted us, perhaps, that Baptism is often mentioned
in the Epistles, and its spiritual benefits ; but "its peculiarity as the *one plenary* remission of sin," it will be urged,
"is not insisted on with such frequency and earnestness
as might be expected—chiefly in one or two passages of
one Epistle, and there obscurely" (in Heb. vi. and x.)
Again, "the doctrine of Absolution is made to rest on
but one or two texts (in Matt. xvi. and John xx.), with
little or no practical exemplification of it in the Epistles,
where it was to be expected. Why," it may be asked,
"are not the Apostles continually urging their converts
to rid themselves of sin after Baptism, as best they can,
by penance, confession, absolution, satisfaction ? Again,
why are Christ's ministers nowhere called Priests? or, at
most, in one or two obscure passages (as in Rom. xv. 16)?
Why is not the Lord's Supper expressly said to be a
Sacrifice ? why is the Lord's Table called an Altar but
once or twice (Matt. v. and Heb. xiii.), even granting
these passages refer to it ? why is consecration of the
elements expressly mentioned only in one passage (1 Cor.
x.) in addition to our Lord's original institution of them?
why is there but once or twice express mention made at
all of the Holy Eucharist, all through the Apostolic
Epistles, and what there is said, said chiefly in one
Epistle ? why is there so little said about Ordination ?
about the appointment of a Succession of Ministers ?
about the visible Church (as in 1 Tim. iii. 15)? why but
one or two passages on the duty of fasting ?"

"In short, is not (it may be asked) the state of the evidence for all these doctrines just this—a few striking texts at most, scattered up and down the inspired Volume, or one or two particular passages of one particular Epistle, or a number of texts which may mean, but need not mean, what they are said by Churchmen to mean, which say something looking like what is needed, but with little strength and point, inadequately and unsatisfactorily? Why then are we thus to be put off? why is our earnest desire of getting at the truth to be trifled with? is it conceivable that, if these doctrines were from God, He would not tell us plainly? why does He make us to doubt? why does 'He keep us in suspense?' *—it is impossible He should do so. Let us, then, have none of these expedients, these makeshift arguments, this patchwork system, these surmises and conjectures, and here a little and there a little, but give us some broad, trustworthy, masterly view of doctrine, give us some plain intelligible interpretation of the sacred Volume, such as will approve itself to all educated minds, as being really gained from the text, and not from previous notions which are merely brought to Scripture, and which seek to find a sanction in it. Such a broad comprehensive view of Holy Scripture is most assuredly fatal to the Church doctrines." "But this (it will be urged) is not all; there are texts in the New Testament actually inconsistent with the Church system of teaching. For example, what can be stronger against the sanctity of particular places, nay of any institutions, persons, or rites at all, than our Lord's declaration, that 'God is a Spirit, and they that worship Him, must worship Him in spirit and in truth'? or against the Eucharistic Sacrifice, than St. Paul's contrast in Heb. x. between the Jewish sacrifices

* John x. 24

and the one Christian Atonement? or can Baptism really have the gifts which are attributed to it in the Catholic or Church system, considering how St. Paul says, that all rites are done away, and that faith is all in all?"

Such is the sort of objection which it is proposed now to consider.

2.

My first answer to it is grounded on the *argumentum ad hominem* of which I have already spoken. That is, I shall show that, if the objection proves anything, it proves too much for the purposes of those who use it; that it leads to conclusions beyond those to which they would confine it; and if it tells for them, it tells for those whom they would not hesitate to consider heretical or unbelieving.

Now the argument in question proves too much, first, in this way, that it shows that external religion is not only not important or necessary, but not allowable. If, for instance, when our Saviour said, "Woman, believe Me, the hour cometh, when ye shall neither in this mountain, nor yet at Jerusalem, worship the Father. . . The hour cometh, and now is, when the true worshippers shall worship the Father in spirit and in truth: for the Father seeketh such to worship Him. God is a Spirit, and they that worship Him must worship Him in spirit and in truth," *—if He means that the external local worship of the Jews was so to be abolished that no external local worship should again be enjoined, that the Gospel worship was but mental, stripped of everything material or sensible, and offered in that simple spirit and truth which exists in heaven, if so, it is plain that all external religion *is* not only not imperative under the

* John iv. 21—24.

Gospel, but forbidden. This text, if it avails for any thing against Sacraments and Ordinances, avails entirely; it cuts them away root and branch. It says, not that they are unimportant, but that they are not to be. It does not leave them at our option. Any interpretation which gives an opening to their existing, gives so far an opening to their being important. If the command to worship in spirit and truth is consistent with the permission to worship through certain rites, it is consistent with the duty to worship through them. Why are *we* to have a greater freedom, if I may so speak, than God Himself? why are *we* to choose what rites we please to worship in, and not He choose them?—as if spirituality consisted, not in doing without rites altogether, (a notion which at least is intelligible,) but in our forestalling our Lord and Master in the choice of them. Let us take the text to mean that there shall be no external worship at all, if we will (we shall be wrong, but we shall speak fairly and intelligibly); but, if there may be times, places, ministers, ordinances of worship, although the text speaks of worshipping in spirit and in truth, then, what is there in it to negative the notion of God's having chosen those times places, ministers, and ordinances, so that if *we* attempt to choose, we shall be committing the very fault of the Jews, who were ever setting up golden calves, planting groves, or consecrating ministers, without authority from God?

And what has been observed of this text, holds good of all arguments drawn, whether from the silence of Scripture about, or its supposed positive statements against, the rites and ordinances of the Church. If obscurity of texts, for instance, about the grace of the Eucharist, be taken as a proof that no great benefit is therein given, it is an argument against there being

any benefit. On the other hand, when certain passages
are once interpreted to refer to it, the emphatic language
used in those passages shows that the benefit is not
small. We cannot say that the subject is unimportant,
without saying that it is not mentioned at all. Either
no gift is given in the Eucharist, or a great gift. If only
the sixth chapter of St. John, for instance, does allude to
it, it shows it is not merely an edifying rite, but an awful
communication beyond words. Again, if the phrase,
" the communication of the Body of Christ," used by St.
Paul, means any gift, it means a great one. You may
say, if you will, that it does not mean any gift at all,
but means only a representation or figure of the communication ; this I call explaining away, but still it is
intelligible ; but I do not see how, if it is to be taken
literally as a real *communication* of something, it can be
other than a communication of *His Body*. Again, though
the Lord's Table be but twice called an Altar in Scripture, yet, granting that it *is* meant in those passages,
it is there spoken of so solemnly, that it matters not
though it be nowhere else spoken of. " We have an Altar,
whereof they have no right to eat which serve the taber-
nacle." We do not know of the existence of the Ordinance except in the knowledge of its importance ; and
in corroboration and explanation of this matter of fact,
let it be well observed that St. Paul expressly declares
that the Jewish rites are *not* to be practised because they
are *not* important.

This is one way in which this argument proves too
much ; so that they who for the sake of decency or edification, or from an imaginative turn of mind, delight in
Ordinances, yet think they may make them for themselves, in that those ordinances bring no special blessing
with them, such men contradict the Gospel as plainly as

those who attribute a mystical virtue to them,—nay more so; for if any truth is clear, it is, that such ordinances as are without virtue are abolished by the Gospel, this being St. Paul's very argument against the use of the Jewish rites.

3.

Now as to the other point of view in which the argument in question proves too much for the purpose of those who use it :—If it be a good argument against the truth of the Apostolical Succession and similar doctrines, that so little is said about them in Scripture, this is quite as good an argument against nearly all the doctrines which are held by any one who is called a Christian in any sense of the word; as a few instances will show.

(1.) First, as to Ordinances and Precepts. There is not a single text in the Bible enjoining infant baptism : the Scripture warrant on which we baptize infants consists of inferences carefully made from various texts. How is it that St. Paul does not in his Epistles remind parents of so great a duty, if it is a duty?

Again, there is not a single text telling us to keep holy the first day of the week, and that *instead* of the seventh. God hallowed the seventh day, yet we now observe the first. Why do we do this? Our Scripture warrant for doing so is such as this : "*since* the Apostles met on the first day of the week, *therefore* the first day is to be hallowed; and *since* St. Paul says the Sabbath is abolished, *therefore* the seventh day (which is the Sabbath) is not to be hallowed :"—these are true inferences, but very indirect surely. The duty is not on the surface of Scripture. We might infer,—though incorrectly, still we might infer,—that St. Paul meant that the command in the second chapter of Genesis was repealed, and that now there is no sacred day at all in the seven, though meetings for prayer on Sunday are right and proper. There is nothing on the surface of Scripture to prove that the sacredness conferred in the beginning on the seventh day now by transference attaches to the first.

Again, there is scarcely a text enjoining our going to Church for joint worship. St. Paul happens in one place of his Epistle to the Hebrews, to warn us against forgetting to assemble together for prayer. Our Saviour says that where two or three are gathered together, He is in the midst of them; yet this alludes in the first instance not to public worship, but to Church Councils and censures, quite a distinct subject. And in the Acts and Epistles we meet with instances or precepts in favour of joint worship; yet there is nothing express to show that it is necessary for all times,—nothing more express than there is to show that in 1 Cor. vii. St. Paul meant that an unmarried state is better at all times,—nothing which does not need collecting and inferring with minute carefulness from Scripture. The first disciples did pray together, and so in like manner the first disciples did not marry. St. Paul tells those who were in a state of distress to pray together so much the more *as they see the day approaching*—and he says that celibacy is "good *for the present distress.*" The same remarks might be applied to the question of community of goods. On the other hand, our Lord did not use social prayer: even when with His disciples He prayed by Himself; and His directions in Matt. vi. about *private* prayer, with the silence which He observes about *public*, might be as plausibly adduced as an argument against public, as the same kind of silence in Scripture concerning turning to the east, or making the sign of the Cross, or concerning commemorations for the dead in Christ, accompanied with its warnings against formality and ceremonial abuses, is now commonly urged as an argument against these latter usages.

Again:—there is no text in the New Testament which enjoins us to "establish" Religion (as the phrase is), or to make it national, and to give the Church certain honour and power; whereas our Lord's words, "My kingdom is not of this world" (John xviii. 36), may be interpreted to discountenance such a proceeding. We consider that it is right to establish the Church on the ground of mere deductions, though of course true ones, from the sacred text; such as St. Paul's using his rights as a Roman citizen.

There is no text which allows us to take oaths. The words of our Lord and St. James look plainly the other way. Why then do we take them? We *infer* that it is allowable to do so, from finding that St. Paul uses such expressions as "I call God for a record upon my soul"— "The things which I write unto you, behold, before God, I lie not" (2 Cor. i. 23; Gal. i. 20); these we *argue*, and rightly, are equivalent to an oath, and a precedent for us.

Again, considering God has said, "Whoso sheddeth man's blood, by man shall his blood be shed," it seems a very singular power which we give to the Civil Magistrate to take away life. It ought to rest, one might suppose, on some very clear permission given in Scripture. Now, on what does it rest? on one or two words of an Apostle casually introduced into Scripture, as far as anything is casual,—on St. Paul's saying in a parenthesis, "he (the magistrate) beareth not the *sword* in vain;" and he is speaking of a *heathen* magistrate, *not* of Christian.

Once more:—On how many texts does the prohibition of polygamy depend, if we set about counting them?

(2.) So much for ordinances and practices : next, consider how Doctrine will stand, if the said rule of interpretation is to hold.

If the Eucharist is never distinctly called a Sacrifice, or Christian Ministers never called Priests, still, let me ask (as I have already done), is the Holy Ghost ever expressly called God in Scripture ? Nowhere ; we infer it from what is said then ; we compare parallel passages.

If the words Altar, Absolution, or Succession, are not in Scripture (supposing it), neither is the word Trinity.

Again : how do we know that the New Testament is inspired ? does it anywhere declare this of itself ? nowhere ; *how*, then, do we know it ? we infer it from the circumstance that the very office of the Apostles who wrote it was to publish the Christian Revelation, and from the Old Testament being said by St. Paul to be inspired.

Again : whence do Protestants derive their common notion, that every one may gain his knowledge of revealed truth from Scripture for himself ?

Again : consider whether the doctrine of the Atonement may not be explained away by those who explain away the doctrine of the Eucharist : if the expressions used concerning the latter are merely figurative, so may be those used of the former.

Again : on how many texts does the doctrine of Original Sin rest, that is, the doctrine that we are individually born under God's displeasure, in consequence of the sin of Adam ? on one or two.

Again : how do we prove the doctrine of justification by faith only ? it is nowhere declared in Scripture. St. Paul does but speak of justification by faith, not by faith only, and St. James actually denies that it is by faith only. Yet we think right to infer, that there is a correct sense in which it is by faith only; though an Apostle has in so many words said just the contrary. Is any of the special Church doctrines about the power of Absolution, the Christian Priesthood, or the danger of sin after Baptism, so disadvantageously circumstanced in point of evidence as this, " articulus," as Luther called it, "stantis ut cadentis ecclesiæ"?

On the whole, then, I ask, on how many special or palmary texts do any of the doctrines or rites which we hold depend? what doctrines or rites would be left to us, if we demanded the clearest and fullest evidence, before we believed anything? what would the Gospel consist of? would there be any Revelation at all left? Some all-important doctrines indeed at first sight certainly would remain in the New Testament, such as the divinity of Christ, the unity of God, the supremacy of divine grace, our election in Christ, the resurrection of the body, and eternal life or death to the righteous or sinners; but little besides. Shall we give up the divinity of the Holy Ghost, original sin, the Atonement, the inspiration of the New Testament, united worship, the Sacraments, and Infant Baptism? Let us do so. Well:—I will venture to say, that then we shall go on to find difficulties as regards those other doctrines, as the divinity of Christ, which at first sight seem to be in Scripture certainly; they are only *more* clearly there than the others, not so clearly stated as to be secured from specious objections. We shall have difficulties about the *meaning* of the word " everlasting," as applied to punishment, about the *compatibility* of divine grace with free-will, about the *possibility* of the resurrection of the body, and about the *sense* in which Christ is God. The inquirer who rejects a doctrine which has but one text in its favour, on the ground that if it were important it would have more, may, even in a case when a doctrine is mentioned often, always find occasion to wonder that still it is not mentioned in this or that particular place, where it might be expected. When he is pressed with such a text as St. Thomas's confession, "My Lord and my God," he will ask, But why did our Lord say but seven days before to St. Mary Magdalen, "I ascend to My Father and your Father, to My God and your God"? When he is pressed with St. Peter's confession, "Lord, Thou knowest all things,—Thou knowest that I love Thee," he will ask, "But why does Christ say of Himself, that He does not know the last day, but only the Father?" Indeed, I may truly say, the more arguments there are for a certain doctrine found in Scripture, the more objections will be found against it; so that, on the whole, after all, the Scripture evidence, even for the divinity of Christ, will be found in fact as little able to satisfy the cautious reasoner, when he is fairly engaged to discuss it, as that for Infant Baptism, great as is the difference of strength in the evidence for the one and for the other. And the history of these last centuries bears out this remark.

I conclude, then, that there must be some fault somewhere in this specious argument; that it does not follow that a doctrine or rite is not divine, because it is not directly stated in Scripture; that there are some wise and unknown reasons for doctrines being, as we find them, not clearly stated there. To be sure, I might take the other alternative, and run the full length of scepticism, and openly deny that any doctrine or duty, whatever it is, is divine, which is not stated in Scripture beyond all contradiction and objection. But for many reasons I cannot get myself to do this, as I shall proceed to show.

2.

The Difficulties of Latitudinarianism.

NO one, I think, will seriously maintain, that any other definite religious *system* is laid down in Scripture at all more clearly than the Church system. It may be maintained, and speciously, that the Church system is not there, or that this or that particular doctrine of some other system seems to be there more plainly than the corresponding Church doctrine ; but that Presbyterianism as a whole, or Independency as a whole, or the religion of Lutherans, Baptists, Wesleyans, or Friends, as a whole, is more clearly laid down in Scripture, and with fewer texts looking the other way— that any of these denominations has less difficulties to encounter than the Creed of the Church,—this I do not think can successfully be maintained. The arguments which are used to prove that the Church system is not in Scripture, may as cogently be used to prove that no system is in Scripture. If silence in Scripture, or apparent contrariety, is an argument against the Church system, it is an argument against system altogether. No system is on the surface of Scripture ; none, but has at times to account for the silence or the apparent opposition of Scripture as to particular portions of it.

I.

This, then, is the choice of conclusions to which we are brought :—*either* Christianity contains no definite mes-

sage, creed, revelation, system, or whatever other name
we give it, nothing which can be made the subject of
belief at all ; *or*, secondly, though there really is a true
creed or system in Scripture, still it is not on the surface
of Scripture, but is found latent and implicit within it,
and to be maintained only by indirect arguments, by
comparison of texts, by inferences from what is said
plainly, and by overcoming or resigning oneself to
difficulties ;—or again, though there is a true creed or
system revealed, it is not revealed in Scripture, but must
be learned collaterally from other sources. I wish in-
quirers to consider this statement steadily. I do not see
that it can be disputed ; and if not, it is very important.
I repeat it ; we have a choice of three conclusions.
Either there is no definite religious information given us
by Christianity at all, or it is given in Scripture in an
indirect and covert way, or it is indeed given, but not in
Scripture. The first is the Latitudinarian view which
has gained ground in this day ; the second is our own
Anglican ground ; the third is the ground of the Roman
Church. If then we will not content ourselves with
merely probable, or (what we may be disposed to call)
insufficient proofs of matters of faith and worship, we
must become either utter Latitudinarians or Roman
Catholics. If we will not submit to the notion of the
doctrines of the Gospel being hidden under the text of
Scripture from the view of the chance reader, we must
submit to believe either that there are no doctrines at all
in Christianity, or that the doctrines are not in Scripture,
but elsewhere, as in Tradition. I know of no other
alternative.

Many men, indeed, will attempt to find a fourth way,
thus: they would fain discern one or two doctrines in
Scripture clearly, and no more ; or some generalized

form, yet not so much as a *body* of doctrine of any character. They consider that a certain message, consisting of one or two great and simple statements, makes up the whole of the Gospel, and that these *are* plainly in Scripture ; accordingly, that he who holds and acts upon these is a Christian, and ought to be acknowledged by all to be such, for in holding these he holds all that is necessary. These statements they sometimes call the essentials, the peculiar doctrines, the vital doctrines, the leading idea, the great truths of the Gospel,—and all this sounds very well ; but when we come to realize what is abstractedly so plausible, we are met by this insurmountable difficulty, that no great number of persons agree together what *are* these great truths, simple views, leading ideas, or peculiar doctrines of the Gospel. Some say that the doctrine of the Atonement is the leading idea ; some, the doctrine of spiritual influence ; some, that both together are the peculiar doctrines ; some, that love is all in all; some, that the acknowledgment that Jesus is the Christ; and some, that the resurrection from the dead ; some, that the announcement of the soul's immortality, is after all the essence of the Gospel, and all that need be believed.

Moreover, since, as all parties must confess, the Catholic doctrine of the Trinity is not brought out in form upon the surface of Scripture, it follows either that it is not included in the leading idea, or that the leading idea is not on the surface. And if the doctrine of the Trinity is not to be accounted as one of the leading or fundamental truths of Revelation, the keystone of the mysterious system is lost ; and, that being lost, mystery will, in matter of fact, be found gradually to fade away from the Creed altogether ; that is, the notion of Christianity as being a revelation of new truths, will gradually fade away, and the Gospel in course of time will be considered scarcely more than the republication of the law of nature. This, I think, will be found to be the historical progress and issue of this line of thought. It is but one shape of Latitudinarianism. If we will have it so, that the doctrines of Scripture should be on the surface of Scripture, though I may have my very definite notion what doctrines *are* on the surface, and you yours, and another his, yet you and he and I, though each of us in appearance competent to judge, though all serious men, earnest, and possessed of due attainments, nevertheless will not agree together *what* those doctrines are ; so that, practically, what I have said will come about in the end, —that (if we are candid) we shall be forced to allow, that there is no system, no creed, no doctrine at all lucidly and explicitly set forth in Scripture ; and thus we are brought to the result, which I have already pointed out : if we will not seek for revealed truth under the surface of Scripture, we must either give up seeking for it, or must seek for it in Tradition,—we must become Latitudinarians or Roman Catholics.

2.

Now of these alternatives, the Roman idea or the Latitudinarian, the latter I do really conceive to be quite out of the question with every serious mind. The Latitudinarian doctrine is this: that every man's view of Revealed Religion is acceptable to God, if he acts up to it ; that no one view is in itself better than another, or at least that we cannot tell which is the better. All that we have to do then is to act consistently with what we hold, and to value others if they act consistently with what they hold ; that to be consistent constitutes sincerity ; that where there is this evident sincerity, it is no matter whether we profess to be Romanists or Protestants, Catholics or Heretics, Calvinists or Arminians, Anglicans or Dissenters, High Churchmen or Puritans, Episcopalians or Independents, Wesleyans or Socinians. Such seems to be the doctrine of Latitude. Now, I can conceive such a view of the subject to be maintainable, supposing God had given us no Revelation,—though even then, (by the way,) and were we even left to the light of nature, belief in His existence and moral government would, one should think, at least be necessary to please Him. "He that cometh to God must believe that He is, and that He is a rewarder of them which diligently seek Him." * But however, not to press this point, one may conceive that, before God had actually spoken to us, He might accept as sufficient a sincere acting on religious opinions of whatever kind ; but that, after a Revelation is given, there is nothing to believe, nothing (to use an expressive Scripture word) to "hold," to "hold fast," that a message comes from God, and contains no subject-matter, or that, containing it (as it must do), it is not important to be received, and is not capable of being learned by any one who takes the proper means of learning it, that there is in it nothing such, that we may depend on our impression of it to be the true impression, may feel we have really gained something, and continue in one and one only opinion about it,—all this is so extravagant, that I really cannot enter into the state of mind of a person maintaining it. I think he is not aware what he is saying. Why should God speak, unless He meant to say something ? Why should He say it, unless He meant us to hear? Why should we be made to hear if it mattered not whether we accepted it or no ? *What* the doctrine is, is another and distinct question ; but

* Heb. xi. 6.

that there is *some* doctrine revealed, and that it is revealed in order that it may be received, and that it really *is* revealed, (I mean, not so hidden that it is a mere matter of opinion, a mere chance, what is true and what is not, and that there are a number of opposite modes of holding it, one as good as another, but) that it is plain in one and the same substantial sense to all who sincerely and suitably seek for it, and that God is better pleased when we hold it than when we do not,—all this seems a truism. Again, *where* it is given us, whether entirely in Scripture, or partly elsewhere,—this too is another and secondary question; though, if some doctrine or other is really given, that it must be given somewhere, is a proposition which cannot be denied, without some eccentricity or confusion of mind, or without some defect in seriousness and candour. I say, first, if there be a Revelation, there must be some essential doctrine proposed by it to our faith; and, if so, the question at once follows, *what* is it, and *how much*, and *where?* and we are forthwith involved in *researches* of some kind or other, somewhere or other; for the doctrine is not written on the sun.

For reasons such as the above, I really cannot conceive a serious man, who realized what he was speaking about, to be a consistent Latitudinarian. He always will reserve from the general proscription his own favourite doctrine, whatever it is; and then holding it, he will be at once forced into the difficulty, which is ours also, but which he would fain make ours only and not his, that of stating clearly what this doctrine of his is, and what are those grounds of it, such, as to enable him to take in just so much of dogmatic teaching as he does take in, and nothing more, to hold so much firmly, and to treat all the rest as comparatively unimportant.

Revelation implies a something revealed, and what is revealed is imperative on our faith, *because* it is revealed. Revelation implies imperativeness; it limits in its very notion our liberty of thought, because it limits our liberty of error, for error is one kind of thought.

If then I am not allowed to hold that Scripture, however implicit in its teaching, is really dogmatic, I shall be led to be, not a Latitudinarian, but a Roman Catholic.   You tell me, that "no creed is to be found in Scripture,— *therefore*, Christianity has no creed."   Indeed! supposing the fact to be as stated (which I do not grant, but supposing it), is this the necessary conclusion?   No: there is another.   Such an inference indeed as the above is a clever controversial way of settling the matter; it is the sort of answer which in the schools of disputation or the courts of law may find a place, where men are not in earnest; but it is an answer without a heart.   It is an excuse for indolence, love of quiet, or worldliness. There is another answer.   I do not adopt it, I do not see I am driven to it, because I do not allow the premisses from which the Latitudinarian argument starts.   I do not allow that there *is* no creed at all contained in Scripture, though I grant it is not on the surface.   But if there *be* no divine message, gospel, or creed producible from Scripture, this would not lead me one inch toward deciding that there was none at all *anywhere*. No; it would make me look *out* of Scripture for it, that is all.   If there is a Revelation, there must be a doctrine; both our reason and our hearts tell us so.   If it is not in Scripture, it is somewhere else; it is to be sought elsewhere.   Should the fact so turn out, (which I deny,) that Scripture is so obscure that nothing can be made of it, even when the true interpretation is elsewhere given, so obscure that every person will have his own interpretation of it, and no two alike, this would drive me, not into Latitudinarianism, but into Romanism. Yes, and it will drive the multitude of men. It is far more certain that Revelation must contain a message, than that that message must be in Scripture. It is a less violence to one's feelings to say that part of it is revealed elsewhere, than to say that nothing is revealed anywhere. There is an overpowering antecedent improbability in Almighty God's announcing that He has revealed something, and then revealing nothing; there is no antecedent improbability in His revealing it elsewhere than in an inspired volume.

And, I say, the mass of mankind will feel it so. It is very well for educated persons, at their ease, with few cares, or in the joyous time of youth, to argue and speculate about the impalpableness and versatility of the divine message, its chameleon-like changeableness, its adaptation to each fresh mind it meets; but when men are conscious of sin, are sorrowful, are weighed down, are desponding, they ask for something to lean on, something external to themselves. It will not do to tell them that whatever they at present hold as true, is enough. They want to be assured that what seems to them true, is true; they want something to lean on, holier, diviner, more stable than their own minds. They have an instinctive feeling that there is an external, eternal truth which is their only stay; and it mocks them, after being told of a Revelation, to be assured, next, that that Revelation tells us nothing certain, nothing which we do not know without it, nothing distinct from our own impressions concerning it, whatever they may be,— nothing such, as to exist independently of that shape and colour into which our own individual mind happens to throw it. Therefore, practically, those who argue for

the vague character of the Scripture informations, and
the harmlessness of all sorts of religious opinions, do not
tend to advance Latitudinarianism one step among the
many,—they advance Romanism. That truth, which
men are told they cannot find in Scripture, they will
seek out of Scripture. They will never believe, they
will never be content with, a religion without doctrines.
The common sense of mankind decides against it. Religion cannot but be dogmatic; it ever has been. All
religions have had doctrines; all have professed to carry
with them benefits which could be enjoyed only on condition of believing the word of a supernatural informant,
that is, of embracing some doctrines or other.

And it is a mere idle sophistical theory, to suppose it
can be otherwise. Destroy religion, make men give it up,
if you can; but while it exists, it will profess an insight
into the next world, it will profess important information
about the next world, it will have points of faith, it will
have dogmatism, it will have anathemas. Christianity,
therefore, ever will be looked on, by the multitude, what
it really is, as a rule of faith as well as of conduct. Men
may be Presbyterians, or Baptists, or Lutherans, or Calvinists, or Wesleyans; but something or other they will
be; a creed, a creed necessary to salvation, they will
have; a creed either in Scripture or out of it; and if in
Scripture, I say, it must be, from the nature of the case,
only indirectly gained from Scripture. Latitudinarianism,
then, is out of the question; and you have your choice,
to be content with inferences from texts *in* Scripture, or
with tradition *out of* Scripture. You cannot get beyond
this; *either* you must take up with us, (or with some
system not at all better off, whether Presbyterianism
or Independency, or the like,) *or* you must go to Rome.
Which will you choose? You may not like us; you

may be impatient and impetuous; you may go forward, but back you cannot go.

3.

But, further, it can scarcely be denied that Scripture, if it does not furnish, at least speaks of, refers to, takes for granted, sanctions, some certain doctrine or message, as is to be believed in order to salvation; and which, accordingly, if not found in Scripture, must be sought for out of it. It says, " He who believeth shall be saved, and he who believeth not shall be damned;" it speaks of "the doctrine of Christ," of " keeping the faith," of " the faith once *delivered* to the saints," and of " delivering that which has been received," recounting at the same time some of the articles of the Apostles' Creed. And the case is the same as regards discipline; rules of worship and order, whether furnished or not, are at least alluded to again and again, under the title of "traditions." Revelation then will be inconsistent with itself, unless it has provided some Creed somewhere. For it declares in Scripture that it has given us a Creed; therefore some creed exists somewhere, whether in Scripture or out of it.

Nor is this all; from the earliest times, so early that there is no assignable origin to it short of the Apostles, one definite system has in fact existed in the Church both of faith and worship, and that in countries far disjoined from one another, and without any appearance (as far as we can detect) of the existence of any other system anywhere; and (what is very remarkable) a system such, that the portion in it which relates to matters of faith (or its theology), accurately fits in and corresponds to that which relates to matters of worship and order (or its ceremonial); as if they were evidently parts of a whole, and not an accidental assemblage of rites on the one hand, and doctrines on the other ;—a system moreover which has existed ever since, and exists at the present day, and in its great features, as in other branches of the Church, so among ourselves;—a system moreover which at least professes to be quite consistent with, and to appeal and defer to, the written word, and thus in all respects accurately answers to that to which Scripture seems to be referring in the notices above cited. Now, is it possible, with this very significant phenomenon standing in the threshold of Christian history, that any sensible man can be of opinion that one creed or worship is as good as another ? St. Paul speaks of one faith, one baptism, one body ; this in itself is a very intelligible hint of his own view of Christianity ; but as if to save his words from misinterpretation, here in history is at once a sort of realization of what he seems to have before his mind.

Under these circumstances, what excuse have we for not recognizing, in this system of doctrine and worship existing in history, that very system to which the Apostles refer in Scripture ? They evidently did not in Scripture say out all they had to say ; this is evident on the face of Scripture, evident from what they do say. St. Paul says, " *The rest* will I set in order when I come." St. John, " I had *many things* to write, but I will not with ink and pen write unto thee ; but I trust I shall shortly see thee, and we shall *speak* face to face." This he says in two Epistles. Now supposing, to take the case of profane history, a collection of letters were extant written by the founders or remodellers of the Platonic or Stoic philosophy, and supposing those masters referred in them to their philosophy, and treated of it in some of its parts, yet without drawing it out in an orderly way, and then secondly, supposing there did exist other and more direct historical sources of various kinds, from which a distinct systematic account of their philosophy might be drawn, that is, one account of it and but one from many witnesses, should we not take it for granted that this *was* their system, that system of which their letters spoke? Should not we accept that system conveyed to us by history with (I will not say merely an antecedent disposition in its favour, but with) a confidence and certainty that it *was* their system; and if we found discrepancies between it and their letters, should we at once cast it aside as spurious, or should we not rather try to reconcile the two together, and suspect that *we* were in fault, that *we* had made some mistake; and even if after all we could not reconcile all parts (supposing it), should we not leave the discrepancies *as* difficulties, and believe in the system notwithstanding? The Apostles refer to a large existing fact, their system, —"the whole counsel of God"; history informs us of a system, as far as we can tell, contemporaneous with, and claiming to be theirs;—what other claimant is there?

Whether, then, the system of doctrine and worship, referred to but not brought out in Scripture, be really latent there or not, whether our hypothesis be right or the Roman view, at any rate a system there is; we see it, we have it external to Scripture. There it stands, however we may determine the further question, whether it is also in Scripture. Whether we adopt our Sixth Article or not, we cannot obliterate the fact that a system does substantially exist in history; all the proofs you may bring of the obscurities or of the unsystematic character of Scripture cannot touch this independent fact; were Scripture lost to us, that fact, an existing Catholic system, will remain. You have your choice to say that Scripture does or does not agree with it. If you think it actually disagrees with Scripture, then you have your choice between concluding either that you are mistaken in so thinking, or that, although this system comes to us as it does, on the same evidence with Scripture, yet it is not divine, while Scripture is. If, however, you consider that it merely teaches things additional to Scripture, then you have no excuse for not admitting it in addition to Scripture. And if it teaches things but indirectly taught in Scripture, then you must admit it as an interpreter or comment upon Scripture. But, whether you say it is an accordant or a discordant witness, whether the supplement, or complement, or interpreter of Scripture, there it stands, that consistent harmonious system of faith and worship, as in the beginning; and, if history be allowed any weight in the discussion, it is an effectual refutation of Latitudinarianism. It is a fact concurring with the common sense of mankind and with their wants. Men want a dogmatic system; and behold, in the beginning of Christianity, and from the beginning to this day, there it stands. This is so remarkable a coincidence that it will always practically weigh against Latitudinarian views. Infidelity is more intelligible, more honest than they are.

Nor does it avail to say, that there were additions made to it in the course of years, or that the feeling of a want may have given rise to it; for what was added after, whatever it was, could not create that to which it was added; and I say that first of all, before there was a time for the harmonious uniform expansion of a system, for the experience and supply of human wants, for the inroads of innovation, and the growth of corruption, and with all fair allowance for differences of opinions as to how much is primitive, or when and where this or that particular fact is witnessed, or what interpretation is to be given to particular passages in historical

documents,—from the first a system exists. And we
have no right to refuse it, merely on the plea that *we* do
not see all the parts of it in Scripture, or that we think
some parts of it to be inconsistent with Scripture ; for
even though some parts were not there, this would not
disprove its truth ; and even though some parts seemed
contrary to what is there, this appearance might after
all be caused simply by our own incompetency to judge
of Scripture.

4.

But perhaps it may here be urged, that I have proved
too much ; that is, it may be asked " If a system of
doctrine is so necessary to Revelation, and appears at
once in the writings of the Apostles' disciples, as in the
Epistles of St. Ignatius, how is it that it is not in the
writings of the Apostles themselves ? how does it happen
that it does appear in the short Epistles of Ignatius, and
does not in the longer Epistles of St. Paul ? so that the
tendency of the foregoing argument is to disparage the
Apostles' teaching, as showing that it is not adapted, and
Ignatius's is adapted, to our wants." But the answer to
this is simple : for though the Apostles' writings do not
on their surface set forth the Catholic system of doctrine,
they certainly do contain (as I have said) a recognition
of its existence, and of its principle, and of portions of it.
If, then, in spite of this, there is no Apostolic system of
faith and worship, all we shall have proved by our argument is, that the Apostles are inconsistent with themselves ; that they recognize the need of such a system,
and do not provide one. How it is they do not draw
out a system, while they nevertheless both recognize
its principle and witness its existence, has often been
discussed, and perhaps I may say something incidentally

on the subject hereafter. Here, I do but observe, that on the one side of the question we have the human heart expecting, Scripture sanctioning, history providing,—a coincidence of three witnesses; and on the other side only this, Scripture not actually providing by itself in form and fulness what it sanctions.

Lastly, I would observe, that much as Christians have differed in these latter or in former ages, as to what *is* the true faith and what the true worship and discipline of Christ, yet one and all have held that Christianity is dogmatic and social, that creeds and forms are not to be dispensed with. There has been an uninterrupted maintenance of this belief from the beginning of Christianity down to this day, with exceptions so partial or so ephemeral as not to deserve notice. I conclude, then, either that the notion of forms and creeds, and of unity by means of them, is so natural to the human mind as to be spontaneously produced and cherished in every age; or that there has been a strong external reason for its having been so cherished, whether in authority, or in argumentative proof, or in the force of tradition. In whatever way we take it, it is a striking evidence in favour of dogmatic religion, and against that unreal form, or rather that mere dream of religion, which pretends that modes of thinking and social conduct are all one and all the same in the eyes of God, supposing each of us to be sincere in his own.

Dismissing, then, Latitudinarianism once for all, as untenable, and taking for granted that there is a system of religion revealed in the Gospel, I come, as I have already stated several times, to one or other of two conclusions: either that it is not all in Scripture, but part in tradition only, as the Romanists say,—or, as the English Church says, that though it is in tradition, yet it can also be gathered from the communications of Scripture. As to the nondescript system of religion now in fashion, viz., that nothing is to be believed but what is clearly stated in Scripture, that all its own doctrines are clearly there and none other, and that, as to history, it is no matter what history says and what it does not say, except so far as it must of course be used to prove the canonicity of Scripture, this will come before us again and again in the following Lectures. Suffice that it has all the external extravagance of Latitudinarianism without any gain in consistency. It is less consistent because it is morally better : Latitudinarianism is less inconsistent because it is intellectually deeper. Both, however, are mere theories in theology, and ought to be discarded by serious men. We must give up our ideal notions, and resign ourselves to facts. We must take things as we find them, as God has given them. We did not make them, we cannot alter them, though we are sometimes tempted to think it very hard that we cannot. We must submit to them, instead of quarrelling with them. We must submit to the indirectness of Scripture,* unless we think it wiser and better to become Romanists : and we must employ our minds rather (if so be) in accounting for the fact, than in excepting against it.

* [It may require explanation, why it was that the author, in this argument against Latitudinarianism, should so earnestly insist on the implicit teaching of Scripture, with history for its explicit interpreter, instead of boldly saying that, not Scripture, but history, is our informant in Christian doctrine. But he was hampered by his belief in the Protestant tenet that *all* revealed doctrine is in Scripture, and, since he could not maintain that it was on the surface of the inspired Word, he was forced upon the (not untrue, but unpractical) theory of the implicit sense, history developing it. *Vide infr.* p. 149.]

3.

On the Structure of the Bible, antecedently considered.

I.

ENOUGH perhaps has now been said by way of opening the subject before us. The state of the case I conceive to be as I have said. The structure of Scripture is such, so irregular and immethodical, that either we must hold that the Gospel doctrine or message is not contained in Scripture (and if so, either that there is no message at all given, or that it is given elsewhere, external to Scripture), or, as the alternative, we must hold that it is but indirectly and covertly recorded there, that is, under the surface. Moreover, since the great bulk of professing Christians in this country, whatever their particular denomination may be, do consider, agreeably with the English Church, that there *are* doctrines revealed (though they differ among themselves as to what), and next that they are *in Scripture*, they must undergo, and resign themselves to an inconvenience which certainly does attach to our Church, and, as they often suppose, to it alone, that of having to infer from Scripture, to prove circuitously, to argue at disadvantage, to leave difficulties unsolved, and to appear to the world weak or fanciful reasoners. They must leave off criticising our proof of our doctrines, because they are not stronger in respect to proof themselves. No matter whether they are Lutherans or Calvinists, Wesleyans or Independents, they have to wind their way through obstacles, in and out, avoiding some things and catching at others, like men making their way in a wood, or over broken ground.

If they believe in consubstantiation with Luther, or in the absolute predestination of individuals, with Calvin, they have very few texts to produce which, in argument, will appear even specious. And still more plainly have these religionists strong texts actually against them, whatever be their sect or persuasion. If they be Lutherans, they have to encounter St. James's declaration, that "by works a man is justified, and not by faith only;"* if Calvinists, God's solemn declaration, that "as He liveth, He willeth not the death of a sinner, but rather that he should live;" if a Wesleyan, St. Paul's precept to "obey them that have the rule over you, and submit yourselves;"† if Independents, the same Apostle's declaration concerning the Church's being "the pillar and ground of the Truth;" if Zuinglians, they have to explain how Baptism is not really and in fact connected with regeneration, considering it is always connected with it in Scripture; if Friends, why they allow women to speak in their assemblies, contrary to St. Paul's plain prohibition; if Erastians, why they forget our Saviour's plain declaration, that His kingdom is not of this world; if maintainers of the ordinary secular Christianity, what they make of the woe denounced against riches, and the praise bestowed on celibacy. Hence, none of these sects and persuasions has any right to ask the question of which they are so fond, "Where in the Bible are the Church doctrines to be found? Where in Scripture, for instance, is Apostolical Succes-

* James ii. 24. † Heb. xiii. 7.

sion, or the Christian Priesthood, or the power of Absolution?" This is with them a favourite mode of dealing with us ; and I in return ask them, *Where* are we told that the Bible contains all that is necessary to salvation ? Where are we told that the New Testament is inspired ? Where are we told that justification is by faith only ? Where are we told that every individual who is elected is saved ? Where are we told that we may leave the Church, if we think its ministers do not preach the Gospel ? or, Where are we told that we may make ministers for ourselves ?

All Protestants, then, in this country,—Churchmen, Presbyterians, Baptists, Arminians, Calvinists, Lutherans, Friends, Independents, Wesleyans, Unitarians,—and whatever other sect claims the Protestant name, all who consider the Bible as the one standard of faith, and much more if they think it the standard of morals and discipline too, are more or less in this difficulty,—the more so, the larger they consider the contents of Revelation to be, and the less, the scantier they consider them ; but they cannot escape from the difficulty altogether, except by falling back into utter scepticism and latitudinarianism, or, on the other hand, by going on to Rome. Nor does it rid them of their difficulties, as I have said more than once, to allege, that all points that are beyond clear Scripture proof are the mere *peculiarities* of each sect ; so that if all Protestants were to agree to put out of sight their respective peculiarities, they would then have a Creed set forth distinctly, clearly, and adequately, in Scripture. For take that single instance, which I have referred to in a former Lecture, the doctrine of the Holy Trinity. Is this to be considered as a mere peculiarity or no ? Apparently a peculiarity ; for on the one hand it is not held by all Protestants, and next, it is not brought out in form in Scripture. First, the word Trinity is not in Scripture. Next I ask, *How* many of the verses of the Athanasian Creed are distinctly set down in Scripture? and further, take particular portions of the doctrine, viz., that Christ is co-eternal with the Father, that the Holy Ghost is God, or that the Holy Ghost proceedeth from the Father and the Son, and consider the kind of texts and the modes of using them, by which the proof is built up. Yet is there a more sacred, a more vital doctrine in the circle of the articles of faith than that of the Holy Trinity? Let no one then take refuge and comfort in the idea that he will be what is commonly called an orthodox Protestant,—I mean, that he will be just this and no more; that he will admit the doctrine of the Trinity, but not that of the Apostolic Succession,—of the Atonement, but not of the Eucharist, —of the influences of grace, but not of Baptism. This is an impossible position : it is shutting one eye, and looking with the other. Shut both or open both. Deny that there is any necessary doctrine in Scripture, or consent to infer indirectly from Scripture what you at present disbelieve.

2.

The whole argument, however, depends of course on the certainty of the fact assumed, viz., that Scripture *is* unsystematic and uncertain in its communications to the extent to which I have supposed it to be. To this point, therefore, I shall, in the Lectures which follow, direct attention. Here, however, I shall confine myself to a brief argument with a view of showing that under the circumstances the fact *must* be so. I observe, then, as follows :—

In what way inspiration is compatible with that per-

sonal agency on the part of its instruments, which the
composition of the Bible evidences, we know not ; but if
anything is certain, it is this,—that, though the Bible is
inspired, and therefore, in one sense, written by God, yet
very large portions of it, if not far the greater part of it,
are written in as free and unconstrained a manner, and
(apparently) with as little apparent consciousness of a
supernatural dictation or restraint, on the part of His
earthly instruments, as if He had had no share in the
work. As God rules the will, yet the will is free,—as
He rules the course of the world, yet men conduct it,—
so He has inspired the Bible, yet men have written it.
Whatever else is true about it, this is true, that we may
speak of the history or the mode of its composition, as
truly as of that of other books ; we may speak of its
writers having an object in view, being influenced by
circumstances, being anxious, taking pains, purposely
omitting or introducing matters, leaving things incom-
plete, or supplying what others had so left. Though
the Bible be inspired, it has all such characteristics as
might attach to a book uninspired,—the characteristics
of dialect and style, the distinct effects of times and
places, youth and age, of moral and intellectual character ;
and I insist on this, lest in what I am going to say, I
seem to forget (what I do not forget), that in spite of its
human form, it has in it the Spirit and the Mind of God.

I observe, then, that Scripture is not one book ; it is a
great number of writings, of various persons, living at
different times, put together into one, and assuming its
existing form as if casually and by accident. It is as if
you were to seize the papers or correspondence of leading men in any school of philosophy or science, which
were never designed for publication, and bring them out
in one volume. You would find probably in the collec-

tion so resulting many papers begun and not finished ; some parts systematic and didactic, but the greater part made up of hints or of notices which assume first principles instead of asserting them, or of discussions upon particular points which happened to require their attention. I say the doctrines, the first principles, the rules, the objects of the school, would be taken for granted, alluded to, implied, not directly stated. You would have some trouble to get at them ; you would have many repetitions, many hiatuses, many things which looked like contradictions ; you would have to work your way through heterogeneous materials, and, after your best efforts, there would be much hopelessly obscure ; and, on the other hand, you might look in vain in such a casual collection for some particular opinions which the writers were known nevertheless to have held, nay to have insisted on.

Such, I conceive, with limitations presently to be noticed, is the structure of the Bible. Parts, indeed, are more regular than others ; parts of the Pentateuch form a regular history. The book of Job is a regular narrative ; some Prophecies are regular, one or two Epistles ; but even these portions are for the most part incorporated in or with writings which are not regular in their form or complete ; and we never can be sure beforehand what we shall find in them, or what we shall not find. They are the writings of men who had already been introduced into a knowledge of the unseen world and the society of Angels, and who reported what they had seen and heard ; and they are full of allusions to a system, a course of things, which was ever before their minds, which they felt both too awful and too familiar to them to be described minutely, which we do not know, and which these allusions, such as they are, but partially disclose to us. Try to make out the history of Rome from the extant letters of some of its great politicians, and from the fragments of ancient annals, histories, laws, inscriptions, and medals, and you will have something like the state of the case, viewed antecedently, as regards the structure of the Bible, and the task of deducing the true system of religion from it.

This being, as I conceive, really the state of the case in substance, I own it seems to me, judging antecedently, very improbable indeed, that it *should* contain the whole of the Revealed Word of God. I own that in my own mind, at first sight, I am naturally led to look not only there, but elsewhere, for notices of sacred truth ; and I consider that they who say that the Bible does contain the whole Revelation (as I do say myself), that they and I, that we, have what is called the *onus probandi*, the burden and duty of proving the point, on our side. Till we prove that Scripture does contain the whole Revealed Truth, it is natural, from its *prima facie* appearance, to suppose that it does not. Why, for instance, should a certain number of letters, more or less private, written by St. Paul and others to particular persons or bodies, contain the whole of what the Holy Spirit taught them ? We do not look into Scripture for a complete history of the secular matters which it mentions ; why should we look for a complete account of religious truth ? You will say that its writers wrote in order to communicate religious truth ; true, but not all religious truth : that is the point. They did not sit down with a design to commit to paper all they had to say on the whole subject, all they could say about the Gospel, " the whole counsel of God " ; but they either wrote to correct some particular error of a particular time or place, or to "stir up the pure minds" of their brethren, or in answer to questions, or to give direction for conduct, or on indifferent matters. For instance, St. Luke says he wrote his Gospel that Christians might know "the certainty of the things in which they had been instructed." Does this imply he told all that was to be told? Anyhow he did *not;* for the other Evangelists add to his narrative. It is then far from being a self-evident truth that Scripture must contain all the revealed counsel of God; rather, the probability at first sight lies the other way.

Nevertheless, at least as regards matters of faith, it *does* (as we in common with all Protestants hold) contain all that is necessary for salvation; it has been overruled to do so by Him who inspired it. By parallel acts of power, He both secretly inspired the books, and secretly formed them into a perfect rule or canon. I shall not prove what we all admit, but I state it, to prevent misapprehension. If asked *how* we know this to be the case, I answer, that the early Church thought so, and the early Church must have known. And, if this answer does not please the inquirer, he may look out for a better as he can. I know of no other. I require no other. For our own Church it is enough, as the Homilies show. It is enough that Scripture has been overruled to contain the whole Christian faith, and that the early Church so taught, though the form of Scripture at first sight might lead to an opposite conclusion. And this being once proved, we see in this state of things an analogy to God's providence in other cases. How confused is the course of the world, yet it is the working out of a moral system, and is overruled in every point by God's will! Or, take the structure of the earth; mankind are placed in fertile and good dwelling-places, with hills and valleys, springs and fruitful fields, with metals and marbles, and coal, and other minerals, with seas and forests; yet this beautiful and fully-furnished surface is the result of (humanly speaking) a series of accidents, of gradual influences and sudden convulsions, of a long history of change and chance.

3.

Yet while we admit, or rather maintain, that the Bible is the one standard of faith, there is no reason why we should suppose the overruling hand of God to go further than we are told that it has gone. That He has overruled matters so far as to make the apparently casual writings of the Apostles a complete canon of saving faith, is no reason why He should have given them a systematic structure, or a didactic form, or a completeness in their subject-matter. So far as we have no positive proof that the Bible is more than at first sight it seems to be, so far the antecedent probability, which I have been insisting on, tells against its being more. Both the history of its composition and its internal structure are opposed to the notion of its being a complete depository of the Divine Will, unless the early Church says that it is. Now the early Church does not tell us this. It does not seem to have considered that a complete code of *morals*, or of Church *government*, or of *rites*, or of *discipline*, is in Scripture; and therefore so far the original improbability remains in force. Again, this antecedent improbability tells, even in the case of the doctrines of faith, as far as this, viz., it reconciles us to the necessity of gaining them only *indirectly* from Scripture, for it is a near thing (if I may so speak) that they are in Scripture at all; the wonder is, that they are *all* there; humanly judging, they would not be there but for divine interposition; and, therefore, since they are there by a sort of accident, it is not strange they are there only in an implicit shape, and only indirectly producible thence. Providence effects His greatest ends by apparent accidents. As in respect to this earth, we do not find minerals or plants arranged within it as in a cabinet—as we do not find the materials for building laid out in order, stone, timber, and iron—as metal is found in ore, and timber on the tree,—so we must not be surprised, but think it great gain, if we find revealed doctrines scattered about high and low in Scripture, in places expected and unexpected. It could not be otherwise, the same circumstances being supposed. Supposing fire, water, and certain chemical and electrical agents in free operation, the earth's precious contents *could* not be found arranged in order and in the light of day without a miracle; and so without a miracle (which we are nowhere told to expect) we could not possibly find in Scripture all sacred truths in their place, each set forth clearly and fully, with its suitable prominence, its varied bearings, its developed meaning, supposing Scripture to be, what it is, the work of various independent minds in various times and places, and under various circumstances. And so much on what might reasonably be expected from the nature of the case.

4.

Structure of the Bible in matter of fact.

I HAVE above insisted much upon this point,—that if Scripture contains any religious system at all, it *must* contain it covertly, and teach it obscurely, because it is altogether most immethodical and irregular in its structure; and therefore, that the indirectness of the Scripture proofs of the Catholic system is not an objection to its cogency, except as it is an objection to the Scripture proofs of every other form of Christianity; and accordingly that we must take our choice (Romanism being for the time put aside) between utter Latitudinarianism and what may be called the Method of Inferences. Now this argument depends evidently on the fact, that Scripture is thus unsystematic in its structure —a fact which it would not be necessary to dwell upon, so obvious is it, except that examining into it will be found to give us a much more vivid apprehension of it, and to throw light upon the whole subject of Scripture teaching. Something accordingly, I have just been observing about it from antecedent probability, and now I proceed, at some length, to inquire into the matter of fact.

I shall refer to Scripture as a record both of historical events and of general doctrine, with a view of exhibiting the peculiar character of its structure, the unostentatious, indirect, or covert manner, which it adopts, for whatever reason, in its statements of whatever kind. This, I say, will throw light on the subject in hand ; for so it is, as soon as we come to see that anything, which has already attracted our notice in one way, holds good in others, that there is a certain law, according to which it occurs uniformly under various circumstances, we gain a satisfaction from that very coincidence, and seem to find a reason for it in the very circumstance that it does proceed on a rule or law. Even in matters of conduct, with which an external and invariable standard might seem to interfere, the avowal, " It is my way," " I always do so," is often given and accepted as a satisfactory account of a person's mode of acting. Order implies a principle ; order in God's Written Word implies a principle or design in it. If I show that the Bible is written throughout with this absence of method, I seem to find an order in the very disorder, and hence become reconciled to it in particular instances. That it is inartificial and obscure as regards the relation of facts, has the effect of explaining its being obscure in statement of doctrines ; that it is so as regards one set of doctrines, seems naturally to account for its being so as regards another. Thus, the argument from analogy, which starts with the profession of being only of a *negative* character, ends with being *positive*, when drawn out into details ; such being the difference between its abstract pretension and its actual and practical force.

First I propose to mention some instances of the unstudied and therefore perplexed character of Scripture, as regards its relation of *facts;* and to apply them, as I go, to the point under discussion, viz., the objection brought against the Church doctrines from the mode in which they too are stated in Scripture; and I shall begin without further preface.

I.

An illustration occurs in the very beginning of the Bible. However we account for it, with which I am not concerned, you will find that the narrative of the Creation, commenced in the first chapter, ends at the third verse of the second chapter; and then begins a fresh narrative, carrying on the former, but going back a little way. The difference is marked, as is well known, by the use of the word "God" in the former narrative, and of "Lord God" in the latter. According to the former, God is said to create man "in His own image; *male and female* created He them" on the sixth day. According to the latter, the Lord God created Adam, and placed him in the garden of Eden, to dress and keep it, and gave him the command about the forbidden fruit, and brought the beasts to him; and *afterwards*, on his finding the want of a helpmeet, caused him to sleep, and took one of his ribs, and thence made woman. This is an instance of the unsolicitous freedom and want of system of the sacred narrative. The second account, which is an expansion of the first, is in the letter opposed to it. Now supposing the narrative contained in the second chapter was *not* in Scripture, but *was* the received Church account of man's creation, it is plain not only would it not be *in*, but it could not even be gathered or proved *from* the first chapter; which makes the argument all the stronger. Evidently not a pretence could be made of *proving* from the first chapter the account of the dressing the garden, the naming the brutes, the sleep, and the creation of Eve from a rib. And most persons in this day would certainly have disbelieved it. Why? Because it wanted *authority?* No. There would be some sense in such a line of argument, but

they would not go into the quest on of authority.
Whether or not it had Catholic tradition in its favour,
whether Catholic tradition were or were not a sufficient
guarantee of its truth, would not even enter into their
minds ; they would not go so far, they would disbelieve
it at once on two grounds : first, they would say Scripture was *silent* about it, nay, that it contradicted it, that
it spoke of man and woman being created both together
on the sixth day ; and, secondly, they would say it was
incongruous and highly improbable, and that the account
of Adam's rib sounded like an idle tradition. If (I say)
they were to set it aside for want of evidence of its
truth, that would be a fair ground ; but I repeat, their
reason for setting it aside (can it be doubted ?) would be,
that it was *inconsistent* with Scripture in actual statement,
and *unlike* it in tone. But it is in Scripture. It seems
then that a statement may seem at variance with a certain passage of Scripture, may bear an improbable
exterior, and yet come from God. Is it so strange then,
so contrary to the Scripture account of the institution,
that the Lord's Supper should also be a Sacrifice, when
it is no interference at all with the truth of the first
chapter of Genesis, that the second chapter also should
be true ? No one ever professed to deduce the second
chapter from the first : all Anglo-Catholics profess to
prove the sacrificial character of the Lord's Supper from
Scripture. Thus the Catholic doctrine of the Eucharist
is not unscriptural, unless the book of Genesis is (what
is impossible, God forbid the thought !) self-contradictory.

Again, take the following account, in the beginning
of the fifth chapter of Genesis, and say whether, if this
passage only had come down to us, and not the chapters
before it, we should not, with our present notions, have
utterly disallowed any traditional account of Eve's

creation, the temptation, the fall, and the history of Cain and Abel:—"This is the book of the generation of Adam. In the day that God created man, in the likeness of God created He him; male and female created He them; and blessed them, and called their name Adam, in the day when they were created. *And* Adam lived an hundred and thirty years, and begat a son in his own likeness, after his image, and called his name Seth." If the contrast between God's likeness and Adam's image be insisted on as intentional, then I would have it observed, how indirect and concealed that allusion is.

Again: I believe I am right in saying that we are nowhere told in Scripture, certainly not in the Old Testament, that the Serpent that tempted Eve was the Devil. The nearest approach to an intimation of it is the last book of the Bible, where the devil is called "that old serpent." Can we be surprised that other truths are but obscurely conveyed in Scripture, when this hardly escapes (as I may say) omission?

Again: we have two accounts of Abraham's denying his wife; also, one instance of Isaac being betrayed into the same weakness. Now supposing we had only one or two of these in Scripture, and the others by tradition, should we not have utterly rejected these others as perversions and untrustworthy? On the one hand, we should have said it was inconceivable that two such passages should occur in Abraham's life; or, on the other, that it was most unlikely that both Abraham and Isaac should have gone to Gerar, in the time of a king of the same name, Abimelech. Yet because St. James says, "Confess your faults *one to another*," if we read that in the early Church there was an usage of secret confession made *to the priest*, we are apt to consider this latter practice, which our Communion Service recognizes, **as a** mere perversion or corruption of the Scripture command, and that the words of St. James are a positive argument against it.

In Deuteronomy we read that Moses fasted for forty days in the Mount, twice; in Exodus only one fast is mentioned. Now supposing Deuteronomy were not Scripture, but merely part of the Prayer Book, should we not say the latter was in this instance evidently mistaken? This is what men do as regards Episcopacy. Deacons are spoken of by St. Paul in his Epistles to Timothy and Titus, and Bishops; but no third order in direct and express terms. The Church considers that there are two kinds of Bishops, or, as the word signifies, overseers; those who have the oversight of single parishes, or priests, and those who have the oversight of many together, or what are now specially called Bishops. People say, "Here is a contradiction to Scripture, which speaks of two orders, not of three." Yes, just as real a contradiction, as the chapter in Deuteronomy is a contradiction of the chapter in Exodus. But this again is to take far lower ground than we need; for we all contend that the doctrine of Episcopacy, even granting it goes beyond the teaching of some passages of Scripture, yet is in exact accordance with others.

Again: in the history of Balaam we read, "God came unto Balaam at night, and said unto him, If the men come to call thee, rise up and *go with them;* but yet the word which I shall say unto thee, that shalt thou speak."* Presently we read, "And God's anger was kindled, *because* he went; and the Angel of the Lord stood in the way for an adversary against him." Now supposing the former circumstance (the permission given him to go) was not in Scripture, but was only the received belief of the Church,

* Numb. xxii. 20.

would it not be at once rejected by most men as inconsistent with Scripture? And supposing a Churchman
were to entreat objectors to consider the strong evidence
in Catholic tradition for its truth, would not the answer
be, "Do not tell us of evidence; we cannot give you a
hearing; your statement is in plain contradiction to the
inspired text, which says that God's *anger* was kindled.
How then can He have told Balaam to go with the men?
The matter stands to reason; we leave it to the private
judgment of any unbiassed person. Sophistry indeed
may try to reconcile the tradition with Scripture; but
after all you are unscriptural, and we uphold the pure
word of truth without glosses and refinements." Now,
is not this just what is done in matters of doctrine?
Thus, because our Lord represents the Father saying,
in the parable of the Prodigal Son, "Bring forth the best
robe, and put it on him; and put a ring on his hand, and
shoes on his feet," * it is argued that this is inconsistent
with the Church's usage (even supposing for argument's
sake it has no Scripture sanction) of doing penance for
sin.

Again: the book of Deuteronomy, being a recapitula-
tion of the foregoing Books, in an address to the Israelites,
is in the position of the Apostolic Epistles. Exodus,
Leviticus, and Numbers, being a very orderly and systematic account of events, are somewhat in the position of
Catholic tradition. Now Deuteronomy differs in some
minute points from the former books. For example: in
Exodus, the fourth commandment contains a reference
to the creation of the world on the seventh day, as the
reason of the institution of the Sabbath: in Deuteronomy,
the same commandment refers it to the deliverance of the
Israelites out of Egypt on that day. Supposing we had

* Luke xv. 22.

only the latter statement in Scripture, and supposing the former to be only the received doctrine of the Church, would not this former, that is, the statement contained in Exodus, that the Sabbatical rest was in memory of God's resting after the Creation, have seemed at once fanciful and unfounded? Would it not have been said, "Why do you have recourse to the mysticism of types? here is a plain intelligible reason for keeping the Sabbath holy, viz., the deliverance from Egypt. Be content with this: —besides, your view is grossly carnal and anthropomorphic. How can Almighty God be said to rest? And it is unscriptural; for Christ says, 'My Father worketh hitherto, and I work.'" Now is it not a similar procedure to argue, that *since* the Holy Eucharist is a "communication of the body and blood of Christ," *therefore* it is not also a mysterious representation of His meritorious Sacrifice in the sight of Almighty God?

2.

Let us proceed to the history of the Monarchy, as contained in the Books of Samuel and Kings, and compare them with the Chronicles. Out of many instances in point, I will select a few. For instance:—

In 2 Kings xv. we read of the reign of Azariah, or Uzziah, king of Judah. It is said, "he did that which was right in the sight of the Lord, according to all that his father Amaziah had done;" and then that "the Lord smote the king, so that he was a leper unto the day of his death;" and we are referred for "the rest of the acts of Azariah, and all that he did," to "the book of the Chronicles of the kings of Judah." We turn to the Chronicles, and find an account of the cause of the visitation which came upon him. "When he was strong, his heart was lifted up to his destruction; for he transgressed

against the Lord his God, and went into the temple of
the Lord to burn incense upon the altar of incense.   And
Azariah the priest went in after him, and with him four-
score priests of the Lord that were valiant men.   And they
withstood Uzziah the king, and said unto him, It apper-
taineth not unto thee, Uzziah, to burn incense unto the
Lord, but to the priests, the sons of Aaron, that are consecrated to burn incense : go out of the sanctuary, for thou
hast trespassed ; neither shall it be for thine honour from
the Lord God.   Then Uzziah was wroth, and had a censer
in his hand to burn incense ; and while he was wroth with
the priests, the leprosy even rose up in his forehead, before
the priests in the house of the Lord, from beside the incense altar.   And Azariah, the chief priest, and all the
priests, looked upon him, and behold he was leprous in
his forehead, and they thrust him out from thence ; yea,
himself hasted also to go out because the Lord had
smitten him.   And Uzziah the king was a leper unto
the day of his death, and dwelt in a several house, being
a leper." *

Now nothing can be more natural than this joint
narrative.   The one is brief, but refers to the other for
the details ; and the other gives them.   Suppose, then,
a captious mind were to dwell upon the remarkable
silence of the former narrative,—magnify it as an objection,—and on the other hand should allude to the
tendency of the second narrative to uphold the priesthood, and should attribute it to such a design.   Should
we think such an argument valid, or merely ingenious,
clever, amusing, yet not trustworthy ?   I suppose the
latter ; yet this instance is very near a parallel to the
case as it stands, between the New Testament and the
doctrine of the Church.   For instance, after St. Paul

* 2 Chron. xxvi. 16—21.

has declared some plain truths to the Corinthians, he says, " Be ye followers of me : *for this cause* have I sent unto you Timotheus, who is my beloved son, and faithful in the Lord, *who shall bring you into remembrance of my ways,* which be in Christ, as I *teach* everywhere in every Church." * He refers them to an authority beyond and beside his epistle,—to Timothy, nay to his doctrine *as* he had taught in every Church. If then we can ascertain, for that I here assume, what was that doctrine taught everywhere in the Church, we have ascertained that to which St. Paul refers us ; and if that doctrine, so ascertained, adds many things in detail to what he has written, develops one thing, and gives a different impression of others, it is no more than such a reference might lead us to expect,—it is the very thing he prepares us for. It as little, therefore, contradicts what is written, as the books of Chronicles contradict the books of Kings; and if it appears to favour the priesthood more than St. Paul does, this is no more than can be objected to the Chronicles compared with the Kings.

Again, after, not teaching, but reminding them about the Lord's Supper, he adds, " *the rest* will I set in order when I come." When then we find the Church has always considered that Holy Sacrament to be not only a feast or supper, but in its fulness to contain a sacrifice, and to require a certain liturgical form, how does this contradict the inspired text, which plainly signifies that something else *is* to come besides what it has said itself ? So far from its being strange that the Church brings out and fills up St. Paul's outline, it would be very strange if it did not. Yet it is not unusual to ascribe these additional details to priestcraft, and without proof to call them corruptions and innovations, in the very spirit

* 1 Cor. iv. 17.

in which freethinkers have before now attributed the books of Chronicles to the Jewish priests, and accused them of bigotry and intolerance.

It is remarkable how frequent are the allusions in the Epistles to *other* Apostolic teaching beyond themselves, that is, besides the written authority. For instance; in the same chapter, "I *praise* you, brethren, that ye *remember* me in all things, and *keep the traditions*, as I delivered them to you." Again, "I have also received," or had by tradition, "of the Lord that which also I delivered unto you," that is, which I gave by tradition unto you. This giving and receiving was not in writing. Again, "If any man seem to be contentious, we have no such custom, neither the churches of God : " he appeals to the received custom of the Church. Again, "I declare unto you the Gospel which I preached unto you, which also ye have received, and wherein ye stand, . . . for I delivered unto you (gave by tradition) first of all that which I also received" (by tradition). Again, "Stand fast, and hold the traditions which ye have been taught, whether by word or our epistle."* Such passages prove, as all will grant, that at the time there were means of gaining knowledge distinct from Scripture, and sources of information in addition to it. When, then, we actually do find in the existing Church system of those times, as historically recorded, such additional information, that information may be Apostolic or it may be not ; but however this is, the mere circumstance that it is in addition, is no proof against its being Apostolic ; that it is extra-scriptural is no proof that it is unscriptural, for St. Paul himself tells us in Scripture, that there are truths not in Scripture, and we may as fairly object to the books of Chronicles, that they are an addition

* 1 Cor. xi. 2, 16, 23 ; xv. 1—3 ; 1 Thess. ii. 15.

to the books of Kings. In saying this, I am not entering into the question which lies between us and the Romanists, whether these further truths are substantive additions or simply developments, whether in faith or in conduct and discipline.

Further: the Chronicles pass over David's great sin, and Solomon's fall; and they insert Manasseh's repentance. The account of Manasseh's reign is given at length in the second book of Kings; it is too long of course to cite, but the following are some of its particulars. Manasseh* "used enchantments and dealt with familiar spirits and wizards;" he "seduced them to do more evil than did the nations whom the Lord destroyed before the children of Israel." "Moreover Manasseh shed innocent blood very much, till he had filled Jerusalem from one end to another." Afterwards, when Josiah had made his reforms, the sacred writer adds,† "Notwithstanding the Lord turned from the *fierceness of His great wrath*, wherewith His anger was kindled against Judah, *because* of all the provocations that *Manasseh* had provoked him withal." And again in Jehoiakim's time,‡ "Surely, at the commandment of the Lord came this upon Judah, to remove them out of His sight for the sins of Manasseh, according to all that he did; and also for the innocent blood, that he shed; for he filled Jerusalem with innocent blood, *which the Lord would not pardon.*" And again in the book of Jeremiah,§ "I will cause them to be removed into all the kingdoms of the earth, *because of Manasseh*, the son of Hezekiah, king of Judah, for that which he did in Jerusalem." Who would conjecture, with such passages of Scripture before him, that Manasseh repented before his death, and was forgiven? but to complete the *illusion* (as

* 2 Kings **xxi.** † 2 Kings xxiii. 26. ‡ 2 Kings xxiv. 3, 4. § Jer. xv. 4.

it may be called), the account of his reign in the book
of Kings ends thus :* " Now the rest of the acts of
Manasseh, and all that he did, and *his sin that he sinned*,
are they not *written in the book of the Chronicles* of the
kings of Judah ? "—not a word about his repentance.
Might it not then be plausibly argued that the books of
Kings precisely limited and defined *what* the Chronicles
were to relate, " *the sin that he sinned ;* " that this was to
be the theme of the history, its outline and ground plan,
and that the absolute silence of the books of Kings about
his repentance was a cogent, positive argument that he
did not repent ? How little do they prepare one for
the following most touching record of him : " When he
was in affliction, he besought the Lord his God, and
humbled himself greatly before the God of his fathers,
and prayed unto Him. And He was entreated of him,
and heard his supplication, and brought him again to
Jerusalem into his kingdom. Then Manasseh knew
that the Lord He was God. . . . And he took away the
strange gods, and the idol out of the house of the Lord,
and the altars that he had built in the mount of the
house of the Lord, and in Jerusalem, and cast them out
of the city," etc. . . . " Now the rest of the acts of
Manasseh, and his prayer unto his God, and the words
of the seers that spake to him in the name of the Lord
God of Israel, behold they are written in the book of
the kings of Israel. . . . So Manasseh slept with his
fathers." † If then the books of Kings were the only
canonical account, and the book of Chronicles part of the
Apocrypha, would not the latter be pronounced an
unscriptural record, a legend and a tradition of men,
not because the evidence for their truth was insufficient, but on the allegation that they contradicted the

* 2 Kings xxi.   † 2 Chron. xxxiii. 12—20,

books of Kings?—at least, is not this what is done as regards the Church system of doctrine, as if it must be at variance with the New Testament, because it views the Gospel from a somewhat distinct point of view, and in a distinct light?

Again; the account given of Jehoash in the Kings is as follows:* "Jehoash did that which was right in the sight of the Lord *all his days, wherein* Jehoiada the priest instructed him." And it ends thus: "His servants arose and made a conspiracy, and slew Joash in the house of Millo:" there is no hint of any great defection or miserable ingratitude on his part, though, as it turns out on referring to Chronicles, the words "all his days, wherein," etc., are significant. In the Chronicles we learn that *after* good Jehoiada's death, whose wife had saved him from Athaliah, and who preserved for him his throne, he went and served groves and idols, and killed Zechariah the son of Jehoiada, when he was raised up by the Spirit of God to protest. Judgments followed,—the Syrians, and then "great diseases," and then assassination. Now, if the apparently simple words, "all the days wherein," etc., are emphatic, why may not our Saviour's words, "If thou bring thy gifts to the *altar,*" be emphatic, or "If thou wouldst be *perfect,*" suggest a doctrine which it does not exhibit?

3.

Now let us proceed to the Gospels; a few instances must suffice.

Considering how great a miracle the raising of Lazarus is in itself, and how connected with our Lord's death, how is it that the three first Gospels do not mention it? They speak of the chief priests taking counsel to put Him

* 2 Kings xii.

to death, but they give no reason; rather they seem to assign other reasons,—for instance, the parables He spoke against them.* At length St. John mentions the miracle and its consequences. Things important then may be true, though particular inspired documents do not mention them. As the raising of Lazarus is true, though not contained at all in the first three Gospels, so the gift of consecrating the Eucharist may have been committed by Christ to the priesthood, though this is only indirectly stated in any of the four. Will you say I am arguing against our own Church, which says that Scripture "contains all things necessary to be believed to salvation"? Doubtless, Scripture *contains* all things necessary to be *believed;* but there may be things *contained* in it, which are not *on the surface,* and things which belong to the *ritual* and not to *belief.* Points of faith may lie *under* the surface, points of observance need not be in Scripture *at all.* The rule for consecrating is a point of ritual; yet it *is* indirectly taught in Scripture, though not brought out, when Christ said, "Do this," for He spoke to the Apostles who were priests, not to His disciples generally.

Again: I just now mentioned the apparent repetition in Genesis of the account of Abraham's denying his wife; a remark which applies to the parallel miracles which occur in the histories of Elijah and Elisha, as the raising of the dead child and the multiplication of the oil. Were only the first of these parallel instances in Scripture, and the second in tradition, we should call the second a corruption or distorted account; and not without some plausibility, till other and contrary reasons were brought. And in like manner, as regards the Gospels, did the account of the feeding of the 4,000

* Matt. xxi 45.

with seven loaves rest on the testimony of Antiquity, most of us would have said, "You see how little you can trust the Fathers ; it was not 4,000 with seven loaves, but 5,000 with five." Again, should we not have pronounced that the discourses in Luke vi., xi., and xii., if they came to us through the Fathers, were the same, only in a corrupt form, as the Sermon on the Mount in Matt. v.—vii. and as chapter xxiii. ? Nay, we should have seized on Luke xi. 41, "But rather give alms of such things as ye have, and behold *all things are clean* unto you," as a symptom of incipient Popery, a mystery already working. Yes, our Saviour's own sacred words (I fear too truly) would have been seized on by some of us as the signs of the dawn of Antichrist. This is a most miserable thought.

Again : St. Matthew, St. Mark, and St. Luke say, that Simon of Cyrene bore Christ's cross ; St. John, that Christ Himself bore it. Both might be true, and both of course were true. He bore it part of the way, and Simon part. Yet I conceive, did we find it was the tradition of the Church that Simon bore it, we should decide, without going into the evidence, that this was a gloss upon the pure scriptural statement. So, in like manner, even supposing that, when St. Paul says, "Ye do *shew forth* the Lord's death till He come," he meant, which I do not grant, by "shew forth," preach, remind each other of, or commemorate among yourselves, and nothing more, (which I repeat I do not grant,) even then it may be that the Holy Eucharist is also a remembrance in God's sight, a pleading before Him the merits of Christ's death, and, so far, a propitiatory offering, even though this view of it were only contained in the immemorial usage of the Church, and were no point of necessary faith contained in Scripture.

Again : Judas is represented as hanging himself in
St. Matthew, yet in the Acts as falling headlong, and his
bowels gushing out. I do not mean to say, of course,
that these accounts are irreconcilable even by us ; but
they certainly differ from each other : do not they differ
as much as the explicit Scripture statement that Confirmation imparts miraculous gifts, differs from the Church
view, not clearly brought out in Scripture, that it is also
an ordinary rite conferring ordinary gifts ?

We know how difficult it is to reconcile the distinct
accounts of the occurrences which took place at the
Resurrection with each other, and our Lord's appearances
to His disciples. For instance :—according to Matt.
xxviii., it might seem that Christ did not appear to His
disciples, till He met them on the mountain in Galilee ;
but in St. Luke and St. John His first appearance was
on the evening of the day of Resurrection. Again : in
the Gospel according to St. Mark and St. Luke, the
Ascension seems to follow immediately on the Resurrection ; but in the Acts our Lord is declared to have
shown Himself to His disciples for forty days. These
forty days are a blank in two Gospels. And in like
manner, even though Scripture be considered to be altogether silent as to the intermediate state, and to pass
from the mention of death to that of the Judgment, there
is nothing in this circumstance to disprove the Church's
doctrine, (if there be other grounds for it,) that there *is*
an intermediate state, and that it has an important place
in the scheme of salvation, that in it the souls of the
faithful are purified and grow in grace, that they pray
for us, and that our prayers benefit them.

Moreover, there is on the face of the New Testament
plain evidence, that often the sacred writers are but
referring to the circumstances it relates, *as* known, and

not narrating them.   Thus St. Luke, after describing our Lord's consecration of the bread at supper time, adds immediately, "*Likewise* also the cup after supper, saying,"* etc. ; he does not narrate it in its place ; he does but allude to it as a thing well known, in the way of a note or memorandum.   Again: St. Mark, in giving an account of St. John Baptist's martyrdom, says, "When his disciples heard of it, they came and took up his corpse and laid it in *the* tomb."†   He is evidently speaking of an occurrence, and of a tomb, which were well known to those for whom he wrote.   If historical facts be thus merely alluded to, not taught, why may not doctrines also?   Here again it will be replied, that Scripture was written to teach doctrine, not history ; but such an answer will not hold good for many reasons.   First, is it true that the Gospels were *not* written to teach us the facts of Christ's life ?   Next, is it true that the account of the institution of the Lord's Supper is a mere abstract historical narrative, and not recorded to direct our practice ?   Further, where is the proof that Scripture *was* intended to teach doctrine ?   This is one of the main points in dispute.   But enough in answer to a gratuitous proposition ; and enough indeed in exemplification of the characteristic of Scripture, which I proposed to consider.

* Luke xxii. 20.

† Mark vi 29. [In the revised Version of 1881, it is translated "in a tomb ;" but μνημεῖον is more than a tomb, it implies a place of *remembrance.*]

5.

The Impression made on the Reader by the Statements of Scripture.

THE characteristics then, of the narrative portion of Scripture are such as I have described; it is unsystematic and unstudied;—from which I would infer, that as Scripture relates *facts* without aiming at completeness or consistency, so it relates *doctrines* also; so that, if it does after all include in its teaching the whole Catholic Creed, (as we of the English Church hold,) this does not happen from any purpose in its writers so to do, but from the overruling providence of God, overruling just so far as this: to secure a certain result, not a certain mode of attaining it,—not so as to interfere with their free and natural manner of writing, but by imperceptibly guiding it; in other words, not securing their teaching against indirectness and disorder, but against eventual incompleteness. From which it follows, that we must not be surprised to find in Scripture doctrines of the Gospel, however momentous, nevertheless taught obliquely, and capable only of circuitous proof;—such, for instance, as that of the Blessed Trinity,—and, among them, the especial Church doctrines, such as the Apostolical Succession, the efficacy of the Holy Eucharist, and the essentials of the Ritual.

The argument, stated in a few words, stands thus:— Since distinct portions of Scripture itself are apparently inconsistent with one another, yet are not really so, therefore it does not follow that Scripture and Catholic doctrine are at variance with each other, even though there may be sometimes a difficulty in adjusting the one with the other.

Now I propose to go over the ground again in somewhat a different way, not confining myself to illustrations from Scripture narrative, but taking others from Scripture teaching also, and that with a view of answering another form which the objection is likely to take.

I.

The objection then may be put thus: "We are told, it seems, in the Prayer Book, of a certain large and influential portion of doctrine, as constituting one great part of the Christian Revelation, that is, of Sacraments, of Ministers, of Rites, of Observances; we are told that these are the appointed means through which Christ's gifts are conveyed to us. Now when we turn to Scripture, we see much indeed of those gifts, viz., we read much of what He has done for us, by atoning for our sins, and much of what He does in us, that is, much about holiness, faith, peace, love, joy, hope, and obedience; but of those intermediate provisions of the Revelation coming between Him and us, of which the Church speaks, we read very little. Passages, indeed, are pointed out to us as if containing notices of them, but they are in our judgment singularly deficient and unsatisfactory; and that, either because the meaning assigned to them is not obvious and natural, but (as we think) strained, unexpected, recondite, and at best but possible, or because they are conceived in such plain, unpretending words, that we cannot imagine the writers meant to say any great thing in introducing them. On the other hand, a silence is observed in certain places, where one might expect the doctrines in question to be mentioned. Moreover, the general tone of the New Testament is to our apprehension a full disproof of them ; that is, it is moral, rational, elevated, impassioned, but there is nothing of what may be called a sacramental, ecclesiastical, mysterious tone in it.

"For instance, let Acts xx. be considered : 'Upon the first day of the week, when the disciples came together to break bread'—who would imagine, from such a mode of speaking, that this was a solemn, mysterious rite ?   The words 'break bread' are quite a familiar expression.

"Or again: 'Christ our Passover is sacrificed for us, therefore let us keep the feast, not with old leaven, neither with the leaven of malice and wickedness, but with the unleavened bread of sincerity and truth.'   Here, if the Church system were true, one might have expected that in mentioning 'keeping the feast,' a reference would be made to the Eucharist, as being the great feast of Christ's sacrifice; whereas, instead of the notion of any literal feast occuring to the sacred writer, a mental feast is the only one he proceeds to mention ; and the unleavened bread of the Passover, instead of suggesting to his mind the sacred elements in the Eucharist, is to him but typical of something moral, 'sincerity and truth.'

"Or again : 'Lo, I am with you alway, even unto the end of the world.' *   This means, we are told, that Christ is with the present Church : *for* when Christ said 'with you,' He meant with you and your descendants ; and the Church, at present so called, is descended from the Apostles and first disciples.   How very covert, indirect, and unlikely a meaning !

* Matt. xxviii. 20.

" Or, to take another instance : How is it proved that the Lord's Supper is generally necessary to salvation ? By no part of Scripture except the sixth chapter of St. John. Now, suppose that a person denies that this passage belongs to that Sacrament, how shall we prove it ? And is it any very strong step to deny it ? Do not many most excellent men now alive deny it ? have not many now dead denied it ? "

This is the objection now to be considered, which lies it would seem in this : that after considering what I have been saying about the statement of facts in Scripture, after all allowances on the score of its unstudied character, there is still a serious difficulty remaining,—that the circumstance that its books were written at different times and places, by different persons, without concert, explains indeed much,—explains indeed why there is no system in it, why so much is out of place, why great truths come in by-the-bye, nay, would explain why others were left out, were there any such ; but it does not explain the case as it stands, it does not explain why a doctrine is not introduced when there is an actual call for it, why a sacred writer should come close up to it, as it were, and yet pass by it ; why, when he does introduce it, he should mention it so obscurely, as not at all to suggest it to an ordinary reader ; why, in short, the tone and character of his writing should be just contrary to his real meaning. This is the difficulty,—strongly, nay almost extravagantly put, but still plausible,—on which I shall now attempt some remarks.

2.

Now there are two attributes of the Bible throughout, which, taken together, seem to meet this difficulty,— attributes which, while at first sight in contrast, have

a sort of necessary connexion, and set off each other—
simplicity and depth. Simplicity leads a writer to say
things without display; and depth obliges him to use
inadequate words. Scripture then, treating of invisible
things, at best must use words less than those things;
and, as if from a feeling that no words can be worthy of
them, it does not condescend to use even the strongest
that exist, but often takes the plainest. The deeper the
thought, the plainer the word; the word and thought
diverge from each other. Again, it is a property of
depth to lead a writer into verbal contradictions; and
it is a property of simplicity not to care to avoid them.
Again, when a writer is deep, his half sentences, paren-
theses, clauses, nay his words, have a meaning in them
independent of the context, and admit of exposition.
There is nothing put in for ornament's sake, or for
rhetoric; nothing put in for the mere sake of anything
else, but all for its own sake; all as the expressions and
shadows of great things, as seeds of thought, and with
corresponding realities. Moreover, when a writer is deep,
or again when he is simple, he does not set about exhausting his subject in his remarks upon it; he says so
much as is in point, no more; he does not go out of
his way to complete a view or to catch at collateral
thoughts; he has something before him which he aims
at, and, while he cannot help including much in his
meaning which he does not aim at, he does aim at one
thing, not at another. Now to illustrate these remarks,
and to apply them.

One of the most remarkable characteristics of Scripture narrative, which I suppose all readers must have
noticed, is the absence of expressions by which the
reader can judge whether the events recorded are presented for praise or blame. A plain bare series of facts

is drawn out ; and whether for imitation or warning, often cannot be decided except by the context, or by the event, or by our general notions of propriety—often not at all. The bearing and drift of the narrative are not given.

For instance, when the prophet Isaiah told Ahaz to ask a sign, he said, " I will not ask, neither *will I tempt* the Lord."   Was this right or wrong ?

When Elisha said to Joash, " Smite on the ground," the king " smote thrice and stayed."   What was the fault of this ?   We should not know it was faulty but by the event, viz., that "the man of God was wroth with him, and said, Thou shouldest have smitten five or six times." *

What was David's sin in numbering the people ?   Or take the account of Moses striking the rock : "And Moses took the rod from before the Lord, as He commanded him.   And Moses and Aaron gathered the congregation together before the rock, and he said unto them, Hear now, ye rebels ; must we fetch you water out of this rock ?   And Moses lifted up his hand, and with his rod he smote the rock twice : and the water came out abundantly, and the congregation drank, and their beasts also."†   I really do not think we should have discovered that there was anything wrong in this, but for the comment that follows : " Because ye believed Me not, to sanctify Me," etc. ; though, of course, when we are told, we are able to point out where their fault lay.

And in that earlier passage in the history of Moses, when his zeal led him to smite the Egyptian, we are entirely left by the sacred narrative to determine for ourselves whether his action was good or bad, or how far one, how far the other.   We are left to a comment, the comment of our own judgment, external to the inspired volume.

* 2 Kings xiii. 18, 19.   † Numb. xx. 9—11.

Or consider the account of Jeroboam's conduct from first to last in the revolt of the ten tribes ; or that of the old prophet who dwelt in Samaria. Is it not plain that Scripture does not interpret itself?

Or consider the terms in which an exceeding great impiety of Ahaz and the high priest is spoken of; and say, if we knew not the Mosaic law, or if we were not told in the beginning of the chapter what the character of Ahaz was, whether we should be able to determine, from the narrative itself, whether he was doing a right or a wrong, or an indifferent action. There is no epithet, no turn of sentence, which betrays the divine judgment of his deed. It passes in the Scripture narrative, as in God's daily providence, silently. I allude to the following passage : "And king Ahaz went to Damascus to meet Tiglath-pileser, king of Assyria, and saw an altar that was at Damascus : and king Ahaz sent to Urijah the priest the fashion of the altar, and the pattern of it, according to all the workmanship thereof. And Urijah the priest built an altar according to all that king Ahaz had sent from Damascus : so Urijah the priest made it against king Ahaz came from Damascus. And when the king was come from Damascus, the king saw the altar ; and the king approached to the altar, and offered thereon. And he burned his burnt-offering, and his meat-offering, and poured his drink-offering, and sprinkled the blood of his peace-offerings upon the altar. And he brought also the brasen altar, which was before the Lord, from the fore-front of the house, from between the altar and the house of the Lord, and put it on the north side of the altar. And king Ahaz commanded Urijah the priest, saying, Upon the great altar burn the morning burnt-offering . . . and the brasen altar shall be for me to inquire by. Thus did

Urijah the priest, according to all that king Ahaz commanded."*

Or, again, how simple and unadorned is the account of St. John Baptist's martyrdom! "Herod had laid hold of John, and bound him and put him in prison for Herodias' sake, his brother Philip's wife; for John said unto him, It is not lawful for thee to have her. And when he would have put him to death, he feared the multitude, because they counted him as a prophet. But when Herod's birthday was kept, the daughter of Herodias danced before them, and pleased Herod. Whereupon, he promised with an oath, to give her whatsoever she would ask. And she, being before instructed of her mother, said, Give me here John Baptist's head in a charger. And the king was sorry: nevertheless for the oath's sake, and them which sat with him at meat, he commanded it to be given her. And he sent, and beheaded John in the prison. And his head was brought in a charger, and given to the damsel; and she brought it to her mother. And his disciples came, and took up the body, and buried it, and went and told Jesus." † Not a word of indignation, of lament, or of triumph! Such is the style of Scripture, singularly contrasted to the uninspired style, most beautiful but still human, of the ancient Martyrologies; for instance, that of the persecution at Lyons and Vienne.

St. Paul's journey to Jerusalem, against the warnings of the prophets, is the last instance of this character of Scripture narrative which shall be given. The facts of it are related so nakedly, that there has been room for maintaining that he was wrong in going thither. That he was right would seem certain, from the way in which he speaks of these warnings: "Behold, I go *bound in the*

* **2** Kings xvi. 10—16.   † Matt. xiv.

Spirit unto Jerusalem, not knowing the things that shall befall me there, save that the Holy Ghost witnesseth in every city, saying, that bonds and afflictions abide me;"[*] and also from Christ's words in the vision: "Be of good cheer, Paul; for as thou *hast testified of Me* in Jerusalem,"[†] etc. Yet though this be abundantly enough to convince us, nevertheless, the impression conveyed by the warning of the disciples at Tyre saying, "through the Spirit, that he should not go up to Jerusalem,"[‡] and by that of Agabus at Cæsarea, and, when he got to Jerusalem, by his attempt to soften the Jews by means of a conformity to the Law, and by his strong words, seemingly retracted, to Ananias, and by his cleverly dividing the Jewish council by proclaiming himself a Pharisee,—the impression, I say, conveyed by all this would *in itself* be (a very false one,) that there was something human in his conduct.

3.

Thus the style of Scripture is plain and colourless, as regards the relation of facts; so that we are continually perplexed what to think about them and about the parties concerned in them. They need a comment,—they are evidently but a text *for* a comment,—they have no comment; and as they stand, may be turned this way or that way, according to the accidental tone of mind in the reader. And often the true comment, when given us in other parts of Scripture, is startling. I think it startling at first sight that Lot, being such as he is represented to be on the whole in the Old Testament, should be called by St. Peter "a just man." I think Ehud's assassination of Eglon a startling act,—the praise given to Jael for killing Sisera, startling. It is evident that the letter of the sacred history conveys to the ordinary

---

[*] Acts xx. 22, 23.   [†] Ib. xxiii. 11.   [‡] Ib. xxi. 4.

reader a very inadequate idea of the facts recorded in it, considered as bodily, substantial, and (as it were) living and breathing transactions.

Equal simplicity is observed in the relation of great and awful events. For instance, consider the words in which is described the vision of God vouchsafed to the elders of Israel. "Then went up Moses and Aaron, and Nadab and Abihu, and seventy of the elders of Israel; and they saw the God of Israel: and there was under His feet as it were a paved work of a sapphire stone, and as it were the body of heaven in his clearness. And upon the nobles of the children of Israel He laid not His hand: also they saw God, and did eat and did drink."* Or consider the account of Jacob's wrestling with the Angel. Or the plain, unadorned way in which the conversations, if I may dare use the word, between Almighty God and Moses are recorded, and His gracious laments, purposes of wrath, appeasement, repentance. Or between the Almighty and Satan, in the first chapter of Job. Or how simply and abruptly the narrative runs, "And [the Serpent] said unto the woman . . . and the woman said unto the serpent;" or, "And the Lord opened the mouth of the ass, and she said to Balaam. . . . and Balaam said unto the ass."† Minds familiarized to supernatural things, minds set upon definite great objects, have no disposition, no time to indulge in embellishment, or to aim at impressiveness, or to consult for the weakness or ignorance of the hearer.

And so in like manner the words in which the celebration of the holy Eucharist is spoken of by St. Luke and St. Paul, viz., "breaking bread," are very simple: they are applicable to a common meal quite as well as to the Sacrament, and they only do not exclude, they in no

* Exod. xxiv. 9—11. † Numb. xxii. 28—29.

respect introduce that full and awful meaning which the
Church has ever put on them. " As He sat at meat
with them, He took bread, and blessed it, and brake,
and gave to them ; and their eyes were opened."* "They
continued stedfastly in the breaking of bread, and in
prayers."† " The first day of the week, when the
disciples came together to break bread. . . . When he
therefore was come up again and had broken bread,
and eaten, and talked a long while even till break of day,
so he departed."‡ " When he had thus spoken, he took
bread, and gave thanks to God in the presence of them
all ; and when he had broken it, he began to eat."§
" The bread which we break, is it not the communion
of the Body of Christ ? "‖ " The Lord Jesus, the same
night in which He was betrayed, took bread ; and when
He had given thanks, He brake it."¶ Now no words
can be simpler than these. What *is* remarkable is the
repeated mention of the very same acts in the same
order—taking, blessing or giving thanks, and breaking.
Certainly the constant use of the word " break" is very
remarkable. For instance, in the ship, why should it be
said, " And when He had thus spoken, He took bread,
and gave thanks ; and when He had *broken* it, He began
to eat," since he *alone* ate it, and did not divide it among
his fellow-passengers ? But supposing the passages had
been a little less frequent, so as not to attract attention
by their similarity, what could be more simple than the
words,—what less adapted to force on the mind any
high meaning ? Yet these simple words, *blessing, breaking, eating, giving*, have a very high meaning put on
them in our Prayer Book, put on them by the Church
from the first ; and a person may be tempted to say

---

* Luke xxiv. 30, 31.   ‡ Acts xx. 7—11.   ‖ 1 Cor. x. 16.
† Acts ii. 42.   § Ib. xxvii. 35.   ¶ Ib. xi. 23, 24.

that the Church's meaning is not borne out by such simple words. I ask, are they more bare and colourless than the narrative of many a miraculous transaction in the Old Testament?

Such is the plain and (as it were) unconscious way in which great things are recorded in Scripture. However, it may be objected that there is no allusion to Catholic doctrines, even where one would think there must have been, had they been in the inspired writer's mind; that is, supposing them part of the Divine Revelation. For instance, if Baptism is so indispensable for the evangelical blessings, why do we hear nothing of the baptism of the Apostles? If Ordinances are so imperative now, why does not our Lord say so, when He says, "Neither in this mountain, nor yet at Jerusalem, shall ye worship the Father"? That is, the tone of the New Testament is unsacramental; and the impression it leaves on the mind is not that of a Priesthood and its attendant system. This may be objected: yet I conceive that a series of Scripture parallels to this, as regards other matters, might easily be drawn out, all depending on this principle, and illustrating it in the case before us; viz., that when the sacred writers were aiming at one thing, they did not go out of their way ever so little to introduce another. The fashion of this day, indeed, is ever to speak about all religious things at once, and never to introduce one, but to introduce all, and never to maintain reserve about any; and those who are imbued with the spirit which this implies, doubtless will find it difficult to understand how the sacred writers could help speaking of what was very near their subject, when it was not their subject. Still we must submit to facts, which abundantly evidence that they could. This omission of the Sacraments in St. Paul and St. John, so far as distinct mention is omitted (for in fact they are frequently mentioned), as little proves that those Apostles were not aware and thinking of them, as St. James's Epistle is an evidence that he did not hold the doctrine of the Atonement, which is not there mentioned. Or consider how many passages there are in the history, in which some circumstance is omitted which one would expect to be inserted. For instance : St. Peter struck off the ear of Malchus when our Lord was seized. St. John gives the names ; St. Matthew and St. Mark relate the occurrence without the names. This is commonly explained on the ground that St. John, writing later than his brother Evangelists, and when all parties were dead, might give the names without exposing St. Peter, if indeed he was still alive, to any civil inconveniences. True, this is an explanation so far ; but what explains their omitting, and St. John omitting, our Lord's miracle in healing the ear, while St. Luke relates it ? Was not this to deliver a half account ? is it not what would be called unnatural, if it were a question, not of history, but of doctrine ?

4.

Now let us review cases in which matters of doctrine, or the doctrinal tone of the composition, is in question. Is the tone of Scripture more unfavourable to the doctrine of a Priesthood than it is to the idea of Christianity, such as we have been brought up to regard it,—I mean of an established, endowed, dignified Church ; and, if its establishment is not inconsistent (as it is not) with the New Testament, why should its mysticalness be ? Certainly, if anything is plain, it is that Scripture represents the very portion of Christians, one and all, to be tribulation, want, contempt, persecution. I do not,—of course not, far from it,—I do not say that the actual present state of the Church Catholic and the text of the New Testament, are not reconcilable ; but is it not a fact, that the first impression from Scripture of what the Church should be, is not fulfilled in what we see around us ?

Again.: I suppose another impression which would be left on an unbiassed reader by the New Testament would be, that the world was soon to come to an end. Yet it has not. As, then, we submit to facts in one case, and do not exercise our so-called right of private judgment to quarrel with our own consciousness that we do live, and that the world does still go on, why should we not submit to facts in the other instance ? and if there be good proof that what the Church teaches is true, and is comformable to given texts of Scripture, in spite of this vague impression from its surface to the contrary, why should we not reconcile ourselves to the conclusion that that impression of its being opposed to a Sacramental or Priestly system is a false impression, is private and personal, or peculiar to a particular age, untrustworthy, in fact false, just as the impression of its teaching that the world was soon to come to an end is false, because it has not been fulfilled ?

Again : I suppose any one reading our Lord's discourses, would, with the Apostles, consider that the Gentiles, even if they were to be converted, yet were not to be on a level with the Jews. The impression His words convey is certainly such. But of this more presently.

Again : it is objected that little is said in the New Testament of the danger of sin after baptism, or of the penitential exercises by which it is to be remedied. Well : supposing it for argument's sake : yet let me ask the previous question. Is there much said in the New

Testament of the chance of sin after baptism at all? Are not all Christians described as if in all important respects sinless? Of course, falling away is spoken of, and excommunication; but grievous sin has no distinct *habitat* among those who are "called to be saints" and members of the Church in the Epistles of St. Paul and St. John. Till we examine Scripture on the subject, perhaps we have no adequate notion how little those Apostles contemplate recurring sin in the baptized. The argument then proves too much: for if silence proves anything, it will prove either that Christians who now live do not fall into gross sin, or that those who have so fallen have forfeited their Christianity.

Again: the first three Gospels contain no declaration of our Lord's divinity, and there are passages which tend at first sight the other way. Now, is there one doctrine more than another the essential and characteristic of a Christian mind? Is it possible that the Evangelists could write any one particle of their records of His life, without having the great and solemn truth steadfastly before them, that He was their God? Yet they do not show this. It follows, that truths may be in the mind of the inspired writers, which are not discoverable to ordinary readers in the tone of their composition. I by no means deny that, now we know the doctrine, we can gather proofs of it from the three Gospels in question, and can discern in them a feeling of reverence towards our Lord, which fully implies it; but no one will say it is on the surface, and such as to strike a reader. I conceive the impression left on an ordinary mind would be, that our Saviour was a superhuman being, intimately possessed of God's confidence, but still a creature; an impression infinitely removed from the truth as really contained and intended in those Gospels.

Again: is the tone of the Epistle of St. James the same as the tone of St. Paul's Epistle to the Ephesians? or that of St. Paul's Epistle to the Romans as that of the same Apostle's Epistle to the Hebrews? Might they not be as plausibly put in opposition with each other, as the Church system is made contrary to Scripture?

Again: consider what the texts are from which Calvinists are accustomed to argue, viz., such as speak of God's sovereign grace, without happening to make mention of man's responsibility. Thus: "He who has begun a good work in you will perform it unto the day of the Lord Jesus," and, "Who are kept by the power of God through faith unto salvation," are taken as irrefragable arguments for final perseverance. If mention in Scripture of God's electing mercy need not exclude man's moral freedom, why need the stress laid in Scripture upon faith and love exclude the necessity of sacraments as instruments of grace?

Again: if silence implies denial or ignorance of the things passed over; if nothing is the sense of Scripture but what is openly declared; if first impressions are everything, what are we to say to the Book of Canticles, which nowhere hints, (nor Scripture afterwards anywhere hints either,) that it has a spiritual meaning? Either, then, the apparent tone of passages of Scripture is not the real tone, or the Canticles is not a sacred book.

Again: is not the apparent tone of the Prophecies concerning Christ of a similarly twofold character, as is shown by the Jewish notion that there were to be two Messiahs, one suffering and one triumphant?

Another illustration which deserves attention, lies in the impression which David's history in the Books of Samuel conveys, compared with that derived from the Chronicles and the Psalms. I am not speaking of verbal discrepancies or difficulties to be reconciled,—the subject which I have already discussed,—but of the tone of the narrative, and the impression thence made upon the reader; and I think that it must be allowed that the idea which we have of David's character from the one document, is very different from that gained from the other two. In the Books of Samuel we have the picture of a monarch, bold, brave, generous, loyal, accomplished, attractive, and duly attached to the cause, and promoting the establishment, of the Mosaic law, but with apparently little permanent and consistent personal religion; his character is sullied with many sins, and clouded with many suspicions. But in the First Book of Chronicles, and in the Psalms, we are presented with the picture of a humble, tender, devotional, and deeply spiritual mind, detached from this world, and living on the thought and in the love of God. Is the impression derived from the New Testament more unfavourable to the Church system (admitting that it is unfavourable), than that of the Books of Samuel to David's personal holiness?

5.

I just now reserved the doctrine of the admission of the Gentiles into the Church, for separate consideration; let us now turn to it. Their call, certainly their equality with the Jews, was but covertly signified in our Lord's teaching. I think it is plainly there signified, though covertly; but, if covertly, then the state of the evidence for the Catholicity of the Christian Church will lie in the same disadvantage in the Gospels as the state of the evidence for its ritual character in the Epistles; and we may as well deny that the Church is Gentile, on the ground that our Lord but indirectly teaches it, as that it is sacramental on the ground that His Apostles indirectly teach it. It is objected that the Church system, the great Episcopal, Priestly, Sacramental system, was an after-thought, a corruption coming upon the simplicity of the primitive and Apostolic religion. The primitive religion, it is said was more simple. More simple! Did objectors never hear that there have been unbelievers who have written to prove that Christ's religion was more simple than St. Paul's—that St. Paul's Epistles are a second system coming upon the three Gospels and changing their doctrine? Have we never heard that some have considered the doctrine of our Lord's Divinity to be an addition upon the "simplicity" of the Gospels? Yes: this has been the belief not only of heretics, as the Socinians, but of infidels, such as the historian Gibbon, who looked at things with less of prejudice than heretics, as having no point to maintain. I think it will be found quite as easy to maintain that the Divinity of Christ was an after-thought, brought in by the Greek Platonists and other philosophers, upon the simple and primitive creed of the Galilean fishermen, as infidels say, as that the Sacramental system came in from the same source as rationalists say.—But to return to the point before us. Let it be considered whether a very plausible case might not be made out by way of proving that our Blessed Lord did not contemplate the evangelizing of the heathen at all, but that it was an after-thought, when His Apostles began to succeed, and their ambitious hopes to rise.

If texts from the Gospels are brought to show that it was no after-thought, such as the mustard-seed, or the labourers of the vineyard, which imply the calling and conversion of the Gentiles, and the implication contained in His discourse at Nazareth concerning the miracles of Elijah and Elisha wrought upon Gentiles, and His significant acts, such as His complying with the prayer of the Canaanitish woman, and His condescension towards the centurion, and, above all, His final command to go into all the world and preach the Gospel to every creature, " and to go teach all nations, baptizing them ;" still it may be asked, Did not the Apostles hear our Lord, and what was *their* impression from what they heard ? Is it not certain that the Apostles did not gather this command from His teaching ? So far is certain : and it is certain that none of us will deny that nevertheless that command comes from Him. Well then, it is plain, that important things may be in Scripture, yet not brought out : is there then any reason why *we* should be more clear-sighted as regards another point of doctrine, than the Apostles were as regards this ? I ask this again : Is there any reason that we, who have not heard Christ speak, should have a clearer apprehension of the meaning of His recorded discourses on a given point, than the Apostles who did ? and if it be said that we have now the gift of the Holy Spirit, which the Apostles had not during our Lord's earthly ministry, then I ask again, where is there any promise that we, as individuals, should be brought by His gracious influences into the perfect truth by merely employing ourselves on the text of Scripture by ourselves ? However, so far is plain, that a doctrine which we see to be plainly contained, nay necessarily presupposed, in our Lord's teaching, did not so impress itself on the Apostles.

These thoughts deserve consideration ; but what I was coming to in particular is this ; I wish you to turn in your mind such texts as the following : "Ye shall be witnesses unto Me both in Jerusalem and in all Judæa and in Samaria, and unto *the uttermost part of the earth.*" An objector would say that " the uttermost part of the earth" ought to be translated "uttermost part of the *land*"—that is, the Holy Land. And he would give this reason to confirm it. "How very unlikely that the whole of the world, except Judæa, should be *straitened up into one clause!* Jerusalem, Judæa, Samaria, mentioned distinctly, and the whole world brought under one word!" And I suppose the Apostles did at the time understand the sentence to mean only the Holy Land. Certainly they did not understand it to imply the absolute and immediate call of the Gentiles as mere Gentiles.

You will say that such texts as Luke xxiv. 47, are decisive: "that repentance and remission of sins should be preached in His Name *among all nations*, beginning at Jerusalem." Far from it; as men nowadays argue, they would say it was not *safe* to rely on such texts. *Among* all nations:" "*into* or *to* all nations," this need not mean more than that the Jews in those nations should be converted. The Jews were scattered about in those days; the Messiah was to collect them together. This text speaks of His doing so, according to the prophecies, wherever they were scattered. To this, the question of the populace relates, "Whither will He go that we shall not find Him? will He go unto the dispersed among the Gentiles, and teach the Gentiles"[*] or Greek Jews? And St. John's announcement also, that He died "not for that nation only, but that also He should gather together in one the children of God that were scattered abroad."[†] And St. Peter's address " to the strangers scattered throughout Pontus, Galatia, Cappadocia, Asia, and Bithynia." And especially on the day of Pentecost, when the same Apostle addressed the Jews, devout men dwelling at Jerusalem, out of every nation under heaven."[‡]

---

[*] John vi. 35. [†] Ib. xi. 51. 52. [‡] Acts ii. 5.

Again : if the words "preach the Gospel to every creature," were insisted on, an objector might say that creature or creation does not mean all men any more than it includes all animals or all Angels, but one part of the creation, the elect, the Jews.*

Here then are instances of that same concise and indirect mode of stating important doctrine in half sentences, or even words, which is supposed to be an objection to the peculiar Church doctrines only. For instance, it is objected that the sacred truth of the procession of the Holy Ghost from the Father, is only contained in the words, " the Spirit of Truth, which *proceedeth rom* the Father :"† the co-equality of the Son to the Father, in the phrase, "who being in the form of God, thought it not robbery *to be equal with* God," and in the Jews' inference from our Lord's words, " He said that God was His Father, making Himself equal with God."‡ The doctrine of original sin depends on a few implications such as this, " *As* in Adam all die, even so in Christ shall all be made alive." § And in like manner the necessity of the Holy Eucharist for salvation, upon the sixth chapter of St. John, in which the subject of Christ's flesh and blood is mentioned, but not a word expressly concerning that Sacrament, which as yet was future. So also, 1 Cor. x. 16, " The cup of blessing," etc., is almost a parenthesis : and the ministerial power of Absolution depends on our Lord's words to His Apostles, " Whosesoever sins ye remit," ‖ etc. ; and the doctrine of the Christian Altar, upon such words as, " If thou bring thy gift to the Altar," etc.   Now I say all these are paralleled by the mode in which our Lord taught the call of the Gentiles : He said, " Preach the Gospel to every crea-

* *Vide* Rom. viii. 19.   § 1 Cor. xv. 22.
† John xv. 26.   ‖ John xx. 23.
‡ Philip. ii. 6 ; John v. 18.

ture." These words need have only meant, "Bring all men to Christianity through Judaism:" make them Jews, that they may enjoy Christ's privileges, which are lodged in Judaism; teach them those rites and ceremonies, circumcision and the like, which hereto have been dead ordinances, and now are living: and so the Apostles seem to have understood them. Yet they meant much more than this; that Jews were to have no precedence of the Gentiles, but the one and the other to be on a level. It is quite plain that our Saviour must have had this truth before His mind, if we may so speak, when He said, "Preach to every creature." Yet the words did not on the surface mean all this. As then they meant more than they need have been taken to mean, so the words, "I am with you alway," or, "Receive ye the Holy Ghost," may mean much more than they need mean; and the early Church may, in God's providence, be as really intended to bring out and settle the meaning of the latter, as St. Peter at Joppa, and St. Paul on his journeys, to bring out the meaning of the former.

To this there are other parallels. For instance: who would have conceived that the doctrine of the Resurrection of the Dead lay hid in the words, "I am the God of Abraham," etc.? Why may not the doctrines concerning the Church lie hid in repositories which certainly are less recondite? Why may not the Church herself, who is called the pillar and ground of the Truth, be the appointed interpreter of the doctrines about herself?

Again: consider how much is contained, and how covertly, in our Saviour's words, "But ye are clean, but not all;"—or in His riding on an ass, and not saying why; or in His saying "Destroy this Temple," when "He spoke of the Temple of His Body." Let it be borne in mind, that a figurative, or, what may be called a sacramental style, was the very characteristic of oriental teaching ; so that it would have been a wilful disrespect in any hearer who took the words of a great prophet in their mere literal and outside sense.

Here, too, the whole subject of prophecy might be brought in. What doctrine is more important than that of the miraculous conception of our Lord ? Yet how is it declared in prophecy ? Isaiah said to Ahaz, " Behold, a Virgin shall conceive, and bear a Son, and shall call His Name Immanuel." The first meaning of these words seems not at all to allude to Christ, but to an event of the day. The great Gospel doctrine is glanced at (as we may say) through this minor event.

6.

These remarks surely suffice on this subject, viz., to show that the impression we gain from Scripture need not be any criterion or any measure of its true and full sense ; that solemn and important truths may be silently taken for granted, or alluded to in a half sentence, or spoken of indeed, yet in such unadorned language that we may fancy we see through it, and see nothing ;—peculiarities of Scripture which result from what is the peculiar character of its teaching, simplicity and depth. Yet even without taking into account these peculiarities, it is obvious, from what meets us daily in the course of life, how insufficient a test is the surface of any one composition, conversation, or transaction, of the full circle of opinions of its author. How different persons are, when we know them, from what they appeared to us in their writings ! how many opinions do they hold, which we did not expect in them ! how many practices and ways have they, how many peculiarities, how many tastes, which we did not imagine! I will give an illustration ;—that great philosopher, Bp. Butler, has written a book, as we know, on the Analogy of Religion. It is distinguished by a grave, profound, and severe style; and apparently is not the work of a man of lively or susceptible mind. Now we know from his history, that, when Bishop, he put up a Cross in his chapel at Bristol. Could a reader have conjectured this from that work? At first sight would it not have startled one who knew nothing of him but from that work? I do not ask whether, on consideration, he would not find it fell in with his work; of course it would, if his philosophy were consistent with itself ; but certainly it is not on the surface of his work. Now might not we say that his work contained the *whole* of his philosophy, and yet say that the use of the Cross was one of his *usages*? In like manner we may say that the Bible is the *whole* of the Divine Revelation, and yet the use of the Cross a divine usage.

But this is not all. Some small private books of his are extant, containing a number of every-day matters, such as of course one could not expect to be able to conjecture from his great work ; I mean, matters of ordinary and almost household life. Yet those who have seen these papers are likely to feel a surprise that they should be Butler's. I do not say that they can give any reason why they should not be so; but the notion we form of any one whom we have not seen, will ever be in its details very different from the true one.

Another series of illustrations might be drawn from the writings of the ancients. Those who are acquainted with the Greek historians know well that they, and particularly the gravest and severest of them, relate events so simply, calmly, unostentatiously, that an ordinary reader does not recognize what events are great and

what little; and on turning to some modern history
in which they are commented on, will find to his surprise that a battle or a treaty, which was despatched in
half a line by the Greek author, is perhaps the turning-
point of the whole history, and was certainly known by
him to be so. Here is the case of the gospels, with
this difference, that they are unsystematic compositions,
whereas the Greek historians profess to be methodical.

Again : instances might easily be given of the silence
of contemporary writers, Greek or Roman, as to great
events of their time, when they might be expected to
notice them; a silence which has even been objected
against the fact of those events having occurred, yet, in
the judgment of the mass of well-informed men, without
any real cogency.

Again : as to Greek poetry, philosophy, and oratory,
how severe and unexceptionable is it for the most part;
yet how impure and disgraceful was the Greek daily
life ! Who shows a more sober and refined majesty
than Sophocles ? yet to him Pericles addressed the
rebuke recorded in the first book of Cicero's Offices.*

7.

I conclude with two additional remarks. I have been
arguing that Scripture is a deep book, and that the peculiar doctrines concerning the Church, contained in the
Prayer Book, are in its depths. Now let it be remarked
in corroboration, first, that the early Church always did
consider Scripture to be what I have been arguing that
it is from its structure,—viz., a book with very recondite
meanings; this they considered, not merely with reference to its teaching the particular class of doctrines in
question, but as regards its entire teaching. They con-

* i. 40.

sidered that it was full of mysteries. Therefore, saying that Scripture has deep meanings, is not an hypothesis invented to meet this particular difficulty, that the Church doctrines are not on its surface, but is an acknowledged principle of interpretation independent of it.

Secondly, it is also certain that the early Church did herself conceal these same Church doctrines. I am not determining whether or not all her writers did so, or all her teachers, or at all times, but merely that, viewing that early period as a whole, there is on the whole a great secrecy observed in it concerning such doctrines (for instance) as the Trinity and the Eucharist ; that is, the early Church did the very thing which I have been supposing Scripture does,—conceal high truths. To suppose that Scripture conceals them, is not an hypothesis invented to meet the difficulty arising from the fact that they are not on the surface; for the early Church, independent of that alleged difficulty, did herself in her own teaching conceal them. This is a second very curious coincidence. If the early Church had reasons for concealment, it may be that Scripture has the same ; especially if we suppose,—what at the very least is no very improbable idea,—that the system of the early Church is a continuation of the system of those inspired men who wrote the New Testament,

6.

External Difficulties of the Canon and the Catholic Creed, compared.

I AM now proceeding to a subject which will in some little degree take me beyond the bounds which I had proposed to myself when I began, but which, being closely connected with that subject, and (as I think) important, has a claim on our attention. The argument which has been last engaging us is this : Objection is made to the indirectness of the evidence from Scripture on which the peculiar Church doctrines are proved ;—I have answered, that sacred *history* is for the most part marked by as much apparent inconsistency, as recorded in one part of Scripture and another, as there is inconsistency as regards *doctrine* in the respective informations of Scripture and the Church ; one event being told us here, another there ; so that we have to compare, compile, reconcile, adjust. As then we do not complain of the history being conveyed in distinct, and at times conflicting, documents, so too we have no fair reason for complaining of the obscurities and intricacies under which doctrine is revealed through its two channels.

I then went on to answer in a similar way the objection, that Scripture was contrary to the teaching of the Church (*i. e.*, to our Prayer Book), not only in specific statements, but in tone ; for I showed that what we call the tone of Scripture, or the impression it makes on the reader, varies so very much according to the reader, that little stress can be laid upon it, and that its tone and the impression it makes would tell against a variety of other points undeniably true and firmly held by us, quite as much as against the peculiar Church doctrines.

In a word, it is as easy to show that Scripture has no contents at all, or next to none, as that it does not contain the special Church doctrines—I mean, the objection which is brought against the Apostolical Succession or the Priesthood being in Scripture, tells against the instruction and information conveyed in Scripture generally. But now I am going to a further point, which has been incidentally touched on, that this same objection is prejudicial not only to the Revelation, whatever it is, contained in Scripture, but to the text of Scripture itself, to the books of Scripture, to their canonicity, to their authority. I have said, the line of reasoning entered on in this objection may be carried forward, and, if it reaches one point, may be made to reach others also. For, first, if the want of method and verbal consistency in Scripture be an objection to the "teaching of the Prayer Book," it is also an objection equally to what is called "Orthodox Protestantism." Further, I have shown that it tells also against the trustworthiness of the sacred history, to the statement of facts contained in any part of Scripture, which is in great measure indirect. And now, lastly, I shall show that it is an objection to the Bible itself, both because that Book cannot be a Revelation which contains neither definite doctrine nor unequivocal matter of fact, and next because the evidence, on which its portions are received, is not clearer or fuller than its own evidence for the facts and doctrines which our Article says it "contains." This is the legitimate consequence of the attempt to invalidate the scripturalness of Catholic doctrine, on the allegation of its want of Scripture proof—an invalidating of Scripture itself; this is the conclusion to which both the argument itself, and the temper of mind which belongs to it, will assuredly lead those who use it, at least in the long run.

There is another objection which is sometimes attempted against Church doctrines, which may be met in the same way. It is sometimes strangely maintained, not only that Scripture does not clearly teach them, but that the Fathers do not clearly teach them; that nothing can be drawn for certain from the Fathers; that their evidence leaves matters pretty much as it found them, as being inconsistent with itself, or of doubtful authority. This part of the subject has not yet been considered, and will come into prominence as we proceed with the present argument.

I purpose, then, now to enlarge on this point; that is, to show that those who object to Church doctrines, whether from deficiency of Scripture proof or of Patristical proof, ought, if they acted consistently on their principles, to object to the canonicity and authority of Scripture; a melancholy truth, if it be a truth; and I fear it is but too true. Too true, I fear, it is *in fact*,— not only that men ought, if consistent, to proceed from opposing Church doctrine to oppose the authority of Scripture, but that the leaven which at present makes the mind oppose Church doctrine, *does* set it, or *will* soon set it, against Scripture. I wish to declare what I think will be found really to be the case, viz., that a battle for the Canon of Scripture is but the next step after a battle for the Creed,—that the Creed comes first in the assault, that is all; and that if we were not defending the Creed, we should at this moment be defending the Canon. Nay, I would predict as a coming event, that minds *are to be* unsettled as to what is Scripture and what is not; and I predict it that, as far as the voice of one person in one place can do, I may defeat my own prediction by making it. Now to consider the subject.

I.

How do we know that the whole Bible is the word of God? Happily at present we are content to believe this, because we have been so taught. It is our great blessedness to receive it on faith. A believing spirit is in all cases a more blessed spirit than an unbelieving. The testimony of unbelievers declares it: they often say, " I wish I *could* believe; I should be happier, if I could; but my *reason* is unconvinced." And then they go on to speak as if they were in a more exalted, though less happy state of mind. Now I am not here to enter into the question of the grounds on which the duty and blessedness of believing rest; but I would observe, that Nature certainly does give sentence against scepticism, against doubt, nay, against a habit (I say a *habit*) of inquiry, against a critical, cold, investigating temper, the temper of what are called shrewd, clear-headed, hard-headed, men, in that, by the confession of all, happiness is attached, not to *their* temper, but rather to confiding, unreasoning faith. I do not say that inquiry may not under circumstances be a duty, as going into the cold and rain may be a duty, instead of stopping at home,— as serving in war may be a duty; but it does seem to me preposterous to confess, that free inquiry leads to scepticism, and scepticism makes one less happy than faith, and yet, that such free inquiry is a merit. What is right and what is happy cannot in the long run and on a large scale be disjoined. To follow after truth can never be a subject of regret; free inquiry does lead a man to regret the days of his childlike faith ; therefore it is not following after truth. Those who measure everything by utility, should on their own principles embrace the obedience of faith for its very expedience; and they should cease this kind of seeking, which begins in doubt.

I say, then, that never to have been troubled with a doubt about the truth of what has been taught us, is the happiest state of mind ; and if any one says, that to maintain this is to admit that heretics ought to remain heretics, and pagans pagans, I deny it. For I have not said that it is a happy thing never to *add* to what you have, but that it is not happier to *take away*. Now true religion is the summit and perfection of false religions : it combines in one whatever there is of good and true, severally remaining in each. And in like manner the Catholic Creed is for the most part the combination of separate truths which heretics have divided among themselves, and err in dividing. So that, in matter of fact, if a religious mind were educated in and sincerely attached to some form of heathenism or heresy, and then were brought under the light of truth, it would be drawn off from error into the truth, not by losing what it had, but by gaining what it had not,—not by being unclothed, but by being "clothed upon," "that mortality may be swallowed up of life." That same principle of faith which attaches it to its original human teaching, would attach it to the truth ; and that portion of its original teaching which was to be cast off as absolutely false, would not be directly rejected, but indirectly rejected *in* the reception of the truth which is its opposite. True conversion is of a positive, not a negative character. This was St. Paul's method of controversy at Athens ; and, if Apologists after him were wont to ridicule the heathen idolatries, it must be considered that belief in the popular mythology was then dying out, and was ridiculed by the people themselves.

All this is a digression : but before returning to my subject, I will just add, that it must not be supposed from my expressing such sentiments, that I have any fear of argument for the cause of Christian truth, as if reason were dangerous to it, as if it could not stand before a scrutinizing inquiry. Nothing is more out of place, though it is too common, than such a charge against the defenders of Church doctrines. They may be right or they may be wrong in their arguments, but argue they do ; they are ready to argue ; they believe they have reason on their side ; but they remind others, they remind themselves, that though argument on the whole will but advance the cause of truth, though so far from dreading it, they are conscious it is a great weapon in their hands ; yet that, after all, if a man does nothing more than argue, if he has nothing deeper at bottom, if he does not seek God by some truer means, by obedience, by faith prior to demonstration, he will either not attain truth, or attain a shallow, unreal view of it, and have a weak grasp of it. Reason will prepare for the reception, will spread the news, and secure the outward recognition of the truth ; but in all we do we ought to seek edification, not mere knowledge. Now to return.

I say, it is our blessedness, if we have no doubts about the Canon of Scripture, as it is our blessedness to have no doubts about the Catholic Creed. And this *is* at present actually our blessedness as regards the Canon ; we have no doubts. Even those persons who unhappily have doubts about the Church system, have no doubts about the Canon,—by a happy inconsistency, *I* say. They ought to have doubts on their principles ; this I shall now show, in the confidence that their belief in the

Canon is so much stronger than their disbelief of the Church system, that if they must change their position, they will rather go on and believe the Church system, than go back to disbelieve the Canon.

2.

Now there are two chief heads of objection made against the Catholic or Church system of doctrine and worship,— external and internal.   It is said, on the one hand, to be uncertain, not only what is in Scripture, but what is in Antiquity, and what not ; for the early Fathers, it is objected, who are supposed to convey the information, contradict each other ; and the most valuable and voluminous of them did not live till two or three hundred years after St. John's death, while the earlier records are scanty ; and moreover that their view of doctrine was from the first corrupted from assignable external sources, pagan, philosophical, or Jewish.   And on the other hand, the system itself may be accused of being contrary to reason and incredible.   Here I shall consider the former of these two objections.

Objectors, then, speak thus : " We are far from denying," they say, " that there is truth and value in the ancient Catholic system, as reported by the Fathers ; but we deny that it is *unmixed* truth.   We consider it is truth and error mixed together : we do not see why the system of doctrine must be taken together as a whole, so that if one part is true, all is true.   We consider that we have a right to take it piecemeal, and examine each part by itself ; that so far as it is true, it is true not as belonging to the ancient system, but for other reasons, as being agreeable to our reason, or to our understanding of Scripture, not because stated by the Fathers ; and, after all, the Church system in question (that is, such doctrines as the mystical power of the Sacraments, the power of the keys, the grace of Ordination, the gifts of the Church, and the Apostolical Succession), has very little authority really primitive. The Fathers whose works we have, not only ought to be of an earlier date, in order to be of authority, but they contradict each other; they declare what is incredible and absurd, and what can reasonably be ascribed to Platonism, or Judaism, or Paganism."

Be it so : well, how will the same captious spirit treat the sacred Canon ? in just the same way. It will begin thus :—" These many writings are put together in one book ; what makes them one ? who put them together ? the printer. The books of Scripture have been printed together for many centuries. But that does not make them one ; what authority had those who put them together to do so ? what authority to put just so many books, neither more nor less ? when were they first so put together ? on what authority do we leave out the Wisdom, or the Son of Sirach, and insert the book of Esther ? Catalogues certainly are given of these books in early times : but not exactly the same books are enumerated in all. The language of St. Austin is favourable to the admission of the Apocrypha.* The Latin Church anciently left out the Epistle to the Hebrews, and the Eastern Church left out the book of Revelation. This so-called Canon did not exist at earliest till the fourth century, between two and three hundred years after St. John's death. Let us then see into the matter with our own eyes. Why should not we be as good judges as the Church of the fourth century, on whose authority we receive it ? Why should one book be divine, because another is ? " This is what objectors would say. Now to follow them into particulars

* De Doctr. Christ., ii. 13.

as far as the first head; viz., as to the evidence itself, which is offered in behalf of the divinity and inspiration of the separate books.

For instance; the first Father who expressly mentions Commemorations for the Dead in Christ (such as we still have in substance at the end of the prayer for the Church Militant, where it was happily restored in 1662, having been omitted a century earlier), is Tertullian, about a hundred years after St. John's death. This, it is said, is not authority early enough to prove that that Ordinance is Apostolical, though succeeding Fathers, Origen, St. Cyprian, Eusebius, St. Cyril of Jerusalem, etc., bear witness to it ever so strongly. "Errors might have crept in by that time; mistakes might have been made; Tertullian is but one man, and confessedly not sound in many of his opinions; we ought to have clearer and more decisive evidence." Well, supposing it : suppose Tertullian, a hundred years after St. John, is the first that mentions it, yet Tertullian is also the first who refers to St. Paul's Epistle to Philemon, and even he without quoting or naming it. He is followed by two writers; one of Rome, Caius, whose work is not extant, but is referred to by Eusebius, who, speaking of *thirteen* Epistles of St. Paul, and as excluding the Hebrews, by implication includes that to Philemon ; and the other, Origen, who quotes the fourteenth verse of the Epistle, and elsewhere speaks of *fourteen* Epistles of St. Paul. Next, at the end of the third century, follows Eusebius. Further, St. Jerome observes, that in his time some persons doubted whether it was St. Paul's (just as Aerius about that time questioned the Commemorations for the Dead), or at least whether it was canonical, and that from internal evidence ; to which he opposes the general consent of external testimony as a sufficient answer. Now, I ask, why do we receive the Epistle to Philemon as St. Paul's, and not the Commemorations for the faithful departed as Apostolical also? Ever after indeed the date of St. Jerome, the Epistle to Philemon was accounted St. Paul's, and so too ever after the same date the Commemorations which I have spoken of are acknowledged on all hands to have been observed as a religious duty, down to three hundred years ago. If it be said that from historical records we have good reasons for thinking that the Epistle of St. Paul to Philemon, with his other Epistles, was read from time immemorial in Church, which is a witness independent of particular testimonies in the Fathers, I answer, no evidence can be more satisfactory and conclusive to a well-judging mind ; but then it is a moral evidence, resting on very little formal and producible proof ; and quite as much evidence can be given for the solemn Commemorations of the Dead in the Holy Eucharist which I speak of. They too were in use in the Church from time immemorial. Persons, then, who have the heart to give up and annul the Ordinance, will not, if they are consistent, scruple much at the Epistle. If in the sixteenth century the innovators on religion had struck the Epistle to Philemon out of Scripture, they would have had just as much right to do it as to abolish these Commemorations ; and those who wished to defend such innovation as regards the Epistle to Philemon, would have had just as much to say in its behalf as those had who put an end to the Commemorations.

If it be said they found nothing on the subject of such Commemorations in Scripture, even granting this for argument's sake, yet I wonder where they found in Scripture that the Epistle to Philemon was written by St. Paul, except indeed in the Epistle itself. Nowhere ; yet they kept the one, they abolished the other—as far, that is, as human tyranny could abolish it. Let us be thankful that they did not also say, "The Epistle to Philemon is of a private nature, and has no marks of inspiration about it. It is not mentioned by name or quoted by any writer till Origen, who flourished at a time when mistakes had begun, in the third century, and who actually thinks St. Barnabas wrote the Epistle which goes under his name ; and he too, after all, just mentions it once, but not as inspired or canonical, and also just happens to speak elsewhere of St. Paul's fourteen Epistles. In the beginning of the fourth century, Eusebius, without anywhere naming this Epistle," (as far as I can discover,) "also speaks of fourteen Epistles, and speaks of a writer one hundred years earlier, who in like manner enumerated thirteen besides the Hebrews. All this is very unsatisfactory. We will have nothing but the pure word of God ; we will only admit what has the clearest proof. It is impossible that God should require us to believe a book to come from Him without authenticating it with the highest and most cogent evidence."

Again : the early Church with one voice testifies in favour of Episcopacy, as an ordinance especially pleasing to God. Ignatius, the very disciple of the Apostles, speaks in the clearest and strongest terms ; and those who follow fully corroborate his statements for three or four hundred years. And besides this, we know the fact, that a succession of Bishops from the Apostles did exist in all the Churches all that time. At the end of that time, one Father, St. Jerome, in writing controversially, had some strong expressions against the divine origin of the ordinance. And this is all that can be said in favour of any other regimen. Now, on the other hand, what is the case as regards the Epistle to the Hebrews ? Though received in the East, it was not received in the Latin Churches, till that same St. Jerome's time. St. Irenæus either does not affirm or actually denies that it is St. Paul's. Tertullian ascribes it to St. Barnabas. Caius excluded it from his list. St. Hippolytus does not receive it. St. Cyprian is silent about it. It is doubtful whether St. Optatus received it. Now, that this important Epistle is part of the inspired word of God, there is no doubt. But why? Because the testimony of the fourth and fifth centuries, when Christians were at leisure to examine the question thoroughly, is altogether in its favour. I know of no other reason, and I consider this to be quite sufficient: but with what consistency do persons receive this Epistle as inspired, yet deny that Episcopacy is a divinely ordained means of grace?

Again: the Epistles to the Thessalonians are quoted by six writers in the first two hundred years from St. John's death; first, at the end of the first hundred, by three Fathers, Irenæus, Clement, and Tertullian; and are by implication acknowledged in the lost work of Caius, at the same time, and are in Origen's list some years after. On the other hand, the Lord's table is always called an Altar, and is called a Table only in one single passage of a single Father, during the first three centuries. It is called Altar in four out of the seven Epistles of St. Ignatius. It is called Altar by St. Clement of Rome, by St. Irenæus, Tertullian, St. Cyprian, Origen, Eusebius, St. Athanasius, St. Ambrose, St. Gregory Nazianzen, St. Optatus, St. Jerome, St. Chrysostom, and St. Austin.* It is once called Table by St. Diony-

---

* It is perhaps unnecessary to say that the sense of the word Altar (θυσια- στήριον) in some of these passages has been contested; as it has been contested whether the Fathers' works are genuine, or the Books of Scripture genuine, or its text free from interpolations. There is no one spot in the

sius of Alexandria. (Johnson's U. S., vol. i., p. 306.) I
do not know on what ground we admit the Epistles to
the Thessalonians to be the writing of St. Paul, yet deny
that the use of Altars is Apostolic.

Again : that the Eucharist is a Sacrifice is declared or
implied by St. Clement of Rome, St. Paul's companion,
by St. Justin, by St. Irenæus, by Tertullian, by St.
Cyprian, and others. On the other hand, the Acts of
the Apostles are perhaps alluded to by St. Polycarp, but
are first distinctly noticed by St. Irenæus, then by three
writers who came soon after (St. Clement of Alexandria,
Tertullian, and the Letter from the Church of Lyons),
and then not till the end of the two hundred years from
St. John's death. Which has the best evidence, the Book
of Acts, or the doctrine of the Eucharistic Sacrifice?

Again : much stress, as I have said, is laid by objectors
on the fact that there is so little evidence concerning
Catholic doctrine in the very first years of Christianity.
Now, how does this objection stand, as regards the Canon
of the New Testament ? The New Testament consists of
twenty-seven books in all, though of varying importance. Of these, fourteen are not mentioned at all till
from eighty to one hundred years after St. John's death,
in which number are the Acts, the Second to the Corinthians, the Galatians, the Colossians, the Two to the

territory of theology but has been the scene of a battle. Anything has been
ventured and believed in the heat of controversy ; but the ultimate appeal
in such cases is the common sense of mankind. Ignatius says, " Be diligent
to use one Eucharist, for there is one Flesh of our Lord Jesus Christ, and
one cup for the union of His Blood ; one Altar, as one Bishop, together
with the Presbytery and deacons, my fellow-servants."—*Ad Phil.* 4. Would
it have entered into any one's mind, were it not for the necessities of his
theory, to take Eucharist, Flesh, Cup, Blood, Bishop, Presbytery, Deacon,
in their ecclesiastical meaning, as belonging to the Visible Church, and the
one word Altar figuratively ?

Thessalonians, and St. James. Of the other thirteen, five, viz., St. John's Gospel, the Philippians, the First of Timothy, the Hebrews, and the First of John, are quoted but by one writer during the same period. Lastly, St. Irenæus, at the close of the second century, quotes all the books of the New Testament but five, and deservedly stands very high as a witness. Now, why may not so learned and holy a man, and so close on the Apostles, stand also as a witness of some doctrines which he takes for granted, as the invisible but real Presence in the Holy Eucharist, the use of Catholic tradition in ascertaining revealed truth, and the powers committed to the Church ?

If men then will indulge that eclectic spirit which chooses part and rejects part of the primitive Church system, I do not see what is to keep them from choosing part and rejecting part of the Canon of Scripture.

3.

There are books, which sin as it would be in us to reject, I think any candid person would grant are presented to us under circumstances less promising than those which attend upon the Church doctrines. Take, for instance, the Book of Esther. This book is not quoted once in the New Testament. It was not admitted as canonical by two considerable Fathers, Melito and Gregory Nazianzen. It contains no prophecy ; it has nothing on the surface to distinguish it from a mere ordinary history ; nay, it has no mark on the surface of its even being a religious history. Not once does it mention the name of God or Lord, or any other name by which the God of Israel is designated. Again, when we inspect its contents, it cannot be denied that there are things in it which at first sight startle us, and make de-

* *

14

mands on our faith. Why then do we receive it? Because we have good reason from tradition to believe it to be one of those which our Lord intended, when He spoke of " the prophets." *

In like manner the Book of Ecclesiastes contains no prophecy, is referred to in no part of the New Testament, and contains passages which at first sight are startling. Again : that most sacred Book, called the Song of Songs, or Canticles, is a continued type from beginning to end. Nowhere in Scripture, as I have already observed, are we told that it is a type ; nowhere is it hinted that it is not to be understood literally. Yet it is only as having a deeper and hidden sense, that we are accustomed to see a religious purpose in it. Moreover, it is not quoted or alluded to once all through the New Testament. It contains no prophecies. Why do we consider it divine? For the same reason ; because tradition informs us that in our Saviour's time it was included under the title of " the Psalms" : and our Saviour, in St. Luke's Gospel, refers to "the Law, the Prophets, and *the Psalms.*"

Objections as plausible, though different, might be urged against the Epistles of St. James, St. Jude, the Second of St. Peter, the Second and Third of St. John, and the Book of Revelation.

Again : we are told that the doctrine of the mystical efficacy of the Sacraments comes from the Platonic philosophers, the ritual from the Pagans, and the Church polity from the Jews. So they do ; that is, in a sense in which much more also comes from the same sources. Traces also of the doctrines of the Trinity, Incarnation, and Atonement, may be found among heathens, Jews, and philosophers; for the Almighty scattered through the world, before His Son came, vestiges and gleams of His

* Luke xxiv. 44.

true Religion, and collected all the separated rays
together, when He set Him on His holy hill to rule the
day, and the Church, as the moon, to govern the night.
In the sense in which the doctrine of the Trinity is
Platonic, doubtless the doctrine of mysteries generally is
Platonic also. But this by the way. What I have here
to notice is, that the same supposed objection can be
and has been made against the books of Scripture too
viz., that they borrow from external sources. Unbelievers
have accused Moses of borrowing his law from the
Egyptians or other Pagans ; and elaborate comparisons
have been instituted, on the part of believers also, by
way of proving it ; though even if proved, and so far as
proved, it would show nothing more than this,—that God,
who gave His law to Israel absolutely and openly, had
already given some portions of it to the heathen.

Again : an infidel historian accuses St. John of borrowing the doctrine of the Eternal Logos or Word from
the Alexandrian Platonists.

Again : a theory has been advocated,—by whom I
will not say,—to the effect that the doctrine of apostate
angels, Satan and his hosts, was a Babylonian tenet,
introduced into the Old Testament after the Jews' return
from the Captivity ; that no allusion is made to Satan,
as the head of the malignant angels, and as having set
up a kingdom for himself against God, in any book
written before the Captivity ; from which circumstance
it may easily be made to follow, that those books of the
Old Testament which were written after the Captivity
are not plenarily inspired, and not to be trusted as canonical. Now, I own I am not at all solicitous to deny
that this doctrine of an apostate Angel and his host was
gained from Babylon : it might still be divine, nevertheless. God who made the prophet's ass speak, and there-

by instructed the prophet, might instruct His Church by means of heathen Babylon. *

In like manner, is no lesson intended to be conveyed to us by the remarkable words of the governor of the feast, upon the miracle of the water changed to wine? " Every man at the beginning doth set forth good wine, and when men have well drunk, then that which is worse; but Thou hast kept the good wine until now." † Yet at first sight they have not a very serious meaning. It does not therefore seem to me difficult, nay, nor even unlikely, that the prophets of Israel should, in the course of God's providence, have gained new truths from the heathen, among whom those truths lay corrupted. The Church of God in every age has been, as it were, on visitation through the earth, surveying, judging, sifting, selecting, and refining all matters of thoughts and practice; detecting what was precious amid what is ruined and refuse, and putting her seal upon it. There is no reason, then, why Daniel and Zechariah should not have been taught by the instrumentality of the Chaldeans. However, this is insisted on, and as if to the disparagement of the Jewish Dispensation by some persons; and under the notion that its system was not only enlarged but altered at the era of the Captivity. And I certainly think it may be insisted on as plausibly as pagan customs are brought to illustrate and thereby to invalidate the ordinances of the Catholic Church; though the proper explanation in the two cases is not exactly the same.

The objection I have mentioned is applied, in the quarter to which I allude, to the Books of Chronicles. These, it has already been observed, have before now been ascribed by sceptics to (what is called) priestly influence: here then is a second exceptional influence, a

* [This principle seems here too broadly enunciated.]   † John ii. 10.

second superstition. In the Second Book of Samuel it is said, "the anger of the Lord was kindled against Israel : and He moved David against them to say, Go, number Israel and Judah." * On the other hand, in Chronicles it is said, "*Satan* stood up against Israel, and provoked David to number Israel."† On this a writer, not of the English Church, says, "The author of the Book of Chronicles . . . *availing himself* of the learning which he had acquired in the East, and *influenced* by a suitable tenderness for the harmony of the Divine Attributes, refers the act of temptation to the malignity of the evil principle." You see in this way a blow is also struck against the more ancient parts of the Old Testament, as well as the more modern. The books written before the Captivity are represented, as the whole discussion would show, as containing a ruder, simpler, less artificial theology ; those after the Captivity, a more learned and refined : God's inspiration is excluded in both cases.

The same consideration has been applied to determine the date and importance of the Book of Job, which has been considered, from various circumstances, external and internal, not to contain a real history, but an Eastern story.

But enough has been said on this part of the subject.

4.

It seems, then, that the objections which can be made to the evidence for the Church doctrines are such as also lie against the Canon of Scripture ; so that if they avail against the one, they avail against both. If they avail against both, we are brought to this strange conclusion, that God has given us a Revelation, yet has revealed

* 2 Sam. xxxiv. 1. † 1 Chron. xxi. 1.

nothing,—that at great cost, and with much preparation, He has miraculously declared His will, that multitudes have accordingly considered they possessed it, yet that, after all, He has said nothing so clearly as to recommend itself as His to a cautious mind ; that nothing is so revealed as to be an essential part of the Revelation nothing plain enough to act upon, nothing so certain that we dare assert that the contrary is very much less certain.

Such a conclusion is a practical refutation of the objection which leads to it. It surely cannot be meant that we should be undecided all our days. We were made for action, and for right action,—for thought, and for true thought. Let us live while we live ; let us be alive and doing ; let us act on what we have, since we have not what we wish. Let us believe what we do not see and know. Let us forestall knowledge by faith. Let us maintain before we have demonstrated. This seeming paradox is the secret of happiness. Why should we be unwilling to go by faith ? We do all things in this world by faith in the word of others. By faith only we know our position in the world, our circumstances, our rights and privileges, our fortunes, our parents, our brothers and sisters, our age, our mortality. Why should Religion be an exception ? Why should we be unwilling to use for heavenly objects what we daily use for earthly ? Why will we not discern, what it is so much our interest to discern, that trust, in the first instance, in what Providence sets before us in religious matters, is His will and our duty ; that thus it is He leads us into all truth, not by doubting, but by believing ; that thus He speaks to us, by the instrumentality of what seems accidental ; that He sanctifies what He sets before us, shallow or weak as it may be in itself, for His high purposes ; that most systems have enough of truth in them, to make it better for us, when we have no choice besides, and cannot discriminate, to begin by taking all (that is not plainly immoral) than by rejecting all; that He will not deceive us if we thus trust in Him. Though the received system of religion in which we are born were as unsafe as the sea when St. Peter began to walk on it, yet " be not afraid." He who could make St. Peter walk the waves, could make even a corrupt or defective creed a mode and way of leading us into truth, even were ours such; much more can He teach us by the witness of the Church Catholic. It is far more probable that her witness should be true, whether about the Canon or the Creed, than that God should have left us without any witness at all.

7.

Internal Difficulties of the Canon and the Catholic Creed, compared.

I SHALL now finish the subject I have commenced, the parallel between the objections adducible against the Catholic system, and those against the Canon of Scripture. It will be easily understood, that I am not attempting any formal and full discussion of the subject, but offering under various general heads such suggestions as may be followed out by those who will. The objections to the evidence for the Canon have been noticed; now let us consider objections that may be made to its contents.

I.

Perhaps the main objection taken to the Church system, is the dislike which men feel of its doctrines. They call them the work of priestcraft, and in that word is summed up all that they hate in them. Priestcraft is the art of gaining power over men by appeals to their consciences; its instrument is mystery; its subject-matter, superstitious feeling. "Now the Church doctrines," it is urged, "invest a certain number of indifferent things with a new and extraordinary power, beyond sense, beyond reason, beyond nature, a power over the soul; and they put the exclusive possessions and use of the things thus distinguished into the hands of the Clergy. Such, for instance, is the Creed; some mysterious benefit is supposed to result from holding it, even though with but a partial comprehension, and the Clergy are practically its sole expounders. Such still more are the Sacraments, which the Clergy only administer, and which are supposed to effect some supernatural change in the soul, and to convey some supernatural gift." This then is the antecedent exception taken against the Catholic doctrines, that they are mysterious, tending to superstition, and to dependence on a particular set of men. And this object is urged, not merely as a reason for demanding fair proof of what is advanced, but as a reason for refusing to listen to any proof whatever, as if it fairly created an insurmountable presumption against the said doctrines.

Now I say, in like manner, were it not for our happy reverence for the Canon of Scripture, we should take like exception to many things in Scripture ; and, since we do not, neither ought we, consistently, to take this exception to the Catholic system ; but if we do take such grounds against that system, there is nothing but the strength of habit, good feeling, and our Lord's controlling grace, to keep us from using them against Scripture also. This I shall now attempt to show, and with that view, shall cite various passages in Scripture which, to most men of this generation, will appear at first sight strange, superstitious, incredible, and extreme. If then, in spite of these, Scripture is nevertheless from God, so again, in spite of similar apparent difficulties, the Catholic system may be from Him also ; and what the argument comes to is this, that the minds of none of us are in such a true state, as to warrant us in judging peremptorily in every case what is from God and what is not. We shrink from the utterances of His providence with offence, as if they were not His, in consequence of our inward ears being attuned to false harmonies. Now for some instances of what I mean.

2.

1. I conceive, were we not used to the Scripture narrative, that we should be startled at the accounts there given us of demoniacs.—For instance : "And He asked him, What is thy name ? And He answered, *My name is Legion*, for we are many."*—Again, consider the passage, "When the unclean spirit is gone out of a man, he walketh through dry places, seeking rest, and findeth none," † etc. ; and in like manner, the account of the damsel who was "possessed of a spirit of divination," or "Python," that is, of a heathen god, in Acts xvi. ; and in connexion with this, St. Paul's assertion "that the things which the Gentiles sacrifice, they sacrifice to devils and not to God,"‡ and this as being so literally true that he deduces a practical conclusion from it, "I would not that ye should have fellowship with devils." But, as regards this instance, we are not at all driven to conjecture, but we know it is really the case, that they who allow themselves to treat the inspired text freely, do at once explain away, or refuse to admit its accounts of this mysterious interference of evil spirits in the affairs of men. Let those then see to it, who call the Fathers credulous for recording similar narratives. If they find fault with the evidence, that is an intelligible objection ; but the common way with objectors is at once and before examination to charge on the narrators of such accounts childish superstition and credulity.

2. If we were not used to the narrative, I conceive we should be very unwilling to receive the account of the serpent speaking to Eve, or its being inhabited by an

---

* Mark v. 9.   † Matt. xii. 43.   ‡ 1 Cor. x. 20.

evil spirit; or, again, of the devils being sent into the swine. We should scoff at such narratives, as fanciful and extravagant. Let us only suppose that, instead of being found in Scripture, they were found in some legend of the middle ages ; should we merely ask for evidence, or simply assume that there was none ? Should we think that it was a case for evidence one way or the other ? Should we not rather say, " This is intrinsically incredible?—it supersedes the necessity of examining into evidence, it decides the case." Should we allow the strangeness of the narrative merely to act as suspending our belief, and throwing the burden of proof on the other side, or should we not rather suffer it to settle the question for us ? Again, should we have felt less distrust in the history of Balaam's ass speaking ? Should we have been reconciled to the account of the Holy Ghost appearing in a bodily shape, and that apparently the shape of an irrational animal, a dove ? And, again, though we might bear the figure of calling our Saviour a lamb, if it occurred once, as if to show that He was the antitype of the Jewish sacrifices, yet, unless we were used to it, would there not be something repugnant to our present habits of mind in calling again and again our Saviour by the name of a brute animal ? Unless we were used to it, I conceive it would hurt and offend us much to read of "glory and honour " being ascribed to Him that sitteth upon the Throne and to the Lamb, as being a sort of idolatry, or at least an unadvised way of speaking. It seems to do too much honour to an inferior creature, and to dishonour Christ. You will see this, by trying to substitute any other animal, however mild and gentle. It is said that one difficulty in translating the New Testament into some of the oriental languages actually is this, that the word in them for Lamb does not carry with it the associations which it does in languages which have had their birth in Christianity. Now we have a remarkable parallel to this in the impression produced by another figure, which was in use in primitive times, when expressed in our own language. The ancients formed an acrostic upon our Lord's Greek titles as the Son of God, the Saviour of men, and in consequence called Him from the first letters ἰχθὺς, or "fish." Hear how a late English writer speaks of it. "This contemptible and disgusting quibble originated in certain verses of one of the pseudo-sibyls. . . . I know of no figure which so revoltingly degrades the person of the Son of God." Such as this is the nature of the comment made in the farther east on the sacred image of the Lamb.

But without reference to such peculiar associations, which vary with place and person, there is in the light of reason a strangeness, perhaps, in God's allowing material symbols of Himself at all; and, again, a greater strangeness in His vouchsafing to take a brute animal as the name of His Son, and bidding us ascribe praise to it. Now it does not matter whether we take all these instances separate or together. Separate, they are strange enough; put them together, you have a law of God's dealings, which accounts indeed for each separate instance, yet does not make it less strange that the brute creation should have so close a connexion with God's spiritual and heavenly kingdom. Here, moreover, it is in place to make mention of the "four beasts" spoken of in the Apocalypse as being before God's throne. Translate the word "living thing," as you may do, yet the circumstance is not less startling. They were respectively like a lion, calf, man, and eagle. To this may be added the figure of the Cherubim in the

Jewish law, which is said to have been a symbol made up of limbs of the same animals. Is it not strange that Angels should be represented under brute images? Consider, then, if God has thus made use of brutes in His supernatural acts and in His teaching, as real instruments and as symbols of spiritual things, what is there strange antecedently in supposing He makes use of the inanimate creation also? If Balaam's ass instructed Balaam, what is there fairly to startle us in the Church's doctrine, that the water of Baptism cleanses from sin, that eating the consecrated Bread is eating His Body, or that oil may be blessed for spiritual purposes, as is still done in our Church in the case of a coronation? Of this I feel sure, that those who consider the doctrines of the Church incredible, will soon, if they turn their thoughts steadily that way, feel a difficulty in the serpent that tempted Eve, and the ass that admonished Balaam.

3.

3. We cannot, it seems, believe that water applied to the body really is God's instrument in cleansing the soul from sin; do we believe that, at Bethesda, an Angel gave the pool a miraculous power? What God has done once, He may do again; that is, there is no antecedent improbability in His connecting real personal benefits to us with arbitrary outward means. Again, what should we say, unless we were familarized with it, to the story of Naaman bathing seven times in the Jordan? or rather to the whole system of mystical signs:—the tree which Moses cast into the waters to sweeten them; Elisha's throwing meal into the pot of poisonous herbs; and our Saviour's breathing, making clay, and the like? Indeed, is not the whole of the Bible, Old and New Testament, engaged in a system of outward signs with

hidden realities under them, which in the Church's teaching is only continued ? Is it not certain, then, that those who stumble at the latter as incredible, will stumble at the former too, as soon as they learn just so much irreverence as to originate objections as well as to be susceptible of them ? I cannot doubt that, unless we were used to the Sacraments, we should be objecting, not only to the notion of their conveying virtue, but to their observance altogether, viewed as mere badges and memorials. They would be called Oriental, suited to a people of warm imagination, suited to the religion of other times, but too symbolical, poetical, or (as some might presume to say) theatrical for us ; as if there were something far more plain, solid, sensible, practical, and edifying in a sermon, or an open profession, or a prayer.

4. Consider the accounts of virtue going out of our Lord, and that, in the case of the woman with the issue of blood, as it were by a natural law, without a distinct application on His part ;—of all who touched the hem of His garment being made whole ; and further, of handkerchiefs and aprons being impregnated with healing virtue by touching St. Paul's body, and of St. Peter's shadow being earnestly sought out,—in the age when religion was purest, and the Church's condition most like a heaven upon earth. Can we hope that these passages will not afford matter of objection to the mind, when once it has brought itself steadily to scrutinize the evidence for the inspiration of the Gospels and Acts ? Will it not be obvious to say, " St. Luke was not an Apostle ; and I do not believe this account of the handkerchiefs and aprons, though I believe the Book of Acts as a whole." Next, when the mind gets bolder, it will address itself to the consideration of the account of the woman with the

issue of blood. Now it is not wonderful that she, poor ignorant woman (as men speak), in deplorable ignorance of spiritual religion (alas! that words should be so misused), dark, and superstitious,—it is not wonderful, I say, that she should expect a virtue from touching our Lord's garment; but that she should obtain it by means of this *opus operatum* of merely touching, and again that He should even commend her faith, will be judged impossible. The notion of virtue going out of Him will be considered as Jewish, pagan, or philosophical.

Yes; the outline of the story will be believed,—the main fact, the leading idea,—not the details. Indeed, if persons have already thought it inherently incredible that the hands of Bishop or priest should impart a power, or grace, or privilege, if they have learned to call it profane, and (as they speak) blasphemous to teach this with the early Church, how can it be less so, to consider that God gave virtue to a handkerchief, or apron, or garment, though our Lord's? What was it, after all, but a mere earthly substance, made of vegetable or animal material? How was it more holy because He wore it? *He* was holy, not *it;* it did not gain holiness by being near Him. Nay: do they not already lay this down as a general principle, that, to suppose He diffuses from His Person heavenly virtue, is a superstition? do not they, on this ground, object to the Catholic doctrine of the Eucharist; and on what other ground do they deny that the Blessed Virgin, whom all but heretics have ever called the Mother of God, was most holy in soul and body, from her ineffable proximity to God? He who gave to the perishing and senseless substances of wool or cotton that grace of which it was capable, should not He rather communicate of His higher spiritual perfections to her in whose bosom He lay, or to those

who now possess Him through the Sacramental means
He has appointed?

5. I conceive that, if men indulge themselves in criti-
cizing, they will begin to be offended at the passage in
the Apocalyse, which speaks of the "number of the
beast." Indeed, it is probable that they will reject that
book of Scripture altogether, not sympathizing with the
severe tone of doctrine which runs through it. Again:
there is something very surprising in the importance
attached to the Name of God and Christ in Scripture.
The Name of Jesus is said to work cures and frighten
away devils. I anticipate that this doctrine will become
a stone of stumbling to those who set themselves to inquire into the trustworthiness of the separate parts of
Scripture. For instance, the narrative of St. Peter's
cure of the impotent man, in the early chapters of the
Acts :—first, "Silver and gold," he says, "have I none;
but such as I have, give I thee; In the Name of Jesus
Christ of Nazareth, rise up and walk." Then, "And
His Name, through faith in His Name, hath made this
man strong." Then the question "By what power, or by
what *name*, have ye done this?" Then the answer, "By
the Name of Jesus Christ of Nazareth . . . even by it
doth this man now stand here before you whole . . .
there is none other name under heaven given among men
whereby we must be saved." Then the threat, that the
Apostles should not "speak at all, nor teach in the Name
of Jesus." Lastly, their prayer that God would grant
"that signs and wonders might be done by the Name of
His Holy Child Jesus." In connexion with which must
be considered, St. Paul's declaration, "that in the Name
of Jesus every knee should bow." * Again : I conceive
that the circumstances of the visitation of the Blessed

* Acts. iii. 4. Phil. ii. 10.

Virgin to Elizabeth would startle us considerably if we lost our faith in Scripture. Again : can we doubt that the account of Christ's ascending into heaven will not be received by the science of this age, when it is carefully considered what is implied in it ? Where is heaven ? Beyond all the stars ? If so, it would take years for any natural body to get there. We say, that with God all things are possible. But this age, wise in its own eyes, has already decided the contrary, in maintaining, as it does, that He who virtually annihilated the distance between earth and heaven, on His Son's ascension, cannot annihilate it in the celebration of the Holy Communion, so as to make us present with Him, though He be on God's right hand in heaven.

4.

6. Further, unless we were used to the passage, I cannot but think that we should stumble greatly at the account of our Lord's temptation by Satan. Putting aside other considerations, dwell awhile on the thought of Satan showing " *all* the kingdoms of the world in a moment of time." * What is meant by this ? How did he show all, and in a moment ? and if by a mere illusion, why from the top of a high mountain ?

Or again : consider the account of our Saviour's bidding St. Peter catch a fish in order to find money in it, to pay tribute with. What should we say if this narrative occurred in the Apocrypha ? Should we not speak of it as an evident fiction ? and are we likely to do less, whenever we have arrived at a proper pitch of unscrupulousness, and what is nowadays called critical acumen, in analyzing and disposing of what we have hitherto received as divine ? Again : I conceive that the blood and

* Luke iv. 5.

water which issued from our Saviour's side, particularly taken with the remarkable comment upon it in St. John's Epistle, would be disbelieved, if men were but consistent in their belief and disbelief. The miracle would have been likened to many which occur in Martyrologies, and the inspired comment would have been called obscure and fanciful, as on a par with various doctrinal interpretations in the Fathers, which carry forsooth their own condemnation with them. Again : the occurrence mentioned by St. John, "Then came there a voice from heaven, saying, I have both glorified it (My Name), and will glorify it again. The people, therefore, that stood by, and heard it, said that it thundered ; others said, An Angel spake to him:"* this, I conceive, would soon be looked upon as suspicious, did men once begin to examine the claims of the Canon upon our faith.

Or again : to refer to the Old Testament. I conceive that the history of the Deluge, the ark, and its inhabitants, will appear to men of modern tempers more and more incredible, the longer and more minutely it is dwelt upon. Or, again, the narrative of Jonah and the whale. Once more, the following narrative will surely be condemned also, as bearing on its face evident marks of being legendary : "And the sons of the prophets said unto Elisha, Behold now, the place where we dwell with thee is too strait for us. Let us go, we pray thee, unto Jordan, and take thence every man a beam, and let us make us a place there, where we may dwell. And he answered, Go ye. And one said, Be content, I pray thee, and go with thy servants. And he answered, I will go. So he went with them. And when they came to Jordan, they cut down wood. But as one was felling a beam, the axe-head fell into the water ; and he cried,

* 2 John xii. 28, 29.

and said, Alas, master! for it was borrowed. And the
man of God said, Where fell it? And he showed him
the place. And he cut down a stick, and cast it in
thither; and the iron did swim. Therefore said he,
Take it up to thee. And he put out his hand, and took
it." *

5.

7. Having mentioned Elisha, I am led to say a word
or two upon his character. Men of this age are full
of their dread of priestcraft and priestly ambition; and
they speak and feel as if the very circumstance of a person claiming obedience upon a divine authority was
priestcraft and full of evil. They speak as if it was
against the religious rights of man (for some such rights
are supposed to be possessed by sinners, even by those
who disown the doctrine of the political rights of man),
as if it were essentially an usurpation for one man to
claim spiritual power over another. They do not ask
for the voucher of his claim, for his commission, but
think the claim absurd. They so speak, that any one
who heard them, without knowing the Bible, would think
that Almighty God had never "given such power unto
men." Now, what would such persons say to Elisha's
character and conduct? Let me recount some few passages in his history, in the Second Book of Kings, and
let us bear in mind what has been already observed of
the character of the Books of Chronicles. When the little
children out of Bethel mocked him, "he cursed them
in the name of the Lord."† This was his first act after
entering on his office. Again: Jehoram, the son of
Ahab, put away Baal, and walked not in the sins of his
father and his mother; but because he did not put away

* 2 Kings vi. 1—7.   † 2 Kings ii. 23.

the false worship of Jeroboam, but kept to his calves, his self-appointed priests, altars, and holy days, which he probably thought a little sin, when he was in distress, and called upon Elisha, Elisha said, "What have I to do with thee? Get thee to the prophets of thy father, and to the prophets of thy mother:"* and went on to say, that, but for the presence of good Jehoshaphat, "I would not look toward thee nor see thee." This was taking (what would now be called) a high tone. Again: the Shunammite was a great woman; he was poor. She got her husband's leave to furnish a "little chamber" for him, not in royal style, but as for a poor minister of God. It had "a bed and a table and a stool and a candlestick," and when he came that way he availed himself of it. The world would think that she was the patron, and he ought to be humble, and to know his place. But observe his language on one occasion of his lodging there. He said to his servant, "Call this Shunammite." When she came, she, the mistress of the house, "stood before him." He did not speak to her, but bade his servant speak, and then she retired; then he held a consultation with his servant, and then he called her again, and she "stood in the door;" then he promised her a son. Again: Naaman was angered that Elisha did not show him due respect: he only sent him a message, and bade him wash and be clean. Afterwards we find the prophet interposing in political matters in Israel and Syria.

Now, it is not to the purpose to account for all this, by saying he worked miracles. Are miracles necessary for being a minister of God? Are miracles the only way in which a claim can be recognized? Is a man the higher minister, the more miracles he does? Are we to

* Ib. iii. 13.

honour only those who minister temporal miracles, and to be content to eat and be filled with the loaves and fishes? Are there no higher miracles than visible ones? John the Baptist did no miracles, yet he too claimed, and gained, the obedience of the Jews. Miracles prove a man to be God's minister; they do not make him God's minister. No matter how a man is proved to come from God, if he is known to come from God. If Christ is with His ministers, according to His promise, even to the end of the world, so that he that despiseth them despiseth Him, then, though they do no miracles, they are in office as great as Elisha. And if Baptism be the cleansing and quickening of the dead soul, to say nothing of Holy Eucharist, they do work miracles. If God's ministers are then only to be honoured when we see that they work miracles, where is place for faith? Are we not under a dispensation of faith, not of sight? Was Elisha great because he was seen to work miracles, or because he could, and did, work them? Is God's minister a proud priest now, for acting as if he came from God, if he does come from Him? Yet men of this generation, without inquiring into his claims, would most undoubtedly call him impostor and tyrant, proud, arrogant, profane, and Antichristian, nay, Antichrist himself, if he, a Christian minister, assume one-tenth part of Elisha's state. Yes, Antichrist;—" If they have called the Master of the house Beelzebub, how much more shall they call them of His household?"*

8. St. John the Baptist's character, I am persuaded, would startle most people, if they were not used to Scripture; and when men begin to doubt about the integrity of Scripture, it will be turned against the authenticity or the authority of the particular passages which

* Matt. x. 25.

relate to it.   Let us realize to ourselves a man living on
locusts and wild honey, and with a hair shirt on, bound
by a leathern girdle.   Our Lord indeed bids us avoid
outward show, and therefore the ostentation of such
austerity would be wrong now, of course ; but what is
there to show that the thing itself would be wrong, if
a person were moved to do it ?   Does not our Saviour
expressly say, with reference to the austerities of St.
John's disciples, that after His departure His own disciples shall resemble them,—"then shall they fast" ? Yet,
I suppose, most persons would cry out now against the
very semblance of the Baptist's life ; and why?   Those
who gave a reason would perhaps call it Jewish.   Yet
what had St. John to do with the Jews, whose religion
was one, not of austerity, but of joyousness and feasting,
and that by divine permission ?   Surely the same feeling
which would make men condemn an austere life now, if
individuals attempted it, which makes them, when they
read of such instances in the early Church, condemn
it, would lead the same parties to condemn it in St.
John, were they not bound by religious considerations ;
and, therefore, I say, if ever the time comes that men
begin to inquire into the divinity of the separate parts
of Scripture, as they do now scrutinize the separate parts
of the Church system, they will no longer be able to
acquiesce in St. John's character and conduct as simply
right and religious.

6.

9. Lastly, I will mention together a number of doctrinal passages, which, though in Scripture, they who
deny that the Fathers contain the pure Gospel, hardly
would consider parts of it, if they were but consistent in
their free speculations.   Such are St. Paul's spiritualizing

the history of Sarah and Hagar; his statement of the
fire trying every man's work in the day of judgment;
his declaring that women must have their heads covered
in church, "because of the Angels;" his charging
Timothy "before the elect Angels;" his calling the
Church "the pillar and ground of the Truth;" the tone
of his observations on celibacy, which certainly, if written
by any of the Fathers, would in this day have been cited
in proof of "the mystery of iniquity" (by which they
mean Romanism) "already working" in an early age;
St. John's remarkable agreement of tone with him in a
passage in the Apocalypse, not to say our Lord's; our
Lord's account of the sin against the Holy Ghost, viewed
in connexion with St. Paul's warning against falling
away, after being enlightened, and St. John's notice of
a sin which is unto death—(this would be considered
opposed to the free grace of the Gospel); our Lord's
strong words about the arduousness of a rich man's getting to heaven; what He says about binding and loos-
ing; about a certain kind of evil spirit going out only by
fasting and prayer; His command to turn the left cheek
to him who smites the right; St. Peter's saying that we
are partakers of a divine nature; and what he says
about Christ's "going and preaching to the spirits in
prison;" St. Matthew's account of the star which guided
the wise men to Bethlehem; St. Paul's statement, that
a woman is saved through childbearing; St. John's
directions how to treat those who hold not "the doctrine
of Christ;"—these and a multitude of other passages
would be adduced, not to prove that Christianity was
not true, or that Christ was not the Son of God, or the
Bible not inspired, or not on *the whole* genuine and
authentic, but that every part of it was not *equally*
divine; that portions, books, particularly of the Old

Testament, were not so; that we must use our own judgment. Nay, as time went on, perhaps it would be said that the Old Testament altogether was not inspired, only the New—nay, perhaps only parts of the New, not certain books which were for a time doubted in some ancient Churches, or not the Gospels according to St. Mark and St. Luke, nor the Acts, because not the writing of Apostles, or not St. Paul's reasonings, only his conclusions. Next, it would be said, that no reliance can safely be placed on single texts; and so men would proceed, giving up first one thing, then another, till it would become a question what they gained of any kind, what they considered they gained, from Christianity as a definite revelation or a direct benefit. They would come to consider its publication mainly as an historical event occurring eighteen hundred years since, which modified or altered the course of human thought and society, and thereby altered what would otherwise have been our state; as something infused into an existing mass, and influencing us in the improved tone of the institutions in which we find ourselves, rather than as independent, substantive, and one, specially divine in its origin, and directly acting upon us.

This is what the Age is coming to, and I wish it observed. We know it denies the existence of the Church as a divine institution: it denies that Christianity has been cast into any particular social mould. Well: but this, I say, is not all; it is rapidly tending to deny the existence of any system of Christianity either; any creed, doctrine, philosophy, or by whatever other name we designate it. Hitherto it has been usual, indeed, to give up the Church, and to speak only of the covenant, religion, creed, matter, or system of the Gospel; to consider the Gospel as a sort of literature or philosophy, open for all to take and appropriate, not confined to any set of men, yet still a real, existing system of religion. This has been the approved line of opinion in our part of the world for the last hundred and fifty years ; but now a further step is about to be taken. The view henceforth is to be, that Christianity does not exist in documents, any more than in institutions ; in other words, the Bible will be given up as well as the Church. It will be said that the benefit which Christianity has done to the world, and which its Divine Author meant it should do, was to give an impulse to society, to infuse a spirit, to direct, control, purify, enlighten the mass of human thought and action, but not to be a separate and definite something, whether doctrine or association, existing objectively, integral, and with an identity, and for ever, and with a claim upon our homage and obedience. And all this fearfully coincides with the symptoms in other directions of the spread of a Pantheistic spirit, that is, the religion of beauty, imagination, and philosophy, without constraint moral or intellectual, a religion speculative and self-indulgent. Pantheism, indeed, is the great deceit which awaits the Age to come.

7.

Let us then look carefully, lest we fall in with the evil tendencies of the times in which our lot is cast. God has revealed Himself to us that we might believe : surely His Revelation is something great and important. He who made it, meant it to be a blessing even to the end of the world : this is true, if any part of Scripture is true. From beginning to end, Scripture implies that God has spoken, and that it is right, our duty, our interest, our safety to believe. Whether, then, we have in our hands the means of exactly proving this or that part of Scripture to be genuine or not, whether we have in our hands the complete proofs of all the Church doctrines, we are more sure that hearty belief in something is our duty, than that it is not our duty to believe those doctrines and that Scripture as we have received them. If our choice lies between accepting all and rejecting all, which I consider it does when persons are consistent, no man can hesitate which alternative is to be taken.

So far then every one of us may say,—Our Heavenly Father gave the world a Revelation in Christ ; we are baptized into His Name. He wills us to believe, *because* He has given us a Revelation. He who wills us to believe *must* have given us an object to believe. Whether I can prove this or that part to my satisfaction, yet, since I can prove all in a certain way, and cannot separate part from part satisfactorily, I cannot be wrong in taking the whole. I am sure that, if there be error, which I have yet to learn, it must be, not in principles, but in mere matters of detail. If there be corruption or human addition in what comes to me, it must be in little matters, not in great. On the whole, I cannot but have God's Revelation, and that, in what I see before me, with whatever incidental errors. I am sure, on the other hand, that the way which the Age follows cannot be right, for it tends to destroy Revelation altogether. Whether this or that doctrine, this or that book of Scripture is fully provable or not, that line of objection to it cannot be right, which, when pursued, destroys Church, Creed, Bible altogether,—which obliterates the very Name of Christ from the world. It is then God's will, under my circumstances, that I should believe what, in the way of Providence, He has put before me to believe. God will not deceive me. I can trust Him. Either every part of the system is pure truth, or, if this or that be an addition, He will (I humbly trust and believe) make such addition harmless to my soul, if I thus throw myself on His mercy with a free and confiding spirit. Doubt is misery and sin, but belief has received Christ's blessing.

This is the reflection which I recommend to all, so far as they have not the means of examining the Evidences for the Church, Creed, and Canon of Scripture; but I must not be supposed to imply, because I have so put the matter, that those who have the means, will not find abundant evidence for the divinity of all three.

8.

Difficulties of Jewish and of Christian Faith compared.

I HAVE been engaged for some time in showing that the Canon of Scripture rests on no other foundation than the Catholic doctrines rest ; that those who dispute the latter should, if they were consistent,—will, when they learn to be consistent,—dispute the former ; that in both cases we believe, mainly, because the Church of the fourth and fifth centuries unanimously believed, and that we have at this moment to defend our belief in the Catholic doctrines merely because they come first, are the first object of attack ; and that if we were not defending our belief in them, we should at this very time be defending our belief in the Canon. Let no one then hope for peace in this day ; let no one attempt to purchase it by concession ;—vain indeed would be that concession. Give up the Catholic doctrines, and what do you gain ? an attack upon the Canon, with (to say the least) the same disadvantages on your part, or rather, in fact, with much greater ; for the circumstance that you have already given up the Doctrines as if insufficiently evidenced in primitive times, will be an urgent call on you, in consistency, to give up the Canon too. And besides, the Church doctrines may also be proved from Scripture, but no one can say that the Canon of Scripture itself can be proved from Scripture to be a Canon; no one can say, that Scripture anywhere enumerates all the books of which it is composed, and puts its seal upon them ever so indirectly, even if it might allowably bear witness to itself.

I.

But here, before proceeding to make some reflections on the state of the case, I will make one explanation, and notice one objection.

In the first place, then, I must explain myself, when I say that we depend for the Canon and Creed upon the fourth and fifth centuries. We depend upon them thus : As to Scripture, former centuries certainly do not speak distinctly, frequently, or unanimously, except of some chief books, as the Gospels : but still we see in them, as we believe, an ever-growing tendency and approximation to that full agreement which we find in the fifth. The testimony given at the latter date is the limit to which all that has been before given converges. For instance, it is commonly said, *Exceptio probat regulam ;* when we have reason to think, that a writer or an age *would* have witnessed so and so, but for this or that, and this or that were mere accidents of his position, then he or it may be said to tend towards such testimony. In this way the first centuries tend towards the fifth. Viewing the matter as one of moral evidence, we seem to see in the testimony of the fifth the very testimony which every preceding century gave, accidents excepted, such as the present loss of documents once extant, or the then existing misconceptions, which want of intercourse between the Churches occasioned. The fifth century acts as a comment on the obscure text of the centuries before it, and brings out a meaning which, with the help of that comment, any candid person sees really to belong to them.

And in the same way as regards the Catholic Creed,

though there is not so much to explain and account for.
Not so much, for no one, I suppose, will deny that in the
Fathers of the fourth century it is as fully developed, and
as unanimously adopted, as it is in the fifth century ;
and, again, there had been no considerable doubts about
any of its doctrines previously, as there were about the
Epistle to the Hebrews or the Apocalypse : or if any,
they were started by individuals, as Origen's about
eternal punishment, not by Churches,—or they were
at once condemned by the general Church, as in the
case of heresies,—or they were not about any primary
doctrine, for instance, the Incarnation or Atonement ; and
all this, in spite of that want of free intercourse which did
occasion doubts about portions of the Canon. Yet, in both
cases, we have at first an inequality of evidence as regards
the constituent parts of what was afterwards universally
received as a whole,—the doctrine of the Holy Trinity,
for instance, and, on the other hand, the four Gospels
being generally witnessed from the first ; but certain other
doctrines, (as the necessity of infant baptism,) being at
first rather practised and assumed, than insisted on,
and certain books, (as the Epistle to the Hebrews and
the Apocalypse,) doubted, or not admitted, in particular
countries. And as the unanimity of the fifth century as
regards the Canon, clears up and overcomes all previous
differences, so the abundance of the fourth as to the
Creed interprets, develops, and combines all that is
recondite or partial, in previous centuries, as to doctrine,
acting in a parallel way as a comment, not, indeed, as in
the case of the Canon, upon a perplexed and disordered,
but upon a concise text. In both cases, the after centuries contain but the termination and summing up of
the testimony of the foregoing.

2.

So much as to the explanation which I proposed to give; the objection I have to notice is this. It is said, that the Fathers might indeed bear witness to a document such as the books of Scripture are, and yet not be good witnesses to a doctrine, which is, after all, but an opinion. A document or book is something external to the mind; it is an object that any one can point at, and if a person about two or three hundred years after Christ, said, "This book of the New Testament has been accounted sacred ever since it was written," we could be as sure of what he said, as we are at the present day, that the particular church we now use was built at a certain date, or that the date in the title-page of a certain printed book is trustworthy. On the other hand, it is urged, a doctrine does not exist, except in the mind of this or that person, it is not a thing you can point at, it is not a something which two persons see at once,—it is an opinion; and every one has his own opinion. I have an opinion, you have an opinion;—if on comparing notes we think we agree, we call it the same opinion, but it is not the same really, only called the same, because similar; and, in fact, probably no two such opinions really do coincide in all points. Every one describes and colours from his own mind. No one then can bear witness to a doctrine being ancient. Strictly speaking, that which he contemplates, witnesses, speaks about, began with himself; it is a birth of his own mind. He may, indeed, have caught it from another, but it is not the same as another man's doctrine, unless one flame is the same as a second kindled from it; and as flame communicated from spirit to sulphur, from sulphur to wood, from wood to coal, from coal to charcoal, burns variously, so, true as it may be that certain doctrines

originated in the Apostles, it does not follow that the
particular form in which we possess them, originated
with the Apostles also. Such is the objection ; that the
Fathers, if honest men, may be credible witnesses of
facts, but not, however honest, witnesses to doctrines.

It admits of many answers :—I will mention two.

1. It does not rescue the Canon from the difficulties
of its own evidence, which is its professed object ; for it
is undeniable that there are books of Scripture, which
in the first centuries particular Fathers, nay, particular
Churches did not receive. What is the good of con-
trasting testimony to facts with testimony to opinions,
when we have not in the case of the Canon that clear
testimony to the facts in dispute, which the objection
supposes ? Lower, as you will, the evidence for the
Creed ; you do nothing thereby towards raising the evidence for the Canon. The first Fathers, in the midst of
the persecutions, had not, as I have said, time and opportunity to ascertain always what was inspired and
what was not ; and, since nothing but an agreement of
many, of different countries, will prove to us what the
Canon is, we must betake ourselves of necessity to the
fourth and fifth centuries, to those centuries which did
hold those very doctrines, which, it seems, are to be rejected as superstitions and corruptions. But if the Church
then was in that miserable state of superstition, which belief in those doctrines is supposed to imply, then I must
contend, that blind bigotry and ignorance were not fit
judges of what was inspired and what was not. I will not
trust the judgment of a worldly-minded partizan, or a
crafty hypocrite, or a credulous fanatic in this matter.
Unless then you allow those centuries to be tolerably
free from doctrinal corruptions, I conceive, you cannot
use them as witnesses of the canonicity of the Old and

New Testament, as we now have them; but, if you do consider the fourth and fifth centuries enlightened enough to decide on the Canon, then I want to know why you call them not enlightened in point of doctrine. The only reason commonly given is, that their Christianity contains many notions and many usages and rites not *in* Scripture, and which, because not *in* Scripture, are to be considered, it seems, as if *against* Scripture. But this surely is no sound argument, unless it is true also that the canonicity itself of the Old and New Testament, not being declared *in* Scripture, is therefore unscriptural. I consider then that the man, whether we call him cautious or sceptical, who quarrels with the testimony for Catholic doctrine, because a doctrine is a mere opinion, and not an objective fact, ought also in consistency to quarrel with the testimony for the Canon, as being that of an age which is superstitious as a teacher and uncritical as a judge.

2. But again : the doctrines of the Church are after all not mere matters of opinion ; they were not in early times mere ideas in the mind to which no one could appeal, each individual having his own, but they were external facts, quite as much as the books of Scripture ; —how so? Because they were embodied in rites and ceremonies. A usage, custom, or monument, has the same kind of identity, is in the same sense common property, and admits of a common appeal, as a book. When a writer appeals to the custom of the Sign of the Cross, or the Baptism of infants, or the Sacrifice or the Consecration of the Eucharist, or Episcopal Ordination, he is not speaking of an opinion in his mind, but of something external to it, and is as trustworthy as when he says that the Acts of the Apostles is written by St. Luke. Now such usages are symbols of common,

not individual opinions, and more or less involve the doctrines they symbolize. Is it not implied, for instance, in the fact of priests only consecrating the Eucharist, that it is a gift which others have not? in the Eucharist being offered to God, that it *is* an offering? in penance being exacted of offenders, that it is right to impose it? in children being exorcised, that they are by nature children of wrath, and inhabited by Satan? On the other hand, when the Fathers witness to the inspiration of Scripture, they are surely as much witnessing to a mere doctrine,—not to the book itself, but to an opinion,—as when they bear witness to the grace of Baptism.

Again, the Creed is a document the same in kind as Scripture, though its wording be not fixed and invariable, or its language. It admits of being appealed to, and is appealed to by the early Fathers, as Scripture is. If Scripture was written by the Apostles, (as it is,) because the Fathers say so, why was not the Creed taught by the Apostles, because the Fathers say so? The Creed is no opinion in the mind, but a form of words pronounced many times a day, at every baptism, at every communion, by every member of the Church:— is it not common property as much as Scripture?

Once more; if Church doctrine is but a hazy opinion, how is it there can be such a thing at all as Catholic consent about it? If, in spite of its being subjective to the mind, Europe, Asia, and Africa could agree together in doctrine in the fourth and fifth centuries (to say nothing of earlier times), why should its subjective character be an antecedent objection to a similar agreement in it between the fourth century and the first? And does not this agreement show that we are able to tell when we agree together, and when we do not? Is it a mere accident, and perhaps a mistake, that Christians then felt sure that they agreed together in creed, and we now feel sure that we do not agree together?

Granting, then, that external facts can be discriminated in a way in which opinions cannot be, yet the Church doctrines are not mere opinions, but ordinances also: and though the books of Scripture themselves are an external fact, yet they are not all of them witnessed by all writers till a late age, and their canonicity and inspiration are but doctrines, not facts, and open to the objections, whatever they are, to which doctrines lie open.

3.

And now, having said as much as is necessary on these subjects, I will make some remarks on the state of the case as I have represented it, and thus shall bring to an end the train of thought upon which I have been engaged. Let us suppose it proved, then, as I consider it has been proved, that many difficulties are connected with the evidence for the Canon, that we might have clearer evidence for it than we have; and again, let us grant that there are many difficulties connected with the evidence for the Church doctrines, that they might be more clearly contained in Scripture, nay, in the extant writings of the first three centuries, than they are. This being assumed, I observe as follows :—

1. There is something very arresting and impressive in the fact, that there should be these difficulties attending those two great instruments of religious truth which we possess. We are all of us taught from the Bible, and from the Creed or the Prayer Book: it is from these that we get our knowledge of God. We are sure they contain a doctrine which is from Him. We are sure of it ; but *how* do we know it ? We are sure the doctrine is from Him, and

(I hesitate not to say) by a supernatural divinely inspired assurance; but *how* do we know the doctrine is from Him? When we go to inquire into the reasons in argument, we find that the Creed or the Prayer Book with its various doctrines rests for its authority upon the Bible, and that these might be more clearly stated in the Bible than they are; and that the Bible, with its various books, rests for its authority on ancient testimony, and that its books might have been more largely and strongly attested than they are. I say, there is something very subduing to a Christian in this remarkable coincidence, which cannot be accidental. We have reason to believe that God, our Maker and Governor, has spoken to us by Revelation; yet why has He not spoken more distinctly? He has given us doctrines which are but obscurely gathered from Scripture, and a Scripture which is but obscurely gathered from history. It is not a single fact, but a double fact; it is a coincidence. We have two informants, and both leave room, if we choose, for doubt. God's ways surely are not as our ways.

2. This is the first reflection which rises in the mind on the state of the case. The second is this: that, most remarkable it is, the Jews were left in the same uncertainty about Christ, in which we are about His doctrine. The precept, " *Search* the Scriptures," and the commendation of the Berœans, who " *searched* the Scriptures daily," surely implies that divine truth was not on the surface of the Old Testament. We do not search for things which are before us, but for what we have lost or have to find. The whole system of the prophecies left the Jews (even after Christ came) where we are—in uncertainty. The Sun of Righteousness did not at once clear up the mists from the Prophetic Word. It was a dark saying to the many, after He came, as well as

before. It is not to be denied that there were and are many real difficulties in the way of the Jews admitting that Jesus Christ is their Messiah. The Old Testament certainly does speak of the Messiah as a temporal monarch, and a conqueror of this world. *We* are accustomed to say that the prophecies must be taken spiritually; and rightly do we say so. True: yet does not this look like an evasion, to a Jew? Is it not much more like an evasion, though it be not, than to say (what the Church does say and rightly) that rites remain, *though* Jewish rites are done away, because *our* rites are not Jewish, but spiritual, gifted with the Spirit, channels of grace? The Old Testament certainly spoke as if, when the Church expanded into all nations, still those nations were to be inferior to the Jews, even if admitted into the Church; and so St. Peter understood it till he had the vision. Yet when the Jews complained, instead of being soothed and consoled, they were met with language such as this: "Friend, I do thee no wrong. . . . Is it not lawful for Me to do what I will with Mine own? Is thine eye evil because I am good?" And, "Nay but, O man, who art thou that repliest against God? Shall the thing formed say to Him that formed it, Why hast Thou made me thus?" *

Again; why were the Jews discarded from God's election? for *keeping* to their Law. Why, this was the very thing they were *told* to do, the very thing which, if *not* done, was to be their ruin. Consider Moses' words: "If thou wilt not observe to do all the words of this law that are written in this book, that thou mayest fear this glorious and fearful Name, The Lord thy God; then the Lord will make thy plagues wonderful, and the plagues of thy seed, even great plagues, and of

* Matt xx. 13—15. Rom. ix. 20.

long continuance, and sore sicknesses, and of long continuance." *   Might they not, or rather did they not,
bring passages like this as an irrefragable argument
against Christianity, that they were told to give up their
Law, that Law which was the charter of their religious
prosperity? Might not their case seem a hard one,
judging by the surface of things, and without reference to "the hidden man of the heart"? *We* know
how to answer this objection; we say, Christianity lay
beneath the letter; that the letter slew those who for
whatever cause went by it; that when Christ came,
He shed a light on the sacred text and brought out its
secret meaning. Now, is not this just the case I have
been stating, as regards Catholic doctrines, or rather a
more difficult case? The doctrines of the Church are
not hidden so deep in the New Testament, as the Gospel
doctrines are hidden in the Old; but they are hidden;
and I am persuaded that were men but consistent, who
oppose the Church doctrines as being unscriptural, they
would vindicate the Jews for rejecting the Gospel.

Much might be said on this subject: I will but add,
by way of specimen, how such interpretations as our
Lord's of "I am the God of Abraham," etc., would,
were we not accustomed to them, startle and offend reasoning men. Is it not much further from the literal
force of the words, than the doctrine of the Apostolical
Succession is from the words, "I am with you alway,
even unto the end of the world"? In the one case we
argue, "Therefore, the Apostles are in one sense *now* on
earth, because Christ says 'with *you alway;*'" in the
other, Christ Himself argues, "therefore in one sense the
bodies of the patriarchs are still alive; for God calls
Himself '*their* God.'" We say, "therefore the Apostles

* Deut. xxviii. 58, **59.**

live in their successors." Christ implies, "therefore the body never died, and therefore it will rise again." His own divine mouth hereby shows us that doctrines may be in Scripture, though they require a multitude of links to draw them thence. It must be added that the Sadducees *did* profess (what they would call) a plain and simple creed ; they recurred to Moses and went by Moses, and rejected all additions to what was on the surface of the Mosaic writings, and thus they rejected what really was in the mind of Moses, though not on his lips. They denied the Resurrection ; they had no idea that it was contained in the books of Moses.

Here, then, is another singular instance of the same procedure on the part of Divine Providence. That Gospel which was to be "the glory of His people Israel,"* was a stumblingblock to them, as for other reasons, so especially *because* it was not on the *surface* of the Old Testament. And all the compassion (if I may use the word) that they received from the Apostles in their perplexity was, "because they *knew* Him not, nor yet the *voice* of the Prophets which are read every Sabbath day, they have fulfilled them in condemning Him."† Or again : "Well spake the Holy Ghost by Esaias the prophet unto our fathers, saying, Go unto this people, and say, Hearing, ye shall hear, and shall not understand,"‡ etc. Or when the Apostles are mildest : "I have great heaviness and continual sorrow in my heart. For I could wish that myself were accursed from Christ for my brethren, my kinsman according to the flesh ;" or "I bear them record that they have a zeal of God, but not according to knowledge." § Moreover, it is observable that the record of their anxiety is preserved

* Luke ii. 32.   ‡ Ib. xxviii. 25, 26.
† Acts xiii. 27.   § Rom. ix. 2, 3 : x. 2.

to us; an anxiety which many of us would call just and rational, many would pity, but which the inspired writers treat with a sort of indignation and severity. "Then came the Jews round about Him, and said unto Him, How long dost Thou make us to doubt?"* or more literally, "How long dost Thou keep our soul in suspense? If thou be the Christ, *tell us plainly.*" Christ answers by referring to His works, and by declaring that His sheep do hear and know Him, and follow Him. If any one will seriously consider the intercourse between our Lord and the Pharisees, he will see that, not denying their immorality and miserable pride, still they had reason for complaining (as men now speak) that "the Gospel was not preached to them,"—that the Truth was not placed before them clearly, and fully, and uncompromisingly, and intelligibly, and logically,—that they were bid to believe on weak arguments and fanciful deductions. †

This then, I say, is certainly a most striking coincidence in addition. Whatever perplexity any of us may feel about the evidence of Scripture or the evidence of Church doctrine, we see that such perplexity is represented in Scripture as the lot of the Jews too; and this circumstance, while it shows that it is a sort of law of God's providence, and thereby affords an additional evidence of the truth of the Revealed System by showing its harmony, also serves to quiet and console, and moreover to awe and warn us. Doubt and difficulty, as regards evidence, seems our lot; the simple question is, What is our duty under it? Difficulty is our lot, as far as we take on ourselves to inquire; the multitude are not able to inquire, and so escape the trial; but when men inquire, this trial at once comes upon them. And surely we may use the

* John x. 24.   † [This is too strongly worded.]

parable of the Talents to discover what our duty is under the trial. Do not those who refuse to go by the hints and probable meaning of Scripture hide their talent in a napkin? and will they be excused?

3. Now in connexion with what has been said, observe the singular coincidence, or rather appositeness, of what Scripture enjoins, as to the duty of going by *faith* in religious matters. The difficulties which exist in the evidence give a deep meaning to that characteristic enunciation. Scripture is quite aware of those difficulties. Objections can be brought against its own inspiration, its canonicity, its doctrines in our case, as in the case of the Jews against the Messiahship of Jesus Christ. It knows them all: it has provided against them, by recognizing them. It says, "Believe," because it knows that, unless we believe, there is no means of our arriving at a knowledge of divine things. If we will doubt, that is, if we will not allow evidence to be sufficient for us which mainly results, considered in its details, in a balance preponderating on the side of Revelation; if we will determine that no evidence is enough to prove revealed doctrine but what is simply overpowering; if we will not go by evidence in which there are (so to say) a score of reasons for Revelation, yet one or two against it, we cannot be Christians; we shall miss Christ either in His inspired Scriptures, or in His doctrines, or in His ordinances.

4

To conclude: our difficulty and its religious solution are contained in the sixth chapter of St. John. After our Lord had declared what all who heard seemed to feel to be a hard doctrine, some in surprise and offence left Him. Our Lord said to the Twelve most tenderly, "Will ye also go away?" St. Peter promptly answered,

No: but observe on what ground he put it: "Lord, *to whom* shall we go?" He did not bring forward evidences of our Lord's mission, though he knew of such. He knew of such in abundance, in the miracles which our Lord wrought: but, still, questions might be raised about the so-called miracles of others, such as of Simon the sorcerer, or of vagabond Jews, or about the force of the evidence from miracles itself. This was not the evidence on which he rested personally, but this,—that if Christ were not to be trusted, there was nothing in the world to be trusted; and this was a conclusion repugnant both to his reason and to his heart. He had within him ideas of greatness and goodness, holiness and eternity, —he had a love of them—he had an instinctive hope and longing after their possession. Nothing could convince him that this unknown good was a dream. Divine life, eternal life was the object which his soul, as far as it had learned to realize and express its wishes, supremely longed for. In Christ he found what he wanted. He says, "Lord, to whom *shall* we go?" implying he must go somewhere. Christ had asked, "Will ye also go *away?*" He only asked about Peter's leaving *Himself;* but in Peter's thought to leave Him was to go somewhere else. He only thought of leaving Him *by* taking another god. That negative state of neither believing nor disbelieving, neither acting this way nor that, which is so much in esteem now, did not occur to his mind as possible. The fervent Apostle ignored the existence of scepticism. With him, his course was at best but a *choice of difficulties*—of difficulties perhaps, but still a choice. He knew of no course without a choice,—choice he must make. Somewhither he must go: whither else? If Christ could deceive him, to whom should he go? Christ's ways might be dark, His words often perplexing, but still he found in Him what he found nowhere else,—amid difficulties, a realization of his inward longings. " Thou hast the words of eternal life."

So far he saw. He might have misgivings at times ; he might have permanent and in themselves insuperable objections ; still, in spite of such objections, in spite of the assaults of unbelief, on the whole, he saw that in Christ which was positive, real, and satisfying. He saw it nowhere else. " Thou," he says, " hast the words of eternal life ; and we *have believed* and *have known* that thou art the Christ, the Son of the Living God." As if he said, " We will stand by what we believed and knew yesterday,—what we believed and knew the day before. A sudden gust of new doctrines, a sudden inroad of new perplexities, shall not unsettle us. We *have* believed, we *have* known : we cannot collect together all the evidence, but this is the abiding deep conviction of our minds. We feel that it is better, safer, truer, pleasanter, more blessed to cling to Thy feet, O merciful Saviour, than to leave Thee. Thou *canst not* deceive us : it is impossible. We will hope in Thee against hope, and believe in Thee against doubt, and obey Thee in spite of gloom."

Now what are the feelings I have described but the love of Christ ? Thus love is the parent of faith.* We

* [To say that "love is the parent of faith" is true, if by "love" is meant, not evangelical charity, the theological virtue, but that desire for the knowledge and drawing towards the service of our Maker, which precedes religious conversion. Such is the main outline, personally and historically, of the inward acceptance of Revelation on the part of individuals, and doe. not at all exclude, but actually requires, the exercise of Reason, and the presence of grounds for believing, as an incidental and necessary part of the process. The preliminary, called in the text "love," but more exactly, a "pia affectio," or "bona voluntas," does not stand in antagonism or in contrast to Reason, but is a sovereign condition without which Reason cannot be brought to bear upon the great work in hand.—*Vid.* Univ. Serm. xii., 20.]

believe in things we see not from love of them : if we did not love, we should not believe. Faith is reliance on the word of another ; the word of another is in itself a faint evidence compared with that of sight or reason. It is influential only when we cannot do without it. We cannot do without it when it is our informant about things which we cannot do without. Things we cannot do without, are things which we desire. They who feel they cannot do without the next world, go by faith (not that sight would not be better), but because they have no other means of knowledge to go by. "To whom shall they go ?" If they will not believe the word preached to them, what other access have they to the next world ? Love of God led St. Peter to follow Christ, and love of Christ leads men now to love and follow the Church, as His representative and voice.

Let us then say, If we give up the Gospel, as we have received it in the Church, to whom shall we go ? It has the words of eternal life in it : where else are they to be found ? Is there any other Religion to choose but that of the Church ? Shall we go to Mahometanism or Paganism ? But we may seek some heresy or sect : true, we may ; but why are they more sure ? are they not a part, while the Church is the whole ? Why is the part true, if the whole is not ? Why is not that evidence trustworthy for the whole, which is trustworthy for a part ? Sectaries commonly give up the Church doctrines, and go by the Church's Bible ; but if the doctrines cannot be proved true, neither can the Bible ; they stand or fall together. If we begin, we must soon make an end. On what consistent principle can I give up part and keep the rest ? No : I see a work before me, which professes to be the work of that God whose being and attributes I feel within me to be real. Why should not this great sight be,—

what it professes to be—His presence ?   Why should not
the Church be divine ?   The burden of proof surely is on
the other side.   I will accept her doctrines, and her rites,
and her Bible,—not one, and not the other, but all,—till
I have clear proof, which is an impossibility, that she is
mistaken.   It is, I feel, God's will that I should do so ;
and besides, I love all that belong to her,—I love her
Bible, her doctrines, her rites, and therefore I believe.

September, 1838.

IV.

THE TAMWORTH READING ROOM.

(Addressed to the Editor of the TIMES. *By Catholicus.)*

I.

Secular Knowledge in contrast with Religion.

SIR,—Sir Robert Peel's position in the country, and his high character, render it impossible that his words and deeds should be other than public property. This alone would furnish an apology for my calling the attention of your readers to the startling language, which many of them doubtless have already observed, in the Address which this most excellent and distinguished man has lately delivered upon the establishment of a Library and Reading-room at Tamworth ; but he has superseded the need of apology altogether, by proceeding to present it to the public in the form of a pamphlet. His speech, then, becomes important, both from the name and the express act of its author. At the same time, I must allow that he has not published it in the fulness in which it was spoken. Still it seems to me right and fair, or rather imperative, to animadvert upon it as it has appeared in your columns, since in that shape it will have the widest circulation. A public man must not claim to harangue the whole world in newspapers, and then to offer his second thoughts to such as choose to buy them at a bookseller's.

I shall surprise no one who has carefully read Sir Robert's Address, and perhaps all who have not, by stating my conviction, that, did a person take it up without looking at the heading, he would to a certainty set it down as a production of the years 1827 and 1828, —the scene Gower Street, the speaker Mr. Brougham or Dr. Lushington, and the occasion, the laying the first stone, or the inauguration, of the then-called London University. I profess myself quite unable to draw any satisfactory line of difference between the Gower Street and the Tamworth Exhibition, except, of course, that Sir Robert's personal religious feeling breaks out in his Address across his assumed philosophy. I say assumed, I might say affected;—for I think too well of him to believe it genuine.

On the occasion in question, Sir Robert gave expression to a theory of morals and religion, which of course, in a popular speech, was not put out in a very dogmatic form, but which, when analyzed and fitted together, reads somewhat as follows :—

Human nature, he seems to say, if left to itself, becomes sensual and degraded. Uneducated men live in the indulgence of their passions; or, if they are merely taught to read, they dissipate and debase their minds by trifling or vicious publications. Education is the cultivation of the intellect and heart, and Useful Knowledge is the great instrument of education. It is the parent of virtue, the nurse of religion; it exalts man to his highest perfection, and is the sufficient scope of his most earnest exertions.

Physical and moral science rouses, transports, exalts, enlarges, tranquillizes, and satisfies the mind. Its attractiveness obtains a hold over us; the excitement attending it supersedes grosser excitements; it makes us know our duty, and thereby enables us to do it ; by taking the mind off itself, it destroys anxiety ; and by providing objects of admiration, it soothes and subdues us.

And, in addition, it is a kind of neutral ground, on which men of every shade of politics and religion may meet together, disabuse each other of their prejudices, form intimacies, and secure co-operation.

This, it is almost needless to say, is the very theory, expressed temperately, on which Mr. Brougham once expatiated in the Glasgow and London Universities. Sir R. Peel, indeed, has spoken with somewhat of his characteristic moderation ; but for his closeness in sentiment to the Brougham of other days, a few parallels from their respective Discourses will be a sufficient voucher.

For instance, Mr. Brougham, in his Discourses upon Science, and in his Pursuit of Knowledge under Difficulties,* wrote about the " pure delight " of physical knowledge, of its " pure gratification," of its " tendency to purify and elevate man's nature," of its "elevating and refining it," of its " giving a dignity and *importance* to the enjoyment of life." Sir Robert, pursuing the idea, shows us its importance even in death, observing, that physical knowledge supplied the thoughts from which " a great experimentalist professed *in his last illness* to derive some pleasure and some consolation, when most other sources of consolation and pleasure were closed to him."

Mr. Brougham talked much and eloquently of " the *sweetness* of knowledge," and "the *charms* of philosophy," of students " smitten with the love of knowledge," of

* [This latter work is wrongly ascribed to Lord Brougham in this passage. It is, however, of the Brougham school.]

" *wooing* truth with the unwearied ardour of a *lover*," of
"keen and overpowering *emotion*, of *ecstasy*," of "the
absorbing *passion* of knowledge," of "the *strength* of the
passion, and the exquisite pleasure of its *gratification*."
And Sir Robert, in less glowing language, but even in a
more tender strain than Mr. Brougham, exclaims, "If I
can only persuade you to enter upon that delightful
path, I am sanguine enough to believe that there *will
be opened to you gradual charms and temptations* which
will induce you to persevere."

Mr. Brougham naturally went on to enlarge upon
"bold and successful adventures in the pursuit;"—such,
perhaps, as in the story of Paris and Helen, or Hero
and Leander; of daring ambition in its course to
greatness," of "enterprising spirits," and their "brilliant
feats," of "adventurers of the world of intellect," and
of "the illustrious vanquishers of fortune." And Sir
Robert, not to be outdone, echoes back "aspirations for
knowledge and distinction," "simple determination of
overcoming difficulties," "premiums on skill and intelligence," "mental activity," "steamboats and railroads,"
"producer and consumer," "spirit of inquiry afloat;"
and at length he breaks out into almost conventical
eloquence, crying, "Every newspaper *teems with notices*
of publications written upon *popular principles*, detailing
all the recent discoveries of science, and their connexion
with improvements in arts and manufactures. *Let me
earnestly entreat you* not to neglect the *opportunity* which
we are now willing to afford you! *It will not be our
fault* if the ample page of knowledge, rich with the spoils
of time, is not unrolled to you! *We tell you*," etc., etc.

Mr. Brougham pronounces that a man by "learning
truths wholly new to him," and by "satisfying himself of
the grounds on which known truths rest," "will enjoy

a *proud consciousness* of having, by his own exertions become a *wiser*, and *therefore* a more *exalted* creature." Sir Robert runs abreast of this great sentiment. He tells us, in words which he adopts as his own, that a man "in becoming *wiser* will become *better*:" he will "rise *at once* in the scale of intellectual and moral existence, and by being accustomed to such contemplations, he will feel the *moral dignity* of his nature *exalted*."

Mr. Brougham, on his inauguration at Glasgow, spoke to the ingenuous youth assembled on the occasion, of "the benefactors of mankind, when they rest from their pious labours, looking down upon the blessings with which their toils and sufferings have clothed the scene of their former existence;" and in his Discourse upon Science declared it to be "no mean reward of our labour to become acquainted with the prodigious genius of those who have almost exalted the nature of man above his destined sphere;" and who "hold a station apart, rising over *all* the great teachers of mankind, and spoken of reverently, as if Newton and La Place were not the names of mortal men." Sir Robert cannot, of course, equal this sublime flight; but he succeeds in calling Newton and others "those mighty spirits which have made the *greatest* (though imperfect) advances towards the understanding of 'the Divine Nature and Power.'"

Mr. Brougham talked at Glasgow about putting to flight the "evil spirits of *tyranny and persecution* which haunted the long night now gone down the sky," and about men "no longer suffering themselves to be led *blindfold in ignorance*;" and in his Pursuit of Knowledge he speaks of Pascal having, "under the influence of certain religious views, during a period of *depression,* conceived scientific pursuits "to be little better than abuse of his time and faculties." Sir Robert, fainter in tone, but true to the key, warns his hearers,— "Do not be deceived by the sneers that you hear against knowledge, which are uttered by men who *want to depress you,* and keep you depressed to the level of their *own contented ignorance.*"

Mr. Brougham laid down at Glasgow the infidel principle, or, as he styles it, "the great truth," which "has gone forth to all the ends of the earth, that man shall no more render account to man for his belief, over which he has himself no control." And Dr. Lushington applied it in Gower Street to the College then and there rising, by asking, "Will any one argue for establishing a *monopoly* to be enjoyed by the few who are of one *denomination* of the Christian Church only?" And he went on to speak of the association and union of all *without exclusion or restriction,* of "friendships cementing the bond of charity, and softening the asperities which *ignorance and separation* have fostered." Long may it be before Sir Robert Peel professes the great principle itself! even though, as the following passages show, he is inconsistent enough to think highly of its application in the culture of the mind. He speaks, for instance, of "this preliminary and fundamental rule, that no works of *controversial divinity* shall enter into the library (applause),"—of "the institution being open to all persons of all descriptions, without reference to political opinions, or *religious creed,*"—and of "an edifice in which men of all political opinions and *all religious feelings* may unite in the furtherance of knowledge, without the *asperities* of party feeling." Now, that British society should consist of persons of different religions, is this a positive standing evil, to be endured at best as unavoidable, or a topic of exultation ? Of exultation, answers Sir Robert ; the greater differences the better, the more the merrier. So we must interpret his tone.

It is reserved for few to witness the triumph of their own opinions ; much less to witness it in the instance of their own direct and personal opponents. Whether the Lord Brougham of this day feels all that satisfaction and inward peace which he attributes to success of whatever kind in intellectual efforts, it is not for me to decide ; but that he has achieved, to speak in his own style, a mighty victory, and is leading in chains behind his chariot-wheels, a great captive, is a fact beyond question.

Such is the reward in 1841 for unpopularity in 1827.

What, however, is a boast to Lord Brougham, is in the same proportion a slur upon the fair fame of Sir Robert Peel, at least in the judgment of those who have hitherto thought well of him. Were there no other reason against the doctrine propounded in the Address which has been the subject of these remarks, (but I hope to be allowed an opportunity of assigning others,) its parentage would be a grave *primâ facie* difficulty in receiving it. It is, indeed, most melancholy to see so sober and experienced a man practising the antics of one of the wildest performers of this wild age ; and taking off the tone, manner, and gestures of the versatile ex-Chancellor, with a versatility almost equal to his own.

Yet let him be assured that the task of rivalling such a man is hopeless, as well as unprofitable. No one can equal the great sophist. Lord Brougham is inimitable in his own line.

2.

Secular Knowledge not the Principle of Moral Improvement.

A DISTINGUISHED Conservative statesman tells us from the town-hall of Tamworth that "in becoming wiser a man will become better ;" meaning by wiser more conversant with the facts and theories of physical science; and that such a man will "rise *at once* in the scale of intellectual and *moral* existence." "That," he adds, "is my belief." He avows, also, that the fortunate individual whom he is describing, by being "accustomed to such contemplations, will feel the *moral dignity of his nature exalted*." He speaks also of physical knowledge as "being the means of useful occupation and rational recreation ;" of "the pleasures of knowledge" superseding "the indulgence of sensual appetite," and of its "contributing to the intellectual and *moral improvement* of the community." Accordingly, he very consistently wishes it to be set before "the female as well as the male portion of the population ;" otherwise, as he truly observes, "great injustice would be done to the well-educated and virtuous women" of the place. They are to "have equal power and equal influence with others." It will be difficult to exhaust the reflections which rise in the mind on reading avowals of this nature.

The first question which obviously suggests itself is *how* these wonderful moral effects are to be wrought under the instrumentality of the physical sciences. Can the process be analyzed and drawn out, or does it act like a dose or a charm which comes into general use empirically? Does Sir Robert Peel mean to say, that whatever be the occult reasons for the result, so it is; you have but to drench the popular mind with physics, and moral and religious advancement follows on the whole, in spite of individual failures? Yet where has the experiment been tried on so large a scale as to justify such anticipations? Or rather, does he mean, that, from the nature of the case, he who is imbued with science and literature, unless adverse influences interfere, cannot but be a better man? It is natural and becoming to seek for some clear idea of the meaning of so dark an oracle. To know is one thing, tŏ do is another; the two things are altogether distinct. A man knows he should get up in the morning,—he lies a-bed; he knows he should not lose his temper, yet he cannot keep it. A labouring man knows he should not go to the ale-house, and his wife knows she should not filch when she goes out charing; but, nevertheless, in these cases, the consciousness of a duty is not all one with the performance of it. There are, then, large families of instances, to say the least, in which men may become wiser, without becoming better; what, then, is the meaning of this great maxim in the mouth of its promulgators?

Mr. Bentham would answer, that the knowledge which carries virtue along with it, is the knowledge how to take care of number one—a clear appreciation of what is pleasurable, what painful, and what promotes the one and prevents the other. An uneducated man is ever mistaking his own interest, and standing in the way of his own true enjoyments. Useful Knowledge is that which tends to make us more useful to ourselves;—a most definite and intelligible account of the matter, and needing no explanation. But it would be a great injustice, both to Lord Brougham and to Sir Robert, to suppose, when they talk of Knowledge being Virtue, that they are Benthamizing. Bentham had not a spark of poetry in him ; on the contrary, there is much of high aspiration, generous sentiment, and impassioned feeling in the tone of Lord Brougham and Sir Robert. They speak of knowledge as something "pulchrum," fair and glorious, exalted above the range of ordinary humanity, and so little connected with the personal interest of its votaries, that, though Sir Robert does *obiter* talk of improved modes of draining, and the chemical properties of manure, yet he must not be supposed to come short of the lofty enthusiasm of Lord Brougham, who expressly panegyrizes certain ancient philosophers who gave up riches, retired into solitude, or embraced a life of travel, smit with a sacred curiosity about physical or mathematical truth.

Here Mr. Bentham, did it fall to him to offer a criticism, doubtless would take leave to inquire whether such language was anything better than a fine set of words "signifying nothing,"—flowers of rhetoric, which bloom, smell sweet, and die. But it is impossible to suspect so grave and practical a man as Sir Robert Peel of using words literally without any meaning at all ; and though I think at best they have not a very profound meaning, yet, such as it is, we ought to attempt to draw it out.

Now, without using exact theological language, we may surely take it for granted, from the experience of facts, that the human mind is at best in a very unformed or disordered state ; passions and conscience, likings and reason, conflicting,—might rising against right, with the prospect of things getting worse. Under these circumstances, what is it that the School of philosophy in which Sir Robert has enrolled himself proposes to accomplish ? Not a victory of the mind over itself—not the supremacy of the law—not the reduction of the rebels—not the unity of our complex nature—not an harmonizing of the chaos—but the mere lulling of the passions to rest by turning the course of thought ; not a change of character, but a mere removal of temptation.   This should be carefully observed.   When a husband is gloomy, or an old woman peevish and fretful, those who are about them do all they can to keep dangerous topics and causes of offence out of the way, and think themselves lucky, if, by such skilful management, they get through the day without an outbreak. When a child cries, the nurserymaid dances it about, or points to the pretty black horses out of window, or shows how ashamed poll-parrot or poor puss must be of its tantarums.   Such is the sort of prescription which Sir Robert Peel offers to the good people of Tamworth.   He makes no pretence of subduing the giant nature, in which we were born, of smiting the loins of the domestic enemies of our peace, of overthrowing passion and fortifying reason ; he does but offer to bribe the foe for the nonce with gifts which will avail for that purpose just so long as they *will* avail, and no longer.

This was mainly the philosophy of the great Tully, except when it pleased him to speak as a disciple of the Porch.   Cicero handed the recipe to Brougham, and Brougham has passed it on to Peel.   If we examine the old Roman's meaning in "*O philosophia, vitæ dux,*" it was neither more nor less than this ;—that, *while* we were thinking of philosophy, we were not thinking of anything else ; we did not feel grief, or anxiety, or passion, or ambition, or hatred all that time, and the only point was to keep thinking of it.   How to keep thinking of it was *extra artem.* If a man was in grief, he was to be amused ; if disappointed, to be excited; if in a rage, to be soothed ; if in love, to be roused to the pursuit of glory. No inward change was contemplated, but a change of external objects ; as if we were all White Ladies or Undines, our moral life being one of impulse and emotion, not subjected to laws, not consisting in habits, not capable of growth. When Cicero was outwitted by Cæsar, he solaced himself with Plato ; when he lost his daughter, he wrote a treatise on Consolation. Such, too, was the philosophy of that Lydian city, mentioned by the historian, who in a famine played at dice to stay their stomachs.

And such is the rule of life advocated by Lord Brougham; and though, of course, he protests that knowledge " must invigorate the mind as well as entertain it, and refine and elevate the character, while it gives listlessness and weariness their most agreeable excitement and relaxation," yet his notions of vigour and elevation, when analyzed, will be found to resolve themselves into a mere preternatural excitement under the influence of some stimulating object, or the peace which is attained by there being nothing to quarrel with. He speaks of philosophers leaving the care of their estates, or declining public honours, from the greater desirableness of Knowledge ; envies the shelter enjoyed in the University of Glasgow from the noise and bustle of the world ; and, *apropos* of Pascal and Cowper, " so mighty," says he, " is the power of intellectual occupation, to make the heart forget, *for the time*, its most prevailing griefs, and to change its deepest gloom to sunshine."

Whether Sir Robert Peel meant all this, which others before him have meant, it is impossible to say ; but I will be bound, if he did not mean this, he meant nothing else, and his words will certainly insinuate this meaning, wherever a reader is not content to go without any meaning at all. They will countenance, with his high authority, what in one form or other is a chief error of the day, in very distinct schools of opinion,—that our true excellence comes not from within, but from without; not wrought out through personal struggles and sufferings, but following upon a passive exposure to influences over which we have no control. They will countenance the theory that diversion is the instrument of improvement, and excitement the condition of right action; and whereas diversions cease to be diversions if they are constant, and excitements by their very nature have a crisis and run through a course, they will tend to make novelty ever in request, and will set the great teachers of morals upon the incessant search after stimulants and sedatives, by which unruly nature may, *pro re natâ*, be kept in order.

Hence, be it observed, Lord Brougham, in the last quoted sentence, tells us, with much accuracy of statement, that "intellectual occupation made the heart" of Pascal or Cowper "*for the time* forget its griefs." He frankly offers us a philosophy of expedients : he shows us how to live by medicine. Digestive pills half an hour before dinner, and a posset at bedtime at the best; and at the worst, dram-drinking and opium,—the very remedy against broken hearts, or remorse of conscience, which is in request among the many, in gin-palaces *not* intellectual.

And if these remedies be but of temporary effect at the utmost, more commonly they will have no effect at all. Strong liquors, indeed, do for a time succeed in their object; but who was ever consoled in real trouble by the small beer of literature or science? "Sir," said Rasselas, to the philosopher who had lost his daughter,

" mortality is an event by which a wise man can never be surprised." "Young man," answered the mourner, "you speak like one that hath never felt the pangs of separation. What comfort can truth or reason afford me? of what effect are they now but to tell me that my daughter will not be restored?" Or who was ever made more humble or more benevolent by being told, as the same practical moralist words it, "to concur with the great and unchangeable scheme of universal felicity, and co-operate with the general dispensation and tendency of the present system of things"? Or who was made to do any secret act of self-denial, or was steeled against pain, or peril, by all the lore of the infidel La Place, or those other "mighty spirits" which Lord Brougham and Sir Robert eulogize? Or when was a choleric temperament ever brought under by a scientific King Canute planting his professor's chair before the rising waves? And as to the "keen" and "ecstatic" pleasures which Lord Brougham, not to say Sir Robert, ascribes to intellectual pursuit and conquest, I cannot help thinking that in that line they will find themselves outbid in the market by gratifications much closer at hand, and on a level with the meanest capacity. Sir Robert makes it a boast that women are to be members of his institution; it is hardly necessary to remind so accomplished a classic, that Aspasia and other learned ladies in Greece are no very encouraging precedents in favour of the purifying effects of science. But the strangest and most painful topic which he urges, is one which Lord Brougham has had the good taste altogether to avoid,—the power, not of religion, but of scientific knowledge, on a death-bed; a subject which Sir Robert treats in language which it is far better to believe is mere oratory than is said in earnest.

Such is this new art of living, offered to the labouring classes,—we will say, for instance, in a severe winter, snow on the ground, glass falling, bread rising, coal at 20d. the cwt., and no work.

It does not require many words, then, to determine that, taking human nature as it is actually found, and assuming that there is an Art of life, to say that it consists, or in any essential manner is placed, in the cultivation of Knowledge, that the mind is changed by a discovery, or saved by a diversion, and can thus be amused into immortality,—that grief, anger, cowardice, self-conceit, pride, or passion, can be subdued by an examination of shells or grasses, or inhaling of gases, or chipping of rocks, or calculating the longitude, is the veriest of pretences which sophist or mountebank ever professed to a gaping auditory. If virtue be a mastery over the mind, if its end be action, if its perfection be inward order, harmony, and peace, we must seek it in graver and holier places than in Libraries and Reading-rooms.

3.

Secular Knowledge not a direct Means of Moral Improvement.

THERE are two Schools of philosophy, in high esteem, at this day, as at other times, neither of them accepting Christian principles as the guide of life, yet both of them unhappily patronized by many whom it would be the worst and most cruel uncharitableness to suspect of unbelief. Mr. Bentham is the master of the one; and Sir Robert Peel is a disciple of the other.

Mr. Bentham's system has nothing ideal about it; he is a stern realist, and he limits his realism to things which he can see, hear, taste, touch, and handle. He does not acknowledge the existence of anything which he cannot ascertain for himself. Exist it may nevertheless, but till it makes itself felt, to him it exists not; till it comes down right before him, and he is very short-sighted, it is not recognized by him as having a co-existence with himself, any more than the Emperor of China is received into the European family of Kings. With him a being out of sight is a being simply out of mind; nay, he does not allow the traces or glimpses of facts to have any claim on his regard, but with him to have a little and not much, is to have nothing at all. With him to speak truth is to be ready with a definition, and to imagine, to guess, to doubt, or to falter, is much the same as to lie. What opinion will such an iron thinker entertain of Cicero's "glory," or Lord Brougham's "truth," or Sir

Robert's "scientific consolations," and all those other airy nothings which are my proper subject of remark, and which I have in view when, by way of contrast, I make mention of the philosophy of Bentham? And yet the doctrine of the three eminent orators, whom I have ventured to criticise, has in it much that is far nobler than Benthamism; their misfortune being, not that they look for an excellence above the beaten path of life, but that whereas Christianity has told us what that excellence is, Cicero lived before it was given to the world, and Lord Brougham and Sir Robert Peel prefer his involuntary error to their own inherited truth. Surely, there is something unearthly and superhuman in spite of Bentham; but it is not glory, or knowledge, or any abstract idea of virtue, but great and good tidings which need not here be particularly mentioned, and the pity is, that these Christian statesmen cannot be content with what is divine without as a supplement hankering after what was heathen.

Now, independent of all other considerations, the great difference, in a practical light, between the object of Christianity and of heathen belief, is this—that glory, science, knowledge, and whatever other fine names we use, never healed a wounded heart, nor changed a sinful one; but the Divine Word is with power. The ideas which Christianity brings before us are in themselves full of influence, and they are attended with a supernatural gift over and above themselves, in order to meet the special exigencies of our nature. Knowledge is not "power," nor is glory "the first and only fair;" but "Grace," or the "Word," by whichever name we call it, has been from the first a quickening, renovating, organizing principle. It has new created the individual, and transferred and knit him into a social body, composed of members each similarly created. It has cleansed man of his moral diseases, raised him to hope and energy, given him to propagate a brotherhood among his fellows, and to found a family or rather a kingdom of saints all over the earth ; —it introduced a new force into the world, and the impulse which it gave continues in its original vigour down to this day. Each one of us has lit his lamp from his neighbour, or received it from his fathers, and the lights thus transmitted are at this time as strong and as clear as if 1800 years had not passed since the kindling of the sacred flame. What has glory or knowledge been able to do like this ? Can it raise the dead ? can it create a polity? can it do more than testify man's need and typify God's remedy?

And yet, in spite of this, when we have an instrument given us, capable of changing the whole man, great orators and statesmen are busy, forsooth, with their heathen charms and nostrums, their sedatives, correctives, or restoratives ; as preposterously as if we were to build our men-of-war, or conduct our iron-works, on the principles approved in Cicero's day. The utmost that Lord Brougham seems to propose to himself in the education of the mind, is to keep out bad thoughts by means of good—a great object, doubtless, but not so great in philosophical conception, as is the destruction of the bad in Christian fact. "If it can be a pleasure," he says, in his Discourse upon the Objects and Advantages of Science, "if it can be a *pleasure to gratify curiosity*, to know what we were ignorant of, to have our *feelings of wonder* called forth, *how pure a delight of this very kind* does natural science hold out to its students ! How wonderful are the laws that regulate the motions of fluids ! Is there anything in all the idle books of tales and horrors, more truly astonish-

ing that the fact, that a few pounds of water may, by
mere pressure, without any machinery, by merely being
placed in one particular way, produce very irresistible
force ? What can be more strange, than that an ounce
weight should balance hundreds of pounds by the in-
tervention of a few bars of thin iron ? Can anything surprise us more than to find that the colour white is a
mixture of all others ? that water should be chiefly composed of an inflammable substance ? Akin to this
pleasure of contemplating new and extraordinary truths
is the *gratification of a more learned curiosity*, by tracing
resemblances and relations between things which to common apprehension seem widely different," etc., etc. And
in the same way Sir Robert tells us even of a *devout*
curiosity. In all cases *curiosity* is the means, *diversion*
of mind the highest end ; and though of course I will
not assert that Lord Brougham, and certainly not that
Sir Robert Peel, denies any higher kind of morality,
yet when the former rises above Benthamism, in which
he often indulges, into what may be called *Broughamism
proper*, he commonly grasps at nothing more real and
substantial than these Ciceronian ethics.

In morals, as in physics, the stream cannot rise higher
than its source. Christianity raises men from earth, for
it comes from heaven ; but human morality creeps,
struts, or frets upon the earth's level, without wings to
rise. The Knowledge School does not contemplate raising man above himself; it merely aims at disposing of
his existing powers and tastes, as is most convenient, or
is practicable under circumstances. It finds him, like the
victims of the French Tyrant, doubled up in a cage in
which he can neither lie, stand, sit, nor kneel, and its
highest desire is to find an attitude in which his unrest
may be least. Or it finds him like some musical instru-

ment, of great power and compass, but imperfect; from
its very structure some keys must ever be out of tune,
and its object, when ambition is highest, is to throw the
fault of its nature where least it will be observed. It leaves
man where it found him—man, and not an Angel—a
sinner, not a Saint; but it tries to make him look as
much like what he is not as ever it can. The poor indulge in low pleasures; they use bad language, swear
loudly and recklessly, laugh at coarse jests, and are rude
and boorish. Sir Robert would open on them a wider
range of thought and more intellectual objects, by teaching
them science; but what warrant will he give us that, if
his object could be achieved, what they would gain in
decency they would not lose in natural humility and
faith? If so, he has exchanged a gross fault for a more
subtle one. "Temperance topics" stop drinking; let
us suppose it; but will much be gained, if those who
give up spirits take to opium? *Naturam expellas furcâ,
tamen usque recurret*, is at least a heathen truth, and
universities and libraries which recur to heathenism may
reclaim it from the heathen for their motto.

Nay, everywhere, so far as human nature remains
hardly or partially Christianized, the heathen law remains
in force; as is felt in a measure even in the most religious places and societies. Even there, where Christianity has power, the venom of the old Adam is not
subdued. Those who have to do with our Colleges give
us their experience, that in the case of the young committed to their care, external discipline may change the
fashionable excess, but cannot allay the principle of sin-
ning. Stop cigars, they will take to drinking parties;
stop drinking, they gamble; stop gambling, and a worse
license follows. You do not get rid of vice by human
expedients; you can but use them according to circum-

stances, and in their place, as making the best of a bad matter. You must go to a higher source for renovation of the heart and of the will. You do but play a sort of "hunt the slipper" with the fault of our nature, till you go to Christianity.

I say, you must use human methods *in their place,* and there they are useful ; but they are worse than useless out of their place. I have no fanatical wish to deny to any whatever subject of thought or method of reason a place altogether, if it chooses to claim it, in the cultivation of the mind. Mr. Bentham may despise verse-making, or Mr. Dugald Stewart logic, but the great and true maxim is to sacrifice none—to combine, and therefore to adjust, all. All cannot be first, and therefore each has its place, and the problem is to find it. It is at least not a lighter mistake to make what is secondary first, than to leave it out altogether. Here then it is that the Knowledge Society, Gower Street College, Tamworth Reading-room, Lord Brougham and Sir Robert Peel, are all so deplorably mistaken. Christianity, and nothing short of it, must be made the element and principle of all education. Where it has been laid as the first stone, and acknowledged as the governing spirit, it will take up into itself, assimilate, and give a character to literature and science. Where Revealed Truth has given the aim and direction to Knowledge, Knowledge of all kinds will minister to Revealed Truth. The evidences of Religion, natural theology, metaphysics,—or, again, poetry, history, and the classics,—or physics and mathematics, may all be grafted into the mind of a Christian, and give and take by the grafting. But if in education we begin with nature before grace, with evidences before faith, with science before conscience, with poetry before practice, we shall be doing much the same as if we were to indulge the appetites and passions, and turn a deaf ear to the reason. In each case we misplace what in its place is a divine gift. If we attempt to effect a moral improvement by means of poetry, we shall but mature into a mawkish, frivolous, and fastidious sentimentalism; —if by means of argument, into a dry, unamiable long-headedness;—if by good society, into a polished outside, with hollowness within, in which vice has lost its grossness, and perhaps increased its malignity;—if by experimental science, into an uppish, supercilious temper, much inclined to scepticism. But reverse the order of things : put Faith first and Knowledge second ; let the University minister to the Church, and then classical poetry becomes the type of Gospel truth, and physical science a comment on Genesis or Job, and Aristotle changes into Butler, and Arcesilas into Berkeley.*

Far from recognizing this principle, the teachers of the Knowledge School would educate from Natural Theology up to Christianity, and would amend the heart through literature and philosophy. Lord Brougham, as if faith came from science, gives out that "henceforth nothing shall prevail over us to praise or to blame any one for " his belief, "which he can no more change than he can the hue of his skin, or the height of his stature." And Sir Robert, whose profession and life give the lie to his philosophy, founds a library into which "no works of controversial divinity shall enter," that is, no Christian doctrine at all ; and he tells us that "an increased sagacity will make men not merely believe in the cold doctrines of Natural Religion, but that it will *so prepare*

* [On the supremacy of each science in its own field of thought, and the encroachments upon it of other sciences, *vide* the author's "University Teaching," Disc. 3, and "University Subjects," No. 7 and 10.]

and temper the spirit and understanding that they will be better *qualified to comprehend the great scheme of human redemption.*"   And again, Lord Brougham considers that " the pleasures of science tend not only to make our lives more agreeable, but better ;" and Sir Robert responds, that " he entertains the hope that there will be the means afforded of useful occupation and rational recreation; that men will prefer the pleasures of knowledge above the indulgence of sensual appetite, and that there is a prospect of contributing to the intellectual and moral improvement of the neighbourhood."

Can the nineteenth century produce no more robust and creative philosophy than this ?

4.

Secular Knowledge not the Antecedent of Moral Improvement.

HUMAN nature wants recasting, but Lord Brougham is all for tinkering it. He does not despair of making something of it yet. He is not, indeed, of those who think that reason, passion, and whatever else is in us, are made right and tight by the principle of self-interest. He understands that something more is necessary for man's happiness than self-love; he feels that man has affections and aspirations which Bentham does not take account of, and he looks about for their legitimate objects. Christianity has provided these; but, unhappily, he passes them by. He libels them with the name of dogmatism, and conjures up instead the phantoms of Glory and Knowledge; *idola theatri,* as his famous predecessor calls them. "There are idols," says Lord Bacon, "which have got into the human mind, from the different tenets of philosophers, and the perverted laws of demonstration. And these we denominate idols of the theatre; because all the philosophies that have been hitherto invented or received, are but so many stage plays, written or acted, as having shown nothing but fictitious and theatrical worlds. Idols of the theatre, or theories, are many, and will probably grow much more numerous; for if men had not, through many ages, *been prepossessed with religion and theology,* and *if civil governments*, but particularly monarchies," (and, I suppose, their ministers, counsellors, functionaries, inclusive,) " *had not been averse to innovations of this kind*, though but intended, so as to make it dangerous and prejudicial to the private fortunes of such as take the bent of innovating, not only by depriving them of advantages, but also of exposing them to contempt and hatred, there would doubtless have been *numerous other sects* of philosophies and theories, introduced, of kin to those that in great variety formerly flourished among the Greeks. And these theatrical fables have this in common with dramatic pieces, that the fictitious narrative is neater, more elegant and pleasing, than the true history."

I suppose we may readily grant that the science of the day is attended by more lively interest, and issues in more entertaining knowledge, than the study of the New Testament. Accordingly, Lord Brougham fixes upon such science as the great desideratum of human nature, and puts aside faith under the nickname of opinion. I wish Sir Robert Peel had not fallen into the snare, insulting doctrine by giving it the name of " controversial divinity."

However, it will be said that Sir Robert, in spite of such forms of speech, differs essentially from Lord Brougham : for he goes on, in the latter part of the Address which has occasioned these remarks, to speak of Science as leading to Christianity. " I can never think it possible," he says, "that a mind can be so constituted, that after being familiarized with the great truth of observing in every object of contemplation that nature presents the manifest proofs of a Divine Intelligence, if you range even from the organization of the meanest weed you trample upon, or of the insect that lives but for an hour, up to the magnificent structure of the heavens, and the still more wonderful phenomena of the soul, reason, and conscience of man ; I cannot believe that any man, accustomed to such contemplations, can return from them with any other feelings than those of enlarged conceptions of the Divine Power, and greater reverence for the name of the Almighty Creator of the universe." A long and complicated sentence, and no unfitting emblem of the demonstration it promises. It sets before us a process and deduction. Depend on it, it is not so safe a road and so expeditious a journey from premiss and conclusion as Sir Robert anticipates. The way is long, and there are not a few half-way houses and traveller's rests along it; and who is to warrant that the members of the Reading-room and Library will go steadily on to the goal he would set before them ? And when at length they come to " Christianity," pray how do the roads lay between it and " controversial divinity " ? Or, grant the Tamworth readers to *begin* with " Christianity" as well as science, the same question suggests itself, What *is* Christianity ? Universal bene- volence ? Exalted morality ? Supremacy of law ? Conservatism ? An age of light ? An age of reason ?— Which of them all ?

Most cheerfully do I render to so religious a man as Sir Robert Peel the justice of disclaiming any insinua- tion on my part, that he has any intention at all to put aside Religion ; yet his words either mean nothing, or they do, both on their surface, and when carried into effect, mean something very irreligious.

And now for one plain proof of this.

It is certain, then, that the multitude of men have neither time nor capacity for attending to many subjects. If they attend to one, they will not attend to the other ;

if they give their leisure and curiosity to this world, they will have none left for the next. We cannot be everything; as the poet says, "*non omnia possumus omnes.*" We must make up our minds to be ignorant of much, if we would know anything. And we must make our choice between risking Science, and risking Religion. Sir Robert indeed says, "Do not believe that you have not time for rational recreation. It is the idle man who wants time for everything." However, this seems to me rhetoric; and what I have said to be the matter of fact, for the truth of which I appeal, not to argument, but to the proper judges of facts,—common sense and practical experience; and if they pronounce it to be a fact, then Sir Robert Peel, little as he means it, does unite with Lord Brougham in taking from Christianity what he gives to Science.

I will make this fair offer to both of them. Every member of the Church Established shall be eligible to the Tamworth Library on one condition—that he brings from the "public minister of religion," to use Sir Robert's phrase, a ticket in witness of his proficiency in Christian knowledge. We will have no "controversial divinity" in the Library, but a little out of it. If the gentlemen of the Knowledge School will but agree to teach town and country Religion first, they shall have a *carte blanche* from me to teach anything or everything else second. Not a word has been uttered or intended in these Letters against Science; I would treat it, as they do *not* treat "controversial divinity," with respect and gratitude. They caricature doctrine under the name of controversy. I do not nickname science infidelity. I call it by their own name, "useful and entertaining knowledge;" and I call doctrine "Christian knowledge:" and, as thinking Christianity something more than useful and entertaining, I want faith to come first, and utility and amusement to follow.

That persons indeed are found in all classes, high and low, busy and idle, capable of proceeding from sacred to profane knowledge, is undeniable ; and it is desirable they should do so. It is desirable that talent for particular departments in literature and science should be fostered and turned to account, wherever it is found. But what has this to do with this general canvass of " *all* persons of all descriptions without reference to religious creed, who shall have attained *the age of fourteen*" ? Why solicit "the working classes, without distinction of party, political opinion, or religious profession ;" that is, whether they have heard of a God or no ? Whence these cries rising on our ears, of "Let me entreat you!" "Neglect not the opportunity!" "It will not be our fault!" "Here is an access for you!" very like the tones of a street preacher, or the cad of an omnibus,—little worthy of a great statesman and a religious philosopher ?

However, the Tamworth Reading-room admits of one restriction, which is not a little curious, and has no very liberal sound. It seems that all "*virtuous* women" may be members of the Library ; that "great injustice would be done to the *well-educated and virtuous* women of the town and neighbourhood" had they been excluded. A very emphatic silence is maintained about women not virtuous. What does this mean ? Does it mean to exclude them, while bad *men* are admitted ? Is this accident, or design, sinister and insidious, against a portion of the community ? What has virtue to do with a Reading-room ? It is to *make* its members virtuous ; it is to "exalt the *moral dignity* of their nature ;" it is to provide "charms and temptations" to allure them from sensuality and riot. To whom but to the vicious ought Sir Robert to discourse about "opportunities," and "access," and "moral improvement;" and who else would prove a fitter experiment, and a more glorious triumph, of scientific influences? And yet he shuts out all but the well-educated and virtuous.

Alas, that bigotry should have left the mark of its hoof on the great "fundamental principle of the Tamworth Institution"! Sir Robert Peel is bound in consistency to attempt its obliteration. But if that is impossible, as many will anticipate, why, O why, while he is about it, why will he not give us just a little more of it? *Cannot* we prevail on him to modify his principle, and to admit into his library none but "well-educated and virtuous" *men?*

5.

Secular Knowledge not a Principle of Social Unity.

SIR ROBERT PEEL proposes to establish a Library which "shall be open to all persons of all descriptions, without reference to political opinions or to religious creed." He invites those who are concerned in manufactories, or who have many workmen, "without distinction of party, political opinions, *or* religious profession." He promises that "in the selection of subjects for public lectures everything calculated to excite religious *or* political animosity shall be excluded." Nor is any "discussion on matters connected with religion, politics, *or* local party differences" to be permitted in the reading-room. And he congratulates himself that he has "laid the foundation of an edifice in which men of all political opinions *and* of all religious feelings may unite in furtherance of Knowledge, without the asperities of "party feeling." In these statements religious difference are made synonymous with "party feeling ;" and, whereas the tree is "known by its fruit," their characteristic symptoms are felicitously described as "asperities," and "animosities." And, in order to teach us more precisely what these differences are worth, they are compared to differences between Whig and Tory—nay, even to "*local* party differences ;" such, I suppose, as about a municipal election, or a hole-and-corner meeting, or a parish job, or a bill in Parliament for a railway.

But, to give him the advantage of the more honourable parallel of the two, are religious principles to be put upon a level even with political ? Is it as bad to be a republican as an unbeliever? Is it as magnanimous to humour a scoffer as to spare an opponent in the House ? Is a difference about the Reform Bill all one with a difference about the Creed? Is it as polluting to hear arguments for Lord Melbourne as to hear a scoff against the Apostles ? To a statesman, indeed, like Sir Robert, to abandon one's party is a far greater sacrifice than to unparliamentary men; and it would be uncandid to doubt that he is rather magnifying politics than degrading Religion in throwing them together; but still, when he advocates concessions in theology *and* politics, he must be plainly told to make presents of things that belong to him, nor seek to be generous with other people's substance. There are entails in more matters than parks and old places. He made his politics for himself, but Another made theology.

Christianity is faith, faith implies a doctrine ; a doctrine propositions; propositions yes or no, yes or no differences. Differences, then, are the natural attendants on Christianity, and you cannot have Christianity, and not have differences. When, then, Sir Robert Peel calls such differences points of "party feeling," what is this but to insult Christianity ? Yet so cautious, so correct a man, cannot have made such a sacrifice for nothing ; nor does he long leave us in doubt what is his inducement. He tells us that his great aim is the peace and good order of the community, and the easy working of the national machine. With this in view, any price is cheap, everything is marketable; all impediments are a nuisance. He does not undo for undoing's sake; he gains more than an equivalent. It is a mistake, too, to say that he considers all differences of opinion as equal in importance ; no, they are only equally in the way. He only compares them together where they *are* comparable,— in their common inconvenience to a minister of State. They may be as little homogeneous as chalk is to cheese, or Macedon to Monmouth, but they agree in interfering with social harmony ; and, since that harmony is the first of goods and the end of life, what is left us but to discard all that disunites us, and to cultivate all that may amalgamate ?

Could Sir Robert have set a more remarkable example of self-sacrifice than in thus becoming the disciple of his political foe, accepting from Lord Brougham his new principle of combination, rejecting Faith for the fulcrum of Society, and proceeding to rest it upon Knowledge ?

" I cannot help thinking," he exclaims at Tamworth, "that *by bringing together in an institution of this kind* intelligent men of all classes and conditions of life, by uniting together, in the committee of this institution, the gentleman of ancient family and great landed possessions with the skilful mechanic and artificer of good character, I cannot help believing that we are *harmonizing* the gradations of society, and binding men together by a *new* bond, which will have *more than ordinary* strength on account of the object which unites us." The old bond, he seems to say, was Religion; Lord Brougham's is Knowledge. Faith, once the soul of social union, is now but the spirit of division. Not a single doctrine but is "controversial divinity; " not an abstraction can be imagined (could abstractions constrain), not a comprehension projected (could comprehensions connect), but will leave out one or other portion or element of the social fabric. We must abandon Religion, if we aspire to be statesmen. Once, indeed, it was a living power, kindling hearts, leavening them with one idea, moulding them on one model, developing them into one polity. Ere now it has been the life of morality : it has given birth to heroes ; it has wielded empire. But another age has come in, and Faith is effete ; let us submit to what we cannot change ; let us not hang over our dead, but bury it out of sight. Seek we out some young and vigorous principle, rich in sap, and fierce in life, to give form to elements which are fast resolving into their inorganic chaos ; and where shall we find such a principle but in Knowledge ?

Accordingly, though Sir Robert somewhat chivalrously battles for the appointment upon the Book Committee of what he calls two " public ministers of religion, holding prominent and responsible offices, endowed by the State," and that *ex officio*, yet he is untrue to his new principle only in appearance : for he couples his concession with explanations, restrictions, and safeguards quite sufficient to prevent old Faith becoming insurgent against young Knowledge. First he takes his Vicar and Curate as "conversant with literary subjects and with literary works," and then as having duties " immediately con- nected with the moral condition and improvement " of the place. Further he admits " it is perfectly right to be *jealous* of all power held by such a tenure : " and he insists on the "fundamental" condition that these sacred functionaries shall permit no doctrinal works to be in- troduced or lectures to be delivered. Lastly, he reserves in the general body the power of withdrawing this in- dulgence " if the existing checks be not sufficient, and the power be *abused*,"—abused, that is, by the vicar and curate ; also he desires to secure Knowledge from being *perverted* to " *evil* or *immoral* purposes"—such perversion of course, if attempted, being the natural

antithesis, or *pendant*, to the vicar's contraband intro-
troduction of the doctrines of Faith.

Lord Brougham will make all this clearer to us. A
work of high interest and varied information, to which
I have already referred, is attributed to him, and at
least is of his school, in which the ingenious author, whoever he is, shows how Knowledge can do for Society
what has hitherto been supposed the prerogative of Faith.
As to Faith and its preachers, he had already compli-
mented them at Glasgow, as "the evil spirits of tyranny
and persecution," and had bid them good morning as
the scared and dazzled creatures of the " long night now
gone down the sky."

"The great truth," he proclaimed in language borrowed
from the records of faith (for after parsons no men quote
Scripture more familiarly than Liberals and Whigs), has
finally *gone forth to all the ends of the earth*, that man
shall no more render account to man for his belief, over
which he has himself no control. Henceforth nothing
shall prevail on us to *praise or to blame* any one for that
which he can no more change than he can the hue of
his skin or the height of his stature." And then he or
his scholar proceeds to his new *Vitæ Sanctorum*, or, as
he calls it, "Illustrations of the Pursuit of Knowledge ;"
and, whereas the badge of Christian saintliness is conflict, he writes of the " Pursuit of Knowledge *under difficulties ;* " and, whereas this Knowledge is to stand in the
place of Religion, he assumes a hortatory tone, a species
of eloquence in which decidedly he has no rival but Sir
Robert. "Knowledge," he says, " is happiness, as well
as power and virtue;" and he demands "the dedication
of our faculties" to it. "The *struggle*," he gravely
observes, which its disciple " has to wage may be a

protracted, but it ought not to be a *cheerless* one : for, if he do not *relax his exertions*, every movement he makes is necessarily a *step forward*, if not towards that distinction which intellectual attainments sometimes confer, at least to that *inward satisfaction and enjoyment* which is always their reward. No one stands in the way of another, or can deprive him of any part of his chance, we should rather say of his certainty, of success ; on the contrary, they are all *fellow-workers*, and may materially *help each other* forward." And he enumerates in various places the virtues which adorn the children of Knowledge— ardour united to humility, childlike alacrity, teachable- ness, truthfulness, patience, concentration of attention, husbandry of time, self-denial, self-command, and heroism.

Faith, viewed in its history through past ages, presents us with the fulfilment of one great idea in particular— that, namely, of an aristocracy of exalted spirits, drawn together out of all countries, ranks, and ages, raised above the condition of humanity, specimens of the capa- bilities of our race, incentives to rivalry and patterns for imitation. This Christian idea Lord Brougham has borrowed for his new Pantheon, which is equally various in all attributes and appendages of mind, with this one characteristic in all its specimens,—the pursuit of Know- ledge. Some of his worthies are low born, others of high degree ; some are in Europe, others in the Anti- podes ; some in the dark ages, others in the ages of light ; some exercise a voluntary, others an involuntary toil ; some give up riches, and others gain them ; some are fixtures, and others adventure much ; some are pro- fligate, and others ascetic ; and some are believers, and others are infidels.

Alfred, severely good and Christian, takes his place in

this new hagiology beside the gay and graceful Lorenzo de Medicis ; for did not the one " import civilization into England," and was not the other "the wealthy and munificent patron of all the liberal arts " ? Edward VI. and Haroun al Raschid, Dr. Johnson and Dr. Franklin, Newton and Protagoras, Pascal and Julian the Apostate, Joseph Milner and Lord Byron, Cromwell and Ovid, Bayle and Boyle, Adrian pope and Adrian emperor, Lady Jane Grey and Madame Roland,—human beings who agreed in nothing but in their humanity and in their love of Knowledge, are all admitted by this writer to one beatification, in proof of the Catholic character of his substitute for Faith.

The persecuting Marcus is a " good and enlightened emperor," and a "delightful" spectacle, when "mixing in the religious processions and ceremonies" of Athens, "re-building and re-endowing the schools," whence St. Paul was driven in derision. The royal Alphery, on the contrary, " preferred his humble parsonage" to the throne of the Czars. West was " nurtured among the quiet and gentle affections of a Quaker family." Kirke White's "feelings became ardently devotional, and he determined to give up his life to the preaching of Christianity." Roger Bacon was "a brother of the Franciscan Order, at that time the great support and ornament of both Universities." Belzoni seized "the opportunity" of Bonaparte's arrival in Italy to "throw off his monastic habit," " its idleness and obscurity," and to engage himself as a performer at Astley's. Duval, "a very able antiquarian of the last century," began his studies as a peasant boy, and finished them in a Jesuits' College. Mr. Davy, " having written a system of divinity," effected the printing of it in thirteen years " with a press of his own construction," and the assistance of his female servant, working off page by page for twenty-six volumes 8vo, of nearly 500 pages each. Raleigh, in spite of "immoderate ambition," was "one of the very chief glories of an age crowded with towering spirits."

Nothing comes amiss to this author; saints and sinners, the precious and the vile, are torn from their proper homes and recklessly thrown together under the category of Knowledge. 'Tis a pity he did not extend his view, as Christianity has done, to beings out of sight of man. Milton could have helped him to some angelic personages, as patrons and guardians of his intellectual temple, who of old time, before faith had birth,

> " Apart sat on a hill retired
> In thoughts more elevate, and reasoned high
> Of providence, foreknowledge, will, and fate,
> Passion and apathy, and glory, and shame,—
> Vain wisdom all, and false philosophy."

And, indeed, he does make some guesses that way, speaking most catholically of being "admitted to a fellowship with those loftier minds" who "by universal consent *held a station apart*," and are "spoken of *reverently*," as if their names were not those "of mortal men;" and he speaks of these "benefactors of mankind, when they *rest* from their *pious* labours, looking down" upon the blessings with which their "*toils and sufferings* have clothed the scene of their former existence."

Such is the oratory which has fascinated Sir Robert; yet we must recollect that in the year 1832, even the venerable Society for Promoting Christian Knowledge herself, catching its sound, and hearing something about sublimity, and universality, and brotherhood, and effort, and felicity, was beguiled into an admission of this singularly irreligious work into the list of publications which she had delegated to a Committee to select *in usum laicorum.*

That a Venerable Society should be caught by the vision of a Church Catholic is not wonderful ; but what could possess philosophers and statesmen to dazzle her with it, but man's need of some such support, and the divine excellence and sovereign virtue of that which Faith once created ?

6.

Secular Knowledge not a Principle of Action.

PEOPLE say to me, that it is but a dream to suppose that Christianity should regain the organic power in human society which once it possessed. I cannot help that; I never said it could. I am not a politician; I am proposing no measures, but exposing a fallacy, and resisting a pretence. Let Benthamism reign, if men have no aspirations; but do not tell them to be romantic, and then solace them with glory; do not attempt by philosophy what once was done by religion. The ascendency of Faith may be impracticable, but the reign of Knowledge is incomprehensible. The problem for statesmen of this age is how to educate the masses, and literature and science cannot give the solution.

Not so deems Sir Robert Peel; his firm belief and hope is, "that an increased sagacity will administer to an exalted faith; that it will make men not merely believe in the cold doctrines of Natural Religion, but that it will so prepare and temper the spirit and understanding, that they will be better qualified to comprehend the great scheme of human redemption." He certainly thinks that scientific pursuits have some considerable power of impressing religion upon the mind of the multitude. I think not, and will now say why.

Science gives us the grounds or premises from which religious truths are to be inferred; but it does not set about inferring them, much less does it reach the inference;—that is not its province. It brings before us phenomena, and it leaves us, if we will, to call them works of design, wisdom, or benevolence; and further still, if we will, to proceed to confess an Intelligent Creator. We have to take its facts, and to give them a meaning, and to draw our own conclusions from them. First comes Knowledge, then a view, then reasoning, and then belief. This is why Science has so little of a religious tendency; deductions have no power of persuasion. The heart is commonly reached, not through the reason, but through the imagination, by means of direct impressions, by the testimony of facts and events, by history, by description. Persons influence us, voices melt us, looks subdue us, deeds inflame us. Many a man will live and die upon a dogma : no man will be a martyr for a conclusion. A conclusion is but an opinion ; it is not a thing which *is*, but which *we are " certain about ; "* and it has often been observed, that we never say we are certain without implying that we doubt. To say that a thing *must* be, is to admit that it *may not* be. No one, I say, will die for his own calculations ; he dies for realities. This is why a literary religion is so little to be depended upon ; it looks well in fair weather, but its doctrines are opinions, and, when called to suffer for them, it slips them between its folios, or burns them at its hearth. And this again is the secret of the distrust and raillery with which moralists have been so commonly visited. They say and do not. Why? Because they are contemplating the fitness of things, and they live by the square, when they should be realizing their high maxims in the concrete. Now Sir Robert thinks better of natural history, chemistry, and astronomy, than of such ethics ; but they too, what are they more than divinity *in posse ?* He protests against " controversial divinity : " is *inferential* much better ?

I have no confidence, then, in philosophers who cannot help being religious, and are Christians by implication. They sit at home, and reach forward to distances which astonish us ; but they hit without grasping, and are sometimes as confident about shadows as about realities. They have worked out by a calculation the lie of a country which they never saw, and mapped it by means of a gazetteer; and like blind men, though they can put a stranger on his way, they cannot walk straight themselves, and do not feel it quite their business to walk at all.

Logic makes but a sorry rhetoric with the multitude ; first shoot round corners, and you may not despair of converting by a syllogism. Tell men to gain notions of a Creator from His works, and, if they were to set about it (which nobody does), they would be jaded and wearied by the labyrinth they were tracing. Their minds would be gorged and surfeited by the logical operation. Logicians are more set upon concluding rightly, than on right conclusions. They cannot see the end for the process. Few men have that power of mind which may hold fast and firmly a variety of thoughts. We ridicule "men of one idea ; " but a great many of us are born to be such, and we should be happier if we knew it. To most men argument makes the point in hand only more doubtful, and considerably less impressive. After all, man is *not* a reasoning animal ; he is a seeing, feeling, contemplating, acting animal. He is influenced by what is direct and precise. It is very well to freshen our impressions and convictions from physics, but to create them we must go elsewhere. Sir Robert Peel "never can think it possible that a mind can be so constituted, that, after being familiarized with the wonderful discoveries which have been made in every part of experimental science, it can retire from such contemplations without more enlarged conceptions of God's providence, and a higher reverence for His name." If he speaks of religious minds, he perpetrates a truism ; if of irreligious, he insinuates a paradox.

Life is not long enough for a religion of inferences ; we shall never have done beginning, if we determine to begin with proof. We shall ever be laying our foundations ; we shall turn theology into evidences, and divines into textuaries. We shall never get at our first principles. Resolve to believe nothing, and you must prove your proofs and analyze your elements, sinking further and further, and finding "in the lowest depth a lower deep," till you come to the broad bosom of scepticism. I would rather be bound to defend the reasonableness of assuming that Christianity is true, than to demonstrate a moral governance from the physical world. Life is for action. If we insist on proofs for everything, we shall never come to action : to act you must assume, and that assumption is faith.

Let no one suppose that in saying this I am maintaining that all proofs are equally difficult, and all propositions equally debatable. Some assumptions are greater than others, and some doctrines involve postulates larger than others, and more numerous. I only say that impressions lead to action, and that reasonings lead from it. Knowledge of premisses, and inferences upon them, —this is not to *live*. It is very well as a matter of liberal curiosity and of philosophy to analyze our modes of thought ; but let this come second, and when there is leisure for it, and then our examinations will in many ways even be subservient to action. But if we commence with scientific knowledge and argumentative proof, or lay any great stress upon it as the basis of personal

Christianity, or attempt to make man moral and religious by Libraries and Museums, let us in consistency take chemists for our cooks, and mineralogists for our masons.

Now I wish to state all this as matter of fact, to be judged by the candid testimony of any persons whatever. Why we are so constituted that Faith, not Knowledge or Argument, is our principle of action, is a question with which I have nothing to do ; but I think it is a fact, and if it be such, we must resign ourselves to it as best we may, unless we take refuge in the intolerable paradox, that the mass of men are created for nothing, and are meant to leave life as they entered it.   So well has this practically been understood in all ages of the world, that no Religion has yet been a Religion of physics or of philosophy.   It has ever been synonymous with Revelation. It never has been a deduction from what we know : it has ever been an assertion of what we are to believe.   It has never lived in a conclusion ; it has ever been a message, or a history, or a vision.   No legislator or priest ever dreamed of educating our moral nature by science or by argument.   There is no difference here between true Religions and pretended.   Moses was instructed, not to reason from the creation, but to work miracles. Christianity is a history supernatural, and almost scenic : it tells us what its Author is, by telling us what He has done.   I have no wish at all to speak otherwise than respectfully of conscientious Dissenters, but I have heard it said by those who were not their enemies, and who had known much of their preaching, that they had often heard narrow-minded and bigoted clergymen, and often Dissenting ministers of a far more intellectual cast; but that Dissenting teaching came to nothing,—that it was dissipated in thoughts which had no point, and inquiries which converged to no centre, that it ended as it began, and sent away its hearers as it found them ;— whereas the instruction in the Church, with all its defects and mistakes, comes to some end, for it started from some beginning. Such is the difference between the dogmatism of faith and the speculations of logic.

Lord Brougham himself, as we have already seen, has recognized the force of this principle. He has not left his philosophical religion to argument; he has committed it to the keeping of the imagination. Why should he depict a great republic of letters, and an intellectual Pantheon, but that he feels that instances and patterns, not logical reasonings, are the living conclusions which alone have a hold over the affections, or can form the character?

Secular Knowledge without Personal Religion tends to Unbelief.

WHEN Sir Robert Peel assures us from the Town-hall at Tamworth that physical science must lead to religion, it is no bad compliment to him to say that he is unreal. He speaks of what he knows nothing about. To a religious man like him, Science has ever suggested religious thoughts ; he colours the phenomena of physics with the hues of his own mind, and mistakes an interpretation for a deduction. "I am sanguine enough to believe," he says, "that that superior sagacity which is most conversant with the course and constitution of Nature will be first to turn a deaf ear to objections and presumptions against Revealed Religion, and to acknowledge the complete harmony of the Christian Dispensation with all that Reason, assisted by Revelation, tells us of the course and constitution of Nature." Now, considering that we are all of us educated as Christians from infancy, it is not easy to decide at this day whether Science creates Faith, or only confirms it ; but we have this remarkable fact in the history of heathen Greece against the former supposition, that her most eminent empirical philosophers were atheists, and that it was their atheism which was the cause of their eminence. "The natural philosophies of Democritus and others," says Lord Bacon, "*who allow no God or mind* in the frame of things, but attribute the structure of the universe to

infinite essays and trials of nature, or what they call
fate or fortune, and assigned the causes of particular
things to the necessity of matter, *without any intermixture
of final causes,* seem, as far as we can judge from the
remains of their philosophy, *much more solid,* and to have
gone deeper into nature, with regard to physical causes,
than the philosophies of Aristotle or Plato: and this only
because they *never meddled with final causes,* which the
others were perpetually inculcating."

Lord Bacon gives us both the fact and the reason for
it. Physical philosophers are ever inquiring *whence*
things are, not *why;* referring them to nature, not to
mind; and thus they tend to make a system a substitute
for a God. Each pursuit or calling has its own dangers,
and each numbers among its professors men who rise
superior to them. As the soldier is tempted to dissi-
pation, and the merchant to acquisitiveness, and the
lawyer to the sophistical, and the statesman to the expedient, and the country clergyman to ease and comfort,
yet there are good clergymen, statesmen, lawyers, merchants, and soldiers, notwithstanding; so there are
religious experimentalists, though physics, taken by
themselves, tend to infidelity; but to have recourse to
physics to *make* men religious is like recommending a
canonry as a cure for the gout, or giving a youngster a
commission as a penance for irregularities.

The whole framework of Nature is confessedly a tissue
of antecedents and consequents; we may refer all things
forwards to design, or backwards on a physical cause.
La Place is said to have considered he had a formula
which solved all the motions of the solar system; shall
we say that those motions came from this formula or
from a Divine Fiat? Shall we have recourse for our
theory to physics or to theology? Shall we assume

Matter and its necessary properties to be eternal, or Mind with its divine attributes? Does the sun shine to warm the earth, or is the earth warmed because the sun shines? The one hypothesis will solve the phenomena as well as the other. Say not it is but a puzzle in argument, and that no one ever felt it in fact. So far from it, I believe that the study of Nature, when religious feeling is away, leads the mind, rightly or wrongly, to acquiesce in the atheistic theory, as the simplest and easiest. It is but parallel to that tendency in anatomical studies, which no one will deny, to solve all the phenomena of the human frame into material elements and powers, and to dispense with the soul. To those who are conscious of matter, but not conscious of mind, it seems more rational to refer all things to one origin, such as they know, than to assume the existence of a second origin such as they know not. It is Religion, then, which suggests to Science its true conclusions; the facts come from Knowledge, but the principles come of Faith.*

There are two ways, then, of reading Nature—as a machine and as a work. If we come to it with the assumption that it is a creation, we shall study it with awe; if assuming it to be a system, with mere curiosity. Sir Robert does not make this distinction. He subscribes to the belief that the man "accustomed to such contemplations, *struck with awe* by the manifold proofs of infinite power and infinite wisdom, will yield more ready and hearty assent—yes, the assent of the heart, and not only of the understanding, to the pious ex-

---

* [This is too absolute, if it is to be taken to mean that the legitimate, and what may be called the objective, conclusion from the fact of Nature viewed in the concrete is not in favour of the being and providence of God. —*Vide* "Essay on Assent," pp. 336, 345, 369, and "Univ. Serm." p. 194.]

clamation, 'O Lord, how glorious are Thy works!'"
He considers that greater insight into Nature will lead
a man to say, "How great and wise is the Creator, who
has done this!" True: but it is possible that his
thoughts may take the form of "How clever is the
creature who has discovered it!" and self-conceit may
stand proxy for adoration. This is no idle apprehension.
Sir Robert himself, religious as he is, gives cause for it;
for the first reflection that rises in his mind, as expressed
in the above passage, *before* his notice of Divine Power
and Wisdom, is, that "the man accustomed to such
contemplations will feel the *moral dignity of his nature
exalted.*" But Lord Brougham speaks out. "The
delight," he says, "is inexpressible of *being able to follow*,
as it were, with our eyes, the marvellous works of the
Great Architect of Nature." And more clearly still:
"One of the most *gratifying treats* which science affords
us is *the knowledge of the extraordinary powers* with
which the human mind is endowed. No man, until he
has studied philosophy, can have a just idea of the great
things for which Providence has fitted his understanding,
the extraordinary disproportion which there is between
his natural strength and the powers of his mind, and the
force which he derives from these powers. When we
survey the marvellous truths of astronomy, we are first
of all lost in the feeling of immense space, and of the
comparative insignificance of this globe and its inhabitants. But there soon arises a *sense of gratification and
of new wonder* at perceiving how so insignificant a
creature has been *able to reach such a knowledge* of the
unbounded system of the universe." So, this is the
religion we are to gain from the study of Nature; how
miserable! The god we attain is our own mind; our
veneration is even professedly the worship of self.

The truth is that the system of Nature is just as much connected with Religion, where minds are not religious, as a watch or a steam-carriage. The material world, indeed, is infinitely more wonderful than any human contrivance; but wonder is not religion, or we should be worshipping our railroads. What the physical creation presents to us in itself is a piece of machinery, and when men speak of a Divine Intelligence as its Author, this god of theirs is not the Living and True, unless the spring is the god of a watch, or steam the creator of the engine. Their idol, taken at advantage (though it is *not* an idol, for they do not worship it), is the animating principle of a vast and complicated system; it is subjected to laws, and it is connatural and co-extensive with matter. Well does Lord Brougham call it "the great architect of nature;" it is an instinct, or a soul of the world, or a vital power; it is not the Almighty God.*

It is observable that Lord Brougham does not allude to any *relation* as existing between his *god* and ourselves. He is filled with awe, it seems, at the powers of the human mind, as displayed in their analysis of the vast creation. Is not this a fitting time to say a word about gratitude towards Him who gave them? Not a syllable. What we gain from his contemplation of Nature is "a gratifying treat," the knowledge of the "great things for which Providence has fitted man's understanding;" our admiration terminates in man; it passes on to no prototype.† I am not quarrelling with his result as illogical or unfair; it is but consistent with the principles with which he started. Take the system of Nature by itself, detached from the axioms of Religion, and I am willing to confess—nay, I have been expressly urging—that it

* [*Vide* "University Teaching," Disc. **2**.]
† [*Vide* "Essays," vol. i. p. 37, etc.]

does not force us to take it for *more* than a system; but why, then, persist in calling the study of it religious, when it can be treated, and is treated, thus atheistically? Say that Religion hallows the study, and not that the study creates Religion. The essence of Religion is the idea of a Moral Governor and a particular Providence; now let me ask, is the doctrine of moral governance and a particular providence conveyed to us through the physical sciences at all? Would they be physical sciences if they treated of morals? Can physics teach moral matters without ceasing to be physics? But are not virtue and vice, and responsibility, and reward and punishment, anything else than moral matters, and are *they* not of the essence of Religion? In what department, then, of physics are they to be found? Can the problems and principles they involve be expressed in the differential calculus? Is the galvanic battery a whit more akin to conscience and will, than the mechanical powers? What we seek is what concerns us, the traces of a Moral Governor; even religious minds cannot discern these in the physical sciences; astronomy witnesses divine power, and physics divine skill; and all of them divine beneficence; but which teaches of divine holiness, truth, justice, or mercy? Is that much of a Religion which is silent about duty, sin, and its remedies? Was there ever a Religion which was without the idea of an expiation?

Sir Robert Peel tells us, that physical science imparts "pleasure and *consolation*" on a death-bed. Lord Brougham confines himself to the "gratifying treat;" but Sir Robert ventures to speak of "consolation." Now, if we are on trial in this life, and if death be the time when our account is gathered in, is it at all serious or real to be talking of "consoling" ourselves at such a time with scientific subjects ?　Are these topics to suggest to us the thought of the Creator or not ?　If not, are they better than story books, to beguile the mind from what lies before it ?　But, if they are to speak of Him, can a dying man find rest in the mere notion of his Creator, when he knows Him also so awfully as His Moral Governor and his Judge ?　Meditate indeed on the wonders of Nature on a death-bed !　Rather stay your hunger with corn grown in Jupiter, and warm yourself by the Moon.

But enough on this most painful portion of Sir Robert's Address.　As I am coming to an end, I suppose I ought to sum up in a few words what I have been saying.　I consider, then, that intrinsically excellent and noble as are scientific pursuits, and worthy of a place in a liberal education, and fruitful in temporal benefits to the community, still they are not, and cannot be, *the instrument* of an ethical training ; that physics do not supply a basis, but only materials for religious sentiment; that knowledge does but occupy, does not form the mind; that apprehension of the unseen is the only known principle capable of subduing moral evil, educating the multitude, and organizing society ; and that, whereas man is born for action, action flows not from inferences, but from impressions,—not from reasonings, but from Faith.

That Sir Robert would deny these propositions I am far from contending ; I do not even contend that he has asserted the contrary at Tamworth.　It matters little to me whether he spoke boldly and intelligibly, as the newspapers represent, or guarded his strong sayings with the contradictory matter with which they are intercalated in his own report.　In either case the drift and the effect of his Address are the same.　He has given his respected name to a sophistical School, and condescended to mimic the gestures and tones of Lord Brougham. How melancholy is it that a man of such exemplary life, such cultivated tastes, such political distinction, such Parliamentary tact, and such varied experience, should have so little confidence in himself, so little faith in his own principles, so little hope of sympathy in others, so little heart for a great venture, so little of romantic aspiration, and of firm resolve, and stern dutifulness to the Unseen! How sad that he who might have had the affections of many, should have thought, in a day like this, that a Statesman's praise lay in preserving the mean, not in aiming at the high; that to be safe was his first merit, and to kindle enthusiasm his most disgraceful blunder! How pitiable that such a man should not have understood that a body without a soul has no life, and a political party without an idea, no unity!

February, 1841.

V.

WHO'S TO BLAME?

(*Addressed to the Editor of* The Catholic Standard. *By Catholicus.*)

I.

The British Constitution on its Trial.

SIR,—I have been much shocked, as I suppose has been the case with most of your readers, at the weekly extracts you have made from the correspondents of the daily prints, descriptive of the state of the British army in the Crimea; and a conviction has been steadily growing, or rather has been formed, in my mind, which the running comments of the Press continually strengthen, that we must go very deep indeed to get at the root of the evil, which lies, not in the men in authority, nor in systems of administration simply in themselves, but in nothing short of the British Constitution itself. I do not expect I shall get others to agree with me in this conclusion at once; I do not ask you, Mr. Editor, to assent to it, but to be patient with me, if, in order to do justice to my own ideas on the subject, I ask for a long hearing—if I even ask to be diffuse, roundabout, discursive, nay, perhaps, prosy, in support of what, at first sight, readers may call my paradox,—for I have no chance of establishing it in any other way.

Nor have I embraced it with any satisfaction to my feelings, certainly not to my Catholic feelings. Indeed, I have a decided view that Catholicism is safer and more free under a constitutional *regime,* such as our own, than under any other. I have no wish for "reforms"; and should be sorry to create in the minds of your readers any sentiment favourable either to democracy or to absolutism. I have no liking for the tyranny whether of autocrat or mob; no taste for being whirled off to Siberia, or tarred and feathered in the far West, by the enemies of my religion. May I live and die under the mild sway of a polity which certainly represses and dilutes the blind fanaticism of a certain portion of my country-men,—a fanaticism which, except for it, would sweep us off these broad lands, and lodge us, with little delay or compunction, in the German Sea! Still, we cannot alter facts; and, if the British Constitution is admirably adapted for peace, but not for war, which is the proposi-tion I shall support, and which seems dawning on the public mind, there is a lesson contained in that circum-stance which demands our attention. The lesson is this —that we were not wise to go to war, if we could possibly have avoided it, at a time when, by a lucky accident, the Duke of Wellington had gained for the nation a military prestige which it had little chance of preserving; and the sooner we know our capabilities and our true mission among the nations of the earth, and get back into a state of peace, in which we are really and truly great, the better for us.

It is not that I am doubting the heroic bravery and fortitude of the British soldier. I am not speaking of the individual soldier, whose great qualities I revere and marvel at, and whom I have been following with my anxieties and prayers ever since he set out on his foreign campaign. I am as little concerned here with the valour of our soldiers, as with the bigotry of our middle class; with the heights of Inkerman, as with the depths of Exeter Hall. I am to speak of our Constitution and of Constitutional Government; and I say that this said Constitutional Government of ours shows to extreme advantage in a state of peace, but not so in a state of war; and that it cannot be otherwise from the nature of things. Surely it is not paradoxical to say as much as this; for no one in this world can secure all things at once, but in every human work there is a maximum of good, short of the best possible. The wonder and the paradox rather would be, if the institutions of England were equally admirable for all contingencies, for war as well as for peace. Certainly martial law and constitutional freedom, the soldier's bayonet and the staff of the policeman, belong to antagonistic classes of ideas, and are not likely to co-operate happily with each other.

Nor, again, do I therefore say that we must never go to war, or that we shall always get the worst off, if we do. I only mean, it is not our strong point. I suppose, if we had no fowling-pieces, we might still manage, like Philoctetes, to knock off our game with bow and arrows. There are always ways of doing things, where there is the will. I am not denying that, with great exertion, we are able to hoist up our complex Constitution, to ease it into position, and fire it off with uncommon effect; but to do so is a most inconvenient, expensive, tedious process; it takes much time, much money, many men, and many lives. We ought in consequence to think twice before we set it to work for a purpose for which it was never made; and this I think we did not do a year ago. We hardly thought once about the matter. With intense self-conceit, we despised our foe,

We treated him as we treated the Pope four years before, and we have caught it. The *Times* put out feelers, this time last year, as to the possibility of the British Lion being persuaded into a more good-humoured, as well as a more prudent course; but that sagacious journal was soon obliged to draw them in again, and to swim down the stream with the boldest. For the said Lion was bent on puffing the Muscovite into space with the mere breath of his growl; and it did not occur to him at the moment, that perhaps it was his own wisdom, and not the Muscovite's merely, to let well alone, and to live upon the capital which a great military genius had made for him in the last war. And so, without reflection, the Lion did what, I am firmly persuaded, neither the Duke nor Sir Robert Peel would have let him do, had they been alive. He believed those counsellors who had the madness to tell him that it was a little war which he was beginning, and he stood rampant forthwith both in the Baltic and in the Black Sea.

But there is a further view of the matter, and it suggests another unpleasant consideration. No one likes to use a cumbrous, clumsy instrument; and, if at war we are, and with institutions not fitted for war, it is just possible we may alter our institutions, under the immediate pressure, in order to make them work easier for the object of war; and then what becomes of King, Lords, and Commons? There are abundant symptoms, on all sides of us, of the presence of a strong temptation to some such temerarious proceeding. Any one, then, who, like myself, is thankful that he is born under the British Constitution,—any Catholic who dreads the knout and the tar-barrel, will, for that very reason, look with great jealousy on a state of things which not only doubles prices and taxes, but which may bring about a sudden infringement and an irreparable injury of that remarkable polity, which the world never saw before, or elsewhere, and which it is so pleasant to live under. I do not mean to say that anything serious will be sensibly experienced in our time, at least in the time of those who are gliding rapidly along to the evening of life ; but it would be no consolation to me to be told that the Constitution will last my day, if I know that the next generation, whom I am watching as they come into active life, would fall under a form of government less favourable to the Church. And I do not think that the Catholics of England, who have shown no little exultation at the war, would gain much by rescuing Turkey from the Russo-Greeks, if, after planting Protestant Liberalism there instead, they found on looking homeward that despotism or democracy had mounted in these islands on the ruins of the aristocracy.

However, it is not my business to prophesy, but to attempt to lay down principles, which I hope to be allowed to do in my next letter.

2.

States and Constitutions.

THE proposition I have undertaken to maintain is this : —That the British Constitution is made for a state of peace, and not for a state of war ; and that war tries it in the same way, to use a homely illustration, that it tries a spoon to use it for a knife, or a scythe or hay-fork to make it do the work of a spade. I expressed myself thus generally, in order to give to those who should do me the honour of reading me the most expeditious insight into the view which I wished to set before them. But, if I must speak accurately, my meaning is this,—that, whereas a Nation has two aspects, internal and external, one as regards its own members, and one as regards foreigners, and whereas its government has two duties, one towards its subjects, and one towards its allies or enemies, the British State is great in its home department, which is its primary object, foreign affairs being its secondary ; while France or Russia, Prussia or Austria, contemplates in the first place foreign affairs, and is great in their management, and makes the home department only its second object. And further, that, if England be great abroad, as she is, it is not so much the State, as the People or Nation, which is the cause of her great-ness, and that not by means but in spite of the Con-stitution, or, if by means of it in any measure, clumsily so and circuitously; on the other hand, that, if foreign powers are ever great in the management of their own people, and make men of them, this they do in spite of their polity, and rather by the accidental qualifications of the individual ruler ; or if by their polity, still with inconvenience and effort. Other explanations I may add to the above as I proceed, but this is sufficient for the present.

Now I hope you will have patience with me, if I begin by setting down what I mean by a State, and by a Constitution.

First of all, it is plain that every one has a power of his own to act this way or that, as he pleases. And, as not one or two, but every one has it, it is equally plain, that, if all exercised it to the full, at least the stronger part of mankind would always be in conflict with each other, and no one would enjoy the benefit of it ; so that it is the interest of every one to give up some portion of his birth-freedom in this or that direction, in order to secure more freedom on the whole ; exchanging a freedom which is now large and now narrow, according as the accidents of his conflicts with others are more or less favourable to himself, for a certain definite range of freedom prescribed and guaranteed by settled engagements or laws. In other words, Society is necessary for the well-being of human nature. The result, aimed at and effected by these mutual arrangements, is called a State or Standing; that is, in contrast with the appearance presented by a people before and apart from such arrangements, which is not a standing, but a chronic condition of commotion and disorder.

And next, as this State or settlement of a people, is brought about by mutual arrangements, that is, by laws or rules, there is need, from the nature of the case, of some power over and above the People itself to maintain and enforce them. This living guardian of the laws is called the Government, and a governing power is thus involved in the very notion of Society. Let the Government be suspended, and at once the State is threatened with dissolution, which at best is only a matter of time.

A lively illustration in point is furnished us by a classical historian. When the great Assyrian Empire broke up, a time of anarchy succeeded; and, little as its late subjects liked its sway, they liked its absence less. The historian thus proceeds : " There was a wise man among the Medes, called Deioces. This Deioces, aspiring to be tyrant, did thus. He was already a man of reputation in his own country, and he now, more than ever, practised justice. The Medes, accordingly, in his neighbourhood, seeing his ways, made him their umpire in disputes. He, on the other hand, having empire in his eye, was upright and just. As he proceeded thus, the dwellers in other towns, who had suffered from unjust decisions, were glad to go to him and to plead their causes, till at length they went to no one else. Deioces now had the matter in his own hands. Accordingly he would no longer proceed to the judgment-seat ; for it was not worth his while, he said, to neglect his private affairs for the sake of the affairs of others. When rapine and lawlessness returned, his friends said, ' We must appoint a king over us;' and then they debated who it should be, and Deioces was praised by every one. So they made him their king ; and he, upon this, bade them to build him a house worthy of his kingly power, and protect him with guards ; and the Medes did so."

Now I have quoted this passage from history, because it carries us a step further in our investigation. It is for the good of the many that the one man, Deioces, is set up ; but who is to keep him in his proper work ? He puts down all little tyrants, but what is to hinder his becoming a greater tyrant than them all? This was actually the case; first the Assyrian tyranny, then anarchy, then the tyranny of Deioces. Thus the unfortunate masses oscillate between two opposite evils,—that of having no governor, and that of having too much of one; and which is the lesser of the two? This was the dilemma which beset the Horse in the fable. He was in feud with the Stag, by whose horns he was driven from his pasture. The Man promised him an easy victory, if he would let him mount him. On his assenting, the Man bridled him, and vaulted on him, and pursued and killed his enemy; but, this done, he would not get off him. Now, then, the Horse was even worse off than before, because he had a master to serve, instead of a foe to combat.

Here then is the problem: the social state is necessary for man, but it seems to contain in itself the elements of its own undoing. It requires a power to enforce the laws, and to rule the unruly; but what law is to control that power, and to rule the ruler? According to the common adage, "Quis custodiat ipsos custodes?" Who is to hinder the governor dispensing with the law in his own favour? History shows us that this problem is as ordinary as it is perplexing.

The expedient, by which the State is kept *in statu* and its ruler is ruled, is called its Constitution; and this has next to be explained. Now a Constitution really is not a mere code of laws, as is plain at once; for the very problem is how to confine power within the law, and in order to the maintenance of law. The ruling power can, and may, overturn law and law-makers, as Cromwell did, by the same sword with which he protects them. Acts of Parliament, Magna Charta, the Bill of Rights, the Reform Bill, none of these are the British Constitution.

What then is conveyed in that word? I would answer as follows:—

As individuals have characters of their own, so have races. Most men have their strong and their weak points, and points neither good nor bad, but idiosyncratic. And so of races: one is brave and sensitive of its honour; another romantic; another industrious, or long-headed, or religious. One is barbarous, another civilized. Moreover, growing out of these varieties or idiosyncrasies, and corresponding to them, will be found in these several races, and proper to each, a certain assemblage of beliefs, convictions, rules, usages, traditions, proverbs, and principles; some political, some social, some moral; and these tending to some definite form of government and *modus vivendi*, or polity, as their natural scope. And this being the case, when a given race has that polity which is intended for it by nature, it is in the same state of repose and contentment which an individual enjoys who has the food, or the comforts, the stimulants, sedatives, or restoratives, which are suited to his *diathesis* and his need. This then is the Constitution of a State: securing, as it does, the national unity by at once strengthening and controlling its governing power. It is something more than law; it is the embodiment of special ideas, ideas perhaps which have been held by a race for ages, which are of immemorial usage, which have fixed themselves in its innermost heart, which are in its eyes sacred to it, and have practically the force of eternal truths, whether they be such or not. These ideas are sometimes trivial, and, at first sight, even absurd: sometimes they are superstitious, sometimes they are great or beautiful; but to those to whom they belong they are first principles, watchwords, common property, natural ties, a cause to fight for, an occasion of self-sacrifice. They are the expres-

sions of some or other sentiment,—of loyalty, of order, **of**
duty, of honour, of faith, of justice, of glory. They are
the creative and conservative influences of Society ; they
erect nations into States, and invest States with Constitutions. They inspire and sway, as well as restrain, the
ruler of a people, for he himself is but one of that **people**
to which they belong.

3.

Constitutional Principles and their Varieties.

IT is a common saying that political power is founded on opinion; this is true, if the word "opinion" be understood in the widest sense of which it is capable. A State depends and rests, not simply on force of arms, not on logic, not on anything short of the sentiment and will of those who are governed. This doctrine does not imply instability and change as inherent characteristics of a body politic. Since no one can put off his opinions in a moment, or by willing it, since those opinions may be instincts, principles, beliefs, convictions, since they may be self-evident, since they may be religious truths, it may be easily understood how a national polity, as being the creation and development of a multitude of men having all the same opinions, may stand of itself, and be most firmly established, and may be practically secure against reverse. And thus it is that countries become settled, with a definite form of social union, and an ascendancy of law and order; not as if that particular settlement, union, form, order, and law were self-sanctioned and self-supported, but because it is founded in the national mind, and maintained by the force of a living tradition. This, then, is what I mean by a State; and, being the production and outcome of a people, it is necessarily for the good of the people, and it has two main elements, power and liberty,—for without power there is no protection, and without liberty there is nothing to protect. The seat of power is the Government; the seat of liberty is the Constitution.

You will say that this implies that every State must have a Constitution; so I think it has, in the sense in which I have explained the word. As the governing power may be feeble and unready, so the check upon its arbitrary exercise may be partial and uncertain; it may be rude, circuitous, abrupt, or violent; it need not be scientifically recognized and defined; but there never has been, there never can be, in any political body, an instance of unmitigated absolutism. Human nature does not allow of it. In pure despotisms, the practical limitation of the ruler's power lies in his personal fears, in the use of the dagger or the bowstring. These expedients have been brought into exercise before now, both by our foes, the Russians, and, still more so, by our friends, the Turks. Nay, when the present war began, some of our self-made politicians put forward the pleasant suggestion that the Czar's assassination at the hands of his subjects, maddened by taxes and blockades, was a possible path to the triumph of the allies.

Such is the lawless remedy which nature finds for a lawless tyranny; and no one will deny that such a savage justice is national in certain states of Society, and has a traditional authority, and may in a certain sense be called Constitutional. As society becomes civilized, the checks on arbitrary power assume a form in accordance with a more cultivated morality. We have one curious specimen of a Constitutional principle, preserved to us in the Medo-Persian Empire. It was a wholesome and subtle provision, adopting the semblance of an abject servility suitable to the idea of a despotism, which proclaimed the judgment of the despot infallible, and his word irrevocable. Alexander felt what it was to do irrevocable acts in the physical order, when, in the plenitude of his sovereignty, he actually killed his friend in the banquet; and, as to the vulgar multitude, this same natural result, the remedy or penalty of reckless power, is expressed in the unpolite proverb, "Give a rogue rope enough, and he will hang himself." With a parallel significance, then, it was made a sacred principle among the Medo-Persians, which awed and sobered the monarch himself, from its surpassing inconvenience, that what he once had uttered had the force of fate. It was the punishment of his greatness, that, when Darius would have saved the prophet Daniel from the operation of a law, which the king had been flattered into promulgating, he could not do so.

A similar check upon the tyranny of power, assuming the character of veneration and homage, is the form and etiquette which is so commonly thrown round a monarch. By irresistible custom, a ceremonial more or less stringent has been made almost to enter into his essential idea, for we know majesty without its externals is a jest; and, while to lay it aside is to relinquish the discriminating badge which is his claim upon the homage of his subjects, to observe it is to surrender himself manicled and fettered into their hands. It is said a king of Spain was roasted to death because the proper official was not found in time to wheel away his royal person from the fire. If etiquette hindered him from saving his own life, etiquette might also interpose an obstacle to his taking the life of another. If it was so necessary for Sancho Panza, governor of Barataria, to eat his dinner with the sanction of the court physician on every dish, other great functionaries of State might possibly be conditions of other indulgences on his part which were less reasonable and less imperative. As for our own most gracious Sovereign

she is honoured with the Constitutional prerogative that
" the king can do no wrong;" that is, he can do no
political act of his own mere will at all.

It is, then, no paradox to say that every State has in
some sense a Constitution; that is, a set of traditions,
depending, not on formal enactment, but on national
acceptance, in one way or other restrictive of the ruler's
power; though in one country more scientifically developed than another, or more distinctly recognized, or
more skilfully and fully adapted to their end. There is a
sort of analogy between the political and the physical sense
of the word. A man of good constitution is one who
has something more than life,—viz., a bodily soundness,
organic and functional, which will bring him safely through
hardships, or illnesses, or dissipations. On the other hand,
no one is altogether without a constitution : to say he
has nothing to fall back upon, when his health is tried, is
almost to pronounce that his life is an accident, and that
he may at any moment be carried off. And, in like
manner, that must be pronounced no State, but a mere
fortuitous collection of individuals, which has no unity
stronger than despotism, or deeper than law.

I am not sure how far it bears upon the main proposition to which these remarks are meant to conduct us,
but at least it will illustrate the general subject, if I ask
your leave to specify, as regards the depository of political
power, four Constitutional principles, distinct in kind
from each other, which, among other parallel ones, have
had an historical existence. If they must have names
given them, they may be called respectively the principles
of co-ordination, subordination, delegation, and participation.

1. As all political power implies unity, the word *co-
ordination* may seem inconsistent with its essential idea :

and yet there is a state of society, in which the limitation of despotism is by the voice of the people so un-
equivocally committed to an external authority, that we
must speak of it as the Constitution of such a State, in
spite of the seeming anomaly. Such is the recognition
of the authority of Religion, as existing in its own substantive institutions, external to the strictly political
framework, which even in pagan countries has been at
times successfully used to curb the extravagances of
absolute power. Putting paganism aside, we find in the
history both of Israel and of Judah the tyranny of kings
brought within due limits by the priests and prophets,
as by legitimate and self-independent authorities. The
same has been the case in Christian times. The Church
is essentially a popular institution, defending the cause
and encouraging the talents of the lower classes, and
interposing an external barrier in favour of high or low
against the ambition and the rapacity of the temporal
power. " If the Christian Church had not existed," says
M. Guizot, " the whole world would have been abandoned
to unmitigated material force." However, as the cor-
rective principle is in this instance external to the State,
though having its root internally in national opinion, it
cannot, except improperly, be termed Constitutional.

2. Next I come to the principle of *subordination,* which
has been commonly found in young, semi-barbarous
states both in Europe and Asia, and has attained its
most perfect form in what is called the Feudal System.
It has had a military origin; and, after the pattern of an
army, is carried out in an hierarchy of chiefs, one under
the other, each of whom in consequence had direct jurisdiction only over a few. First came the *suzerain,* or lord
paramount, who had the allegiance of a certain number
of princes, dukes, counts, or even kings. These were his

feudatories,—that is, they owed him certain military services, and held their respective territories of him. Their vassals, in turn, were the barons, each under his own prince or duke, and owing him a similar service. Under the barons were the soldiers, each settled down on his own portion of land, with the peasants of the soil as his serfs, and with similar feudal duties to his own baron. A system like this furnished a most perfect expedient against absolutism. Power was distributed among many persons, without confusion or the chance of collision ; and, while the paucity of vassals under one and the same rule gave less scope to tyrannical excesses, it created an effective public opinion, which is strongest when the relation between governor and governed is most intimate. Moreover, if any one were disposed to play the tyrant, there were several distinct parties in a condition to unite against him ; the barons and lower class against the king, the king and the lower classs against the barons. The barbarities of the middle ages have been associated in men's minds with this system ; but, whatever they were,—they surely took place in spite of it, not through it,—just as the anti-Catholic virulence of the present race of Englishmen is mitigated, not caused, by the British Constitution.

3. By the principle of *delegation*, I mean that according to which power is committed for a certain time to individuals, with a commensurate responsibility, to be met whenever that time has expired. Thus the Roman Dictator, elected on great emergencies, was autocrat during the term of his rule. Thus a commander of an army has unfettered powers to do what he will, while his command continues ; or the captain of a ship ; but afterwards his acts are open to inquiry, and, if so be, to animadversion. There are great

advantages to a system like this; it is the mode of bringing out great men, and of working great measures. You choose the fittest man for each department; you frankly trust him, you heap powers upon him, you generously support him with your authority, you let him have his own way, you let him do his best. Afterwards you review his proceedings; you reward or censure him. Such, again, in fact, is with us the liberty of the press, censorship being simply unconstitutional, and the courts of law, the remedy against seditious, libellous, or demoralizing publications. Here, too, your advantage is great; you form public opinion, and you ascertain the national mind.

4. The very opposite to this is the principle of *participation.* It is that by which a People would leave nothing to its rulers, but has itself, or by its immediate instruments, a concurrent part in everything that is done. Acting on the notion that no one is to be trusted, even for a time, and that every act of its officials is to be jealously watched, it never commits power without embarrassing its exercise. Instead of making a venture for the transcendent, it keeps fast by a safe mediocrity. It rather trusts a dozen persons than one to do its work. This is the great principle of boards and officers, engaged in checking each other, with a second apparatus to check the first apparatus, and other functionaries to keep an eye on both of them,—Tom helping Jack, and Jack waiting for Bill, till the end is lost in the means. Such seems to have been the principle of the military duties performed by the Aulic Council in Germany, which virtually co-operated with Napoleon in his victories in that country. Such is the great principle of committees of taste, which have covered this fair land with architectural monstrosities. And as being closely allied to the

principle of comprehension and compromise (a principle, necessary indeed, in some shape, but admitting of ruinous excess), it has had an influence on our national action in matters more serious than architecture or sculpture. And it has told directly upon our political efficiency.

4.

Characteristics of the Athenians.

Now at length I am drawing near the subject which I have undertaken to treat, though Athens is both in leagues and in centuries a great way off England after all. But first to recapitulate :—a State or polity implies two things, Power on the one hand, Liberty on the other; a Rule and a Constitution. Power, when freely developed, results in contralization ; Liberty in self-government. The two principles are in antagonism from their very nature; so far forth as you have rule, you have not liberty ; so far forth as you have liberty, you have not rule. If a People gives up nothing at all, it remains a mere People, and does not rise to be a State. If it gives up everything, it could not be worse off, though it gave up nothing. Accordingly, it always must give up something; it never can give up everything ; and in every case the problem to be decided is, what is the most advisable compromise, what point is the *maximum* of at once protection and independence.

Those political institutions are the best which subtract as little as possible from a people's natural independence as the price of their protection. The stronger you make the Ruler, the more he can do for you, *but* the more he also can do against you; the weaker you make him, the less he can do against you, *but* the less also he can do for you. The Man promised to kill the Stag; but he fairly owned that he must be first allowed to mount the Horse.

Put a sword into the Ruler's hands, it is at his option to use or not use it against you; reclaim it, and who is to use it for you? Thus, if States are free, they are feeble; if they are vigorous, they are high-handed. I am not speaking of a nation or a people, but of a State as such; and I say, the more a State secures to itself of rule and centralization, the more it can do for its subjects externally; and the more it grants to them of liberty and self-government, the less it can do against them internally: and thus a despotic government is the best for war, and a popular government the best for peace.

Now this may seem a paradox so far as this;—that I have said a State cannot be at once free and strong, whereas the combination of these advantages is the very boast which we make about our own island in one of our national songs, which runs,—

> " Britannia, *rule* the waves!
> Britons never shall be *slaves*."

I acknowledge the force of this authority; but I must recall the reader's attention to the distinction which I have just been making between a Nation and a State. Britons are free, considered as a State; they are strong, considered as a Nation;—and, as a good deal depends on this distinction, I will illustrate it, before I come to the consideration of our own country, by the instance of that ancient and famous people whose name I have prefixed to this portion of my inquiry,—a people who, in most respects, are as unlike us, as beauty is unlike utility, but who are in this respect, strange to say, not dissimilar to the Briton.

So pure a democracy was Athens, that, if any of its citizens was eminent, he might be banished by the rest for this simple offence of greatness. Self-government was developed there in the fullest measure, as if provision was not at all needed against any foe. Nor indeed, in the earlier period of Athens, was it required; for the poverty of the soil, and the extent of seaboard as its boundary, secured it against both the cupidity and the successful enterprise of invaders. The chief object, then, of its polity was the maintenance of internal order; but even in this respect solicitude was superfluous, according to its citizens themselves, who were accustomed to boast that they were attracted, one and all, in one and the same way, and moulded into a body politic, by an innate perception of the beautiful and true, and that the genius and cultivation of mind, which were their characteristics, served them better for the observance of the rules of good fellowship and for carrying on the intercourse of life, than the most stringent laws and the best appointed officers of police.

Here then was the extreme of self-government carried out; and the State was intensely free. That in proportion to that internal freedom was its weakness in its external relations, its uncertainty, caprice, injustice, and untrustworthiness, history, I think, abundantly shows. It may be thought unfair to appeal to the age of Philip and Demosthenes, when no Greek State could oppose a military organization worthy of such a foe as Macedon; but at no anterior period had it shown a vigour and perseverance similar to the political force of the barbaric monarchy, which extinguished its liberties. It was simply unable to defend and perpetuate that democratical license which it so inordinately prized.

Had Athens then no influence on the world outside of it, because its political influence was so baseless and fluctuating? Has she gained no conquests, exercised no rule, affected no changes, left no traces of herself upon the nations? On the contrary, never was country able to do so much; never has country so impressed its image upon the history of the world, except always that similarly small strip of land in Syria. And moreover,—for this I wish to insist upon, rather than merely concede,—this influence of hers was in consequence, though not by means, of her democratical *regime*. That democratical polity formed a *People*, who could do what democracy itself could not do. Feeble all together, the Athenians were superlatively energetic one by one. It was their very keenness of intellect individually which made them collectively so inefficient. This point of character, insisted on both by friendly and hostile orators in the pages of her great historian, is a feature in which Athens resembles England. Englishmen, indeed, do not go to work with the grace and poetry which, if Pericles is to be believed, characterized an Athenian; but Athens may boast of her children as having the self-reliance, the spirit, and the unflagging industry of the individual Englishman.

It was this individualism which was the secret of the power of Athens in her day, and remains as the instrument of her influence now. What was her trade, or her colonies, or her literature, but private, not public achievments, the triumph, not of State policy, but of personal effort? Rome sent out her colonies, as Russia now, with political foresight; modern Europe has its State Universities, its Royal Academies, its periodical scientific Associations; it was otherwise with Athens. There, great things were done by citizens working in their private capacity; working, it must be added, not so much from patriotism as for their personal advantage; or, if with patriotism, still with little chance of State encouragement or reward. Socrates, the greatest of her moralists, and since his day one of her chief glories, lived unrecognized and unrewarded, and died under a judicial sentence. Xenophon conducted his memorable retreat across Asia Minor, not as an Athenian, but as the mercenary or volunteer of a Persian Prince. Miltiades was of a family of adventurers, who by their private energy had founded a colony, and secured a lordship in the Chersonese ; and he met his death while prosecuting his private interests with his country's vessels. Themistocles had a double drift, patriotic and traitorous, in the very acts by which he secured to the Greeks the victory of Salamis, having in mind that those acts should profit him at the Persian court, if they did not turn to his account at home. Perhaps we are not so accurately informed of what took place at Rome, when Hannibal threatened the city ; but certainly Rome presents us with the picture of a strong State at that crisis, whereas, in the parallel trial, the Athens of Miltiades and Themistocles shows like the clever, dashing population of a large town.

We have another sample of the genius of her citizens in their conduct at Pylos. Neither they, nor their officers, would obey the orders of the elder Demosthenes, who was sent out to direct the movements of the fleet. In vain did he urge them to fortify the place ; they did nothing ; till, the bad weather detaining them on shore, and inaction becoming tedious, suddenly they fell upon the work with a will ; and, having neither tools nor carriages, hunted up stones where they could find them ready in the soil, made clay do the office of mortar, carried the materials on their backs, supporting them with their clasped hands, and thus finished the necessary works in the course of a few days.

By this personal enterprise and daring the Athenians were distinguished from the rest of Greece. "They are fond of change," say their Corinthian opponents in the

Lacedemonian Council; "quick to plan and to perform, venturing beyond their power, hazarding beyond their judgment, and always sanguine in whatever difficulties. They are alive, while you, O Lacedemonians, dawdle; and they love locomotion, while you are especially a home-people. They think to gain a point, even when they withdraw; but with you, even to advance is to surrender what you have attained. When they defeat their foe, they rush on; when they are beaten, they hardly fall back. What they plan and do not follow up, they deem an actual loss; what they set about and gain, they count a mere instalment of the future; what they attempt and fail in here, in anticipation they make up for there. Such is their labour and their risk from youth to age; no men enjoy so little what they have, for they are always getting, and their best holiday is to do a stroke of needful work; and it is a misfortune to them to have to undergo, not the toil of business, but the listlessness of repose."

I do not mean to say that I trace the Englishman in every clause of this passage; but he is so far portrayed in it as a whole, as to suggest to us that perhaps he too, as well as the Athenian, has that inward spring of restless independence, which makes a State weak, and a Nation great.

5.

Parallel Characteristics of Englishmen.

I HOPE I have now made it clear, that, in saying that a
free State will not be strong, I am far indeed from saying that a People with what is called a free Constitution
will not be active, powerful, influential, and successful.
I am only saying that it will do its great deeds, not
through the medium of its government, or *politically*,
but through the medium of its individual members, or
nationally.   Self-government, which is another name for
political weakness, may really be the means or the
token of national greatness.   Athens, as a State, was
wanting in the elements of integrity, firmness, and consistency ; but perhaps that political deficiency was the
very condition and a result of her intellectual activity.

I will allow more than this readily.   Not only in cases
such as that of Athens, is the State's loss the Nation's
gain, but further, most of those very functions which in
despotisms are undertaken by the State may be performed in free countries by the Nation.   For instance,
roads, the posts, railways, bridges, aqueducts, and the
like, in absolute monarchies, are governmental matters ;
but they may be left to private energy, where self-
government prevails.   Letter-carriage indeed involves
an extent of system and a punctuality in work, which is
too much for any combination of individuals ; but the
care of Religion, which is a governmental work in Russia,
and partly so in England, is left to private competition

in the United States. Education, in like manner, is sometimes provided by the State, sometimes left to religious denominations, sometimes to private zeal and charity. The Fine Arts sometimes depend on the patronage of Court or Government; sometimes are given in charge to Academies; sometimes to committees or vestries.

I do not say that a Nation will manage all these departments equally well, or so well as a despotic government; and some departments it will not be able to manage at all. Did I think it could manage all, I should have nothing to write about. I am distinctly maintaining that the war department it cannot manage; that is my very point. It cannot conduct a war; but not from any fault in the nation, or with any resulting disparagement to popular governments and Constitutional States, but merely because we cannot have all things at once in this world, however big we are, and because, in the nature of things, one thing cannot be another. I do not say that a Constitutional State never must risk war, never must engage in war, never will conquer in war; but that its strong point lies in the other direction. If we would see what liberty, independence, self-government, a popular Constitution, can do, we must look to times of tranquillity. In peace a self-governing nation is prosperous in itself, and influential in the wide world. Its special works, the sciences, the useful arts, literature, the interests of knowledge generally, material comfort, the means and appliances of a happy life, thrive especially in peace. And thus such a nation spreads abroad, and subdues the world, and reigns in the admiration and gratitude and deference of men, by the use of weapons which war shivers to pieces. Alas! that mortals do not know themselves, and will not (according to the proverb) cut their coat according to their cloth! "*Optat ephippia bos.*" John Bull, like other free, self-governing nations, would undertake a little war just now, as if it were his *forte*,—as great lawyers have cared for nothing but a reputation for dancing gracefully, and literary men have bought a complex coat-of-arms at the Heralds' College. Why will we not content to be human? why not content with the well-grounded consciousness that no polity in the world is so wonderful, so good to its subjects, so favourable to individual energy, so pleasant to live under, as our own? I do not say, why will we go to war? but, why will we not think *twice* first? why do we not ascertain our actual position, our strength, our weakness, before we do so?

For centuries upon centuries England has been, like Attica, a secluded land; so remote from the highway of the world, so protected from the flood of Eastern and Northern barbarism, that her children have grown into a magnanimous contempt of external danger. They have had "a cheap defence" in the stormy sea which surrounds them; and, from time immemorial, they have had such skill in weathering it, that their wooden walls, to use the Athenian term, became a second rampart against the foe, whom wind and water did not overwhelm. So secure have they felt in those defences, that they have habitually neglected others; so that, in spite of their valour, when a foe once gained the shore, be he Dane, or Norman, or Dutch, he was encountered by no sustained action or organized resistance, and became their king. These, however, were rare occurrences, and made no lasting impression; they were not sufficient to divert them from pursuing, or to thwart them in attaining, the amplest measures of liberty. Whom had the people to fear? not even their ships, which could not, like military, become a paid force encircling a tyrant, and securing him against their resistance.

To these outward circumstances of England, determining the direction of its political growth, must be added the character of the people themselves. There are races to whom consanguinity itself is not concord and unanimity, but the reverse. They fight with each other, for lack of better company. Imaginative, fierce, vindictive, with their clans, their pedigrees, and their feuds, snorting war, spurning trade or tillage, the old Highlanders, if placed on the broad plains of England, would have in time run through their national existence, and died the death of the sons of Œdipus. But, if you wish to see the sketch of a veritable Englishman in strong relief, refresh your recollection of Walter Scott's "Two Drovers." He is indeed rough, surly, a bully and a bigot; these are his weak points : but if ever there was a generous, good, tender heart, it beats within his breast. Most placable, he forgives and forgets : forgets, not only the wrongs he has received, but the insults he has inflicted. Such he is commonly ; for doubtless there are times and circumstances in his dealings with foreigners in which, whether when in despair or from pride, he becomes truculent and simply hateful ; but at home his bark is worse than his bite. He has qualities, excellent for the purposes of neighbourhood and intercourse ;—and he has, besides, a shrewd sense, and a sobriety of judgment, and a practical logic, which passion does not cloud, and which makes him understand that good-fellowship is not only commendable, but expedient too. And he has within him a spring of energy, pertenacity, and perseverance, which makes him as busy and effective in a colony as he is companionable at home. Some races do not move at all ; others are ever jostling against each other; the Englishman is ever stirring, yet never treads too hard upon his fellow-countryman's toes. He does his work neatly, silently, in his own place; he looks to himself, and can take care of himself; and he has that instinctive veneration for the law, that he can worship it even in the abstract, and thus is fitted to go shares with others all around him in that political sovereignty, which other races are obliged to concentrate in one ruler.

There was a time when England was divided into seven principalities, formed out of the wild warriors whom the elder race had called in to their own extermination. What would have been the history of those kingdoms if the invaders had been Highlanders instead of Saxons? But the Saxon Heptarchy went on, without any very desperate wars of kingdom with kingdom, pretty much as the nation goes on now. Indeed, I much question, supposing Englishmen rose one morning and found themselves in a Heptarchy again, whether its seven portions would not jog on together, much as they do now under Queen Victoria, the union in both cases depending, not so much on the government and the governed, but on the people, viewed in themselves, to whom peaceableness, justice, and non-interference are natural.

It is an invaluable national quality to be keen, yet to be fair to others; to be inquisitive, acquisitive, enterprising, aspiring, progressive, without encroaching upon his next neighbour's right to be the same. Such a people hardly need a Ruler, as being mainly free from the infirmities which make a ruler necessary. Law, like medicine, is only called for to assist nature; and, when nature does so much for a people, the wisest policy is, as far as possible, to leave them to themselves. This,

then, is the science of government with English Statesmen, to leave the people alone ; a free action, a clear
stage, and they will do the rest for themselves. The
more a Ruler meddles, the less he succeeds ; the less he
initiates, the more he accomplishes ; his duty is that of
overseeing, facilitating, encouraging, guiding, interposing
on emergencies. Some races are like children, and
require a despot to nurse, and feed, and dress them, to
give them pocket money, and take them out for airings.
Others, more manly, prefer to be rid of the trouble oi
their affairs, and use their Ruler as their mere manager
and man of business. Now an Englishman likes to take
his own matters into his own hands. He stands on his
own ground, and does as much work as half a dozen men
of certain other races. He can join too with others, and
has a turn for organizing, but he insists on its being voluntary. He is jealous of no one, except kings and governments, and offensive to no one except their partisans
and creatures.

This, then, is the people for private enterprise ; and
of private enterprise alone have I been speaking all
along. What a place is London in its extent, its com-
plexity, its myriads of dwellings, its subterraneous works !
It is the production, for the most part, of individual
enterprise. Waterloo Bridge was the greatest architectural achievement of the generation before this ; it was
built by shares. New regions, with streets of palaces
and shops innumerable, each shop a sort of shrine or
temple of this or that trade, and each a treasure-house
of its own merchandize, grow silently into existence, the
creation of private spirit and speculation. The gigantic
=ystem of railroads rises and asks for its legal *status :*
prudent statesmen decide that it must be left to private
companies, to the exclusion of Government. Trade is to

be encouraged : the best encouragement is, that it should be free. A famine threatens; one thing must be avoided, —any meddling on the part of Government with the export and import of provisions.

Emigration is in vogue : out go swarms of colonists, not, as in ancient times, from the Prytaneum, under State guidance and with religious rites, but each by himself, and at his own arbitrary and sudden will. The ship is wrecked ; the passengers are cast upon a rock,— or make the hazard of a raft. In the extremest peril, in the most delicate and most anxious of operations, every one seems to find his place, as if by magic, and does his work, and subserves the rest with coolness, cheerfulness, gentleness, and without a master. Or they have a fair passage, and gain their new country ; each takes his allotted place there, and works in it in his own way. Each acts irrespectively of the rest, takes care of number one, with a kind word and deed for his neighbour, but still as fully understanding that he must depend for his own welfare on himself. Pass a few years, and a town has risen on the desert beach, and houses of business are extending their connexions and influence up the country. At length, a company of merchants make the place their homestead, and they protect themselves from their enemies with a fort. They need a better defence than they have provided, for a numerous host is advancing upon them, and they are likely to be driven into the sea. Suddenly a youth, the castaway of his family, half-clerk, half-soldier, puts himself at the head of a few troops, defends posts, gains battles, and ends in founding a mighty empire over the graves of Mahmood and Aurungzebe.

It is the deed of one man ; and so, wherever we go all over the earth, it is the solitary Briton, the London, agent, or the *Milordos*, who is walking restlessly about, abusing the natives, and raising a colossus, or setting the Thames on fire, in the East or the West. He is on the top of the Andes, or in a diving-bell in the Pacific, or taking notes at Timbuctoo, or grubbing at the Pyramids, or scouring over the Pampas, or acting as prime minister to the king of Dahomey, or smoking the pipe of friendship with the Red Indians, or hutting at the Pole. No one can say beforehand what will come of these various specimens of the independent, self-governing, self-reliant Englishman. Sometimes failure, sometimes openings for trade, scientific discoveries, or political aggrandizements. His country and his government have the gain; but it is he who is the instrument of it, and not political organization, centralization, systematic plans, authoritative acts. The polity of England is what it was before,—the Government weak, the Nation strong,—strong in the strength of its multitudinous enterprise, which gives to its Government a position in the world, which that Government could not claim for itself by any prowess or device of its own.

6.

Reverse of the Picture.

THE social union promises two great and contrary advantages, Protection and Liberty,—such protection as shall not interfere with liberty, and such liberty as shall not interfere with protection. How much a given nation can secure of the one, and how much of the other, depends on its peculiar circumstances. As there are small frontier territories, which find it their interest to throw themselves into the hands of some great neighbour, sacrificing their liberties as the price of purchasing safety from barbarians or rivals, so too there are countries which, in the absence of external danger, have abandoned themselves to the secure indulgence of freedom, to the jealous exercise of self-government, and to the scientific formation of a Constitution. And as, when liberty has to be surrendered for protection, the Horse must not be surprised if the Man whips or spurs him, so, when protection is neglected for the sake of liberty, he must not be surprised if he suffers from the horns of the Stag.

Protected by the sea, and gifted with a rare energy, self-possession, and imperturbability, the English people have been able to carry out self-government to its limits, and to absorb into its constitutional action many of those functions which are necessary for the protection of any country, and commonly belong to the Executive ; and triumphing in their marvellous success they have thought no task too hard for them, and have from time to time attempted more than even England could accomplish. Such a crisis has come upon us now, and the Constitution has not been equal to the occasion. For a year past we have been conducting a great war on our Constitutional *routine*, and have not succeeded in it. If we continue that *routine*, we shall have more failures, with France or Russia (whichever you please) to profit by it : —if we change it, we change what after all is Constitutional. It is this dilemma which makes me wish for peace,—or else some *Deus è machinâ*, some one greater even than Wellington, to carry us through. We cannot depend upon Constitutional *routine*.

People abuse *routine*, and say that all the mischief which happens is the fault of *routine ;*—but can they get out of *routine*, without getting out of the Constitution ? That is the question. The fault of a *routine* Executive, I suppose, is not that the Executive always goes on in one way,—else, system is in fault,—but that it goes on in a bad way, or on a bad system. We must either change the system, then,—our Constitutional system ; or not find fault with its *routine*, which is according to it. The present Parliamentary Committee of Inquiry, for instance, is either a function and instrument of the *routine* system,—and therefore is making bad worse,—or is not, —and then perhaps it is only the beginning of an infringement of the Constitution. There may be Constitutional failures which have no Constitutional remedies, unwilling as we may be to allow it. They may be necessarily incidental to a free self-governing people.

The Executive of a nation is the same all over the world, being, in other words, the administration of the nation's affairs ; it differs in different countries, not in its nature and office, nor in its ends, acts, or functions, but in its characteristics, as being prompt, direct, effective, or the contrary ; that is, as being strong or feeble. If it pursues its ends earnestly, performs its acts vigorously and discharges its functions successfully, then it is a strong Executive ; if otherwise, it is feeble. Now, it is obvious, the more it is concentrated, that is, the fewer are its springs, and the simpler its mechanism, the stronger it is, because it has least friction and loss of power ; on the other hand, the more numerous and widely dispersed its centres of action are, and the more complex and circuitous their inter-action, the more feeble it is. It is strongest, then, when it is lodged in one man out of the whole nation ; it is feeblest, when it is lodged, by participation or conjointly, in every man in it. How can we help what is self-evident ? If the English people lodge power in the many, not in the few, what wonder that its operation is roundabout, clumsy, slow, intermittent, and disappointing ? And what is the good of finding fault with the *routine,* if it is after all the principle of the *routine,* or the system, or the Constitution, which causes the hitch ? You cannot eat your cake and have it ; you cannot be at once a self-governing nation and have a strong government. Recollect Wellington's question in opposition to the Reform Bill, " How is the King's Government to be carried on ? " We are beginning to experience its full meaning.

A people so alive, so curious, so busy as the English, will be a power in themselves, independently of political arrangements ; and will be on that very ground jealous of a rival, impatient of a master, and strong enough to cope with the one and to withstand the other. A government is their natural foe ; they cannot do without it altogether, but they will have of it as little as they can. They will forbid the concentration of power ; they will multiply its seats, complicate its acts, and make it safe by making it inefficient. They will take care that it is the worst-worked of all the many organizations which are found in their country. As despotisms keep their subjects in ignorance, lest they should rebel, so will a free people maim and cripple their government, lest it should tyrannize.

This is human nature; the more powerful a man is, the more jealous is he of other powers. Little men endure little men; but great men aim at a solitary grandeur. The English nation is intensely conscious of itself; it has seen, inspected, recognized, appreciated, and warranted itself. It has erected itself into a personality, under the style and title of John Bull. Most neighbourly is he when let alone; but irritable, when commanded or coerced. He wishes to form his own judgment in all matters, and to have everything proved to him; he dislikes the thought of generously placing his interests in the hands of others, he grudges to give up what he cannot really keep himself, and stickles for being at least a sleeping partner in transactions which are beyond him. He pays his people for their work, and is as proud of them, if they do it well, as a rich man of his tall footmen.

Policy might teach him a different course. If you want your work done well, which you cannot do yourself, find the best man, put it into his hand, and trust him implicitly. An Englishman is too sensible not to understand this in private matters; but in matters of State he is afraid of such a policy. He prefers the system of checks and counter-checks, the division of power, the imperative concurrence of disconnected officials, and his own supervision and revision,—the method of hitches, cross-purposes, collisions, dead-locks, to the experiment of treating his public servants as gentlemen. I am not quarelling with what is inevitable in his system of self-government; I only say that he cannot expect his work done in the best style, if this is his mode of providing for it. Duplicate functionaries do but merge responsibility; and a jealous master is paid with formal, heartless service. Do your footmen love you across the gulf which you have fixed between them and you? and can you expect your store-keepers and harbour-masters at Balaklava not to serve you by rule and precedent, not to be rigid in their interpretation of your orders, and to commit themselves as little as they can, when you show no belief in their zeal, and have no mercy on their failures?

England, surely, is the paradise of little men, and the purgatory of great ones. May I never be a Minister of State or a Field-Marshal! I'd be an individual, self-respecting Briton, in my own private castle, with the *Times* to see the world by, and pen and paper to scribble off withal to some public print, and set the world right. Public men are only my *employés*; I use them as I think fit, and turn them off without warning. Aberdeen, Gladstone, Sidney Herbert, Newcastle, what are they muttering about services and ingratitude? were they not paid? hadn't they their regular quarter-day? Raglan, Burgoyne, Dundas,—I cannot recollect all the fellows' names,—can they merit aught? can they be profitable to me their lord and master? And so, having no tenderness or respect for their persons, their antecedents, or their age,—not caring that in fact they are serving me with all their strength, not asking whether, if they manage ill, it be not, perchance, because they are in the fetters of Constitutional red tape, which have weighed on their hearts and deadened their energies, till the hazard of failure and the fear of censure have quenched the spirit of daring, I think it becoming and generous,—during, not after their work, not when it is ended, but in the very agony of conflict,—to institute a formal process of inquiry into their demerits, not secret, not indulgent to their sense of honour, but in the hearing of all Europe, and amid the scorn of the world,—hitting down, knocking over, my workhouse apprentices, in order that they may get up again, and do my matters for me better.

How far these ways of managing a crisis can be amended in a self-governing Nation, it is most difficult to say. They are doubly deplorable, as being both unjust and impolitic. They are kind, neither to ourselves, nor to our public servants ; and they so unpleasantly remind one of certain passages of Athenian history, as to suggest that perhaps they must ever more or less exist, except where a despotism, by simply extinguishing liberty, effectually prevents its abuse.

7.

English Jealousy of Law Courts.

PEOPLE account for the mismanagement existing in the department of the military service, on the ground that war is a novelty in this generation, and that it will be corrected after the successive failures of a few years. This doubtless has something to do with our failure, but it is not a full explanation of it ; else, there would be no mis-managements in time of peace. But, if mismanagements exist in peace as well as in war, then we may conclude that they are some defect in our talent for organization ; a defect, the more unaccountable, because Englishmen are far from wanting in this faculty, as is shown by the great undertakings of our master builders and civil engineers. Yet all the time that private men have been directing matters and men on a large scale to definite ends, there has been a general feeling in the community that a govern-ment proceeding is a blunder or a job. From the Irish famines of 1822 to that of 1845 and following years, I think I recollect instances in point, though I have got no list to produce. As to the latter occasion, it is commonly said that to this day the Irish will not believe, in spite of the many millions voted to them by Parliament, that their population has not been deliberately murdered by the Government. This was a far larger instance of mis-management than that which the present Parliamentary Committee will bring to light. How then shall we ac-count for the phenomenon of the incapable Executive of a capable people better than by saying, that, for the very reason the people is capable, its Executive is incapable, as I have been urging all along? It is true, there are public departments of acknowledged efficiency, as the Post Office and the Police ; but these only show what the Executive could be, if the Nation gave it fair play.

And thus I might end my remarks on the subject, which have already been discursive and excursive, beyond the patience of most readers ; and yet I think it worth while, Mr. Editor, to try it a little more, if I gain your consent to my doing so. For I have not yet brought out so clearly as I wish, the relation of the Nation to the Executive, as it exists in this corner of the earth.

The functions of the Executive are such as police, judicature, religion, education, finance, foreign transactions, war. The acts of the Executive are such as the appointment, instruction, supervision, punishment, and removal of its functionaries. The end of the Executive is to perform those functions by means of those acts with despatch and success; that is, so to appoint, instruct, superintend, and support its functionaries, as effectually to protect person and property, to dispense justice, to uphold religion, to provide for the country's expenses, to promote and extend its trade, to maintain its place in the political world, and to make it victorious and formidable. These things, and such as these, are the end,— the direct, intelligible end.—of the Executive ; and to secure their accomplishment, and to secure men to accomplish them, one would suppose would be the one and only object of all Executive government; but it is not the only object of the English.

A very few words will explain what I mean. John, Duke of Marlborough, obtained for the town of Witney a monopoly of blanket-making : accordingly, I believe, Witney at one time supplied the whole nation with blankets of such size and quality as the men of Witney chose. Looking at this as a national act, one would say, that the object of the nation was, not to provide itself with best blankets, but with Witney blankets ; and, did a foreigner object that the blankets were not good, he would speak beside the mark, and be open to the retort, "Nobody said they were good ; what we maintain is that they come from Witney." Now, applying this illustration to our present circumstances, I humbly submit that, though the end of every Executive, as such, is to do its work well, cheaply, and promptly, yet, were the French in the Crimea to judge us by this principle, and to marvel at our choosing neither means or men in accordance with it, they would be simply criticising what they did not understand. The Nation's object never was that the Executive should be worked in the best possible way, but that the Nation should work it. It is altogether a family concern on a very large scale : the Executive is more or less in commission, and the commission is the Nation itself. It vests in itself, as represented by its different classes, in perpetuity, the prerogative of jobbing the Executive. Nor is this so absurd as it seems :—the Nation has two ends in view, quite distinct from the proper end of the Executive itself ; — first, that the Government should not do too much, and next, that itself should have a real share in the Government. The balance of power, which has been the mainspring of our foreign politics, is the problem of our home affairs also. The great State Commission must be distributed in shares, in correspondence with the respective pretensions of its various expectants. Some States are cemented by loyalty, others by religion ; but ours by self-interest, in a large sense of the word. Each element of the political structure demands its special retainer; and power is committed, not to the highest capacity, but to the largest possible constituency. The general public, the constituency, the press, the aristocracy, the capital of the country, the mercantile interest, the Crown, the Court, the great Constitutional parties, Whig and Tory, the great religious parties, Church and Dissent, the country gentlemen, the professions—all must have their part and their proportion in the administration. Such is the will of the Nation, which had rather that its institutions should be firm and stable, than that they should be effective.

But the Sovereign, perhaps it will be said, is the source of all jurisdiction in the English body political, as Tudor monarchs asserted, and Constitutional lawyers have handed down to us;—yes, as the Merovingian king, not the Mayor of the Palace, was ruler of France, and as the Great Mogul, not the Company, is the supreme power in Hindostan. Could Victoria resume at her will that power which the Tudors exercised, but which slipped out of the hands of the Stuarts? The Pope, too, leaves his jurisdiction in the hands of numberless subordinate authorities, patriarchs, metropolitans, bishops, sacred congregations, religious orders; he, however, can, if he pleases, recall what he has given, and sometimes, in fact, he does put them all aside. I think it would astonish the public if, to take a parallel case, our gracious Sovereign, *motu proprio*, were to resume the management of the Crown lands, or re-distribute the dioceses without an Act of Parliament. Let us dismiss from our minds the fictions of antiquarians; the British people divide among themselves the executive powers of the Crown :—and now to give some illustrations in point.

The end of the Judicature is justice. The functionaries

are commonly a jury, made up of men, not specially prepared for their occasional office, but chosen for it as representatives of a class, and performing it under the direction
of a properly educated and experienced dignitary, called
by courtesy the Judge. When I was young, I recollect
being shocked at hearing an eminent man inveigh against
this time-honoured institution, as if absurdly unfitted to
promote the ends of the Law. He was answered by an
able lawyer, who has since occupied the judicial bench;
and he, instead of denying that precise allegation, argued
that the institution had a beneficial *political* effect on the
classes who were liable to serve as jurymen, as associating
them with the established order of things, and investing
them with salutary responsibilities. There is a good
deal in this reason:—a still more plausible defence, I
think, may be found in the consideration of the inexpe-
diency of suffering the tradition of Law to flow separate
from that of popular feeling, whereas there ought to be
a continual influx of the national mind into the judicial
conscience; and, unless there was this careful adjustment
between law and politics, the standards of right and
wrong, set up at Westminster, would diverge from those
received by the community at large, and the Nation
might some day find itself condemned and baffled by its
own supreme oracle of truth. This would be gravely
inconvenient; accordingly, as the Star Chamber recognized the royal decisions as precedents in law, and
formed a tradition of the Court, so it is imperative, in our
better state of things, that Public Opinion should give
the law to Law, and should rule those questions which
directly bear upon any matter of national concern. By
the expedient, then, of a Jury, the good of the country is
made to take the lead of private interest; for better far is
it that injustice should be done to a pack of individuals,

than that the maxims of the Nation should at any time incur the animadversion of its own paid officials, and a deadlock in State matters should be the result of so unfortunate an antagonism.

What makes me think that this is the real meaning of a jury, is what has lately taken place in a parallel way in the Committee of Privy Council on the baptismal controversy. My lords refused to go into the question of the truth of the doctrine in dispute, or into the meaning of the language used in the Prayer Book ; they merely asserted that a certain neutral reading of that language, by which it would bear contrary senses, was more congenial with the existing and traditional sentiments of the English people. They felt profoundly that it would never do to have the Church of the Nation at variance in opinion with the Nation itself. In other words, neither does English law seek justice, nor English religion seek truth, as ultimate and simple ends, but such a justice and such a truth as may not be inconsistent with the interests of large conservatism.

Again, I have been told by an eminent lawyer, that, in another ecclesiastical dispute which came before the Queen's Bench, a Chief Justice, now no more, rather than commit the Court to an unpopular decision, reversed the precedents of several centuries. No one could suspect that upright Judge of cowardice, time-serving, or party prejudice. The circumstances explained the act. Those precedents were out of keeping with the present national mind, which must be the perpetual standard and authoritative interpreter of the law ; and, as the Minister for Foreign Affairs instructs the Queen's representative at a Congress, what to think and say, so it is the Nation's right to impose upon the Judges the duty of expounding certain points of law in a sense agreeable to its high and mighty self. Accordingly the Chief Justice's decision on the occasion in question resulted in giving the public (as Lord John Russell expressed it as regards the Baptismal question) "great satisfaction." For satisfaction, peace, liberty, conservative interests, were the supreme end of the law, and not mere raw justice, as such. It is another illustration of the same spirit, though it does not strictly fall under our subject, that, at the public meeting held to thank that earnest and energetic man, Mr. Maurice, for the particular complexion of one portion of his theology, a speaker congratulated him on having, in questioning or denying eternal punishment, given (not a more correct, but) a "more genial" interpretation to the declarations of Holy Scripture.

Much, again, might be said upon the Constitutional rights of wealth, as tending to the weakening of the Executive. Wealth does not indeed purchase the higher appointments in the Law, but it can purchase situations, not only in the clerical, but in the military and civil services, and in the legislature. It is difficult to draw the line between such recognized transactions, and what is invidiously called corruption. As to parliamentary matters, I can easily understand the danger of that mode of proceeding, which I have called Constitutional, being carried too far. I can do justice to the feeling which, on a late occasion, if I recollect rightly, caused a will to be set aside, which provided for the purchase of a peerage. We must, of course, draw the line somewhere; but if you take your stand on principle, as it is the fashion to do, then I cannot go along with you, and have never been able to see the specific wickedness (where oaths are not broken or evaded) of buying a seat in Parliament, as contrasted with the purchase of an eligible incumbency. It must not be forgotten, that, from the time of Sir

Robert Walpole, bribes, to use an uncivil word, have been necessary to our Constitutional *regime ;*—visions of a higher but impracticable system having died away with Bolingbroke's " Patriot King."

This is but one instance of what is seen in so many various ways, that our Executive is on principle subordinate to class interests; we consider it better that it should work badly, than work to the inconvenience and danger of our national liberties. Such is self-government. Ideal standards, generous motives, pure principles, precise aims, scientific methods, must be excluded, and national utility must be the rule of administration. It is not a high system, but no human system is such. The knout and the tar-barrel aforementioned are not more defensible modes of proceeding, and are less pleasant than ours. Under ours, the individual is consulted for far more carefully than under despotism or democracy. Injustice is the exception; a free and easy mode of living is the rule. It is a venal *régime ; que voulez-vous ?* improvement may make things worse. It succeeds in making things pleasant at home ; whether it succeeds in war is another question.

8.

English Jealousy of Church and Army.

IN spite of the administrative weakness, characteristic of the English Constitution, from its defects in organization, from the interference of traditional principles and extraneous influences in its working, and from the corruption and jobbing incident to it, still so vast are its benefits in the security which it offers to person and property, in the freedom of speech, locomotion, and action, in the religious toleration, and in the general tranquillity and comfort, which go with it ; and again, so numerous and various are the material and mechanical advantages which the energy of the people has associated with it, that, I suppose, England is, in a political and national point of view, the best country to live in in the world. It has not the climate, it has not the faith, it has not the grace and sweetness, the festive cheerfulness, the social radiance, of some foreign cities and people ; but nowhere else surely can you have so much your own way, nowhere can you find ready to your hand so many of your wants and wishes. Take things as a whole, and the Executive and Nation work well, viewed in their results. What is it to the average Englishman that a jury sometimes gives an unjust verdict, that seats in Parliament are virtually bought, that the prizes of the Establishment are attained by interest, not merit, that political parties and great families monopolize the government, and share among themselves its places and appointments, or that the public press is every now and then both cowardly and tyrannical,—what is all this compared with the upshot of the whole national and political system ?

Look at things as a philosopher, and you will learn resignation, or rather thankful content, by perceiving that they all so hang together, that on the whole you cannot make them much better, nor can gain much more without losing much. No idea or principle of political society includes in its operation all conceivable good, or excludes all evil; that is the best form of society which has most of the good, and least of the bad. In the English ideal, the Nation is the centre,—"l'Etat c'est moi : " and everything else is dependent and subservient. We are carried back in our thoughts to the fable of Menenius Agrippa, though with a changed adaptation. The Nation is the sacred seat of vital heat and nourishment, the original element, and the first principle, and the number one of the State framework, and in its various members we find, not what is most effective or exquisite of its kind, but accessories compatible with the supremacy of that digestive and nutritive apparatus. The whole body politic is in unity : "cujus participatio ejus in id ipsum." The kingly office does not give scope for the best of conceivable kings, but for the chief of a self-governing people ; the ministers of state, the members of Parliament, the judges, are not intended to be perfect in their own kind respectively, but national statesmen, councillors and lawyers ; the bishops and commanders of the forces, the squires and the justices of the peace, belong to a Constitutional clergy, soldiery, and magistracy. I will not say that nothing admits of improvement, or what is called "reform," in such a society ; I will not attempt to determine the limits of improvement ; still a limit there is, and things must remain in substance what they are, or "Old England" will cease to be. Let us be merciful to ourselves; as in our own persons, one by one, we consult for our particular constitution of mind and body, and avoid efforts and aims, modes of exercise and diet, which are unsuitable to it, so in like manner those who appreciate the British Constitution aright will show their satisfaction at what it does well, resignation as to what it cannot do, and prudence in steering clear of those problems which are difficult or dangerous in respect to it. Such men will not make it dance on its lame leg. They will not go to war, if they can help it, for the conduct of war is not among its *chef-d'œuvres*, as I now, for positively the last time, will explain.

Material force is the *ultima ratio* of political society everywhere. Arms alone can keep the peace; and, as all other professions are reducible to system and rule, there is of course a science and an art of war. This art is learned like other arts by study and practice; it supposes the existence of expounders and instructors, an experimental process, a circulation of ideas, a traditionary teaching, and an aggregation of members,—in a word, a school. Continuity, establishment, organization, are necessary to the idea of a school and a craft. In other words, if war be an art, and not a matter of haphazard and pell-mell fighting, as under the walls of Troy, it requires what is appropriately called a standing army, that is, an army which has a *status*. Unless we are in a happy valley, or on a sea-protected island, we must have a standing army, or we are open to hostile attack.

But, when you have got your standing army, how are you to keep it from taking the wrong side, and turning upon you, like elephants in Eastern fights, instead of repelling your foe? Thus it was that the Prætorians, the Gothic mercenaries, the medieval Turks, and later Janizzaries, became the masters and upsetters of the Emperors, Caliphs, and Sultans who employed them. This formidable difficulty has been fatal to the military profession in popular governments, who in alarm have thrown the national defence upon the Nation, aided, as it might happen, by foreign mercenaries paid by the job. In such governments, the war department has not been the science of arms, but a political institution. An army has been raised for the occasion from off the estates and homesteads of the land, being soldiers of the soil, as rude as they were patriotic. When a danger threatened, they were summoned from plough or farm-yard, formed into a force, marched against the enemy, with whatever success in combat, and then marched home again. Which of the two would be the greater,—the inconvenience or the insufficiency of such a mode of waging war? Thus we have got round again to the original dilemma of the Horse, the Stag, and the Man; the Horse destined to feel at his flanks the Man's spurs, or the Stag's horns,—a Standing Army, or no profession of arms. In this difficulty, we must strike a balance and a compromise, and then get on as well as we can with a conditional Standing Army and a smattering in military science. Such has been the course adopted by England; and her insular situation, hitherto impregnable, has asked for nothing more.

Every sovereign State will naturally feel a jealousy of the semblance of an *imperium in imperio;* though not every State is in a condition to give expression to it. England has indulged that jealousy to the full, and has assumed a bearing towards the military profession much the same as she shows towards the ecclesiastical. There is indeed a close analogy between these two powers, both in them-

selves and in their relation to the State ; and, in order
to explain the position of the army in England, I cannot do better than refer to the position which in this
country has been assigned to the Church. The Church
and the Army are respectively the instruments of moral
and material force ; and are real powers in their own
respective fields of operation. They necessarily have
common sympathies, and an intense *esprit de corps*.
They are in consequence the strongest supports or the
most formidable opponents of the State to which they
belong, and require to be subjected, beyond any mistake,
to its sovereignty. In England, sensitively suspicious
of combination and system, three precautions have been
taken in dealing with the soldier and the parson,—(I
hope I may be familiar without offence),—precautions
borrowed from the necessary treatment of wild animals,
—(1) to tie him up, (2) to pare his claws, and (3) to keep
him low ; then he will be both safe and useful ;—the
result is a National Church, and a Constitutional Army.

1. In the first place, we tie both parson and soldier up,
by forbidding each to form one large organization. We
prohibit an organized religion and an organized force.
Instead of one corporation in religion, we only allow of
a multitude of small ones, as chapters and rectories,
while we ignore the Establishment as a whole, deny it
any legal *status*, and recognize the Dissenting bodies.
For Universities we substitute Colleges, with rival interests, that the intellect may not be too strong for us, as is
the case with some other countries ; but we freely multiply
local schools, for they have no political significance.
And, in like manner, we are willing to perfect the discipline and appointment of regiments, but we instinc-
tively recoil from the idea of an Army. We toast indeed
" The Army," but as an abstraction. as we used to drink to

"The Church," before the present substitution of "The Clergy of all denominations," which has much more of reality in it. Moreover, while, we have a real reason for sending our troops all over the world, shifting them about, using them for garrison duty, and for the defence of dependencies, we are thereby able also to divide and to hide them from each other. Nor is this all : if any organization requires a directing mind at the head of it, it is an army ; but, faithful to our Constitutional instincts, we have committed its command, *ex abundanti cautelâ*, to as many, I believe, as five independent boards, whose concurrence is necessary for a practical result. Nay, as late occurrences have shown, we have thought it a lesser evil, that our troops should be starved in the Crimea for want of the proper officer to land the stores, and that clothing and fuel shall oscillate to and fro between Balaklava and Malta, than that there should be the chance of the smallest opening for the introduction into our political system of a power formidable to nationalism. Thus we tie up both parson and soldier.

2. Next, in all great systems and agencies of any kind, there are certain accessories, absolutely necessary for their efficiency, yet hardly included in their essential idea. Such, to take a very small matter, is the use of the bag in making a pudding. Material edifices are no part of religion ; but you cannot have religious services without them ; nor can you move field-pieces without horses, nor get together horses without markets and transports. The greater part of these supplemental articles the English Constitution denies to its religious Establishment altogether, and to its Army, when not on active service. Fabrics of worship it encourages ; but it gives no countenance to such ecclesiastical belongings as the ritual and ceremonial of religion, synods, religious orders, sisters of

charity, missions, and the like, necessary instruments of
Christian faith, which zealous Churchmen, in times of
spiritual danger, decay, or promise, make vain endea-
vours to restore. And such in military matters are the
commissariat, transport, and medical departments, which
are jealously suppressed in time of peace, and hastily
and grudgingly restored on the commencement of hos-
tilities. The Constitutional spirit allows to the troops
arms and ammunition, as it allows to the clergy Ordination and two sacraments, neither being really dangerous,
while the supplements, which I have spoken of, are
withheld. Thus it cuts their claws.

3. And lastly, it keeps them low. Though lawyers
are educated for the law, and physicians for medicine,
it is felt among us to be dangerous to the Constitution to
have real education either in the clerical or military profession. Neither theology nor the science of war is
compatible with a national *regime*. Military and naval
science is, in the ordinary Englishman's notion, the
bayonet and the broadside. Religious knowledge comes
by nature; and so far is true, that Anglican divines
thump away in exhortation or in controversy, with a
manliness, good sense, and good will as thoroughly John
Bullish as the stubbornness of the Guards at Inkerman.
Not that they are forbidden to cultivate theology in private as a personal accomplishment, but that they must
not bring too much of it into the pulpit, for then they
become "extreme men," Calvinists or Papists, as it may
be. A general good education, a public school, and a
knowledge of the classics, make a parson; and he is
chosen for a benefice or a dignity, not on any abstract
ground of merit, but by the great officers of State, by
members of the aristocracy, and by country gentlemen,
or their nominees, men who by their position are a suffi-

cient guarantee that the nation will continually flow into the Establishment, and give it its own colour. And so of the army ; it is not so many days ago that a gentleman in office assured the House of Commons (if he was correctly reported) that the best officers were those who had a University education ; and I doubt not it is far better for the troops to be disciplined and commanded by good scholars than by incapables and dunces. But in each department professional education is eschewed, and it is thought enough for the functionary to be a gentleman. A clergyman is the " resident gentleman " in his parish; and no soldier must rise from the ranks, because he is not " company for gentlemen."

Let no man call this satire, for it is most seriously said ; nor have I intentionally coloured any one sentence in the parallel which I have been drawing out ; nor do I speak as grumbling at things as they are ;—I merely want to look facts in the face. I have been exposing what I consider the weak side of our Constitution, not exactly because I want it altered, but because people should not consider it the strong side. I think it a necessary weakness ; I do not see how it can be satisfactorily set right without dangerous innovations. We cannot in this world have all things as we should like to have them. Not that we should not try for the best, but we should be quite sure that we do not, like the dog in the fable, lose what we have, in attempting what we cannot have. Not that I deny that, even with a Constitution adapted for peace, British energy and pluck may not, as it has done before, win a battle, or carry through a war. But after all, reforms are but the first steps in revolution, as medicine is often a diluted poison. Enthusiasts have from time to time thought otherwise. There was Dr. Whately in 1826, who maintained that the Establishment was in degrading servitude, that it had a dog's collar round its neck, that the position of Bishops was intolerable, and that it was imperative to throw off State control, keeping the endowments.* And there is the *Times* newspaper in 1855, which would re-organize the Army, and put it on a scientific basis, satisfactory indeed to the military critic, startling to the Constitutional politician.

Mr. Macaulay gives us a warning from history. " The Constitution of England," he says, " was only one of a large family. In the fifteenth century, the government of Castile seems to have been as free as that of our own country. That of Arragon was, beyond all question, more so even than France ; the States-General alone could impose taxes. Sweden and Denmark had Constitutions of a different description. Let us overleap two or three hundred years, and contemplate Europe at the commencement of the eighteenth century. Every free Constitution, save one, had gone down. That of England had weathered the danger, and was riding in full security. What, then, made us to differ ? The progress of civilization introduced a great change. War became a science, and, as a necessary consequence, a trade. The great body of the people grew every day more reluctant to undergo the inconvenience of military service, and thought it better to pay others for undergoing them. That physical force which in the dark ages had belonged to the nobles and the commons, and had, far more than any charter or any assembly, been the safeguard of their privileges, was transferred entire to the king. The great mass of the population, destitute of all military discipline and organization, ceased to exercise any influence by force on political transactions. Thus absolute monarchy

* [I am informed that Dr. Whately never acknowledged the work here referred to as his own.]

was established on the Continent; England escaped, but she escaped very narrowly. If Charles had played the part of Gustavus Adolphus, if he had carried on a popular war for the defence of the Protestant cause in Germany, if he had gratified the national pride by a series of victories, if he had formed an army of 40,000 or 50,000 devoted soldiers, we do not see what chance the nation would have had of escaping from despotism."

These are very different times; but, however steady and self-righting is John Bull, however elastic his step, and vigorous his arm, I do not see how the strongest and healthiest build can overcome difficulties which lie in the very nature of things.

And now, however circuitously, I have answered my question, "Who's to blame for the untoward events in the Crimea?" They are to blame, the ignorant, intemperate public, who clamour for an unwise war, and then, when it turns out otherwise than they expected, instead of acknowledging their fault, proceed to beat their zealous servants in the midst of the fight for not doing impossibilities.

March, 1855.

VI.

AN INTERNAL ARGUMENT FOR CHRISTIANITY.

THE word "remarkable" has been so hacked of late in theological criticism—nearly as much so as "earnest" and "thoughtful"—that we do not like to apply it without an apology to the instance of a recent work, called "Ecce Homo," which we propose now to bring before the reader. In truth, it presents itself as a very convenient epithet, whenever we do not like to commit ourselves to any definite judgment on any subject before us, and prefer to spread over it a broad neutral tint to painting it distinctly white, red, or black. A man, or his work, or his deed, is "remarkable" when he produces an effect; be he effective for good or for evil, for truth or for falsehood—a point which, as far as that expression goes, we by adopting it, leave it for others or for the future to determine. Accordingly it is just the word to use in the instance of a Volume in which what is trite and what is novel, what is striking and what is startling, what is sound and what is untrustworthy, what is deep and what is shallow, are so mixed up together, or at least so vaguely suggested, or so perplexingly confessed, —which has so much of occasional force and circumambient glitter, of pretence and of seriousness,—as to make it impossible either with a good conscience to praise it, or without harshness and unfairness to condemn. Such a book is at least likely to be effective, whatever else it is or is not ; it may be safely called remarkable ; and therefore we apply the epithet "remarkable" to this *Ecce Homo*.

It is remarkable, then, on account of the sensation which it has made in religious circles. In the course of a few months it has reached a third edition, though it is a fair-sized octavo, and not an over-cheap one. And it has received the praise of critics and reviewers of very distinct shades of opinion. Such a reception must be owing either to the book itself, or to the circumstances of the day in which it has appeared, or to both of these causes together. Or, as seems to be the case, the needs of the day have become a call for some such work ; and the work, on its appearance, has been thankfully welcomed, on account of its professed object, by those whose needs called for it. The author includes himself in the number of these ; and while providing for his own wants he has ministered to theirs. This is what we especially mean by calling his book "remarkable." It deserves remark, because it has excited it.

I.

Disputants may maintain, if they please, that religious doubt is our appropriate, our normal state ; that to cherish doubts is our duty ; that to complain of them is impatience ; that to dread them is cowardice ; that to overcome them is inveracity ; that it is even a happy state, a state of calm philosophic enjoyment, to be conscious of them ;—but after all, unavoidable or not, such a state is not natural, and not happy, if the voice of mankind is to decide the question. English minds, in particular, have too much of a religious temper in them, as a natural gift, to acquiesce for any long time in positive, active doubt. For doubt and devotion are incompatible with each other ; every doubt, be it greater or less, stronger or weaker, involuntary as well as voluntary, acts upon devotion, so far forth, as water sprinkled, or dashed, or poured out upon a flame. Real and proper doubt kills faith, and devotion with it ; and even involuntary or half-deliberate doubt, though it does not actually kill faith, goes far to kill devotion ; and religion without devotion is little better than a burden, and soon becomes a superstition. Since, then, this is a day of objection and of doubt about the intellectual basis of Revealed Truth, it follows that there is a great deal of secret discomfort and distress in the religious portion of the community, the result of that general curiosity in speculation and inquiry which has been the growth among us of the last twenty or thirty years.

The people of this country, being Protestants, appeal to Scripture, when a religious question arises, as their ultimate informant and decisive authority in all such matters ; but who is to decide for them the previous question, that Scripture is really such an authority ? When, then, as at this time, its divine authority is the very point to be determined, that is, the character and extent of its inspiration and its component parts, then they find themselves at sea, without the means of directing their course. Doubting about the authority of Scripture, they doubt about its substantial truth ; doubting about its truth, they have doubts concerning the Object which it sets before their faith, about the historical accuracy and objective reality of the picture which it presents to us of our Lord. We are not speaking of wilful doubting, but of those painful misgivings, greater or less, to which we have already referred. Religious Protestants, when they think calmly on the subject, can hardly conceal from themselves that they have a house without logical foundations, which contrives indeed for the pre-

sent to stand, but which may go any day,—and where
are they then?

Of course Catholics will bid them receive the canon
of Scripture on the authority of the Church, in the spirit
of St. Augustine's well-known words: "I should not
believe the Gospel, were I not moved by the authority
of the Catholic Church." But who, they ask, is to be
voucher in turn for the Church, and for St. Augustine?—is
it not as difficult to prove the authority of the Church
and her doctors as the authority of the Scriptures? We
Catholics answer, and with reason, in the negative; but,
since they cannot be brought to agree with us here, what
argumentative ground is open to them? Thus they seem
drifting, slowly perhaps, but surely, in the direction of
scepticism.

2.

It is under these circumstances that they are invited,
in the Volume of which we have spoken, to betake themselves to the contemplation of our Lord's character, as
it is recorded by the Evangelists, as carrying with it
its own evidence, dispensing with extrinsic proof, and
claiming authoritatively by itself the faith and devotion
of all to whom it is presented. Such an argument, of
course, is as old as Christianity itself; the young man
in the Gospel calls our Lord "Good Master," and St.
Peter introduces Him to the first Gentile converts as one
who "went about doing good;" and in these last times
we can refer to the testimony even of unbelievers in behalf of an argument which is as simple as it is constraining. "Si la vie et la mort de Socrate sont d'un sage,"
says Rousseau, "la vie et la mort de Jésus sont d'un
Dieu." And he clenches the argument by observing,
that were the picture a mere conception of the sacred

writers, "l'inventeur en serait plus étonnant que le héros."
The force of this argument lies in its directness ; it comes
to the point at once, and concentrates in itself evidence,
doctrine, and devotion.   In theological language, it is the
motivum credibilitatis, the *objectum materiale,* and the *for-
male,* all in one ; it unites human reason and supernatural
faith in one complex act ; and it comes home to all men,
educated and ignorant, young and old.   And it is the
point to which, after all and in fact, all religious minds
tend, and in which they ultimately rest, even if they do
not start from it.   Without an intimate apprehension of
the personal character of our Saviour, what professes to
be faith is little more than an act of ratiocination.   If
faith is to live, it must love ; it must lovingly live in the
Author of faith as a true and living Being, *in Deo vivo et
vero ;* according to the saying of the Samaritans to their
townswoman : " We now believe, not for thy saying, for
we ourselves have heard Him."   Many doctrines may
be held implicitly ; but to see Him as if intuitively is
the very promise and gift of Him who is the object of
the intuition.   We are constrained to believe when it is
He that speaks to us about Himself.

Such undeniably is the characteristic of divine faith
viewed in itself : but here we are concerned, not simply
with faith, but with its logical antecedents ; and the
question returns on which we have already touched, as a
difficulty with Protestants,—how can our Lord's Life, as
recorded in the Gospels, be a logical ground of faith,
unless we set out with assuming the truth of those
Gospels ; that is, without assuming, as proved, the original
matter of doubt ?   And Protestant apologists, it may be
urged—Paley, for instance—show their sense of this
difficulty when they place the argument drawn from our
Lord's character only among the auxiliary Evidences of

Christianity. Now the following answer may fairly be made to this objection; nor need we grudge Protestants the use of it, for, as will appear in the sequel, it proves too much for their purpose, as being an argument for the divinity not only of Christ's mission, but of that of His Church also. However, we say this by the way.

It may be maintained then, that, making as large an allowance as the most sceptical mind, when pressed to state its demands in full, would desire, we are at least safe in asserting that the books of the New Testament, taken as a whole, were existing about the middle of the second century, and were then received by Christians, or were in the way of being received, and nothing else but they were received, as the authoritative record of the origin and rise of their Religion. In that first age they were the only account of the mode in which Christianity was introduced to the world. Internal as well as external evidence sanctions us in so speaking. Four Gospels, the book of the Acts of the Apostles, various Apostolic writings, made up then, as now, our sacred books. Whether there was a book more or less, say even an important book, does not affect the general character of the Religion as those books set it forth. Omit one or other of the Gospels, and three or four Epistles, and the outline and nature of its objects and its teaching remain what they were before the omission. The moral peculiarities, in particular, of its Founder are, on the whole, identical, whether we learn them from St. Matthew, St. John, St. Peter, or St. Paul. He is not in one book a Socrates, in another a Zeno, and in a third an Epicurus. Much less is the religion changed or obscured by the loss of particular chapters or verses, or even by inaccuracy in fact, or by error in opinion, (supposing *per impossibile* such a charge could be made good,) in particular portions of a book. For argument's sake, suppose that the three first Gospels are an accidental collection of traditions or legends, for which no one is responsible, and in which Christians had faith because there was nothing else to put faith in. This is the limit to which extreme scepticism can proceed, and we are willing to commence our argument by granting it. Still, starting at this disadvantage, we should be prepared to argue, that if, in spite of this, and after all, there be shadowed out in these anonymous and fortuitous documents a Teacher *sui generis,* distinct, consistent, and original, then does that picture, thus accidentally resulting, for the very reason of its accidental composition, only become more marvellous; then is He an historical fact, and again a supernatural or divine fact;—historical from the consistency of the representation, and because the time cannot be assigned when it was not received as a reality; and supernatural, in proportion as the qualities with which He is invested in those writings are incompatible with what it is reasonable or possible to ascribe to human nature viewed simply in itself. Let these writings be as open to criticism, whether as to their origin or their text, as sceptics can maintain; nevertheless the representation in question is there, and forces upon the mind a conviction that it records a fact, and a superhuman fact, just as the reflection of an object in a stream remains in its general form, however rapid the current, and however many the ripples, and is a sure warrant to us of the presence of the object on the bank, though that object be out of sight.

3.

Such, we conceive, though stated in our own words, is the argument drawn out in the pages before us, or rather

**

such is the ground on which the argument is raised; and the interest which it has excited lies, not in its novelty, but in the particular mode in which it is brought before the reader, in the originality and precision of certain strokes by which is traced out for us the outline of the Divine Teacher. These strokes are not always correct; they are sometimes gratuitous, sometimes derogatory to their object; but they are always determinate; and, being such, they present an old argument before us with a certain freshness, which, because it is old, is necessary for its being effective.

We do not wonder at all, then, at the sensation which the Volume is said to have caused at Oxford, and among Anglicans of the Oxford school, after the wearisome doubt and disquiet of the last ten years; for it has opened the prospect of a successful issue of inquiries in an all-important province of thought, where there seemed to be no thoroughfare. Distinct as are the liberal and Catholicizing parties in the Anglican Church both in their principles and their policy, it must not be supposed that they are also as distinct in the members that compose them. No line of demarcation can be drawn between the one collection of men and the other, in fact; for no two minds are altogether alike; and individually, Anglicans have each his own shade of opinion, and belong partly to this school, partly to that. Or rather, there is a large body of men who are neither the one nor the other; they cannot be called an intermediate party, for they have no discriminating watchwords; they range from those who are almost Catholic to those who are almost Liberals. They are not Liberals, because they do not glory in a state of doubt; they cannot profess to be "Anglo-Catholics," because they are not prepared to give an internal assent to all that is put forth by the

Church as truth of revelation. These are the men who, if they could, would unite old ideas with new; who cannot give up tradition, yet are loth to shut the door to progress; who look for a more exact adjustment of faith with reason than has hitherto been attained; who love the conclusions of Catholic theology better than the proofs, and the methods of modern thought better than its results; and who, in the present wide unsettlement of religious opinion, believe indeed, or wish to believe, Scripture and orthodox doctrine, taken as a whole, and cannot get themselves to avow any deliberate dissent from any part of either, but still, not knowing how to defend their belief with logical exactness, or at least feeling that there are large unsatisfied objections lying against parts of it, or having misgivings lest there should be such, acquiesce in what is called a practical belief, that is, accept revealed truths, only because such acceptance of them is the safest course, because they are probable, and because to hold them in consequence is a duty, not as if they felt absolutely certain, though they will not allow themselves to be actually in doubt. Such is about the description to be given of them as a class; though, as we have said, they so materially differ from each other, that no general account of them will apply strictly to any individual in their body.

Now, it is to this large class which we have been describing that such a work as that before us, in spite of the serious errors which they will not be slow to recognize in it, comes as a friend in need. They do not stumble at the author's inconsistencies or shortcomings; they are arrested by his professed purpose, and are profoundly moved by his successful hits (as they may be called) towards fulfilling it. Remarks on the Gospel history, such as Paley's, they feel to be casual and superficial;

such as Rousseau's to be vague and declamatory; they wish to justify with their intellect all that they believe with their heart; they cannot separate their ideas of religion from its revealed Object; but they have an aching dissatisfaction within them, that they should be apprehending Him so feebly, when they should fain (as it were) see and touch Him as well as hear. When, then, they have logical grounds presented to them for holding that the recorded picture of our Lord is its own evidence, that it carries with it its own reality and authority, that His " revelatio " is " revelata " in the very act of being a " revelatio," it is as if He Himself said to them, as He once said to His disciples, " It is I, be not afraid ; " and the clouds at once clear off, and the waters subside, and the land is gained for which they are looking out.

The author before us, then, has the merit of promising what, if he could fulfil it, would entitle him to the gratitude of thousands. We do not say, we are very far from thinking that he has actually accomplished so high an enterprise, though he seems to be ambitious enough to hope that he has not come far short of it. He somewhere calls his book a treatise ; he would have done better to call it an essay ; nor need he have been ashamed of a word which Locke has used in his work on the Human Understanding. Before concluding, we shall take occasion to express our serious sense, how very much his execution falls below his purpose ; but certainly it is a great purpose which he sets before him, and for that he is to be praised. And there is at least this singular merit in his performance, as he has given it to the public, that he is clear-sighted and fair enough to view our Lord's work in its true light, as including in it the establishment of a visible Kingdom or Church. In proportion, then, as we shall presently find it our duty to pass some severe remarks upon his Volume, as it comes before us, so do we feel bound, before doing so, to give some specimens of it in that point of view in which we consider it really to subserve the cause of Revealed Truth. And in the sketch which we are now about to give of the first steps of his investigation, we must not be understood to make him responsible for the language in which we shall exhibit them to our readers, and which will unavoidably involve our own corrections of his argument, and our own colouring.

4

Among a people, then, accustomed by the most sacred traditions of their Religion to a belief in the appearance, from time to time, of divine messengers for their instruction and reformation, and to the expectation of One such messenger still to come, the last and greatest of all, who should also be their king and deliverer as well as their teacher, suddenly is found, after a long break in the succession, and a period of national degradation, a prophet of the old stamp, in one of the deserts of the country —John, the son of Zachary. He announces the promised kingdom as close at hand, calls his countrymen to repentance, and institutes a rite symbolical of it. The people seem disposed to take him for the destined Saviour ; but, instead, he points out to them a private person in the crowd which is flocking about him ; and henceforth the interest which his own preaching has excited centres in that Other. Thus our Lord is introduced to the notice of His countrymen.

Thus brought before the world, He opens His mission. What is the first impression it makes upon us ? Admiration of its singular simplicity and directness, both as to object and work. Such of course ought to be its character, if it was to be the fulfilment of the ancient, long-expected promise; and such it was, as our Lord proclaimed it. Other men, who do a work, do not at once set about it as their object; they make several failures; they are led on to it by circumstances; they miscalculate their powers; or they are drifted from the first in a different direction from that which they had chosen; they do most where they are expected to do least. But our Lord said and did. "He formed one plan and executed it" (p. 18).

In the next place, what was that plan? Let us consider the force of the words in which, as the Baptist before Him, He introduced His ministry: "The kingdom of God is at hand." What was meant by the kingdom of God? "The conception was no new one, but familiar to every Jew" (p. 19). At the first formation of the nation and state of the Israelites, the Almighty had been their King; when a line of earthly kings was introduced, then God spoke by the prophets. The existence of the theocracy was the very constitution and boast of Israel, as limited monarchy, liberty, and equality are the boast respectively of certain modern nations. Moreover, the Gospel proclamation ran, " "Pœnitentiam agite; for the kingdom of heaven is at hand :" here again was another and recognized token of a theophany; for the mission of a prophet, as we have said above, was commonly a call to reformation and expiation of sin.

A divine mission, then, was a falling back upon the original covenant between God and His people; but again, while it was an event of old and familiar occurrence, it ever had carried with it in its past instances something new in connexion with the circumstances under which it took place. The prophets were accustomed to give interpretations, or to introduce modifications of the letter of the Law, to add to its conditions and to enlarge its application. It was to be expected, then, that now, when the new Prophet to whom the Baptist pointed, opened His commission, He too, in like manner, would be found to be engaged in a restoration, but in a restoration which should be a religious advance; and that the more, if He really was the special, final Prophet of the theocracy, to whom all former prophets had looked forward, and in whom their long and august line was to be summed up and perfected. In proportion as His work was to be more signal, so would His new revelations be wider and more wonderful.

Did our Lord fulfil these expectations? Yes; there was this peculiarity in His mission, that He came, not only as one of the prophets in the kingdom of God, but as the King Himself of that kingdom. Thus His mission involves the most exact return to the original polity of Israel, which the appointment of Saul had disarranged, while it recognizes also the line of Prophets, and infuses a new spirit into the Law. Throughout His ministry our Lord claimed and received the title of King, which no prophet ever had done before. On His birth, the wise men came to worship "the King of the Jews." "Thou art the Son of God, Thou art the King of Israel," cried Nathaniel after His baptism; and on His cross the charge recorded against Him was that He professed to be "King of the Jews." "During His whole public life," says the author, "He is distinguished from the other prominent characters of Jewish history by His unbounded personal pretensions. He claims expressly the character of that Divine Messiah for which the ancient prophets had directed the nation to look."—P. 25.

He is, then, a King, as well as a Prophet; but is He as one of the old heroic kings, David or Solomon? Had such been His pretension, He had not, in His own words, "discerned the signs of the times." It would have been a false step in Him, into which other would-be champions of Israel, before and after Him, actually fell, and in consequence failed. But here this young Prophet is from the first distinct, decided, and original. His contemporaries, indeed, the wisest, the most experienced, were wedded to the notion of a revival of the barbaric kingdom. "Their heads were full of the languid dreams of commentators, the unpracticable pedantries of men who live in the past" (p. 27). But He gave to the old prophetic promises an interpretation which they could undeniably bear, but which they did not immediately suggest; which we can maintain to be true, while we can deny it to be imperative. He had His own prompt, definite conception of the restored theocracy; it was His own, and not another's; it was suited to the new age; it was triumphantly carried out in the event.

5

In what, then, did He consider His royalty to consist? First, what was it not? It did not consist in the ordinary functions of royalty; it did not prevent His payment of tribute to Cæsar; it did not make Him a judge in questions of criminal or of civil law, in a question of adultery, or in the adjudication of an inheritance; nor did it give Him the command of armies. Then perhaps, after all, it was but a figurative royalty, as when the Eridanus is called "fluviorum rex," or Aristotle "the prince of philosophers." No; it was not a figurative royalty either. To call oneself a king, without being one, is playing with edged tools—as in the story of the innkeeper's son, who was put to death for calling himself "heir to the crown." Christ certainly knew what He was saying. "He had provoked the accusation of rebellion against the Roman government: He must have known that the language He used would be interpreted so. Was there then nothing substantial in the royalty He claimed? Did He die for a metaphor?" (p. 28.) He meant what He said, and therefore His kingdom was literal and real; it was visible; but what were its visible prerogatives, if they were not those in which earthly royalty commonly consists? In truth, He passed by the lesser powers of royalty to claim the higher. He claimed certain divine and transcendent functions of the original theocracy, which had been in abeyance since that theocracy had been infringed, which even to David had not been delegated, which had never been exercised except by the Almighty. God had created, first the people, next the state, which He deigned to govern. "The origin of other nations is lost in antiquity" (p. 33); but "this people," runs the sacred word, "have I formed for Myself." And "He who first called the nation did for it the second work of a king: He gave it a law" (p. 34). Now it is very striking to observe that these two incommunicable attributes of divine royalty, as exemplified in the history of the Israelites, are the very two which our Lord assumed. He was the Maker and the Lawgiver of His subjects. He said in the commencement of His ministry, "*Follow* Me;" and He added, and I will make you"—you in turn—"fishers of men." And the next we read of Him is, that His disciples came to Him on the Mount, and He opened His mouth and *taught* them. And so again, at the end of it, "Go ye, make *disciples* of all nations, *teaching* them." "Thus the very works for which the [Jewish] nation chiefly hymned their Jehovah, He undertook in His name to do. He undertook to be the Father of an everlasting state, and the Legislator of a world-wide society" (p. 36) ; that is, showing Himself, according to the prophetic announcement, to be "*Admirabilis, consiliarius, pater futuri sæculi, princeps pacis.*"

To these two claims He added a third : first, He chooses the subjects of His kingdom ; next, He gives them a law ; but thirdly, He judges them—judges them in a far truer and fuller sense than in the old kingdom even the Almighty judged His people. The God of Israel ordained national rewards and punishments for national obedience or transgression ; He did not judge His subjects one by one ; but our Lord takes upon Himself the supreme and final judgment of every one of His subjects, not to speak of the whole human race (though, from the nature of the case, this function cannot belong to His present visible kingdom). " He considered, in short, heaven and hell to be in His hand " (p. 40).

We shall mention one further function of the new King and His new kingdom : its benefits are even bound up with the maintenance of this law of political unity. "To organize a society, and to bind the members of it together by the closest ties, were the business of His life. For this reason it was that He called men away from their homes, imposed upon some a wandering life, upon others the sacrifice of their property, and endeavoured by all means to divorce them from their former connexions, in order that they might find a new home in the Church. For this reason He instituted a solemn initiation, and for this reason He refused absolutely to any one a dispensation from it. For this reason, too . . . He established a common feast, which was through all ages to remind Christians of their indissoluble union " (p. 92). But *cui bono* is a visible kingdom, when the great end of our Lord's ministry is moral advancement and preparation for a future state? It is easy to understand, for instance, how a sermon may benefit, or personal example, or religious friends, or household piety. We can learn to imitate a saint or a martyr, we can cherish a lesson, we can study a treatise, we can obey a rule; but what is the definite advantage to a preacher or a moralist of an external organization, of a visible kingdom? Yet Christ says, "Seek ye *first* the kingdom of God," as well as "His justice." Socrates wished to improve man, but he laid no stress on their acting in concert in order to secure that improvement; on the contrary, the Christian law is political, as certainly as it is moral.

Why is this? It arises out of the intimate relation between Him and His subjects, which, in bringing them all to Him as their common Father, necessarily brings them to each other. Our Lord says, "Where two or three are gathered together in My name, I am in the midst of them." Fellowship between His followers is made a distinct object and duty, because it is a means, according to the provisions of His system, by which in some special way they are brought near to Him. This is declared, still more strikingly than in the text we have just quoted, in the parable of the Vine and its Branches, and in that (if it is to be called a parable) of the Bread of Life. The almighty King of Israel was ever, indeed, invisibly present in the glory above the Ark, but He did not manifest Himself there or anywhere else as a present cause of spiritual strength to His people; but the new King is not only ever present, but to every one of His subjects individually is He a first element and perennial source of life. He is not only the head of His kingdom, but also its animating principle and its centre of power. The author whom we are reviewing does not quite reach the great doctrine here suggested, but he goes near it

in the following passage : " Some men have appeared
who have been 'as levers to uplift the earth and roll it in
another course.' Homer by creating literature, Socrates
by creating science, Cæsar by carrying civilization inland
from the shores of the Mediterranean, Newton by starting
science upon a career of steady progress, may be said to
have attained this eminence. But these men gave a single
impact like that which is conceived to have first set the
planets in motion. Christ claims to be a perpetual
attractive power, like the sun, which determines their
orbit. They contributed to men some discovery, and
passed away ; Christ's discovery is Himself. To humanity struggling with its passions and its destiny He
says, Cling to Me ;—cling ever closer to Me. If we
believe St. John, He represented Himself as the Light
of the world, as the Shepherd of the souls of men, as the
Way to immortality, as the Vine or Life-tree of humanity" (p. 177). He ends this beautiful passage, of
which we have quoted as much as our limits allow, by
saying that " He instructed His followers to hope for life
from feeding on His Body and Blood."

6

O si sic omnia ! Is it not hard, that, after following
with pleasure a train of thought so calculated to warm
all Christian hearts, and to create in them both admiration and sympathy for the writer, we must end our notice
of him in a different tone, and express as much dissent
from him and as serious blame of him as we have hitherto been showing satisfaction with his object, his intention, and the general outline of his argument ? But so it
is. In what remains to be said we are obliged to speak
of his work in terms so sharp that they may seem to be
out of keeping with what has gone before. With what-

er abruptness, we must suddenly shift the scene, and manifest our disapprobation of portions of his book as plainly as we have shown an interest in it. We have praised it in various points of view. It has stirred the hearts of many; it has recognized a need, and gone in the right direction for supplying it. It serves as a token, and a hopeful token, of what is going on in the minds of numbers of men external to the Church. It is so far a good book, and, we trust, will work for good. Especially as we have seen, is it interesting to the Catholic, as acknowledging the visible Church to be our Lord's own creation, as the direct fruit of His teaching, and the destined instrument of His purposes. We do not know how to speak in an unfriendly tone of an author who has done so much as this; but at the same time, when we come to examine his argument in its details, and study his chapters one by one, we find, in spite of, and mixed up with, what is true and original, and even putting aside his patent theological errors, so much bad logic, so much of rash and gratuitous assumption, so much of half-digested thought, that we are obliged to conclude that it would have been much wiser in him, instead of publishing what he seems to confess, or rather to proclaim, to be the jottings of his first researches upon sacred territory, to have waited till he had carefully traversed and surveyed and mapped the whole of it. We now proceed to give a few instances of the faults of which we complain.

His opening remarks will serve as an illustration. In p. 41 he says, "We have not rested upon *single* passages, nor drawn from the *fourth Gospel.*" This, we suppose, must be his reason for ignoring the passage in Luke ii. 49: "Did you not know that I must be about My Father's business?" for he directly contradicts it, by gratuitously imagining that our Lord came for St. John's baptism with the same intention as the penitents around Him; and that, in spite of His own words, which we suppose are to be taken as another "single passage," "So it becometh us to fulfil all justice" (Matt. iii. 15). It must be on this principle of ignoring single passages such as these, even though they admit of combination, that he goes on to say of our Lord, that "in the agitation of mind caused by His baptism, and by the Baptist's designation of Him as the future Prophet, He retired into the wilderness," and there "He matured the plan of action which we see Him executing from the moment of His return into society" (p. 9); and that not till then was He "conscious of miraculous power" (p. 12). This neglect of the sacred text, we repeat, must be allowed him, we suppose, under cover of his acting out his rule of abstaining from single passages and from the fourth Gospel. Let us allow it; but at least he ought to adduce passages, single or many, for what he actually does assert. He must not be allowed arbitrarily to add to the history, as well as cautiously to take from it. Where, then, we ask, did he learn that our Lord's baptism caused Him "agitation of mind," that He "matured His plan of action in the wilderness," and that He then first was "conscious of miraculous power"?

But again: it seems he is not to refer to "single passages or the fourth Gospel;" yet, wonderful to say, he actually does open his formal discussion of the sacred history by referring to a passage from that very Gospel, —nay, to a particular text, which is not to be called "single," only because it is not so much as a single text, but an unfair half text, and half a text such, that, had he taken the whole of it, he would have been obliged to admit that the part which he puts aside just runs counter to his interpretation of the part which he recognizes. The words are these, as they stand in the Protestant version : " Behold the Lamb of God, which taketh away the sin of the world." Now, it is impossible to deny that " which taketh away," etc., fixes and limits the sense of " the Lamb of God ; " but our author notices the latter half of the sentence, only in order to put aside the light which it throws upon the former half; and instead of the Baptist's own interpretation of the title which he gives to our Lord, he substitutes another, radically different, which he selects for himself out of one of the Psalms. He explains " the Lamb " by the well-known image, which represents the Almighty as a shepherd and His earthly servants as sheep—innocent, safe, and happy under His protection. " The Baptist's opinion of Christ's character, then," he says, " is summed up for us in the title he gives Him—the Lamb of God, taking away the sins of the world. There *seems* to be, in the last part of this description, an allusion to the usages of the Jewish sacrificial system ; and, in order to explain it fully, it would be necessary to anticipate much which will come more conveniently later in this treatise. *But* when we remember that the Baptist's mind was *doubtless* full of imagery drawn from the Old Testament, and that the conception of a lamb of God makes the subject of one of the most striking of the Psalms, *we shall perceive what he meant to convey by this phrase*" (pp. 5, 6). This is like saying, to take a parallel instance, "Isaiah declares, 'Mine eyes have seen the King, the Lord of hosts ;' *but*, considering that doubtless the prophet was well acquainted with the first and second books of Samuel, and that Saul, David, and Solomon are the three great kings there represented, we shall easily perceive that, by 'seeing the King,' he meant to say that he saw Uzziah, king of Judah, in the last year of whose reign he had the vision. As to the phrase 'the Lord of hosts,' which seems to refer to the Almighty, we will consider its meaning by-and-by:"—but, in truth, it is difficult to invent a paralogism, in its gratuitous inconsecutiveness parallel to his own.

7.

We must own that, with every wish to be fair to this author, we never recovered from the perplexity of mind which this passage, in the very threshold of his book, inflicted on us. It needed not the various passages, constructed on the same argumentative model, which follow it in his work, to prove to us that he was not only an *incognito*, but an enigma. "Ergo," is the symbol of the logician :—what is the scientific method of a writer whose symbols, profusely scattered through his pages are "probably," "it must be," "doubtless," "on this hypothesis," "we may suppose," and "it is natural to think," and that at the very time that he pointedly discards the comments of school theologians? Is it possible that he can mean us to set aside, in his own favour, the glosses of all that went before him, and to exchange our old lamps for his new ones? Men have been at fault, when trying to determine whether he was an orthodox believer on his road to liberalism, or a liberal on his road to orthodoxy: this doubtless may be to some a perplexity ; but our own difficulty is, whether he comes to us as an investigator or rather as a prophet, as one unequal or superior to the art of reasoning. Undoubtedly he is an able man ; but what can he possibly mean by startling us with such eccentricities of argumentation as are quite familiar with him? Addison somewhere bids his readers bear in mind.

that if he is ever especially dull, he always has a special reason for being so ; and it is difficult to reconcile one's imagination to the supposition that this anonymous writer, with so much religious thought as he certainly evidences, is without some recondite reason for seeming so inconsequent, and does not move by some deep subterraneous process of investigation, which, if once brought to light, would clear him of the imputation of castle-building.

There is always a danger of misconceiving an author who has no antecedents by which we may measure him. Taking his work as it lies, we can but wish that he had kept his imagination under control ; and that he had more of the hard head of a lawyer, and the patience of a philosopher. He writes like a man who cannot keep from telling the world his first thoughts, especially if they are clever or graceful ; he has come for the first time upon a strange world, and his remarks upon it are too often obvious rather than striking, and crude rather than fresh. What can be more paradoxical than to interpret our Lord's words to Nicodemus, "Unless a man be born again," etc., of the necessity of external religion, and as a lesson to him to profess his faith openly and not to visit Him in secret ? (p. 86). What can be more pretentious, not to say vulgar, than his paraphrase of St. John's passage about the woman taken in adultery ? "In His burning embarrassment and confusion," he says, " He stooped down so as to hide His face. . . . They had a glimpse perhaps of the glowing blush upon His face," etc. (p. 104.)

We should be very sorry to use a severe word concerning an honest inquirer after truth, as we believe this anonymous writer to be ; but we will confess that Catholics, kindly as they may wish to feel towards him, are scarcely even able, from their very position, to give his work the enthusiastic reception which it has received from some other critics. The reason is plain; those alone can speak of it from a full heart, who feel a need, and recognize in it a supply of that need. We are not in the number of such ; for they who have found, have no need to seek. Far be it from us to use language savouring of the leaven of the Pharisees. We are not assuming a high place, because we thus speak, or boasting of our security. Catholics are both deeper and shallower than Protestants ; but in neither case have they any call for a treatise such as this *Ecce Homo*. If they live to the world and the flesh, then the faith which they profess, though it is true and distinct, is dead; and their certainty about religious truth, however firm and unclouded, is but shallow in its character, and flippant in its manifestations. And in proportion as they are worldly and sensual, will they be flippant and shallow.* But their faith is as inde- lible as the pigment which colours the skin, even though it is skin-deep. This class of Catholics is not likely to take interest in a pictorial *Ecce Homo*. On the other hand, where the heart is alive with divine love, faith is as deep as it is vigorous and joyous ; and, as far as Catho- lics are in this condition, they will feel no drawing to- wards a work which is after all but an arbitrary and unsatisfactory dissection of the Object of their devotion. Faith, be it deep or shallow, does not need Evidences. That individual Catholics may be harassed with doubts, particularly in a day like this, we are not denying ; but, viewed as a body, Catholics, from their religious condi- tion, are either too deep or too shallow to suffer from those elementary difficulties, or that distress of mind,

* [On this whole subject, *vide* "Difficulties felt by Anglicans," etc., Lecture IX.]

and need of argument, which serious Protestants so often experience.

We confess, then, as Catholics, to some unavoidable absence of cordial feeling in following the remarks of this author, though not to any want of real sympathy; and we seem to be justified in our indisposition by his manifest want of sympathy with us. If we feel distant towards him, his own language about Catholicity, and (what may be called) old Christianity, seems to show that that distance is one of fact, one of mental position, not any fault in ourselves. Is it not undeniable, that the very life of personal religion among Catholics lies in a knowledge of the Gospels? It is the character and conduct of our Lord, His words, His deeds, His sufferings, His work, which are the very food of our devotion and rule of our life. "Behold the Man," which this author feels to be an object novel enough to write a book about, has been the contemplation of Catholics from the first age when St. Paul said, "The life that I now live in the flesh, I live in the faith of the Son of God, who loved me, and delivered Himself for me." As the Psalms have ever been the manual of our prayer, so have the Gospels been the subject-matter of our meditation. In these latter times especially, since St. Ignatius, they have been divided into portions, and arranged in a scientific order, not unlike that which the Psalms have received in the Breviary. To contemplate our Lord in His person and His history is with us the exercise of every retreat, and the devotion of every morning. All this is certainly simple matter of fact; but the writer we are reviewing lives and thinks at so great a distance from us, as not to be cognizant of what is so patent and so notorious a truth. He seems to imagine that the faith of a Catholic is the mere profession of a formula. He deems it important to disclaim, in the outset of his work, all reference to the theology of the Church. He eschews with much precision, as something almost profane, the dogmatism of former ages. He wishes "to trace" our Lord's "biography from point to point, and accept those conclusions—not which Church doctors or even Apostles have sealed with their authority—but which the facts themselves, critically weighed, appear to warrant."—(Preface.) Now, what Catholics, what Church doctors, as well as Apostles, have ever lived on, is not any number of theological canons or decrees, but, we repeat, the Christ Himself, as He is represented in concrete existence in the Gospels.* Theological determinations about our Lord are far more of the nature of landmarks or buoys to guide a discursive mind in its reasonings, than to assist a devotional mind in its worship. Common sense, for instance, tells us what is meant by the words, "My Lord and my God;" and a religious man, upon his knees, requires no commentator; but against irreligious speculators, Arius or Nestorius, a denunciation has been passed, in Ecumenical Council, when "science falsely so-called" encroached upon devotion. Has not this been insisted on by all dogmatic Christians over and over again? Is it not a representation as absolutely true as it is trite? We had fancied that Protestants generally allowed the touching beauty of Catholic hymns and meditations; and after all is there not That in all Catholic churches which goes beyond any written devotion, whatever its force or its pathos? Do we not believe in a Presence in the sacred Tabernacle, not as a form of words, or as a notion, but as an Object as real as we are real? And if before that Presence we need neither profession of faith nor even manual of devotion,

* [*Vide* "Essay on Assent," ch. iv. and v.]

what appetite can we have for the teaching of a writer who not only exalts his first thoughts about our Lord into professional lectures, but implies that the Catholic Church has never known how to point Him out to her children?

8.

It may be objected, that we are making too much of so accidental a slight as is contained in his allusion to "Church doctors," especially as he mentions Apostles in connexion with them; but it would be affectation not to recognize in other places of his book an undercurrent of antagonism to us, of which the passage already quoted is but a first indication. Of course he has quite as much right as another to take up an anti-Catholic position, if he will; but we understand him to be putting forth an investigation, not a polemical argument: and if, instead of keeping his eyes directed towards his own proper subject, he looks to the right or left, hitting at those who view things differently from himself, he is damaging the ethical force of a composition which claims to be, and mainly is, a serious and manly search after religious truth. Why cannot he let us alone? Of course he cannot avoid seeing that the lines of his own investigation diverge from those drawn by others; but he will have enough to do in defending himself, without making others the object of his attack. He is virtually opposing Voltaire, Strauss, Renan, Calvin, Wesley, Chalmers, Erskine, and a host of other writers, but he does not denounce *them ;* why then does he single out, misrepresent, and anathematize a a main principle of Catholic orthodoxy. It is as if he could not keep his hand off us, when we crossed his path. We are alluding to the following magisterial passage:

" If He (our Lord) meant anything by His constant

denunciation of hypocrites, there is nothing which He could have visited with sterner censure than that *short cut to belief* which many persons take, when, overwhelmed with difficulties which beset their minds, and afraid of damnation, they *suddenly* resolve to strive no longer, but, giving their minds a holiday, to rest content with *saying* that they believe, and acting *as if* they did. A melancholy end of Christianity indeed ! Can there be such a disfranchised pauper class among the citizens of the New Jerusalem ? " (p. 79).

He adds shortly afterwards :

" Assuredly, those who represent Christ as presenting to man an abtruse theology, and saying to them peremptorily, ' Believe or be damned,' have the coarsest conception of the Saviour of the world " (p. 80).

Thus he delivers himself : Believe or be damned is so detestable a doctrine, that if any man denies that it *is* detestable, I pronounce him to be a hypocrite ; to be without any true knowledge of the Saviour of the world ; to be the object of His sternest censure ; and to have no part or place in the Holy City, the New Jerusalem, the eternal Heaven above.—Pretty well for a virtuous hater of dogmatism ! We hope we shall show less dictatorial arrogance than his in the answer which we proceed to make to him.

Whether or not there are persons such as he describes, Catholics, or, Protestant converts to Catholicism, —men who profess a faith which they do not believe, under the notion that they shall be eternally damned if they do not profess it without believing,—we really do not know—we never met with such ; but since facts do not concern us here so much as principles, let us, for argument's sake, grant that there are such men. Our author believes they are not only " many," but enough to form a "class;" and he considers that they act in this preposterous manner under the sanction, and in accordance with the teaching, of the religious bodies to which they belong. Especially there is a marked allusion in his words to the Athanasian Creed and the Catholic Church. Now we answer him thus:

It is his charge against the teachers of dogma that they impose on men as a duty, instead of believing, to "act as if they did" believe:—now in fact this is the very kind of profession which, if it is all that a candidate has to offer, absolutely shuts him out from admission into Catholic communion. We suppose, that by belief of a thing this writer understands an inward conviction of its truth;—this being supposed, we plainly say that no priest is at liberty to receive a man into the Church who has not a real internal belief, and cannot say from his heart, that the things taught by the Church are true. On the other hand, as we have said above, it is the very characteristic of the profession of faith made by numbers of educated Protestants, and it is the utmost extent to which they are able to go in believing, to hold, not that Christian doctrine is certainly true,* but that it has such a semblance of truth, it has such considerable marks of probability upon it, that it is their duty to accept and act upon it as if it were true beyond all question or doubt: and they justify themselves, and with much reason, by the authority of Bishop Butler. Undoubtedly, a religious man will be led to go as far as this, if he cannot go farther; but unless he can go farther, he is no catechumen of the Catholic Church. We wish all men to believe that her creed is true; but till they do so believe, we do not wish, we have no permission, to make them her members. Such a faith as this author speaks of to condemn—(our books call it "*practical* certitude")—does not rise to the level of the *sine qua non*, which is the condition prescribed for becoming a Catholic. Unless a a convert so believes that he can sincerely say, "After all, in spite of all difficulties, objections, obscurities, mysteries, the creed of the Church undoubtedly comes from God, and is true, because He who gave it is the Truth," such a man, though he be outwardly received into her fold, will receive no grace from the sacraments, no sanctification in baptism, no pardon in penance, no life in communion. We are more consistently dogmatic than this author imagines; we do not enforce a principle by halves; if our doctrine is true, it must be received as such; if a man cannot so receive it, he must wait till he can. It would be better, indeed, if he now believed ; but since he does not as yet, to wait is the best he can do under the circumstances. If we said anything else than this, certainly we should be, as the author thinks we are, encouraging hypocrisy. Nor let him turn round on us and say that by thus proceeding we are laying a burden on souls, and blocking up the entrance into that fold which was intended for all men, by imposing hard conditions on candidates for admission ; for, as we shall now show, we have already implied a great principle, which is an answer to this objection, and which the Gospels exhibit and sanction, but which he absolutely ignores.

9.

Let us avail ourselves of his own quotation. The Baptist said, "Behold the Lamb of God." Again he says, "This is the Son of God." "Two of his disciples heard him speak, and they followed Jesus." They believed John to be "a man sent from God" to teach them, and therefore they believed his word to be true.

We suppose it was not hypocrisy in them to believe in John's word; rather they would have been guilty of gross inconsistency or hypocrisy, had they professed to believe that he was a divine messenger, and yet had refused to take his word concerning the Stranger whom he pointed out to their veneration. It would have been "saying that they believed," and *not* "acting as if they did;" which at least is not better than saying and acting. Now was not the announcement which John made to them "a short cut to belief"? and what the harm of it? They believed that our Lord was the promised Prophet, without making direct inquiry about Him, without a new inquiry, on the ground of a previous inquiry into the claims of John himself to be accounted a messenger from God. They had already accepted it as truth that John was a prophet; but again, what a prophet said must be true; else he would not be a prophet; now, John said that our Lord was the Lamb of God; this, then, certainly was a sacred truth.

Now it might happen, that they knew exactly and for certain what the Baptist meant in calling our Lord "a Lamb;" in that case they would believe Him to be that which they knew the figurative word meant, as used by the Baptist. But, as our author reminds us, the word has different senses; and though the Baptist explained his own sense of it on the first occasion of using it, by adding "that taketh away the sin of the world," yet when he spoke to the two disciples he did not thus explain it. Now let us suppose that they went off, taking the word each in his own sense, the one understanding by it a sacrificial lamb, the other a lamb of the fold; and let us suppose that, as they were on their way to our Lord's home, they became aware of this difference between their several impressions, and disputed with each other which was the right interpretation. It is clear that they would agree so far as this, viz., that, in saying that the proposition was true, they meant that it was true in that sense in which the Baptist spoke it, whatever that was; moreover, if it be worth noticing, they did after all even agree, in some vague way, about the meaning of the word, understanding that it denoted some high characteristic, or office, or ministry. Anyhow, it was absolutely true, they would say, that our Lord was a Lamb, whatever it meant; the word conveyed a great and momentous fact, and if they did not know what that fact was, the Baptist did, and they would accept it in its one right sense, as soon as he or our Lord told them what that was.

Again, as to that other title which the Baptist gave our Lord, "the Son of God," it admitted of half a dozen meanings. Wisdom was "the only begotten;" the Angels were the sons of God; Adam was a son of God; the descendants of Seth were sons of God; Solomon was a son of God; and so is "the just man." In which of these senses, or in what sense, was our Lord the Son of God? St. Peter, as the after-history shows us, knew, but there were those who did not know; the centurion who attended the crucifixion did not know, and yet he confessed that our Lord was the Son of God. He knew that our Lord had been condemned by the Jews for calling Himself the Son of God, and therefore he cried out, on seeing the miracles which attended his death, "Indeed this *was* the Son of God." His words evidently imply, "I do not know precisely what He meant by so calling Himself; but this I do know,—what He said He was, that He is; whatever He meant, I believe Him; I believe that His word about Himself is true, though I cannot prove it to be so, though I do not even understand it; I believe His word, for I believe *Him*."

Now to return to the accusation which has led to these remarks. Our author says that certain persons are hypocrites, because they "take a short cut to belief, suddenly resolving to strive no longer, but to rest content with saying they believe." Does he mean by "a short cut," believing on the word of another? As far as we see, he can mean nothing else ; yet how *can* he really mean this and mean to blame this, with the Gospels before him? He cannot mean it, if he pays any deference to the Gospels, because the very staple of the sacred narrative, from beginning to end, is a call on all men to believe what is not proved, not plain, to them, on the warrant of divine messengers ; because the very form of our Lord's teaching is to substitute authority for argument ; because the very principle of His grave earnestness, the very key to His regenerative mission, is the intimate connexion of faith with salvation. Faith is not simply trust in His legislation, as the writer says ; it is definitely trust in His word, whether that word be about heavenly things or earthly ; whether it is spoken by His own mouth, or through His ministers. The Angel who announced the Baptist's birth, said, "Thou shalt be dumb, because thou believest not my words." The Baptist's mother said of Mary, "Blessed is she that believed." The Baptist himself said, "He that believeth on the Son hath everlasting life ; and he that believeth not the Son shall not see life, but the wrath of God abideth on him." Our Lord, in turn said to Nicodemus, "We speak that we do know, and ye receive not our witness ; he that believeth not is condemned already, because he hath not believed in the Name of the Only-begotten Son of God." To the Jews, "He that heareth My word, and believeth on Him that sent Me, shall not come into condemnation." To the Capharnaites, "He that believeth on Me hath everlasting life." To St. Thomas, "Blessed are they that have not seen, and yet have believed." And to the Apostles, "Preach the Gospel to every creature; he that believeth not shall be damned."

How is it possible to deny that our Lord, both in the text and in the context of these and other passages, made faith in a message, on the warrant of the messenger, to be a condition of salvation, and enforced it by the great grant of power which He emphatically conferred on His representatives? "Whosoever shall not receive you," He says, "nor hear your words, when ye depart, shake off the dust of your feet." "It is not ye that speak, but the Spirit of your Father." "He that heareth you, heareth Me; he that despiseth you, despiseth Me; and he that despiseth Me, despiseth Him that sent me." "I pray for them that shall believe on Me through their word." "Whose sins ye remit, they are remitted unto them; and whose sins ye retain, they are retained." "Whatsoever ye shall bind on earth shall be bound in heaven." "I will give unto thee the keys of the kingdom of heaven; and whatsoever thou shalt bind on earth shall be bound in heaven, and whatsoever thou shalt loose on earth shall be loosed in heaven." These characteristic and critical announcements have no place in this author's gospel; and let it be understood, that we are not asking why he does not determine the exact doctrines contained in them—for that is a question which he has reserved (if we understand him) for a future Volume—but why he does not recognize the principle they involve—for that is a matter which falls within his present subject.

10

It is not well to exhibit some sides of Christianity, and not others; this we think is the main fault of the author we have been reviewing. It does not pay to be eclectic in so serious a matter of fact. He does not overlook, he boldly confesses, that a visible organized Church was a main part of our Lord's plan for the regeneration of mankind. "As with Socrates," he says, "argument is everything, and personal authority nothing ; so with Christ, personal authority is all in all, and argument altogether unemployed" (p. 94). Our Lord rested His teaching, not on the concurrence and testimony of His hearers, but on His own authority. He imposed upon them the declarations of a Divine Voice. Why does this author stop short in the delineation of principles which he has so admirably begun ? Why does he denounce "short cuts," as a mental disfranchisement, when no cut can be shorter that to "believe and be saved" ? Why does he denounce religious fear as hypocritical, when it is written, "He that believeth not shall be damned" ? Why does He call it dishonest in a man to sacrifice his own judgment to the word of God, when, unless he did so, he would be avowing that the Creator knew less than the creature ? Let him re-collect that no two thinkers, philosophers, writers, ever did, ever will agree, in all things with each other. No system of opinions, ever given to the world, approved it-self in all its parts to the reason of any one individual by whom it was mastered. No revelation then is con-ceivable, which does not involve, almost in its very idea as being something new, a collision with the human intel-lect, and demands accordingly, if it is to be accepted, a sacrifice of private judgment on the part of those to whom it is addressed. If a revelation be necessary, then also in consequence is that sacrifice necessary. One man will have to make a sacrifice in one respect, another in an-other, all men in some.

We say, then, to men of the day, Take Christianity, or leave it ; do not practise upon it ; to do so is as unphilosophical as it is dangerous. Do not attempt to halve a spiritual unit. You are apt to call it a dishonesty in us to refuse to follow out our reasonings, when faith stands in the way ; is there no intellectual dishonesty in your self-trust ? First, your very accusation of us is dishonest ; for you keep in the background the circumstance, of which you are well aware, that such a refusal on our part to back Reason against Faith, is the necessary consequence of our accepting an authoritative Revelation ; and next you profess to accept that Revelation yourselves, whilst you dishonestly pick and choose, and take as much or as little of it as you please. You either accept Christianity, or you do not : if you do, do not garble and patch it ; if you do not, suffer others to submit to it ungarbled.

June, 1866,

INDEX.

CARDINAL NEWMAN'S WORKS.

PAROCHIAL and PLAIN SERMONS. Edited by the Rev. W. J. COPELAND, B.D. late Rector of Farnham, Essex. 8 vols. Cabinet Edition. Crown 8vo. 5s. each. Popular Edition. 8 vols. Crown 8vo. 3s. 6d. each.

SELECTION, adapted to the SEASONS of the ECCLESIASTICAL YEAR, from the 'Parochial and Plain Sermons.' Edited by the Rev. W J. COPELAND, B.D. late Rector of Farnham, Essex. Crown 8vo. 5s.

FIFTEEN SERMONS PREACHED before the UNIVERSITY of OXFORD, between 1826 and 1843. Crown 8vo. 5s.

SERMONS BEARING upon SUBJECTS of the DAY. Edited by the Rev. W. J. COPELAND, B.D. late Rector of Farnham, Essex. Crown 8vo. 5s.

DISCOURSES ADDRESSED to MIXED CONGREGATIONS. Crown 8vo. 6s.

SERMONS PREACHED on VARIOUS OCCASIONS. Crown 8vo. 6s.

LECTURES on the DOCTRINE of JUSTIFICATION. Crown 8vo. 5s.

An ESSAY on the DEVELOPMENT of CHRISTIAN DOCTRINE Cabinet Edition. Crown 8vo. 6s. Cheap Edition. Crown 8vo. 3s. 6d.

The IDEA of a UNIVERSITY DEFINED and ILLUSTRATED. Crown 8vo. 7s.

An ESSAY in AID of a GRAMMAR of ASSENT. Cabinet Edition. Crown 8vo. 7s. 6d. Cheap Edition. Crown 8vo. 3s. 6d.

The VIA MEDIA of the ANGLICAN CHURCH. Illustrated in Lectures, Letters and Tracts written between 1830 and 1841. With Notes, 2 vols. Crown 8vo. 6s. each. Vol. I. Prophetical Office of the Church. Vol II. Occasional Letters and Tracts.

CERTAIN DIFFICULTIES FELT by ANGLICANS in CATHOLIC TEACHING CONSIDERED. (2 vols.) Vol. I. Twelve Lectures. Crown 8vo. 7s. 6d. Vol. II. Letters to Dr. Pusey concerning the Blessed Virgin, and to the Duke of Norfolk in Defence of the Pope and Council. Crown 8vo. 5s. 6d.

The PRESENT POSITION of CATHOLICS in ENGLAND. Crown 8vo. 7s. 6d.

APOLOGIA PRO VITA SUA. Cabinet Edition. Crown 8vo. 6s. Cheap Edition. Crown 8vo. 3s. 6d.

London : LONGMANS, GREEN, & CO.

ESSAYS on BIBLICAL and on ECCLESIASTICAL MIRACLES.
Cabinet Edition. Crown 8vo. 6s. Cheap Edition. Crown 8vo. 3s. 6d.

DISCUSSIONS and ARGUMENTS on VARIOUS SUBJECTS.
Cabinet Edition. Crown 8vo. 6s. Cheap Edition. Crown 8vo. 3s. 6d.
CONTENTS.—1. How to accomplish it. 2. The Antichrist of the Fathers.
3. Scripture and the Creed. 4. Tamworth Reading Room. 5. Who's to Blame
6. An Argument for Christianity.

ESSAYS CRITICAL and HISTORICAL. Cabinet Edition. 2 vols
Crown 8vo. 12s. Cheap Edition. 2 vols. Crown 8vo. 7s.
CONTENTS.—1. Poetry. 2. Rationalism. 3. Apostolical Tradition. 4. De la
Mennais. 5. Palmer on Faith and Unity. 6. St. Ignatius. 7. Prospects of
the Anglican Church. 8. The Anglo-American Church. 9. Countess of
Huntingdon. 10. Catholicity of the Anglican Church. 11. The Antichrist of
Protestants. 12. Milman's Christianity. 13. Reformation of the Eleventh
Century. 14. Private Judgment. 15. Davison. 16. Keble.

HISTORICAL SKETCHES. 3 vols. Crown 8vo. 6s. each.
CONTENTS.—1. The Turks. 2. Cicero. 3. Apollonius. 4. Primitive
Christianity. 5. Church of the Fathers. 6. St. Chrysostom. 7. Theodoret.
8. St. Benedict. 9. Benedictine Schools. 10. Universities. 11. Northmen and
Normans. 12. Medieval Oxford. 13. Convocation of Canterbury.

The ARIANS of the FOURTH CENTURY. Cabinet Edition. Crown
8vo, 6s. Cheap Edition. Crown 8vo. 3s. 6d.

SELECT TREATISES of ST. ATHANASIUS in CONTROVERSY
with the ARIANS. Freely Translated. 2 vols. Crown 8vo. 15s.

THEOLOGICAL TRACTS. Crown 8vo. 8s.
CONTENTS.—1. Dissertatiunculæ. 2. On the Text of the Seven Epistles of
St. Ignatius. 3. Doctrinal Causes of Arianism. 4. Apollinarianism. 5. St.
Cyril's Formula. 6. Ordo de Tempore. 7. Douay Version of Scripture.

VERSES on VARIOUS OCCASIONS. Cabinet Edition. Crown
8vo. 6s. Cheap Edition. Crown 8vo. 3s. 6d.

LOSS and GAIN: The Story of a Convert. Crown 8vo. 6s.

CALLISTA: A Tale of the Third Century. Cabinet Edition. Crown
8vo. 6s. Cheap Edition. Crown 8vo. 3s. 6d.

The DREAM of GERONTIUS. 16mo. 6d. sewed; 1s. cloth.

London: LONGMANS, GREEN, & CO.

A

SELECT LIST OF WORKS

PUBLISHED BY

LONGMANS, GREEN, & CO.

LONDON AND NEW YORK.

MESSRS. LONGMANS, GREEN, & CO.

Issue the undermentioned Lists of their Publications, which may be had post free on application to them at 39 Paternoster Row, London, E.C.:

1. MONTHLY LIST OF NEW WORKS AND NEW EDITIONS.

2. QUARTERLY LIST OF ANNOUNCEMENTS AND NEW WORKS.

3. NOTES ON BOOKS: BEING AN ANALYSIS OF THE WORKS PUBLISHED DURING EACH QUARTER.

4. CATALOGUE OF SCIENTIFIC WORKS.

5. CATALOGUE OF MEDICAL AND SURGICAL WORKS.

6. CATALOGUE OF SCHOOL BOOKS AND EDUCATIONAL WORKS.

7. CATALOGUE OF BOOKS FOR ELEMENTARY SCHOOLS AND PUPIL TEACHERS.

8. CATALOGUE OF THEOLOGICAL WORKS BY DIVINES AND MEMBERS OF THE CHURCH OF ENGLAND.

9. CATALOGUE OF WORKS IN GENERAL LITERATURE.

CARDINAL NEWMAN'S WORKS.

Parochial and Plain Sermons. Edited by REV. W. J. COPELAND, B.D., late Rector of Farnham, Essex. 8 vols. Sold separately. Crown 8vo. Cabinet Edition, 5s. each; Popular Edition, 3s. 6d. each.

CONTENTS OF VOL. I.:—Holiness necessary for Future Blessedness—The Immortality of the Soul—Knowledge of God's Will without Obedience—Secret Faults—Self-Denial the Test of Religious Earnestness—The Spiritual Mind—Sins of Ignorance and Weakness—God's Commandments not Grievous—The Religious Use of Excited Feelings—Profession without Practice—Profession without Hypocrisy—Profession without Ostentation—Promising without Doing—Religious Emotion—Religious Faith Rational—The Christian Mysteries—The Self-Wise Inquirer—Obedience the Remedy for Religious Perplexity—Times of Private Prayer—Forms of Private Prayer—The Resurrection of the Body—Witnesses of the Resurrection—Christian Reverence—The Religion of the Day—Scripture a Record of Human Sorrow—Christian Manhood.

CONTENTS OF VOL. II.:—The World's Benefactors—Faith without Sight—The Incarnation—Martyrdom—Love of Relations and Friends—The Mind of Little Children—Ceremonies of the Church—The Glory of the Christian Church—St. Paul's Conversion viewed in Reference to his Office—Secrecy and Suddenness of Divine Visitations—Divine Decrees—The Reverence Due to the Blessed Virgin Mary—Christ, a Quickening Spirit—Saving Knowledge—Self-Contemplation—Religious Cowardice—The Gospel Witnesses—Mysteries in Religion—The Indwelling Spirit—The Kingdom of the Saints—The Gospel, a Trust Committed to us—Tolerance of Religious Error—Rebuking Sin—The Christian Ministry—Human Responsibility—Guilelessness—The Danger of Riches—The Powers of Nature—The Danger of Accomplishments—Christian Zeal—Use of Saints' Days.

CARDINAL NEWMAN'S WORKS.

Parochial and Plain Sermons.—*Continued.*

CONTENTS OF VOL. III.:—Abraham and Lot—Wilfulness of Israel in Rejecting Samuel—Saul—Early Years of David—Jeroboam—Faith and Obedience—Christian Repentance—Contracted Views in Religion—A particular Providence as revealed in the Gospel—Tears of Christ at the Grave of Lazarus—Bodily Suffering—The Humiliation of the Eternal Son—Jewish Zeal a Pattern to Christians—Submission to Church Authority—Contest between Truth and Falsehood in the Church—The Church Visible and Invisible—The Visible Church an Encouragement to Faith—The Gift of the Spirit—Regenerating Baptism—Infant Baptism—The Daily Service—The Good Part of Mary—Religious Worship a Remedy for Excitements—Intercession—The Intermediate State.

CONTENTS OF VOL. IV.:—The Strictness of the Law of Christ—Obedience without Love, as instanced in the Character of Balaam—Moral Consequences of Single Sins—Acceptance of Religious Privileges Compulsory—Reliance on Religious Observances—The Individuality of the Soul—Chastisement amid Mercy—Peace and Joy amid Chastisement—The State of Grace—The Visible Church for the Sake of the Elect—The Communion of Saints—The Church a Home for the Lonely—The Invisible World—The Greatness and Littleness of Human Life—Moral Effects of Communion with God—Christ Hidden from the World—Christ Manifested in Remembrance—The Gainsaying of Korah—The Mysteriousness of our Present Being—The Ventures of Faith—Faith and Love—Watching—Keeping Fast and Festival.

CONTENTS OF VOL. V.:—Worship, a Preparation for Christ's Coming—Reverence, a Belief in God's Presence Unreal Words—Shrinking from Christ's Coming—Equanimity—Remembrance of Past Mercies—The Mystery of Godliness—The State of Innocence—Christian Sympathy—Righteousness not of us, but in us—The Law of the Spirit—The New Works of the Gospel—The State of Salvation—Transgressions and Infirmities—Sins of Infirmity—Sincerity and Hypocrisy—The Testimony of Conscience—Many called, Few chosen—Present Blessings—Endurance, the Christian's Portion—Affliction, a School of Comfort—The Thought of God, the Stay of the Soul—Love, the One Thing Needful—The Power of the Will.

CONTENTS OF VOL. VI.:—Fasting, a Source of Trial—Life, the Season of Repentance—Apostolic Abstinence, a Pattern for Christians—Christ's Privations, a Meditation for Christians—Christ the Son of God made Man—The Incarnate Son, a Sufferer and Sacrifice—The Cross of Christ the Measure of the World—Difficulty of realising Sacred Privileges—The Gospel Sign Addressed to Faith—The Spiritual Presence of Christ in the Church—The Eucharistic Presence—Faith the Title for Justification—Judaism of the Present Day—The Fellowship of the Apostles—Rising with Christ—Warfare the Condition of Victory—Waiting for Christ—Subjection of the Reason and Feelings to the Revealed Word—The Gospel Palaces—The Visible Temple—Offerings for the Sanctuary—The Weapons of Saints—Faith Without Demonstration—The Mystery of the Holy Trinity—Peace in Believing.

CONTENTS OF VOL. VII.:—The Lapse of Time—Religion, a Weariness to the Natural Man—The World our Enemy—The Praise of Men—Temporal Advantages—The Season of Epiphany—The Duty of Self-Denial—The Yoke of Christ—Moses the Type of Christ—The Crucifixion—Attendance on Holy Communion—The Gospel Feast—Love of Religion, a new Nature—Religion Pleasant to the Religious—Mental Prayer—Infant Baptism—The Unity of the Church—Steadfastness in the Old Paths.

CONTENTS OF VOL. VIII.:—Reverence in Worship—Divine Calls—The Trial of Saul—The Call of David—Curiosity, a Temptation to Sin—Miracles no Remedy for Unbelief—Josiah, a Pattern for the Ignorant—Inward Witness to the Truth of the Gospel—Jeremiah, a Lesson for the Disappointed—Endurance of the World's Censure—Doing Glory to God in Pursuits of the World—Vanity of Human Glory—Truth Hidden when not Sought after—Obedience to God the Way to Faith in Christ—Sudden Conversions—The Shepherd of our Souls—Religious Joy—Ignorance of Evil.

Sermons Preached on Various Occasions. Crown 8vo. Cabinet Edition, 6s.; Popular Edition, 3s. 6d.

CONTENTS:—Intellect the Instrument of Religious Training—The Religion of the Pharisee and the Religion of Mankind—Waiting for Christ—The Secret Power of Divine Grace—Dispositions for Faith—Omnipotence in Bonds—St. Paul's Characteristic Gift—St. Paul's Gift of Sympathy—Christ upon the Waters—The Second Spring—Order, the Witness and Instrument of Unity—The Mission of St. Philip Neri—The Tree beside the Waters—In the World, but not of the World—The Pope and the Revolution.

CARDINAL NEWMAN'S WORKS.

Selection, Adapted to the Seasons of the Ecclesiastical Year, from the 'Parochial and Plain Sermons.' Edited by the REV. W. J. COPELAND, B.D. Crown 8vo. Cabinet Edition, 5s.; Popular Edition, 3s. 6d.

CONTENTS :—*Advent:* Self-Denial the Test of Religious Earnestness—Divine Calls—The Ventures of Faith—Watching. *Christmas Day:* Religious Joy. *New Year's Sunday:* The Lapse of Time. *Epiphany:* Remembrance of Past Mercies—Equanimity—The Immortality of the Soul—Christian Manhood—Sincerity and Hypocrisy—Christian Sympathy. *Septuagesima:* Present Blessings. *Sexagesima:* Endurance, the Christian's Portion. *Quinquagesima:* Love, the One Thing Needful. *Lent:* The Individuality of the Soul—Life the Season of Repentance—Bodily Suffering—Tears of Christ at the Grave of Lazarus—Christ's Privations, a Meditation for Christians—The Cross of Christ the Measure of the World. *Good Friday:* The Crucifixion. *Easter Day:* Keeping Fast and Festival. *Easter Tide:* Witnesses of the Resurrection—A Particular Providence as Revealed in the Gospel—Christ Manifested in Remembrance—The Invisible World—Waiting for Christ. *Ascension:* Warfare the Condition of Victory. *Sunday after Ascension:* Rising with Christ. *Whitsun Day:* The Weapons of Saints. *Trinity Sunday:* The Mysteriousness of Our Present Being. *Sundays after Trinity:* Holiness Necessary for Future Blessedness—The Religious Use of Excited Feelings—The Self-Wise Inquirer—Scripture a Record of Human Sorrow—The Danger of Riches—Obedience without Love, as instanced in the Character of Balaam—Moral Consequences of Single Sins—The Greatness and Littleness of Human Life—Moral Effects of Communion with God—The Thought of God the Stay of the Soul—The Power of the Will—The Gospel Palaces—Religion a Weariness to the Natural Man—The World our Enemy—The Praise of Men—Religion Pleasant to the Religious—Mental Prayer—Curiosity a Temptation to Sin—Miracles no Remedy for Unbelief—Jeremiah, a Lesson for the Disappointed—The Shepherd of our Souls—Doing Glory to God in Pursuits of the World.

Sermons Bearing upon Subjects of the Day. Edited by the REV. W. J. COPELAND, B.D., late Rector of Farnham, Essex. Crown 8vo. Cabinet Edition, 5s.; Popular Edition, 3s. 6d.

CONTENTS :—The Work of the Christian—Saintliness not Forfeited by the Penitent—Our Lord's Last Supper and His First—Dangers to the Penitent—The Three Offices of Christ—Faith and Experience—Faith unto the World—The Church and the World—Indulgence in Religious Privileges—Connection between Personal and Public Improvement—Christian Nobleness—Joshua a Type of Christ and His Followers—Elisha a Type of Christ and His Followers—The Christian Church a Continuation of the Jewish—The Principles of Continuity between the Jewish and Christian Churches—The Christian Church an Imperial Power—Sanctity the Token of the Christian Empire—Condition of the Members of the Christian Empire—The Apostolic Christian—Wisdom and Innocence—Invisible Presence of Christ—Outward and Inward Notes of the Church—Grounds for Steadfastness in our Religious Profession—Elijah the Prophet of the Latter Days—Feasting in Captivity—The Parting of Friends.

Fifteen Sermons Preached before the University of Oxford, between A.D. 1826 and 1843. Crown 8vo. Cabinet Edition, 5s.; Popular Edition, 3s. 6d.

CONTENTS :—The Philosophical Temper, first enjoined by the Gospel—The Influence of Natural and Revealed Religion respectively—Evangelical Sanctity the Perfection of Natural Virtue—The Usurpations of Reason—Personal Influence, the Means of Propagating the Truth—On Justice as a Principle of Divine Governance—Contest between Faith and Sight—Human Responsibility, as independent of Circumstances—Wilfulness, the Sin of Saul—Faith and Reason, contrasted as Habits of Mind—The Nature of Faith in Relation to Reason—Love, the Safeguard of Faith against Superstition—Implicit and Explicit Reason—Wisdom, as contrasted with Faith and with Bigotry—The Theory of Developments in Religious Doctrine.

CARDINAL NEWMAN'S WORKS.

Discourses Addressed to Mixed Congregations. Crown 8vo. Cabinet Edition, 5s.; Popular Edition, 3s. 6d.

CONTENTS :—The Salvation of the Hearer the Motive of the Preacher—Neglect of Divine Calls and Warnings—Men not Angels—The Priests of the Gospel—Purity and Love—Saintliness the Standard of Christian Principle—God's Will the End of Life—Perseverance in Grace—Nature and Grace—Illuminating Grace—Faith and Private Judgment—Faith and Doubt—Prospects of the Catholic Missioner—Mysteries of Nature and of Grace—The Mystery of Divine Condescension—The Infinitude of Divine Attributes—Mental Sufferings of Our Lord in His Passion—The Glories of Mary for the Sake of Her Son—On the Fitness of the Glories of Mary.

Lectures on the Doctrine of Justification. Crown 8vo. Cabinet Edition, 5s. ; Popular Edition, 3s. 6d.

CONTENTS :—Faith considered as the Instrumental Cause of Justification—Love considered as the Formal Cause of Justification—Primary Sense of the term 'Justification'—Secondary Senses of the term 'Justification'—Misuse of the term 'Just' or 'Righteous'—The Gift of Righteousness—The Characteristics of the Gift of Righteousness—Righteousness viewed as a Gift and as a Quality—Righteousness the Fruit of our Lord's Resurrection—The Office of Justifying Faith—The Nature of Justifying Faith—Faith viewed relatively to Rites and Works—On Preaching the Gospel—Appendix.

On the Development of Christian Doctrine. Crown 8vo. Cabinet Edition, 6s.; Popular Edition, 3s. 6d.

On the Idea of a University. Crown 8vo. Cabinet Edition, 7s.; Popular Edition, 3s. 6d.

An Essay in Aid of a Grammar of Assent. Crown 8vo. Cabinet Edition, 7s. 6d.; Popular Edition, 3s. 6d.

Two Essays on Miracles. 1. Of Scripture. 2. Of Ecclesiastical History. Crown 8vo. Cabinet Edition, 6s. ; Popular Edition, 3s. 6d.

Discussions and Arguments. Crown 8vo. Cabinet Edition, 6s.; Popular Edition, 3s. 6d.

1. How to accomplish it. 2. The Antichrist of the Fathers. 3. Scripture and the Creed. 4. Tamworth Reading-room. 5. Who's to Blame? 6. An Argument for Christianity.

Essays, Critical and Historical. 2 vols. Crown 8vo. Cabinet Edition, 12s.; Popular Edition, 7s.

1. Poetry. 2. Rationalism. 3. Apostolic Tradition. 4. De la Mennais. 5. Palmer on Faith and Unity. 6. St. Ignatius. 7. Prospects of the Anglican Church. 8. The Anglo-American Church. 9. Countess of Huntingdon. 10. Catholicity of the Anglican Church. 11. The Antichrist of Protestants. 12. Milman's Christianity. 13. Reformation of the XI. Century. 14. Private Judgment. 15. Davison. 16. Keble.

CARDINAL NEWMAN'S WORKS.

Apologia Pro Vita Sua. Crown 8vo. Cabinet Edition, 6s. ;
Popular Edition, 3s. 6d.

Verses on Various Occasions. Crown 8vo. Cabinet Edition, 6s. ;
Popular Edition, 3s. 6d.

Historical Sketches. 3 vols. Crown 8vo. Cabinet Edition, 6s. each;
Popular Edition, 3s. 6d. each.

   1. The Turks. 2. Cicero. 3. Apollonius. 4. Primitive Christianity.
5. Church of the Fathers. 6. St. Chrysostom. 7. Theodoret. 8. St.
Benedict. 9. Benedictine Schools. 10. Universities. 11. Northmen and
Normans. 12. Mediæval Oxford. 13. Convocation of Canterbury.

The Arians of the Fourth Century. Crown 8vo. Cabinet Edition,
6s.; Popular Edition, 3s. 6d.

**Select Treatises of St. Athanasius in Controversy with the
Arians.** Freely translated. 2 vols. Crown 8vo. Cabinet Edition,
15s.

Theological Tracts. Crown 8vo. Cabinet Edition, 8s.

   1. Dissertatiunculæ. 2. On the Text of the Seven Epistles of St.
Ignatius. 3. Doctrinal Causes of Arianism. 4. Apollinarianism. 5. St.
Cyril's Formula. 6. Ordo de Tempore. 7. Douay Version of Scriptures.

The Via Media of the Anglican Church. 2 vols. Crown 8vo.
Cabinet Edition, 6s. each ; Popular Edition, 3s. 6d. each.
   Vol. I. Prophetical Office of the Church.
   Vol. II. Occasional Letters and Tracts.

**Certain Difficulties felt by Anglicans in Catholic Teaching Con-
sidered.** 2 vols.
   Vol. I.   Twelve Lectures. Crown 8vo. Cabinet Edition, 7s. 6d.;
            Popular Edition, 3s. 6d.
   Vol. II.   Letters to Dr. Pusey concerning the Blessed Virgin, and to
            the Duke of Norfolk in defence of the Pope and Council.
            Crown 8vo. Cabinet Edition, 5s. 6d. ; Popular Edition,
            3s. 6d.

Present Position of Catholics in England. Crown 8vo. Cabinet
Edition, 7s. 6d. ; Popular Edition, 3s. 6d.

Loss and Gain. The Story of a Convert. Crown 8vo. Cabinet
Edition, 6s. ; Popular Edition, 3s. 6d.

Callista. A Tale of the Third Century. Crown 8vo. Cabinet
Edition, 6s. ; Popular Edition, 3s. 6d.

The Dream of Gerontius. 16mo, sewed, 6d.; cloth, 1s.

CARDINAL NEWMAN'S WORKS.

POPULAR EDITION.

Parochial and Plain Sermons. 8 vols. Each	.	. 3s. 6d.
Sermons preached on Various Occasions	. .	. 3s. 6d.
Selection, from the Parochial and Plain Sermons	.	. 3s. 6d.
Sermons bearing on Subjects of the Day	. .	. 3s. 6d.
Sermons preached before the University of Oxford	.	. 3s. 6d.
Discourses addressed to Mixed Congregations	.	. 3s. 6d.
Lectures on the Doctrine of Justification	.	. 3s. 6d.
On the Development of Christian Doctrine	.	. 3s. 6d.
On the Idea of a University	. .	. 3s. 6d.
An Essay in Aid of a Grammar of Assent	.	. 3s. 6d.
Biblical and Ecclesiastical Miracles	. .	. 3s. 6d.
Discussions and Arguments on Various Subjects	.	. 3s. 6d.
Essays, Critical and Historical. 2 vols. Each	.	. 3s. 6d.
Historical Sketches. 3 vols. Each	.	. 3s. 6d.
The Arians of the Fourth Century	. .	. 3s. 6d.
The Via Media of the Anglican Church. 2 vols. Each	.	3s. 6d.
Difficulties felt by Anglicans considered. 2 vols. Each	.	3s. 6d.
Present Position of Catholics in England	.	. 3s. 6d.
Apologia pro Vita Sua	. .	. 3s. 6d.
Verses on Various Occasions	. .	. 3s. 6d.
Loss and Gain	. .	. 3s. 6d.
Callista	. .	. 3s. 6d.

BARRAUD.—**Saint Thomas of Canterbury and Saint Elizabeth of Hungary** : Historical Dramas. By CLEMENT WILLIAM BAR-RAUD, S.J. Crown 8vo. 5s.

FOUARD.—**The Christ, The Son of God.** A Life of Our Lord and Saviour Jesus Christ. By the ABBÉ CONSTANT FOUARD, Honorary Cathedral Canon, Professor of the Faculty of Theology at Rouen, etc., etc. Translated from the Fifth Edition with the Author's sanction. By GEORGE F. X. GRIFFITH. With an Introduction by CARDINAL MANNING. Third Edition. With 3 Maps. 2 vols. Crown 8vo. 14s.

'In erudition the author is to the full up to the level of any writers, Catholic or Protestant, who have as yet attempted the same task, while his reliableness in matters of dogma gives him an enormous scientific advantage over non-Catholics.'—*Dublin Review.*

Saint Peter and the First Years of Christianity. By the ABBÉ CONSTANT FOUARD. Translated by GEORGE F. X. GRIFFITH. Crown 8vo. 9s.

LYONS.—Christianity or Infallibility—Both or Neither. By the Rev. DANIEL LYONS. Crown 8vo. 5s.

'His method is thoroughly popular, and while he has admirably succeeded in avoiding that didactic and argumentative style which is apt to repel the ordinary reader of our day, he nevertheless leaves the distinct impression that his reasoning is based on sound logic, and strengthened by such authorities as would command the attention of every theological student.

'The work is full of erudition, as is shown by the numerous notes indicating a wide range of pertinent and careful reading. . . . The book is a solid and timely contribution to the theological literature of the day.'—*American Ecclesiastical Review.*

CLARKE.—A Pilgrimage to the Holy Coat of Treves. With an Account of its History and Authenticity. By RICHARD F. CLARKE, S.J. With Illustrations. Crown 8vo. 4s.

CHRISTIAN BIOGRAPHIES :

Henri Dominique Lacordaire. A Biographical Sketch. By H. L. SIDNEY LEAR. With Frontispiece. Crown 8vo. 3s. 6d.

A Christian Painter of the Nineteenth Century ; being the Life of Hippolyte Flandrin. By H. L. SIDNEY LEAR. Crown 8vo. 3s. 6d.

Bossuet and his Contemporaries. By H. L. SIDNEY LEAR. Crown 8vo. 3s. 6d.

Fénelon, Archbishop of Cambrai. A Biographical Sketch. By H. L. SIDNEY LEAR. Crown 8vo. 3s. 6d.

A Dominican Artist. A Sketch of the Life of the Rev. Père Besson, of the Order of St. Dominic. By H. L. SIDNEY LEAR. Crown 8vo. 3s. 6d.

The Life of Madame Louise de France, Daughter of Louis XV., also known as the Mother Thérèse de S. Augustin. By H. L. SIDNEY LEAR. Crown 8vo. 3s. 6d.

The Revival of Priestly Life in the Seventeenth Century in France. Charles de Condren—S. Philip Neri and Cardinal de Berulle—S. Vincent de Paul—S. Sulpice and Jean Jacques Olier. By H. L. SIDNEY LEAR. Crown 8vo. 3s. 6d.

Life of S. Francis de Sales, Bishop and Prince of Geneva. By H. L. SIDNEY LEAR. Crown 8vo. 3s. 6d.

Henri Perreyve. By A. GRATRY, PRÊTRE DE L'ORATOIRE, Professeur de Morale Evangélique à la Sorbonne, et Membre de l'Académie Française. Translated, by special permission, by H. L. SIDNEY LEAR. With Portrait. Crown 8vo. 3s. 6d.

FÉNELON.—Spiritual Letters to Men. By Archbishop Fénelon. Translated by H. L. Sidney Lear, author of 'Life of Fénelon,' 'Life of S. Francis de Sales,' etc. etc. 16mo. 2s. 6d.

Spiritual Letters to Women.—By Archbishop Fénelon. Translated by H. L. Sidney Lear, author of 'Life of Fénelon,' 'Life of S. Francis de Sales,' etc. etc. 16mo. 2s. 6d.

DRANE.— The History of St. Dominic, Founder of the Friar Preachers. By Augusta Theodora Drane, author of 'The History of St. Catherine of Siena and her Companions.' With 32 Illustrations. 8vo. 15s.

JAMESON—Works by Mrs. Jameson :

Sacred and Legendary Art. With 19 Etchings and 197 Woodcuts. 2 vols. Cloth, gilt top. 20s. *net.*

Legends of the Madonna : The Virgin Mary as Represented in Sacred and Legendary Art. With 27 Etchings and 165 Woodcuts. 1 vol. Cloth, gilt top. 10s. *net.*

Legends of the Monastic Orders. With 11 Etchings and 88 Woodcuts. 1 vol. Cloth, gilt top. 10s. *net.*

History of the Saviour, His Types and Precursors. Completed by Lady Eastlake. With 13 Etchings and 281 Woodcuts. 2 vols. Cloth, gilt top. 20s. *net.*

MANUALS OF CATHOLIC PHILOSOPHY.

(*Stonyhurst Series.*)

Edited by RICHARD F. CLARKE, S.J.

Logic. By Richard F. Clarke, S.J. Crown 8vo. 5s.

First Principles of Knowledge. By John Rickaby, S.J. Crown 8vo. 5s.

Moral Philosophy (Ethics and Natural Law). By Joseph Rickaby, S.J. Crown 8vo. 5s.

General Metaphysics. By John Rickaby, S.J. Crown 8vo. 5s.

Psychology. By Michael Maher, S.J. Crown 8vo. 6s. 6d.

Natural Theology. By Bernard Boedder, S.J. Crown 8vo. 6s. 6d.

Political Economy. By Charles S. Devas. Crown 8vo. 6s. 6d.

LONDON AND NEW YORK: LONGMANS, GREEN, & CO.
5000/2/93